T0026867

THE
MYTHIC
DREAM

Also by Dominik Parisien & Navah Wolfe

THE STARLIT WOOD: NEW FAIRY TALES

ROBOTS VS. FAIRIES

THE
MYTHIC
DREAM

EDITED BY DOMINIK PARISIEN
& NAVAH WOLFE

SAGA PRESS

LONDON SYDNEY **NEW YORK** TORONTO NEW DELHI

SAGA ⧓ PRESS
AN IMPRINT OF SIMON & SCHUSTER, INC.

1230 AVENUE OF THE AMERICAS, NEW YORK, NEW YORK 10020

This book is a work of fiction. Any references to historical events, real people, or real places are used fictitiously. Other names, characters, places, and events are products of the authors' imaginations, and any resemblance to actual events or places or persons, living or dead, is entirely coincidental. | Introduction and compilation copyright © 2019 by Dominik Parisien & Navah Wolfe | "Phantoms of the Midway" © 2019 by Seanan McGuire | "The Justified" © 2019 by Ann Leckie | "Fisher-Bird" © 2019 by T. Kingfisher | "A Brief Lesson in Native American Astronomy" © 2019 by Rebecca Roanhorse | "Bridge of Crows" © 2019 by JY Yang | "Labbatu Takes Command of the Flagship *Heaven Dwells Within*" © 2019 by Arkady Martine | "Wild to Covet" © 2019 by Sarah Gailey | "¡Cuidado! ¡Que Viene El Coco!" © 2019 by Carlos Hernandez | "He Fell Howling" © 2019 by Stephen Graham Jones | "Curses Like Words, Like Feathers, Like Stories" © 2019 by Kat Howard | "Across the River" © 2019 by Leah Cypess | "Sisyphus in Elysium" © 2019 by Jeffrey Ford | "Kali_Na" © 2019 by Indrapramit Das | "Live Stream" © 2019 by Alyssa Wong | "Close Enough for Jazz" © 2019 by John Chu | "Buried Deep" © 2019 by Naomi Novik | "The Things Eric Eats Before He Eats Himself" © 2019 by Carmen Maria Machado | "Florilegia; or, Some Lies About Flowers" © 2019 by Amal El-Mohtar | All rights reserved, including the right to reproduce this book or portions thereof in any form whatsoever. For information, address Saga Press Subsidiary Rights Department, 1230 Avenue of the Americas, New York, NY 10020. | SAGA PRESS and colophon are trademarks of Simon & Schuster, Inc. | For information about special discounts for bulk purchases, please contact Simon & Schuster Special Sales at 1-866-506-1949 or business@simonandschuster.com. | The Simon & Schuster Speakers Bureau can bring authors to your live event. For more information or to book an event, contact the Simon & Schuster Speakers Bureau at 1-866-248-3049 or visit our website at www.simonspeakers.com. | Interior design by Tom Daly and Erika Genova | The text for this book was set in Adobe Garamond Pro. | First Saga Press trade paperback edition September 2019 | 10 9 8 7 6 5 4 3 2 1 | CIP data for this book is available from the Library of Con-gress. | ISBN 978-1-4814-6238-9 (pbk) | ISBN 978-1-4814-6239-6 (hardcover) | ISBN 978-1-4814-6240-2 (ebook)

For Talya, Hillela, Chayim, Moshe, and Elisha.
We made our own myths together.
—N. W.

For Kelsi, who looks at trees and sees stories.
—D. P.

CONTENTS

INTRODUCTION..XI
by Dominik Parisien & Navah Wolfe

PHANTOMS OF THE MIDWAY.......................1
by Seanan McGuire
(Hades and Persephone)

THE JUSTIFIED 24
by Ann Leckie
(Hathor and the Destruction of Mankind)

FISHER-BIRD...49
by T. Kingfisher
(The Labors of Hercules)

A BRIEF LESSON IN NATIVE AMERICAN ASTRONOMY 67
by Rebecca Roanhorse
(Deer Hunter and White Corn Maiden)

BRIDGE OF CROWS 82
by JY Yang
(The Cowherd and the Weaver Girl)

LABBATU TAKES COMMAND
OF THE FLAGSHIP *HEAVEN DWELLS WITHIN* 97
by Arkady Martine
(Inanna Takes Command of Heaven/Inanna & Enki)

WILD TO COVET..112
by Sarah Gailey
(Thetis)

¡CUIDADO! ¡QUE VIENE EL COCO! 134
by Carlos Hernandez
(El Coco)

HE FELL HOWLING.....................................163
by Stephen Graham Jones
(Lycaon)

CURSES LIKE WORDS, LIKE FEATHERS, LIKE STORIES 181
by Kat Howard
(The Children of Lir)

ACROSS THE RIVER 192
by Leah Cypess
(The Legend of Akdamot/The Legend of Rabbi Meir and the Sambatyon)

SISYPHUS IN ELYSIUM 207
by Jeffrey Ford
(Sisyphus)

KALI_NA 220
by Indrapramit Das
(Kali)

LIVE STREAM 243
by Alyssa Wong
(Artemis and Acteon)

CLOSE ENOUGH FOR JAZZ 262
by John Chu
(Idunn and Her Golden Apples)

BURIED DEEP 282
by Naomi Novik
(Ariadne and the Minotaur)

THE THINGS ERIC EATS BEFORE HE EATS HIMSELF 313
by Carmen Maria Machado
(Erysichthon)

FLORILEGIA; OR, SOME LIES ABOUT FLOWERS 320
by Amal El-Mohtar
(Blodeuwedd)

ACKNOWLEDGMENTS 339
ABOUT THE EDITORS 341
ABOUT THE CONTRIBUTORS 343

INTRODUCTION

ONCE, WE GATHERED, IN THE DARK, AROUND FIRES,
and we told stories of the gods who controlled our fates and moved the
world, the mortals who shaped the destiny of nations and crossed swords
or wits with beings of supreme power, of why things *were* and *are*.

At its core, myth is meaning-making through storytelling, a way of
understanding people, places, natural phenomena. Why does the sun
rise, why do the stars shine, how did that island come to be, how did
that hero rise or fall, what are the origins of life? From the Greek word
"mythos," meaning "speech, thought, or story," myth is a way of making
sense of things through narrative. Myth was storytelling of significance,
meant to impart wisdom of the world, the secret workings of the universe, life itself.

We still gather and tell such stories, by fires, through printed books,
by the light of computers.

There is a tendency to speak of myth as symbolic, metaphorical, but
it can also be literal. There are many cultures today for whom ancient
narratives are truth, not fantasy. Myth is not a thing of the distant past.
While it is rooted in the past, in stories that have endured millennia

upon millennia, it remains, it endures. And throughout time, new tellers made old stories new, changing details to fit the time, the place, to better frame a drought, a famine, a changing political landscape. Myth provides the basis for systems of belief, for truths literal or symbolic, for fields of study, for understanding. It is narrative with power.

And myth doesn't just belong to nations—it belongs to us. We create our own myths as we shape our world, grow our own personal and national mythologies that help us make sense of the institutions we build, the decisions we make. Myth is ancient origin story, but it is also the origin story we tell ourselves as we build our present and our future. Myths, ancient and modern, illustrate truths both subtle and overt, beliefs we hold, or held.

Mythic stories are universal. Or so we claim. Myths occur in all cultures, in so many similar ways, but much of what we mean by the universality of myths is their subtext, their themes, their widespread nature. In the specifics, many mythic stories reinforce traditional power structures, patriarchy, sexism, racism. Myths help make meaning of the world—but the world changes. And so myths change in their retelling. Sometimes in subtle ways, other times drastically. One generation's hero can be another's villain.

The Mythic Dream is a confluence of those elements—it is a way of engaging with classic narratives by recontextualizing them, giving them new perspectives, new worlds to inhabit. Those reimaginings in turn can help us create meaning for the world today, or illustrate truths perhaps obscured in the myth's original version. Here, many of our authors have used those classic tales to interrogate issues of gender, politics, sexuality, patriarchy, power dynamics, and family. They've used those grand narratives to tell very *human* stories.

Mythic personalities who were once supporting characters, who used to be blurred figures on the edges of their own stories, take center stage. Instead of focusing on Actaeon, Artemis takes the lead. Achilles becomes a side note in his mother's tale. Blodeuwedd becomes far more than just flowers. And Idunn, once barely more than a provider to the gods, is the one who holds all the cards. There are reversals at play here, too. A terrifying bogeyman becomes the greatest source of comfort. A curse of lycanthropy is embraced as a gift.

These stories are the dreams of classic myths. Dreams take private and public elements, and filter them through our subconscious. With *The Mythic Dream* we asked our authors to filter classic myths through their dreaming minds, to parse their private lives, their imagination, the world around them, and to bring all those elements they've absorbed consciously and unconsciously to their narratives. For some, the myth was a roadmap to new adventures; the journey is immediately recognizable, but the sights are quite different. For others, the individual elements are familiar, but their travels took them down very different paths. But for all these dreamers, the destination was the same: an adventure or perspective that feels wholly new, and yet rooted in ancient truths.

Madeleine L'Engle once wrote, "When we lose our myths we lose our place in the universe." So we invite you in to *The Mythic Dream*, to join us as we reimagine our collective past, explore our present, and take hold of our future through the lens of classic myths.

—Dominik Parisien & Navah Wolfe

THE
MYTHIC
DREAM

PHANTOMS OF
THE MIDWAY

BY
—
SEANAN McGUIRE

THE SKY OVER INDIANA WAS DOROTHY GALE BLUE,
that shade of sun-bleached denim that spoke of faded dreams and dying
youth and all the wasted days of summer. Aracely squinted up at the sky
and wondered what they'd called that color before Baum came along
with his silver slippers and his golden roads and his green, green fantasies
of a better world. Probably nothing. Some things were so much a part of
the way the world *was* that they never stood out until someone pointed
out that it wasn't always, hadn't always, couldn't always be that way.

People in Indiana lived and died under this sky, and they thought it
was exactly right, and she thought that was exactly wrong. She lowered
her eyes and walked on, cutting a path across the boneyard as around
her, the carnival bloomed like some incredible flower. Tents for petals,

people for pollen, and the straight metal spine of the Ferris wheel for a stem, rising from the dry-baked ground one piece at a time. It was a miracle of modern engineering, the way the whole thing broke down and came back together, and she didn't understand it and would only be in the way if she tried to help, so she kept walking, waving to people who weren't too busy to wave back, smiling at the rest, so they wouldn't have to worry she'd feel slighted when they didn't drop everything to say hello to the boss's daughter.

The carousel sang as it was tested, calliope music drifting sweet as a dream over the field. A speaker buzzed with static louder than a beehive, sweeter than any honey. The garden Aracely had been cultivated for took shape, light and color and glorious, controlled chaos, and she breathed it in with a grateful heart, filling her lungs from tip to top with home, home, *home*. She did all right in motel rooms and trailers, but there was nothing like the honest, open air of the carnival.

Her mama's tent was already up, walls fluttering gently in the breeze, neon sign above the door flickering to draw the midway moths inside. The buzz of the needle cut through the tarp, and Aracely relaxed that tiny bit more. Everything was normal.

She swept the hanging door aside with one hand and stepped through, into the surprising brightness of the tent. Her mother's lighting array had been refined over more seasons than Aracely had been alive, until it would have taken a grand search to find a place—any place—with better visibility. The racks of inks and books of flash were in their places, and her mother sat, regal, next to Charlie, who drove the main wagon, his face pressed into the table, her needle pressed against his skin. A river unspooled behind it, waters dark and deep and beautiful, filled with mystery.

"Hi, Mama," said Aracely.

"Hello, sweetheart. You have a good nap?" Her mother didn't look away from her work, and that, too, was normal; that was the way things were supposed to go.

Aracely, who had been sleeping when the carnival pulled into this new resting place, nodded. "I did," she said. More shyly, she added, "I like to be asleep when we arrive."

Being asleep when the engines stilled and the unloading began meant waking to a garden already coming into bloom, a busy hive of chaos and choices. She hated to see the fields empty, knowing they would only be full—only be fully alive—for such a little time before the carnival moved on again, and the silences returned.

"I know, baby." Her mother reached for a cloth, wiped the tattoo, and went back to work. The carnie stretched out on her table didn't make a sound. "Run along, now. I have a list to get through before we open."

Technically, tattoos could be done anywhere with light and power, and Daisy had done her share of work in roadside motels or while parked at rest stops. But there was something about the carnival air that the carnies swore sped their healing, and there was no advertisement like someone walking around with a smug smile and a bandage on back or bicep. Daisy only tattooed her employees on arrival day: after that, it would be townies until they rolled out again, and that made time on her table rare and precious.

Aracely nodded. "All right, Mama. I love you."

"Love you, too, flower," said Daisy, and then her tall, dream-dazed daughter was gone, leaving her alone with the buzz of the needle and the man on her table, who might as well have been a corpse for all the word he offered.

"You dead there, Charlie? Because I'm not wasting any more of this ink on a dead man."

"Just thinking, Daisy."

"Thinking about what?"

"Aracely."

Most men with the show, they'd said that, they would have had concern for their anatomy immediately after. Aracely was seventeen, sweet and kind and lovely as a summer morning, and her mother protected her like she was the last rose in the world. Daisy had her reasons. No one questioned that. She looked down at Charlie, thoughtful, needle in her hand shaking and ready to sting.

"What about her, Charlie?"

"She doesn't know much outside the show, does she?"

Daisy shook her head, aware he couldn't see her, unable to put her answer, vast and awkward as it was, into words. Born in the back of the boneyard, that was Aracely, her first breath full of popcorn and sawdust and the tinkling song of the calliope. Raised where walls were either tin or canvas, where everything could change in an afternoon—that was Aracely too, daughter of the midway, anchored to the open road. Her life was an eternal summer, bracketed by deep-dreaming winters that passed without comment, leaving her exactly as she'd been before the snow fell.

"Her daddy's people were town," she said finally. "We don't go there anymore. No point to it. He didn't want to know her when she was just getting started, he doesn't get to know her now."

"How's she going to take it when she has to leave?"

Daisy sucked in a sharp breath, putting the needle down before she could do something they'd both regret. Her art was more important than her anger. A flare of temper could last a moment, but a line malformed by a hand that pressed down a bit too hard, a needle wielded in anger . . .

Those were things that would last, and they would shame her. More than anything else, Daisy was a woman who hated to be shamed.

"She never has to leave, Charlie, so you set that thought out of your head," said Daisy, picking her needle up again. "There's nothing in the world outside that she can't find right here."

Charlie, if he thought otherwise, was clever enough to keep his own counsel. The needle flashed and buzzed, and nothing more was said, and too much went unspoken.

Aracely walked the midway as it came alive, a smile on her lips and a song trapped against her tongue, filling her with the heat of its hum. She walked the whole shape of the show, learning every inch of the land, every step of what was going to become her home, transformed by the sweet alchemy of light and sound and intention into something bright, and beautiful, and temporary.

Always temporary.

She stopped at the edge of the space portioned off for their use, melancholy washing over her like a wave, so that she had to press a hand against her chest to keep her heart from beating itself free and flying away. It wasn't fair. Everyone else had a home that was allowed to endure more than the span of a season, but *her* home, *her* place had to disappear every time the wind changed.

Was it so wrong to wish for something that could *last*?

A piece of unsecured rope fluttered in the breeze. She glanced toward it and went still, gazing at the distant shape of a farmhouse. No: it wasn't a farmhouse. She'd seen plenty of those, scattered across America's heartland like a gambler's dice across a felted table. They possessed a certain similarity of form and function, all drawn from the same blueprints, all with their own detail and design. Farmhouses were like people. You knew them when you saw them, and every one of them was different, and every one of them was the same.

This was a mansion. This was the kind of house where movie stars lived, the kind of house that got written up in the magazines that Adam who ran the hoochie-koo show liked to read, the ones he always hid when he saw her coming. Aracely didn't understand why: there was nothing shameful in pictures of nice houses, or interviews with the nice people who lived in them. But Adam acted like he couldn't think of anything worse, like she had no idea there was a world outside the carnival, and so Aracely went along with it. She didn't want to make him uncomfortable.

She went along with a lot of things for the sake of not making anyone else uncomfortable. She thought, sometimes, that *she* was uncomfortable, and then realized if she started dwelling on *that*, she would never do anything ever again, because the impossibility of living her life without doing harm would be too much for her narrow shoulders to carry.

This house didn't look like it worried about doing harm. This house didn't look like it worried about much of anything. It was tall, and every line it had was perfectly straight, except where the architect's hand had decided it should be bent, had coaxed an angle into an arch or a corner into a curve. It was white as bone, and it was beautiful, and Aracely couldn't imagine anything more wonderful than seeing it up close.

She started to step across the line the roustabouts had chalked on the ground and stopped, overcome with indecision. She wasn't allowed to leave the carnival. That was her mother's first and strictest rule. She could murder a man out of boredom, she could lie and cheat and steal and howl down the heavens if that was what she needed to do, but she couldn't leave the show. She had *never* left the show, not really; had been packed away with all its other pieces ever since she could remember, always traveling within the tenuous shell of "carnival." She'd talked to townie kids who said they envied her freedom to travel the country and see the world, not confined in classrooms and expectations, but she thought maybe freedom was one of those things that looked different depending on which side of the cage door you were standing on.

Almost without thinking about it, she lifted a foot, set it down, and was standing suddenly outside the chalk, outside the carnival, outside the shell of everything she'd ever known. Aracely gasped. The wind took the sound and made it disappear.

She took another step. Then she took another step, and another after that, and she was suddenly running across the open field, that thieving wind blowing through her hair, urging her onward. The delicate spring grass bent and broke under her feet, filling the air with the smell of green, growing things, of life beginning and ending in the same careless, carefree step. She didn't stop. She didn't slow. She was running—for the first time in her life she was running—through a world that didn't know her mother's name, that didn't know she was the flower of the midway, too precious to pluck, too delicate to—

The stone that turned under her foot knew nothing of malice, nor of carnivals, nor of runaway midway princesses fleeing gilded cages. It was an accident, nothing more, but it was enough to send Aracely tumbling head over heels down the slope, over and over again, until a strong hand caught her ankle and jerked her to a sudden, bone-jarring halt.

Aracely lay facedown, panting, trying to reconcile the end of her flight with the way the world had turned itself upside-down and wrong-side-up all at the same time. Her chest was tight. Her knees burned, and she knew when she looked at herself, she'd find grass stains and mud and a hundred other proofs of her transgressions.

"My mother's going to *kill* me," she moaned.

A voice—a *new* voice, a *strange* voice, unfamiliar as a motel room in the light of morning—laughed, and the hand holding her ankle let go. "Maybe I should have let you keep rolling, then. A broken neck isn't pleasant, but nobody's mother ever killed them after they were already dead."

Aracely stiffened. New voices meant townies, and townies meant danger. She'd listened to the older ladies talking when they didn't think she was close enough to hear, cigarettes cupped in their hands and secrets hidden in every honeyed syllable. They were her oracles, the grand dames of the carnival, and when she was old enough and wise enough to know everything they knew, she would be allowed to go wherever she wanted. That was how it was, for flowers. They were delicate when they were fresh, but once they'd had time to dry and wither, they were strong. They could perfume the world.

"It's all right. I'm not mad at you or nothing. Lots of people fall down in this field." The voice paused. "Well, I suppose not *lots*. That would take having lots of people hanging around, and that doesn't so much happen anymore."

Aracely hesitated. Whoever it was didn't talk like any townie she'd ever met. Carefully, she pushed herself up onto her hands and twisted around to look over her shoulder.

The girl—woman—girl behind her offered a lopsided smile of greeting, raising one hand in the smallest possible iteration of a wave. "Hi."

She was striking. Not beautiful: there wasn't enough softness to her for beauty. There were girls at the carnival that everyone agreed were beautiful, who could stop traffic when they walked the midway, who could talk townies into anything they wanted. This girl wasn't one of them. She wasn't quite a woman yet, either; she had the same softness and smokiness that Aracely had, like she could still decide to go in any number of directions, rather than growing up to be one singular thing.

Sometimes girls who weren't beautiful could be handsome, but that wasn't this girl, with her hair like coal and her eyes like cinders, with the scars of a bad burn pulling the skin of one cheek upward in a permanent, secretive smile. There were men at the carnival who would say that scar had ruined her, and even without hearing them speak aloud, Aracely felt a wave of hot, terrible hatred for them and their judging eyes. They didn't have the right to judge. They never could.

"Something wrong?" asked the girl, smile fading.

Aracely's hate turned into horror in her belly. She thought—the stranger thought—she thought Aracely was staring at her scars. It was plain as anything.

It was awful.

"No," said Aracely. "I just took a worse tumble than I thought, I guess. I'm sorry. I'm . . ." *I'm away from the carnival for the first time in my life, I'm scared, I'm not supposed to be here, I'm never leaving again.* ". . . I'm Aracely."

"Pretty name," said the stranger, and offered her hand. The only one she could offer, Aracely realized: her other hand was as burnt as her face, and hung, stiff as an old tree branch, at the end of a motionless arm.

I want to kiss her scars, Aracely thought, and her ears burned as she took the offered hand and let herself be tugged to her feet.

"I didn't choose it; my mama gave it to me," she said.

"Still, it suits you," said the stranger. "I'm Joanna."

"That suits you, too." Aracely realized she was still holding Joanna's hand and dropped it, cheeks flaring red. It felt as if there wasn't any blood left for the rest of her body, with the way it was rushing to her face. "I—I mean, you—I mean, do you live around here?"

"In a manner of speaking." Joanna jerked her chin, indicating something beyond Aracely. Aracely turned, and there was the house—the big, white, impossible house that had lured her away from the carnival. The mansion in the middle of nowhere, the house that shouldn't have existed.

"I came back after the fire," said Joanna. "I couldn't think of anyplace I wanted to go. This was home. Didn't matter if it had gotten a little singed-up and smoky. Same thing happened to me. It didn't seem right to leave without fixing what we'd lost."

There was a story in every sentence, and Aracely knew if she peeled them back, if she looked them straight in the eye, she'd find things she didn't want to see. Instead, she smoothed the wrinkles from her skirt and sighed.

"I'm with the carnival that's setting up over the ridge," she said. "I'm sorry to have disturbed you."

Joanna raised an eyebrow. "Carnival?" she asked. "I own the land for a mile around here, and this is the first I'm hearing of a carnival."

The blood that had been rushing to Aracely's face drained away, leaving her pale as paper. "I . . . Our frontman was supposed to make sure everything was in order," she said. "He has the papers." Or did he? She never left the carnival boundary, not under normal circumstances. How would she know if everything was being done correctly?

There was never enough money. She knew *that*. There was never enough money, and the Ferris wheel needed repairing, and half the games were privately owned, they came and went like flowers in the fall, undependable, nothing you could pin a midway on. Her mother had been making concessions on their rent for years, letting them have their spaces for less than she should have, just to be sure of having steady attractions to sell towns on allowing the carnival to stop there.

A big, empty field, near a house that had almost burned down . . . it would have seemed like a good place to set up without paying.

News of disasters travels fast. They could have been states away when the fire happened and still have heard about it, her mother filing the information for a dry spell, a time when an unguarded field would be a necessary thing. News that it had been rebuilt, that someone was living there, well. That wasn't as interesting. It wouldn't have traveled nearly as fast.

"I have to go," said Aracely.

"I suppose you do," said Joanna—and was it Aracely's imagination, or did the other girl's face fall, just a little, the expression dampened by her scars? "No one lingers here for long."

Aracely wanted to tell her no, no, she wasn't running *away* from Joanna; she was running *toward* the carnival, toward her mother, toward the answers to the uncomfortable questions she was asking herself. She wanted to stay where Joanna was more than almost anything she could think of, wanted to keep looking at this beautiful girl with her tousled hair and her suspicious eyes, wanted to daydream about what it would feel like to run her fingers down both sides of her face at once, to read the secret stories tangled in her scars. Her throat was dry; her tongue was strangled. All she could do was shake her head, and turn, and flee.

When she reached the ridge, she looked back.

Joanna was gone.

So was the house.

The carnival had continued to unfold while Aracely was running, was tumbling, was falling, although she did not know it yet, into the fringes of a thing that looked very much like love. As she walked along the familiar, ever-changing aisles, lights twinkling on every side, the Ferris wheel turning gently in the distance, she worried.

To any other girl, it might have seemed strange for a house to be there one moment and gone the next: houses were meant, after all, to be rooted, stationary things. But Aracely had grown up with the carnival.

It moved. If it stopped moving, it would die. She hadn't heard of houses that did the same: that didn't mean they weren't out there. Maybe the house had simply wandered off for a little while, and would be back when it felt like it.

The entrance to her mother's tent was closed, but the buzzing of the needle had stopped. Aracely tugged it aside and peeked through. "Mama?"

Daisy looked up from cleaning her needles and smiled. "There's my girl," she said. "Everything coming together out there?"

"Not from anything I've done," said Aracely, stepping inside. "Mama, did we pay to set up here? Do we have permits?"

"Aracely, what . . ." Daisy stopped mid-sentence, eyes narrowing. "What have you done to your dress?"

"It's not nice to answer a question with a question," said Aracely. "You taught me that."

"I also taught you to respect your mother, and not to go getting grass and mud all over your clothes. Where have you *been*?"

Aracely lifted her chin, trying to look brave. She wasn't sure what brave looked like, but she thought she could do it, if she didn't flinch. "I went running in the grass. It's beautiful out there, Mama, you wouldn't believe how—"

But her mother was on her feet, eyes wide and horrified, cleaning rag and tattoo gun forgotten in her haste to cross the tent and grasp Aracely's shoulders, fingers digging in until they left paths of pain behind them. "You went outside the carnival?" she asked, and her voice was as shrill as the screams from the roller coaster, the ones that hung in the air like a promise of bigger fears to come. "You left the boundary?"

"I wasn't hurt! I met the girl who owns this land, Mama, and she's beautiful too, she's not like a townie at all. She lives in the house past the ridge." The house that wasn't there. But that was all right, because it would come back. Right? That was probably the real difference between a carnival and a house. Houses had to stay on the same land all the time, planted like roses, while carnivals went wherever they wanted to go, like wildflowers.

"Did she touch you?" Daisy's hands grasped tighter, tighter, until Aracely gasped and pulled away, shoulders throbbing.

"Mama, *stop*! You're scaring me!"

"Answer the question!"

Aracely took another step back, and did the unthinkable.

She lied.

"No, Mama. She didn't want to get her hands dirty."

Lies are meant to be false things that seem believable, but this lie didn't seem believable to Aracely. She couldn't imagine Joanna—beautiful Joanna, with her house that is and isn't there—being afraid of a little mud, especially not when that mud came from land that she already owned.

Daisy relaxed, and Aracely did the same, knowing her deception had been successful. A pang of pain shot through her heart. She was a bad girl now. She was a girl who could deceive her mother, and not even feel a little bit sorry for it.

"Good," said Daisy. "I don't know what possessed you to leave the carnival, but you must never, *never* do that again, and even more, you must never, *never* let an outsider touch you. You're delicate. People like that, in places like this, they don't understand how to be kind to delicate things. I won't have you risking yourself like that. All right?"

Aracely didn't answer. Daisy grabbed her again and shook her by the shoulders, seeming to have forgotten her own warning.

"All right?" she repeated.

"All right, Mama," said Aracely.

This time Daisy let go of her own accord. "Good girl," she said, voice barely above a whisper. "Good, good girl."

Aracely turned and fled the tent, and Daisy did not pursue her.

The sun dipped lower in the sky. Not quite sunset, when the midway would light up like a summer morning and the townies would start rolling in, drawn by the lights and the sound and the promise of something better than their quiet, ordinary homes, but getting closer.

Dawn was a distant memory, the moment closer to tomorrow than yesterday.

Aracely stumbled between the familiar attractions, clutching the front of her gown and trying to swallow the fear that had grown in her breast with every panicked word that dropped from her mother's lips. Daisy wasn't supposed to lose her temper. Not with *her*. Daisy was her mother, her sole protector in a world full of dangerous things, and if Daisy was a danger, too, well . . .

Aracely didn't know what she'd do if her mother had somehow become another danger in a world she'd always known was out to do her harm. She was innocent, yes, and she was delicate, but she was both those things because it had been safer than the alternative. If she allowed herself to be innocent and delicate and naïve, her mother would take care of everything, and the dangers of the wider world would never be able to consume her.

"You look lost."

Aracely froze. Charlie emerged from the shadows between two tents, a bandage on his arm and a rolled cigarette in his hand, sweet smoke drifting up to tint the air. He looked at her frankly, assessing her fear. Aracely clutched her gown tighter, the fabric bunching under her fingers.

"What happened, Aracely?" he asked, and his voice was kind—kinder than her mother's had been, kinder than she would ever have expected it to be. "Somebody hurt you?"

Silent, she nodded, unable to make her traitor tongue admit who had done the hurting.

Charlie sighed, taking a long drag on his cigarette as he considered the mud on her hem and the grass stains on her skirt. When he spoke again, it was to ask, "You go off the grounds?"

This time, her nod had a sliver of defiance in it. She glared at him, her fingers unclenching from her gown as she silently dared him to say something, anything, against her going wherever she liked.

Instead, he smiled. "Good girl. You're almost grown. You have the right to leave if you want to. It's not right to keep you cooped up. You're

not the first person born to the midway, and I daresay you won't be the
last—the world may be shutting shows like ours down as fast as it can
manage, but people keep making babies, and we've got a little time yet.
That doesn't mean you have to stay here. You can't choose the carnival if
you've never once been outside it."

"Mama says I do," said Aracely.

"Your mother . . ." Charlie paused, choosing his words as carefully
as he could. "Your mother worries about you. That's all. Mothers always
worry about daughters. Yours maybe more than most. But she has her
reasons."

"What are they?" Aracely narrowed her eyes. "Everyone says she has
her reasons, everyone says she's doing the best she can, but everyone also
acts like it's normal for me to always be in the carnival, even when they
come and go as they please. I've never even been inside the Walmart!"

Her last complaint was delivered with such an indignant wail that
it was all Charlie could do not to laugh. He sobered quickly enough,
regarding her with steady eyes.

"You know it wasn't easy, birthing you," he said. "Your mother
thought she'd lost you, a whole bunch of times, both before and after you
were outside her belly and looking at the world. If she's a little protective,
you can blame it partially on that."

"But I didn't *do* that," said Aracely. "It's not my fault if I was sickly
when I was born. I didn't decide any of that, and it's not fair to keep
holding it against me. I've never done anything wrong, not on purpose.
I just wanted to see the house."

Charlie stilled. Finally, in a soft voice, he asked, "The house?"

"On the other side of the field. I met the girl who lives there. She
didn't know we were coming. Charlie, did we not pay our rental fees?
Are we here when we're not supposed to be?" Aracely looked at him
anxiously. "I don't want to have to move along when we've just gotten
everything set up, but if we don't have permission, I guess that could be
what we have to do."

"There's no house there," said Charlie, voice still soft, like he was afraid that to raise it would be to shatter some thin and impossible peace. "This field . . . the people who owned it all died. The bank owns all the land for almost a mile, and we did all our rental paperwork through them, exactly as we're meant to do. I don't know who you met, girl, but there's no way she lived in a house that doesn't exist, and there's no way she gets to say whether or not we're allowed to linger here."

Aracely stared at him, eyes gone wide and heart gone narrow until it felt like it was barely beating at all, like she was on the verge of toppling over. Then she turned and fled, not deeper into the midway, but out, toward the boundary line, toward the vast and formless freedom of the fields behind. Charlie swore and ran in the opposite direction, fleeing toward Daisy's tent.

Two figures running, both as fleet as fear can make them, one heading for a secret, the other for a story. See how they run, these children of the carnival sky! The man, with his fresh tattoo still aching on his skin, who remembers rumors, yes, stories that will linger after he is gone, who knows that everything is about to change. The girl, as guarded and sheltered as any hothouse flower, perfectly adapted to the climate of the carnival, where walk things that are neither here nor there, now nor then . . . living nor dead.

She ran not because she knew the shape of the story she was becoming, but because she didn't know it; because she was afraid, as all sheltered things are, of the aching unknown.

He ran because he understood.

Aracely was younger, more frightened, and less aware of her own limitations; when she ran, it was with the wholehearted abandon of a young thing, and this time, when she crested the ridge and saw the house set out before her like the shadow of a dream, she did not lose her footing. She ran, and ran, and ran, until her feet were pounding up the front steps of a house that shouldn't exist, until her hands were hammering on the door. Was this how people knocked? She had seen it in movies and on television, but she had never really had the chance to try it for herself. Doors in the carnival worked a little differently. Knocking on a tent could knock it over; knocking on a tin-walled trailer was loud and hollow at the same time, taking so little effort that a child could do it.

Knocking on wood was different. The house felt solid, like she was beating her fists on bone, and when she pulled back for another volley, the skin on the sides of her hands was red and hot.

The door swung open. Joanna stood framed in the entryway, only blackness behind her, a quizzical expression on her beautiful, scarred face. "Aracely?" she asked. "What are you doing here?"

"Are you real?" Aracely blurted.

Joanna's confusion melted into sad resignation—and yes, acceptance. "Ah," she said. "Someone told you. I guess that was going to happen, once you went back to your carnival and told people you'd seen me."

Aracely said nothing.

"I'm real. I was real, anyway, before the fire. I don't know if you'd consider me real now. Are ghosts real?" Joanna looked at her, sidelong and thoughtful. "Are *you* real? The living can't see the dead, usually. They sure can't touch us. You didn't have any trouble touching me."

"Dead?" whispered Aracely.

"In the fire," said Joanna. "We all died. I woke up alone in the ashes. I think . . . I think I stayed for my horses." She waved a hand, indicating the rear of the house, the fields that rolled on behind it. "They died so quickly that they didn't realize it had happened. They're all still here, with me. I guess they will be until someone comes along and paves these hills to build condos or shopping malls or something. Even ghost horses don't want to stick around to argue with bulldozers."

"What happened?"

"Bad wiring in the walls. It was over a century old, and I guess every generation had decided it could be somebody else's problem, until the place went up in the middle of the night, and no one made it outside to watch the burning." Joanna reached up and touched the scar on the side of her face. "I could wish these away if I wanted to, be the girl who'd never known what it was to burn, but it feels like that would be cheating, somehow. If I get to stay here, I should stay here as the aftermath, not the anticipation. How is it that you don't know this?"

"Why should I know it?" asked Aracely. "I've never been outside the carnival before."

Joanna hesitated. Then, without stepping out of the entryway, she extended her hand toward Aracely. When the other girl took it, she sighed, the sound as soft and sad as wind rustling through the boughs of an old oak.

"I thought you knew," she said. "Aracely . . . did none of them ever tell you that you were dead?"

Charlie burst into Daisy's tent to find her sitting with an open bottle of wine and a book of baby pictures, drinking from the one as she wept over the second. Her head was bowed, her shoulders slumped; she looked years older than she had when they'd rolled into town, a comfortable caravan that carried its secrets inside closed boxes, where no one would ever have to see.

"She gone?" Daisy asked, not looking up.

Charlie stopped. "Daisy," he said. "What did you do?"

"You were with us," said Daisy. She turned another page. When was the last time he'd seen that book? When was the last time he'd seen a camera pointed at Aracely, for that matter? "She was such a beautiful child. Remember? Always running around like she thought she was going to get her feet nailed to the ground. So busy. I used to watch her go and wonder what it would take to make her stop. Seemed like it would need a miracle."

Charlie frowned. "Daisy . . ."

"Didn't take a miracle. Not unless you think 'miracle' is another way of saying 'truck.' Only mercy was that she didn't see it coming. She ran out into the road so fast, and the brakes were old, and there wasn't time for her to suffer." Daisy looked up, a tear running down her cheek. "Guess there wasn't time for her to notice, either, because she came running straight over to me, little pigtails bobbing in a breeze that blew right through her, and she didn't seem to realize her body was lying in the dust, like a ticket stub at the end of the night. She asked me to play with her."

Charlie was silent.

"It took everything I had and then some to not start screaming, but I kept my wits about me, and by the time the sun went down, I had a ghost trap drawn all the way along the midway. By the time we rolled out, every truck and every trailer we owned was safe for a haunting. As long as she stays in bounds—and I've pushed them further every year, so she could have truck stops and motel rooms and convenience stores along with all the rest—she's solid, she's real, she's growing like any other girl would grow."

"But she's dead," said Charlie softly.

"She's *mine*." Daisy bared her teeth in a snarl. "*My* daughter, *my* flower, *my* responsibility. She's always been able to be happy here, despite her circumstances. She's always known that she was loved, and how many townie children dream of growing up to run away with the carnival? I gave her the life she would have wanted, if she'd been in a place to choose."

"You didn't give her any life at all," Charlie countered. "She's a shade. That poor child. Does she have any idea?"

"How could she?" For a moment, Daisy's expression was pure smugness. "She's grown up within the confines of the carnival. She's changed with every passing year, exactly as a living girl would. There's nothing stopping her from being happy, from doing everything she could ever want to do, as long as everything she ever wants is within reach of the midway lights." The smugness faded, replaced by sudden sorrow. "Or she would have been happy, if she'd only been content. Is she gone?"

Charlie nodded slowly. "I think so. She ran from me when I told her there was no house."

"Then I'll have to go and get her back." Daisy set the book aside and stood. Her skirt was hiked high enough to show the garlands of wheat and roses tattooed around her calves, climbing ever higher toward the secret mysteries she had shared with no one since Aracely's birth. Charlie felt his cheeks redden, but didn't look away.

Daisy stepped toward him, spreading her empty hands in supplication. "Will you help me?" she asked.

He didn't want to. Dead was dead and living was living, and the two were meant to exist side by side, not share a single space. But Aracely . . . she'd been dead for so long, and he'd never known. She'd been *happy*, despite her circumstances. Did he really have the right to refuse her mother?

"I will," he said, and Daisy smiled.

They walked toward each other, all unknowing of their unison, drawn by forces greater than the moment, forces that had been building for years. Since a fire; since an accident; since a mother's stubborn love had refused to let go what should have been gone and buried. Four people on the green hills between carnival and crypt, between midway and mansion.

Daisy walked with her head high and her skirts bundled above her knees, a jar of salt in one hand and a jar of grave dirt in the other. Her witchery was not complicated, old and slow and comfortable in its working, pouring like molasses into the world, stirred and spelled and carefully tended. She worked the way her mother had taught her, the way she would have taught her own daughter, had it not been so dangerous to teach those workings to the dead.

Charlie walked beside her in silence, his own hands empty and his own heart pounding. He was a simple man. He ferried the carnival from one location to the next, and all he asked in exchange was a paycheck and a clear map of his next destination. This was a bit beyond him. Had he been asked, he would have said he didn't understand why he remained, why he didn't turn and run back to the comforting, ordinary shadows of the midway, which lit up the sky behind them like a beacon. The crowds would be coming soon. The night was on the cusp of beginning.

From the other direction came Aracely and Joanna, hand in hand, which granted them both more power than they yet understood, for to hold a ghost's substance is to hold their strength, and they were powerful as specters go, both of them able to pass among the living, if only for a little while, both of them prepared to fight instead of fleeing. They were what their circumstances had made of them, the flower and the fallen, and they walked with the smooth, easy steps of teenagers who had never been quite allowed to cross the line into adulthood.

Aracely's childhood had been a dream given to her by her mother, but it was hers all the same, and the length of her limbs and the clearness of her eyes belonged to her entirely. Some gifts, once given, can't be taken back. She walked with her fingers tangled in her new companion's, like bones buried in the same earth, and she felt the wind blow through her, and she was not afraid. Part of her, she thought, had always known; had simply been waiting for permission to remember. Part of her was less afraid of letting go than it was of holding on.

They were not lovers, both of them scarce seventeen and dead besides, both of them trying to decide what they wanted to become, as the long years of their existence stretched out in front of them, an endless line of tickets to spend at any midway they chose. But they might be. Aracely flushed when she tried to look too long at Joanna, who she thought still burned, somewhere deep inside, a body built around a cinder in the shape of a heart. And as for Joanna, she couldn't look Aracely in the eye without tasting honey on her tongue, without feeling her skin grow tight and hot in a way that had nothing at all to do with flames. So they were not lovers, no, but one day . . .

Time was on their side. It had been since the moment that they died.

They met at the center of the field, and the carnival shone on the hill behind Daisy and Charlie, and the house that was and was not there flickered ivory and ash behind Joanna and Aracely. Daisy looked at their joined hands and felt her heart break, just a little, just enough to let the light pour in. Aracely looked at the anguish in her mother's eyes and forgave her, just a little, just enough to let the love inside again.

"You should have told me," said Aracely.

"Ghost children don't always grow up," said Daisy. "Living children do. If I lied, it was so you'd be able to stand here like this, and not be trapped forever where you were."

"Were you ever going to tell me?"

Daisy rolled her shoulders in a shrug, and said nothing.

"Are you coming home?" asked Charlie. It was a blunt question, and it fell into the delicate web of things unspoken like a stone. Aracely looked at him.

"Should I?" she asked.

"Yes," said Daisy.

"No," said Joanna.

"Only if you want to," said Charlie.

Aracely was silent for a long beat before slowly, finally, she let go of Joanna's hand. The other girl flickered for a moment, like a sheet whipping in the wind. Only for a moment, though, and moments pass.

"Mama," said Aracely. "Why could I grow up inside the carnival?"

"It's a ghost trap," said Daisy. "I designed it that way. To protect you."

Aracely nodded. "Then this is my answer. When you drive away, I won't come with you."

Daisy made a small, pained sound of wordless longing.

"Winter where you like: I won't be there," said Aracely. "But when you come back in the spring, you can collect us both."

Joanna shot her a surprised look.

"I need some time to think, and then I need to see what else is out there in the world," said Aracely.

"Baby . . ." said Daisy.

"No, Mama. You owe me this."

Daisy looked at her. Then, slowly, she nodded.

"All right, baby," she said. "I'll see you in the spring."

There is a carnival that tours the Midwestern United States on a shifting schedule, like all touring shows of its kind. It is among the last of a dying breed, but still it moves, and still it unfurls like a flower whenever it lands, the petals of the midway spreading wide. People who've seen it say there's something special there; something that may endure when the other traveling shows have closed.

"It's like a haunted house," one said, when interviewed by a local paper. "It's a little shivery, but you want to be there anyway. You want to know what happens next."

What she didn't say—what none of them ever say—was that as she was leaving on the first night the show was in town, she had looked back over her shoulder and seen two girls, barely blurring into women, appear at the top of the Ferris wheel. Their hands had been locked together, tight as chains, and their eyes had been on the moon, and even with all that distance between herself and them, she would have sworn that they were smiling.

Author's Note

I have always loved the story of Hades and Persephone. It shares a great deal of its shape with the ballad of Tam Lin, which was the subject of my thesis in school. I wanted to sort of prod at the places where those stories aligned, and where they fell away from each other. My favorite part of the story has always been that Hades, in Greek myth, is really the nerd of gods. So why would he steal this one perfect flower? What sort of situation would need to arise for him to even consider taking such a step? And the carnival, of course, is always a perfect place to interrogate a myth, because it's a liminal space we create ourselves, out of canvas and paint and anticipation; we can unravel any story we want there. I was raised on carnival ground. I never intend to stop picking it to pieces.

Seanan McGuire

THE JUSTIFIED

BY
—
ANN LECKIE

HET HAD EATEN NOTHING FOR WEEKS BUT BONY, gape-mawed fish—some of them full of neurotoxin. She'd had to alter herself so she could metabolize it safely, which had taken some doing. So when she ripped out the walsel's throat and its blood spurted red onto the twilit ice, she stared, salivary glands aching, stomach growling. She didn't wait to butcher her catch but sank her teeth into skin and fat and muscle, tearing a chunk away from its huge shoulder.

Movement caught her eye, and she sprang upright, walsel blood trickling along her jaw, to see Dihaut, black and silver, walking toward her across the ages-packed snow and ice. She'd have known her sib anywhere, but even if she hadn't recognized them, there was no mistaking their crescent-topped standard, Months and Years, tottering behind them on two thin, insectile legs.

But sib or not, familiar or not, Het growled, heart still racing, muscles poised for flight or attack. She had thought herself alone and unwatched. Had made sure of it before she began her hunt. Had Dihaut been watching her all this time? It would be like them.

For a brief moment she considered disemboweling Dihaut, leaving them dying on the ice, Months and Years in pieces beside them. But that would only put this off until her sib took a new body. Dihaut could be endlessly persistent when they wished, and the fact that they had come all the way to this frigid desert at the farthest reaches of Nu to find her suggested that the ordinary limits of that persistence—such as they were—could not be relied on. Besides, she and Dihaut had nearly always gotten along well. Still, she stayed on the alert, and did not shift into a more relaxed posture.

"This is the Eye of Merur, the Noble Dihaut!" announced Months and Years as Dihaut drew near. Its high, thready voice cut startlingly through the silence of the snowy waste.

"I know who they are," snarled Het.

The standard made a noise almost like a sniff. "I only do my duty, Noble Het."

Dihaut hunched their shoulders. Their face, arms, torso, and legs were covered with what looked like long, fine fur but, this being Dihaut, was likely feathers. Mostly black, but their left arm and leg, and part of their torso, were silver-white. "Hello, sib," they said. "Sorry to interrupt your supper. Couldn't you have fled someplace warmer?"

Het had no answer for this—she'd asked herself the same question many times in the past several years.

"I see you've changed your skin," Dihaut continued. "It does look odd, but I suppose it keeps you warm. Would you mind sharing the specs?" They shivered.

"It's clothes," said Het. "A coat, and boots, and gloves."

"Clothes!" Dihaut peered at her more closely. "I see. They must be very confining, but I suppose it's worth it to be warm. Do you have any you could lend me? Or could whoever supplied you with yours give me some, too?"

"Sorry," growled Het. "Not introducing you." Actually, she hadn't even introduced herself. She'd stolen the clothes, when the fur she'd grown hadn't kept her as warm as she'd hoped.

Dihaut made a wry "huh," their warm breath puffing from their mouth in a small cloud. "Well. I'm sorry to be so blunt." They gave a regretful smile, all Dihaut in its acknowledgment of the pointlessness of small talk. "I'm very sorry to intrude on whatever it is you're doing down here—I never was quite clear on why you left, no one was, except that you were angry about something. Which . . ." They shrugged. "If it were up to me"—they raised both finely feathered hands, gestured vaguely to the dead walsel with the silver one—"I'd leave you to it."

"Would you." She didn't even try to sound as though she believed them.

"Truly, sib. But the ruler of Hehut, the Founder and Origin of Life on Nu, the One Sovereign of This World, wishes for you to return to Hehut." At this, Months and Years waved its thin, sticklike arms as though underlining Dihaut's words. "She'd have sent others before me, but I convinced her that if you were brought back against your wishes, your presence at court would not be as delightful as usual." They shivered again. "Is there somewhere warmer we can talk?"

"Not really."

"I don't mean any harm to the people you've been staying with," said Dihaut.

"I haven't been staying with anyone." She gestured vaguely around with one blood-matted hand, indicating the emptiness of the ice.

"You must have been staying with someone, sib. I know there are no approved habitations here, so they must be unauthorized, but that's no concern of mine unless they should come to Merur's attention. Or if they have Animas. Please tell me, sib, that they don't have unauthorized Animas here? Because you know we'll have to get rid of them if they do, and I'd really like to just go right back to Hehut, where it's actually warm."

Unbidden, her claws extended again, just a bit. She had never spoken to the people who lived here, but she owed them. It was by watching them that she'd learned about the poisonous fish. Otherwise the toxin might have caught her off guard, even killed her. And then she'd have found herself resurrected again in Hehut, in the middle of everything she'd fled.

"They don't have Animas," she told Dihaut. "How could they?" When their bodies died, they died.

"Thank all the stars for that!" Dihaut gave a relieved, shivery sigh. "As long as they stay up here in this freezing desert with their single, cold lives, we can all just go on pretending they don't exist. So surely we can pretend they don't exist in their presumably warmer home?"

"Your standard is right behind you," Het pointed out. "Listening."

"It is," Dihaut agreed. "It always is. There's nowhere in the world we can really be away from Merur. We always have to deal with the One Ruler. Even, in the end, the benighted unauthorized souls in this forsaken place." They were, by now, shivering steadily.

"Can't she leave anyone even the smallest space?" asked Het. "Some room to be apart, without her watching? For just a little while?"

"It's usually us watching for her," put in Dihaut.

Het waved that away. "Not a single life anywhere in the world that she doesn't claim as hers. She makes *certain* there's nowhere to go!"

"Order, sib," said Dihaut. "Imagine what might happen if everyone went running around free to do whatever they liked with no consequences. And she *is* the Founder and Origin of Life on Nu."

"Come on, Dihaut. I was born on *Aeons*, just before Merur left the ship and came down to Nu. There were already people living here. I remember it. And even now it depends who you ask. Either Merur

27

arrived a thousand years ago in *Aeons* and set about pulling land from beneath the water and creating humans, or else she arrived and brought light and order to humans she found living in ignorance and chaos. I've heard both from her own mouth at different times. And you know better. You're the historian."

They tried that regretful half smile again, but they were too cold to manage it. "I tell whichever story is more politic at the moment. And there are, after all, different sorts of truth. But please." They spread their hands, placatory. "I beg you. Come with me back to Hehut. Don't make me freeze to death in front of you."

"Noble Dihaut," piped their standard, "Eye of Merur, I am here. Your Anima is entirely safe."

"Yes," shivered Dihaut, "but there isn't a new body ready for me yet, and I hate being out of things for very long. Please, sib, let's go back to my flier. We can argue about all of this on the way back home."

And, well, now that Dihaut had found her, it wasn't as though she had much choice. She said, with ill grace, "Well fine, then. Where's your flier?"

"This way," said Dihaut, shivering, and turned. They were either too cold or too wise to protest when Het bent to grab the dead walsel's tusk and drag it along as she followed.

It rained in Hehut barely more often than it snowed in the icy waste Het had left, but rivers and streams veined Hehut under the bright, uninterrupted blue of the sky, rivers and streams that pooled here and there into lotus-veiled lakes and papyrus marshes, and the land was lush and green.

The single-lived working in the fields looked up as the shadow of Dihaut's flier passed over them. They made a quick sign with their left hands and turned back to the machines they followed. Small boats dotted the river that snaked through the fields, single-lived fishers hauling in nets, here and there the long, gilded barque of one of the Justified shining in the sun. The sight gave Het an odd pang—she had not ever been given much to nostalgia, or to dwelling on memories of her various childhoods, none of which to her recall had been particularly childish, but she was struck with a sudden, almost tangible memory of sunshine on her skin, and the sound of water lapping at the hull of a boat. Not, she was sure, a single moment but a composite of all the times she'd fled to the river, to fish, or walk, or sit under a tree and stare at the water flowing by. To be by herself. As much as she could be, anyway.

"Almost there," said Dihaut, reclined in their seat beside her. "Are you going to change?" They had shed their feathers on the flight here and now showed black and silver skin, smooth and shining.

Het had shed her coat, boots, and gloves but left her thick and shaggy fur. It would likely be uncomfortable in the heat, but she was reluctant to let go of it; she couldn't say why. "I don't think I have time."

"Noble Eyes of Merur," said Months and Years, upright at Dihaut's elbow, "we will arrive at Tjenu in fifteen minutes. The One Sovereign will see you immediately."

Definitely no time to change. "So urgent?" asked Het. "Do you know what this is about?"

"I have my suspicions." Dihaut shrugged one silver shoulder. "It's probably better if Merur tells you herself."

So this was something that no one—not even Merur's own Eyes— could safely talk about. There were times when Merur was in no mood to be tolerant of any suggestion that her power and authority might be incomplete, and at those times even admitting knowledge of some problem could end with one's Anima deleted altogether.

Tjenu came into view, its gold-covered facade shining in the hot sun, a wide, dark avenue of smooth granite stretching from its huge main doors straight across the gardens to a broad entrance in the polished white walls. The Road of Souls, the single-lived called it, imagining that it was the route traveled by the Animas of the dead on their way to judgment at Dihaut's hands. As large as the building was—a good kilometer on each of its four sides, and three stories high—most of Tjenu was underground. Or so Dihaut had told her. Het had only ever been in the building's sunlit upper reaches. At least while she was alive, and not merely an Anima awaiting resurrection.

Dihaut's flier set down within Tjenu's white walls, beside a willow-edged pond. Coming out, Het found Great Among Millions, her own standard, waiting, hopping from one tiny foot to the other, feathery fingers clenched into minuscule fists, stilled the next moment, its black pole pointing perfectly upright, the gold cow horns at its top polished and shining.

"Eye of Merur," it said, its voice high and thin. "Noble Het, the Justified, the Powerful, Servant of the One Sovereign of Nu. The Ruler of all, in her name of Self-Created, in her name of She Caused All to Be, in her name of She Listens to Prayers, in her name of Sustainer of the Justified, in her name of—"

"Stop," Het commanded. "Just tell me what she wants."

"Your presence, gracious Het," it said, with equanimity. Great Among Millions had been her standard for several lifetimes, and was used to her. "Immediately. Do forgive the appearance of impertinence, Noble Het. I only relay the words of the One Sovereign. I will escort you to your audience."

Months and Years, coming out of the flier, piped, "Great Among Millions, please do not forget the Noble Het's luggage."

"What luggage?" asked Het.

"Your walsel, Noble Eye," replied Months and Years, waving a tiny hand. "What's left of it. It's starting to smell."

"Just dispose of it," said Het. "I've eaten as much of it as I'm going to."

Great Among Millions gave a tiny almost-hop from one foot to the other, and stilled again. "Noble Het, you have been away from Tjenu, from Hehut itself, without me, for fifty-three years, two months, and three days." It almost managed to sound as though it was merely stating a fact, and not making a complaint. But not quite.

"It's good to see you again, too," Het said. Her standard unclenched its little fists and gestured toward the golden mass of Tjenu. "Yes," Het acknowledged. "Let's go."

The vast audience chamber of the One Sovereign of Nu was black-ceilinged, inlaid with silver and copper stars that shone in the light of the lamps below. Courtiers, officials, and supplicants, alone or in small scattered groups, murmured as Het passed. Of course. There was no mistaking her identity, furred and unkempt as she was—Great Among Millions followed her.

She crossed the brown, gold-flecked floor to where it changed, brown shading to blue and green in Merur's near presence, where one never set foot without direct invitation—unless, of course, one was an Eye, in which case one's place in the bright-lit vicinity of Merur was merely assumed, a privilege of status.

Stepping into the green, Great Among Millions tottering behind her, Het cast a surreptitious glance—habitual, even after so long away!—at those so privileged. And stopped, and growled. Among the officials standing near Merur, three bore her Eye. There were four Eyes; Het herself was one. Dihaut, who Het had left with their flier, was another. There should only have been two Eyes here.

"Don't be jealous, Noble Het," whispered Great Among Millions, its thready voice sounding in her ear alone. "You were gone so very long." Almost accusing, that sounded.

"She *replaced* me," Het snarled. She didn't recognize whoever it was who, she saw now, held an unfamiliar standard, but the Justified changed bodies so frequently. If there was a new Eye, why should Merur call on Het? Why not leave her be?

"And you left *me* behind," continued Great Among Millions. "Alone. They asked and asked me where you were and I did not know, though I wished to." It made a tiny, barely perceptible stomp. "They put me in a storeroom. In a box."

"Het, my Eye, approach!" Merur, calling from where she sat under

31

her blue-canopied pavilion, alone but for those three Eyes, and the standards, and smaller lotus- and lily-shaped servants that always attended her.

And now, her attention turned from Merur's other Eyes, Het looked fully at the One Sovereign herself. Armless, legless, her snaking body cased in scales of gold and lapis, Merur circled the base of her polished granite chair of state, her upper body leaning onto the seat, her head standard human, her hair in dozens of silver-plaited braids falling around her glittering gold face. Her dark eyes were slit-pupiled.

Het had seen Merur take such a shape before—as well as taking new bodies at need or at whim, the Justified could to some degree alter a currently held body at will. But there were limits to such transformations, and it had been long, long centuries since Merur had taken this sort of body.

She should have concealed her surprise and prostrated herself, but instead she stood and stared as Great Among Millions announced, in a high, carrying voice, "The fair, the fierce, the Burning Eye of the One Sovereign of Nu, the Noble Het!"

"My own Eye!" said Merur. "I have need of you!"

Het could not restrain her anger, even in the face of the One Sovereign of Nu. "I count four Eyes in this court, Sovereign—those three over there, and the Noble Dihaut. There have always been four. Why should you need me to be a fifth?" Behind her, Great Among Millions made a tiny noise.

"I shed one body," admonished Merur, her voice faintly querulous, "only to reawaken and find you gone. For decades you did not return. Why? No one accused you of any dereliction of duty, let alone disloyalty. You had suffered no disadvantage; your place as my favored Eye was secure. And now, returning, you question my having appointed someone to fill the office you left empty! You would do better to save your anger for the enemies of Nu!"

"I can't account for my heart," said Het crossly. "It is as it is."

This seemed to mollify Merur. "Well, you always have had a temper. And it is this very honesty that I have so missed. Indeed, it is what I require of you!" Here Merur lowered her voice and looked fretfully from one side to the other, and the standards and flower-form servitors scuttled back a few feet. "Het, my Eye. This body is . . . imperfect. It will not obey me as it should, and it is dying, far sooner than it ought. I need to move to a new one."

"Already?" Het's skin prickled with unease.

"This is not the first time a body has grown imperfectly," Merur said, her voice low. "But I should have seen the signs long before I entered it. Someone must have concealed them from me! It is impossible that this has happened through mere incompetence.

"I have dealt with the technicians. I have rooted out any disloyalty in Tjenu. But I cannot say the same of all Hehut, let alone all of Nu. And this body of mine will last only a few months longer, but no suitable replacement, one untampered with by traitors, will be ready for a year or more. And I cannot afford to leave Nu rulerless for so long! My Eyes I trust—you and Dihaut, certainly, after all this time. The Justified are for the most part reliable, and the single-lived know that Dihaut will judge them. But I have never been gone for more than a few days at a time. If this throne is empty longer, it may encourage the very few wayward to stir up the single-lived, and if, in my absence, enough among the Justified can be led astray—no. I cannot be gone so long unless I am certain of order."

Dismayed, Het snarled. "Sovereign, what do you expect me to do about any of this?"

"What you've always done! Protect Nu. All trace of unrest, of disorder, must be prevented. You've rid Nu of rebellion before. I need you to do it again."

That shining silver river, the fishers, the lilies and birds had all seemed so peaceful. So much as they should be, when Het and Dihaut had flown in. "Unrest? What's the cause this time?"

33

"The cause!" Merur exclaimed, exasperated. "There is no *cause*. There never has been! The worthy I give eternal life and health; they need only reach out their hands for whatever they desire! The unworthy are here and gone, and they have all they need and occupation enough, or if not, well, they seal their own fate. There has never been any *cause*, and yet it keeps happening—plots, rumors, mutterings of discontent. My newest Eye"—Merur did not notice, or affected not to notice, Het's reaction to that—"is fierce and efficient. I do not doubt her loyalty. But I am afraid she doesn't have your imagination. Your vision. Your *anger*. Two years ago I sent her out to deal with this, and she returned saying there was no trouble of any consequence! She doesn't *understand*! Where does this keep coming from? Who is planting such ideas in the minds of my people? Root it out, Het. Root it out from among my people, trace it back to its origin, and destroy it so that Nu can rest secure while my next body grows. So that we can at last have the peace and security I have always striven for."

"Sovereign of Nu," growled Het. "I'll do my best."

What choice did she have, after all?

She should have gone right to Dihaut. The first place to look for signs of trouble would be among the Animas of the recently dead. But she was still out of sorts with Dihaut, still resented their summoning her back here. They'd made her share their company on the long flight back to Hehut and never mentioned that Merur had *replaced* her. They might have warned her, and they hadn't. She wasn't certain she could keep her temper with her sib, just now. Which maybe was why they'd kept silent about it, but still.

Besides, that other Eye had doubtless done the obvious first thing, and gone to Dihaut herself. And to judge from what Merur had said, Dihaut must have found nothing, or nothing to speak of. They would give Het the same answer. No point asking again.

She wanted time alone. Time that was hers. She didn't miss the cold—already her thick fur was thinning without any conscious direction on her part. But she did miss the solitude, and the white landscape stretching out seemingly forever, silent except for the wind and her own heart, the hiss of blood in her ears. There was nothing like that here.

She left Tjenu and walked down to the river in the warm early-evening sunlight. Willows shaded the banks, and the lilies in the occasional pool, red and purple and gold, were closing. The scent of water and flowers seized her, plucking at the edges of some memory. Small brown fishing boats sat in neat rows on the opposite bank, waiting for morning. The long, sleek shape of some Justified Noble's barque floated in the middle of the channel, leaf green, gilded, draped with hangings and banners of blue and yellow and white.

She startled two children chasing frogs in the shallows. "Noble," the larger of them said, bowing, pushing the smaller child beside them into some semblance of a bow. "How can we serve you?"

Don't notice my presence, she thought, but of course that was impossible. "Be as you were. I'm only out for a walk." And then, considering the time, "Shouldn't you be home having dinner?"

"We'll go right away," said the older child.

The smaller, voice trembling, said, "Please don't kill us, Noble Het."

Het frowned, and looked behind her, only to see Great Among Millions a short way off, peering at her from behind a screen of willow leaves. "Why would I do such a thing?" Het asked the child. "Are you rebels, or criminals?"

The older child grabbed the younger one's arm, held it tight. "The Noble Het kills who she pleases," they said. The smaller child's eyes filled with tears. Then both children prostrated themselves. "How fair is your face, beautiful Het!" the older child cried into the mud. "The powerful, the wise and loving Eye of the One Sovereign! You see everything and strike where you wish! You were gone for a long time, but now you've returned and Hehut rejoices."

She wanted to reassure them that she hadn't come down to the river to kill them. That being late for dinner was hardly a capital offense. But the words wouldn't form in her mouth. "I don't strike where I wish," she said instead. "I strike the enemies of Nu."

"May we go, beautiful one?" asked the elder child, and now their voice was trembling too. "You commanded us to go home to dinner, and we only want to obey you!"

She opened her mouth to ask this child's name, seized as she was with a sudden inexplicable desire to mention it to Dihaut, to ask them to watch for this child when they passed through judgment, to let Dihaut know she'd been favorably impressed. So well-spoken, even if it was just a hasty assemblage of formulaic phrases, of songs and poetry they must have heard. But she feared asking would only terrify the child further. "I'm only out for a walk, child," she growled, uncomfortably resentful of this attention, even as she'd enjoyed the child's eloquence. "Go home to dinner."

"Thank you, beautiful one!" The elder child scrambled to their feet, pulled the smaller one up with them.

"Thank you!" piped the smaller child. And they both turned and fled. Het watched them go, and then resumed her walk along the riverside. But the evening had been soured, and soon she turned back to Tjenu.

The Thirty-Six met her in their accustomed place, a chamber in Tjenu walled with malachite and lapis, white lily patterns laid into the floor. There were chairs and benches along the edge of the room, but the Thirty-Six stood stiff and straight in the center, six rows of six, white linen kilts perfectly pressed, a gold and silver star on each brow.

"Eye of Merur," said the first of the Thirty-Six. "We're glad you're back."

"They're glad you're back," whispered Great Among Millions, just behind Het's right shoulder. "*They* didn't spend the time in a box."

Each of the Thirty-Six had their own demesne to watch, to protect. Their own assistants and weapons to do the job with. They had been asked to do this sort of thing often enough. Over and over.

Het had used the walk here from the river to compose herself. To take control of her face and her voice. She said, her voice smooth and calm, "The One Ruler of Nu, Creator of All Life on Nu, wishes for us to remove all traces of rebellion, once and for all. To destroy any hint of corruption that makes even the thought of rebellion possible." No word from the silent and still Thirty-Six. "Tell me, do you know where that lies?"

No reply. Either none of them knew, or they thought the answer so obvious that there was no need to say it. Or perhaps they were suspicious of Het's outward calm.

Finally, the first of the Thirty-Six said, "Generally, problems begin among the single-lived, Noble Het. But we can't seem to find the person, or the thing, that sends their hearts astray time after time. The only way to accomplish what the One Sovereign has asked of us would be to kill every single-lived soul on Nu and let Dihaut sort them one from another."

"Are you recommending that?" asked Het.

"It would be a terrible disruption," said another of the Thirty-Six. "There would be so many corpses to dispose of."

"We'd want more single-lived, wouldn't we?" asked yet another. "Grown new, free of the influence that corrupts them now. It might . . ." She seemed doubtful. "It might take care of the problem, but, Eye of Merur, I don't know how many free tanks we have. And who would take care of the new children? It would be a terrible mess that would last for decades. And I'm not sure that . . . It just seems wrong." She cast a surreptitious glance toward the first of the Thirty-Six. "And forgive me, Noble Eye of Merur, but surely the present concern of the One Sovereign is to reduce chaos and disorder. At the current moment."

So that, at least, was well-enough known, or at least rumored. "The newest Eye," said Het, closing her still-clawed hands into fists, willing herself to stand still. Willing her voice to stay clear and calm. Briefly she considered leaving here, going back to the river to catch fish and listen to the frogs. "Did she request your assistance? And did you suggest this to her, the eradication of the single-lived so that we could begin afresh?"

"She thought it was too extreme," said the first of the Thirty-Six. Was that a note of disappointment in her voice? "It seems to me that the Sovereign of Nu found that Eye's service in this instance to be less than satisfactory."

"You think we should do it?" Het asked her.

"If it would rid us of the trouble that arises over and over," the first of the Thirty-Six agreed.

"If I order this, then," Het persisted, clenching her hands tighter, "you would do it?"

"Yes," the foremost of the Thirty-Six agreed.

"Children, as well?" Het asked. Didn't add, *Even polite, well-spoken children who maybe only wanted some time to themselves, in the quiet by the river?*

"Of course," the first of the Thirty-Six replied. "If they're worthy, they'll be back. Eventually."

With a growl Het sprang forward, hands open, claws flashing free of her fingertips, and slashed the throat of the first of the Thirty-Six. As she fell, blood splashed onto the torso and the spotless linen kilt of the Thirty-Six beside her. For a moment, Het watched the blood pump satisfyingly out of the severed artery to pool on the white-lilied floor, and thought of the walsel she'd killed the day before.

But this was no time to indulge herself. She looked up and around. "Anyone else?"

Great Among Millions skittered up beside her. "Noble Het! Eye of Merur! There is currently a backlog of Justified waiting for resurrection. And none of your Thirty-Six have bodies in the tanks."

Het shrugged. The Thirty-Six were all among the Justified. "She'll be back. Eventually." At her feet the injured Thirty-Six breathed her choking last, and for the first time in decades Het felt a sure, gratifying satisfaction. She had been made for this duty, made to enjoy it, and she had nothing left to herself but that, it seemed. "The single-lived come and go," she declared to the remaining Thirty-Six. "Who has remained the same all this time?"

Silence.

"Oh, dear," said Great Among Millions.

The nurturing and protection of Nu had always required a good deal of death, and none of the Thirty-Six had ever been squeamish about it, but so often in recent centuries that death had been accomplished by impersonal, secondhand means—narrowly targeted poison, or engineered microbes let loose in the river. But Het—Het had spent the last several decades hunting huge, sharp-tusked walsel, two or three times the mass of a human, strong and surprisingly fast.

None of the remaining Thirty-Six would join her. Fifteen of them fled. The remaining twenty she left dead, dismembered, their blood pooling among the lilies, and then she went down to the riverbank.

The single-lived fled before her—or before Great Among Millions, not following discreetly now but close behind her, token and certification of who she was. The little fishing boats pulled hastily for the other bank, and their single-lived crews dropped nets and lines where they stood, ran from the river, or cowered in the bottom of their small craft.

Het ignored them all and swam for the blue-and-yellow barque.

The single-lived servants didn't try to stop her as she pulled herself aboard and strode across the deck. After all, where Het went the necessities of order followed. Opposing the Eye of Merur was not only futile, but suicidal in the most ultimate sense.

Streaming river water, claws extended, Het strode to where the barque's Justified owners sat at breakfast, a terrified servant standing beside the table, a tray holding figs, cheese, and a bowl of honey shaking in her trembling hands.

The three Justified stared at Het as she stood before them, soaking wet, teeth bared. Then they saw Great Among Millions close behind her. "Protector of Hehut," said one, a man, as all three rose. "It's an honor." There was, perhaps, the smallest hint of trepidation in his voice. "Of course we'll make all our resources available to you. I'll have the servants brought—"

Het sprang forward, sliced open his abdomen with her claws, then tore his head from his neck. She made a guttural, happy sound, dropped the body, and tossed the head away.

The servant dropped the tray and fled, the bowl of honey bouncing and rolling, fetching up against the corpse's spilled, sliced intestines.

Het sank her teeth into the second Justified's neck, felt him struggle and choke, the exquisite salt tang of his blood in her mouth. This was oh, so much better than hunting walsel. She tore away a mouthful of flesh and trachea.

The third Justified turned to flee, but then stopped and cried, "I am loyal, Noble Eye! The Noble Dihaut will vindicate me!"

Het broke her neck and then stood a moment contemplating the feast before her, these three bodies, warm and bloody and deliciously fresh. She hadn't gotten to do this often enough, in recent centuries. She lifted her head and roared her satisfaction.

A breeze filled and lifted the barque's blue and yellow and white linen hangings. The servants had fled; there was no one alive on the deck but Het and Great Among Millions now. "Rejoice!" it piped. "The Protector of Hehut brings order to Nu!"

Het grinned, and then dove over the side, into the river, on her way to find more of the Justified.

The day wore on, and more of the Justified met bloody, violent ends at Het's hands—and teeth. At first they submitted; after all, they were Justified, and their return was assured, so long as they were obedient subjects of the One Sovereign. But as evening closed in, the Justified began to try to defend themselves.

And more of the houses were empty, their owners and servants fled.

But in this latest, on the outskirts of Hehut, all airy windowed corridors and courtyards, Het found two Justified huddled in the corner of a white-and-gold-painted room, a single-lived servant standing trembling between them and Het.

"Move," growled Het to the servant.

"Justification!" cried one of the Justified. Slurring a bit—was she drunk?

"We swear!" slurred the other. Drunk as well, then.

Neither of them had the authority to make such a promise. Even if they had, the numbers of Justified dead ensured that no newly Justified would see resurrection for centuries, if ever. Despite all of this, the clearly terrified servant stayed.

Het roared her anger. Picked up the single-lived—they were strong, and large as single-lived went, but no match for Het. She set them aside, roughly, and sank her claws into one of the Justified, her teeth into the other. Screams filled her ears, and blood filled her mouth as she tore away a chunk of flesh.

All day her victims had provided her with more than her fill of blood, and so she had drunk sparingly so far. But now, enraged even further by the cowardice of these Justified—of their craven, empty promise to their servant—she drank deep, and still filled with rage, she tore the Justified into bloody fragments that spattered the floor and the wall.

She stopped a moment to appreciate her handiwork. With one furred hand she wiped blood and scraps of muscle off her tingling lips.

Her tingling lips.

The two Justified had barely moved, crouched in their corner. They had slurred their speech, as though they were drunk.

Or as though they were poisoned.

She knew what sort of poison made her lips tingle like this, and her fingertips, now she noticed. Though it would take far more neurotoxin to make her feel this much than even a few dozen skinny, gape-mawed fish would provide. How much had she drunk?

41

Het looked around the blood-spattered room. The single-lived servant was gone. Great Among Millions stood silent and motionless, its tall, thin body crusted with dried blood. Nothing to what covered Het.

She went out into the garden, with its pools and fig trees and the red desert stretching beyond. And found two of Merur's lily standards—She Brings Life and Different Ages. Along with Months and Years. And Dihaut.

"Well, sib," they said, with their regretful smile. "They always send me after you. Everyone else is too afraid of you. I told the One Sovereign it was better not to send forces you'd only chew up. Poison is much easier, and much safer for us."

Het swayed, suddenly exhausted. Dihaut. She'd never expected them to actively take her side, when it came to defying Merur, but she hadn't expected them to poison her.

What *had* she expected? That Merur would approve her actions? No, she'd known someone would come after her, one way or another. And then?

"You can try to alter your metabolism," Dihaut continued, "but I doubt you can manage it quickly enough. The dose was quite high. We needed to be absolutely sure. Honestly, I'm surprised you're still on your feet."

"You," said Het, not certain what she had to say beyond that.

She Gives Life and Different Ages skittered up and stopped a meter or so apart, facing Het. Between them an image of Merur flickered into visibility. Not snakelike, as Het knew her current body to be, but as she appeared in images all over Nu: tall, golden, face and limbs smooth and symmetrical, as though cut from basalt and gilded.

"Het!" cried Merur. "My own Eye! What can possibly have made you so angry that you would take leave of your senses and betray the life and peace of Nu in this way?"

"I was carrying out your orders, Sovereign of Nu!" Het snarled. "You wanted me to remove all possibility of rebellion in Hehut."

"And all of Nu!" piped Great Among Millions, behind Het. Still covered in dried blood.

"I had not thought such sickness and treason possible from anyone Justified as long as you have been," said Merur. "Dihaut."

"Sovereign," said Dihaut, and their smile grew slightly wider. Het growled.

Merur said, "You have said to me before today that I have been too generous. That I have allowed too many of the long-Justified to escape judgment. I did not believe you, but now, look! My Eyes have not been subject to judgment in centuries, and that, I think, has been a mistake. I would like it known that not even the highest of the Justified will be excused if they defy me. Het, before you die, hear Dihaut's judgment."

She was exhausted, and her lips had gone numb. But that was all.

Was she really poisoned? Well, she was, but only a little. Or so it seemed, so far. Maybe she could overpower Dihaut, rip out their throat, and flee. The standards wouldn't stop her.

And then what? Where would she go, that Merur would not eventually follow?

"Sovereign of Nu," said Dihaut, bowing toward Merur's simulacrum. "I will do as you command." They turned to Het. "Het, sib, your behavior this past day is extreme even for you. It calls for judgment, as our Sovereign has said. It is that judgment that keeps order in Hehut, on all of Nu. And perhaps if everyone, every life, endured the same strict judgment as the single-lived pass through, these things would never have happened."

Silence. Not a noise from Great Among Millions, behind Het. Over Dihaut's shoulder, Months and Years was utterly still.

"The One Sovereign has given me the duty of making those judgments. And I must make them, no matter my personal feelings about each person I judge, for the good of Nu."

"That is so," agreed Merur's simulacrum.

"Then from now on, everyone—single-lived or Justified, whoever they may be—every Anima that passes through Tjenu must meet the same judgment. No preference will be given to those who have been resurrected before, not in judgment, and not in the order of resurrection. From now on everyone must meet judgment equally. Including the Sovereign of Nu."

The simulacrum of Merur frowned. "I did not hear you correctly just now, Dihaut."

They turned to Merur. "You've just said that it was a mistake not to subject your Eyes to judgment, and called on me to judge Het. But I can't judge her without seeing that what she has done to the Justified this past day is only what you have always asked her to do to the single-lived. She has done precisely what you demanded of her. It wasn't the fact that Het was unthreatened by judgment that led her to do these things—it was you, yourself."

"You!" spat Merur's simulacrum. "You dare to judge me!"

"You gave me that job," said Dihaut, Months and Years still motionless behind them. "And I will do it. You won't be resurrected on Nu without passing my judgment. I have made certain of this, within the past hour."

"Then it was you behind this conspiracy all along!" cried Merur. "But you can't prevent me returning. I will awake on *Aeons*."

"*Aeons* is far, far overhead," observed Het, no less astonished at what she'd just heard than by the fact that she was still alive.

"And there was no conspiracy," said Dihaut. "Or there wasn't until you imagined one into being. Your own Eyes told you as much. But this isn't the first time you've demanded the slaughter of the innocent so that you can feel more secure. Het only gave me an opportunity, and an example. I will do as you command me. I will judge. Withdraw to *Aeons* if you like. The people who oversee your resurrection on Nu, who have the skills and the access, won't be resurrected themselves until you pass my judgment." They gave again that half-regretful smile. "You've already removed some of those who would have helped you, when you purged

Tjenu of what you assumed was disloyalty to you, Sovereign." The image of Merur flickered out of sight, and She Brings Life and Different Ages scuttled away.

"I'm not poisoned," said Het.

"I should hope not!" exclaimed Dihaut. "No, you left your supper, or your breakfast, or whatever it was, on my flier. I couldn't help being curious about it." They shrugged. "There wasn't much of that neuro-toxin in the animal you left behind, but there was enough to suggest that something in that food chain was very toxic. And knowing you, you'd have changed your metabolism rather than just avoid eating whatever it was. Merur, of course, didn't know that. So when she said she wanted you stopped, I made the suggestion. . . ." They waved one silver hand.

"So all that business with the single-lived servant, promising her Jus-tification if she would defend those two . . ."

"This late in the day the Justified were already beginning to resist you—or try, anyway," Dihaut confirmed, with equanimity. "If these had stood meekly as you slaughtered them, you might have suspected some-thing. And you might not have drunk enough blood to feel the poison. I had to make you even more angry at the people you killed than you already were."

Het growled. "So you *tricked* me."

"You're not the only one of Merur's Eyes, sib, to find that if you truly served in the way you were meant to, you could no longer serve Merur's aims. It's been a long, long time since I realized that for all Merur says I'm to judge the dead with perfect, impartial wisdom, I can never do that so long as she rules here. She has always assumed that her personal good is the good of Nu. But those are not the same thing. Which I think you have recently realized."

"And now *you'll* be Sovereign over Nu," Het said. "Instead of Merur."

"I suppose so," agreed Dihaut. "For the moment, anyway. But maybe not openly—it would be useful if Merur still called herself the One Sovereign but stayed above on *Aeons* and let us do our jobs without interference." They shrugged again and gave that half smile of theirs. "Maybe she can salvage her pride by claiming credit for having tricked you into stopping your over-enthusiastic obedience, and saving everyone. In fact, it might be best if she can pretend everything's going on as it was before. We'll still be her Eyes at least in name, and we can make what changes we like."

Het would have growled at them again, but she realized she was too tired. It had been a long, long day. "I don't want to be anyone's Eye. I want to be out of this." She didn't miss the cold, but she wanted that solitude. That silence. Or the illusion of it, which was all she'd really had. "I want to be somewhere that isn't here."

"Are you sure?" Dihaut asked. "You've become quite popular among the single-lived, today. They call you beautiful, and fierce, and full of mercy."

She thought of the children by the river. "It's meaningless. Just old poetry rearranged." Still she felt it, the gratification that Dihaut had surely meant her to feel. She was glad that she'd managed to spare those lives. That the single-lived of Hehut might remember her not for having slaughtered so many of them, but for having spared their lives. Or perhaps for both. "I want to go."

"Then go, sib." Dihaut waved one silver hand. "I'll make sure no one troubles you."

"And the unauthorized lives there? Or elsewhere on Nu?"

"No one will trouble them either," Dihaut confirmed equably. "So long as they don't pose a threat to Hehut. They never did pose a threat to Hehut, only to Merur's desire for power over every life on Nu."

"Thank you." Her skin itched, her fur growing thicker just at the thought of the cold. "I don't think I want you to come get me. When I die, I mean. Or at least, wait a while. A long time." Dihaut gestured assent, and Het continued, "I suppose you'll judge me, then. Who'll judge you, when the time comes?"

"That's a good question," replied Dihaut. "I don't know. Maybe you, sib. Or maybe by then no one will have to pass my judgment just to be allowed to live. We'll see."

That idea was so utterly alien to Het that she wasn't sure how to respond to it. "I want some peace and quiet," she said. "Alone. Apart." Dihaut gestured assent.

"Don't leave me behind, Noble Het!" piped Great Among Millions. "Beautiful Het! Fierce Het! Het full of mercy! I don't want them to put me in a box in a storeroom again!"

"Come on, then," she said, impatiently, and her standard skittered happily after her as she went to find a flier to take her away from Hehut, back to the twilit ice, and to silence without judgment.

Author's Note

We often talk about Ancient Egypt as though it was one simple, static thing, unchanging until, maybe, the Ptolemies arrived on the scene. But "Ancient Egypt" covers some three thousand years, and while some things may have been broadly true all through those millennia, myths and religious stories changed, were consciously edited and adapted to fit the circumstances of the time, or the intentions of the writer. There was no internally consistent, static whole that myths and beliefs added up to, no one official "right" version of any story.

So given that this is a body of (often fragmentary) myths from a huge range of time, which was always changing to fit the needs of the moment, why stay in the past? Why not move far, far into the future? And the story of the goddess Sekhmet's destruction of mankind is so intriguing. Some older translations of the text suggest that mankind rebels against Re because he's become old, but more recent translations don't offer any reason at all for it. And the goddess sent to put the rebellion down is the nurturing, healing Hathor, who manifests as Sekhmet, the Powerful, the Lady of Slaughter. Who even Re himself can't stop, once she's let loose. She's so dangerous you'd think the gods would be glad to be rid of her, but in other stories Sekhmet, seemingly always angry, leaves Egypt and has to be searched for and cajoled to come back. Those plentiful ambiguities and elisions are irresistible to me.

Ann Leckie

FISHER-BIRD

BY
—
T. KINGFISHER

FISHER-BIRD HAD A CREST LIKE IRON AND EYES AS
dark as the last scale on a blacksnake's snout. She had a white collar and
a gray band and a belt the color of dried blood.

Fisher-Bird had a chatterjack voice that she used to cuss with, and
she flew like the air had personally offended her. Her beak was long and
shaped like a spearpoint, and she could see the ripples fish made when
they even thought of swimming.

Fisher-Bird knew things. Not like crows know things, or ravens—
not that you can ever find a raven around these parts. Not like whip-
poor-wills know the taste of your soul or thrushes know the color of
music. But nothing happened in the woods or along the stream without
it reaching Fisher-Bird eventually.

There's a story about the red belt, and why Fisher-Bird's got one and her husband doesn't. There's always a story. I don't say this one's true.

Time was, Fisher-Bird was perched on a branch over the stream, looking at the fish being lazy in the water. She was thinking maybe it'd be a good thing to dive down there, put the fear of god in a couple of 'em, or at least the fear of Fisher-Bird, when she heard a crack and a crash coming through the woods.

A man came down the deer-trail, staggering like he couldn't see. His face was swelled up and puffy, and his breath squeaked through his throat. He had blood coming out of his ears and out his nose and even oozing out from under his fingernails.

Fisher-Bird looked at him out of her right eye. He was a big man. His arms were tree-trunk thick, and he was so shaggy it looked like he was wearing a shirt. Fisher-Bird had to look twice to see he wasn't, just a mountain lion skin draped over his shoulders like the cat was going for a piggyback ride.

Then she looked out of her left eye, and she saw he had god-blood in him, thick and stringy as spiderwort sap, the kind that clogs up your veins and makes you a hero even if you'd rather just be an ordinary soul. *Poor bastard*, thought Fisher-Bird.

He fell into the stream and shoved his head into the water. All the fish remembered they had somewhere else to be, and Fisher-Bird was left alone on her branch, just watching the shaggy man soak his head in the stream.

When he came up for air, his eyes were slitted open and some of the blood was gone, but his cheeks were still huge and puffed up with lumps. Fisher-Bird saw two holes in a couple of the lumps, and she knew right off what had happened. The shaggy man had pissed off Old Lady Cottonmouth. She's not an evil snake, no matter what people say, but she wants respect and she doesn't suffer fools.

"Damn, hon," said Fisher-Bird. "You look like hammered shit."

The shaggy man froze. "Who said that?" he asked.

Now, this pricked up Fisher-Bird's crest, right enough. She wasn't used to humans who could hear the language of birds, unless they were witches or somebody walking around in human skin who couldn't lay claim to it by birth. "You heard me?"

"I heard you," said the man, trying to pry his eyes open with his fingers, "but I don't *see* you."

"Up here on the branch," said Fisher-Bird, and she dipped her beak, polite-like. "You see me?"

The man stared at her for a little bit, then said, "You're a bird."

"You're quick."

"Are you a devil sent to torment me?"

Fisher-Bird thought this was so funny that she let out one of her long chattering laughs—*"krk-krk-krk-krrrk!"* And then, "Hon, you showed up at my stream and ruined my fishing. I don't think you've got the right end of who's tormenting who." (She didn't really mind the fish, but she wasn't about to give up the moral high ground so fast.)

"Oh," said the man, after a minute. He dunked his head in the water again and swirled it around. He had long curly hair that hung down his back in wet hanks, until it ran into the cat skin coat.

When he came up for air, he said, "Sorry about the fish."

Fisher-Bird was so charmed by a human apologizing for anything that she said, "Aw, nah, don't worry yourself about it. You look like you've messed with worse than a fish today."

"Nest of cottonmouths," he said. "Whole ball all tangled together and chasing anybody who got too close. I was s'posed to clear 'em out."

"Aw, that's a shame," said Fisher-Bird. "You gonna die now?"

He shook his head and scooped up some mud, slapping it across his cheeks. "I don't die easy," he said.

Fisher-Bird hopped a little closer on the branch. "Lotta people don't die easy, but they take a couple bites from Old Lady Cottonmouth and they learn how pretty damn quick."

He grunted. "There were dozens," he said. "I'd chop one's head off and two more would show up. Never seen a thing like it."

"Shit, hon, that was a snake wedding you interrupted. No wonder they were pissed."

Whatever the man might have thought about that was lost as he slapped more mud on his face, then down his arms where the snakes had bit him.

"Are you really here?" he asked after a minute.

This was a pretty peculiar question, but humans are peculiar creatures. Fisher-Bird turned her head so she could look at him out of one eye at a time. "Are *you*?"

The shaggy man groaned. "I mean, I got bit pretty bad," he admitted. "And I think a bird's talking to me, but maybe it's the poison."

"Could be, could be," said Fisher-Bird agreeably. "Or I could have nabbed a toad and got a beak full of moonshine, and now I think a human's talking to me."

". . . Shit," said the shaggy man, with feeling, and flopped down on the streambank.

Fisher-Bird waited a polite length of time, while the mosquitoes hummed to each other, then said, "You dead yet, hon?"

"No."

"How 'bout now?"

"I'm not dying. I told you." He sat up. Fisher-Bird had to admit that he did look better. The swelling was going down, and he'd stopped bleeding from under his nails. "I don't die. Name's Stronger."

"Stronger," said Fisher-Bird, rolling the word around in her beak. "Stronger than what?"

"Everything."

"Krrk-krrk-krk-krk-krk!" She laughed at him. "Modest, ain'tcha?"

"It's true," he said. He didn't sound all that happy about it. He glanced around the stream and walked over to a big boulder half-buried in the gravel. "Look."

He put his hands under the boulder. His arms flexed and the veins popped out, thick and ugly as nightcrawlers, and then he scooped the boulder up and tossed it a couple yards over his shoulder with a crash.

Water rushed into the muddy hole he'd left, and little squirmy things went running in all directions, except for the crawfish, who waved their claws and wanted a fight. Fisher-Bird dropped off her branch, scooped up a crawfish, and proceeded to beat it to pieces on another rock that hadn't been flung quite so far away.

"Pretty—good," she said, between smacking the crawfish around. "Don't—see—that—much."

"Yeah," said Stronger. He sat back down. "It's not so great. I break things."

"What—kind—of—things—*gulp!*"

"People."

Fisher-Bird cleaned the last bits of shell off her beak with one gray foot. "I see that'd be a problem."

"Yeah. Now I got to do a bunch of jobs for my mother-in-law to make up for it."

"Why your mother-in-law?"

"It was her people I broke."

"Ah." Fisher-Bird cocked her head. "That why you were off fighting snakes?"

"Yeah." He began to pick bits of drying mud off his face. "That was one of the jobs. And the mountain lion I got here, that was one, too."

"Big lion."

"Yeah. There's others. Had to kill a boar that was tearing up the farm."

Fisher-Bird nodded. Boars were bad news. They didn't bother her much, of course, but they could take a field and turn it into a wreckage of trampled mud in less time than Fisher-Bird could open up a crayfish.

"And a mad bull, and a bunch of mares that had a very peculiar diet, and do not *talk* to me about stables and . . . well, it's been a long month."

"Is that all you're doing? Putting down livestock?"

Stronger didn't look particularly pleased by this summation. "I caught a doe."

Fisher-Bird snorted. "What did you do, stand in one place for a little while? We got more does than fish around here."

"A *specific* doe."

"Oh, well, that's different."

"My mother-in-law says go kill it, but my sister-in-law says if I do she'll gut me like a hog, because that's her pet deer and it got loose, and I said she shouldn't ought to let it wander around loose, and then she got pissed at me and said she'd let her deer go where it damn well pleased." Stronger rubbed his face. "So I finally just went out and grabbed it and carried it back over my shoulder. Which it did *not* like. I had hoofprints in personal places."

"Still, pet deer. That's honorary livestock."

"I got my cousin's girdle."

Fisher-Bird had been looking for more crawfish, but she stopped and turned her head real slow to look at him. ". . . You got that kinda family, do you?"

"No!" And when Fisher-Bird gave him a steady look, "Well . . . all right. My mother-in-law's married to her brother and they say *her* daddy was a cannibal."

"Take an old bird's advice, son, and get the hell away from those people. Marrying kin ain't good, but you start eating each other and all bets are off."

"Look, I didn't know about that bit when I married in. Anyway, that's what the jobs are for. I finish these, and I'm free and clear and they let me go. I'm gonna move west and never talk to these people again." Stronger rubbed his forehead. "And it wasn't like that with my cousin. I just went and asked politely. Wasn't much of a job. I think my mother-in-law was hoping she'd be mad, but I explained all about it and brought her a bottle of the good stuff, and she said my mother-in-law was always a bad one and she'd be happy to do anything to spit in her eye."

"Well, gettin' away is good," said Fisher-Bird. "I approve of that."

Stronger nodded gloomily. "I don't even like most of them, and that's leaving aside that my mother-in-law keeps trying to kill me."

Fisher-Bird, no stranger to family infighting, nodded wisely. "Some people come outta the egg mad."

Stronger finished flaking the mud off his face. "You're still a bird," he said, almost accusingly.

"Yeah, I'd get used to that."

"If you're a bird, then why can you talk?"

"Shit, son," said Fisher-Bird, and let loose a long string of curses that made Stronger sit up and take notice. "I've always been able to talk. Question is how you're listening."

Stronger shook his head. "Dunno. Never could before."

Fisher-Bird scratched her beak. "Any of those snakes bite your ears?"

The man looked puzzled for a minute, then put his finger in his ear and wiggled it around like he was cleaning earwax. He winced. "Yeah. One got me right up there by the ear."

"There you go," said Fisher-Bird, pleased. "You make a friend of a snake, they'll lick your ears, let you hear the language of birds."

"These snakes weren't friendly."

"Yeah, but spit's spit."

He thought for a few minutes. "Huh. You know, I got some birds I gotta clean out for my mother-in-law. You think this'll help me?"

"What kinda birds?" She hopped down a little closer.

"Weird ones. Feathers like metal. You shoot at 'em and it bounces right off and makes a noise like you're shaking buckshot in a tin can."

"Oh, *them*. Stimps." She grimaced as well as one can with a beak.

"What?"

"Stimps. They're herons, more or less, but their great-great-grand-daddy did a favor for the Iron-Wife and got her blessing. Now they got iron feathers and think they're better'n the rest of us."

"I'm supposed to drive 'em off. They're a real menace over at the lake. They drop feathers that'll cut you all to ribbons."

"Hmm." Fisher-Bird thought it over. She had no great love of humans, but he'd apologized about the fish and that was a pretty fine thing. And she had even less love of herons, who took fish and frogs and a lot of other critters that rightly belonged in Fisher-Bird's gullet, let alone magic herons who thought they owned the place. But most of all, she had an active loathing of stimps, who'd chased one of Fisher-Bird's cousins out of the swamp and had a few nasty words for her when they did it.

"Yeah, okay." The chance to get one back at the stimps was too good to pass up. "Best do it soon, though, before they start nesting. Once you get a couple dozen of them together in a tree, cackling and raising up eggs, it's a problem. And it ain't right to mess with other people's eggs, even stimps."

"So I should just ask 'em to leave, then?"

Fisher-Bird rolled her eyes. "Not unless you got a few hours to waste, listening to a stimp insult you. No, they ain't gonna go on their own."

"Well, I can't get to them. They're in a marshy bit, and if I walk out there, I'm hip-deep in muck. I try to grab one, they'll be miles away, throwin' those nasty sharp feathers at me."

Fisher-Bird preened under her wing. "Come back tomorrow," she said.

"What?"

"Tomorrow. Come back then. Maybe I can help you; maybe I can't."

Stronger looked like he might argue for a minute; then he closed his mouth and nodded. "All right, then. Thank you."

Polite sort of human, Fisher-Bird thought. Worth helping out the polite ones. Particularly if it got rid of those stuck-up stimps.

Just the thought made her chuckle. *"Krk-krk-krk-krk!"*

"All right," said Fisher-Bird, when Stronger came back the next day. "What you want is poison. You got any?"

"I *had* a whole bunch of dead cottonmouths," said Stronger sourly. "But I didn't realize I'd need them."

"Nah, that wouldn't have worked. That stuff dries out too fast, goes all to lumps. Need something nasty that'll mix with tar."

"I got rat poison back home," said Stronger.

"Yeah, that's fine. Now, you got arrows?"

"Arrows?"

"Shit, son, don't tell me humans don't use arrows no more."

"I guess . . . ?" Stronger looked doubtful. "I haven't shot a bow since I was little. I got a gun."

"Can't poison a bullet, son. You need some arrows, and you need to wrap the point with some cloth. Then you mix up some tar and some rat poison and dip the points in that. Make it good and drippy."

"If I can't put a bullet in the stimp, how'm I gonna put an arrow in one?"

"You ain't," said Fisher-Bird. "You're gonna smack 'em with the arrow and leave goop all over those shiny metal feathers of theirs. Then they go to preen and they'll get a mouthful of rat poison."

Stronger thought this over. "Ye-e-e-e-s . . . ," he said slowly. "Could work. But I still don't know how to get to the stimps in the first place. They're out in the marsh and the mud, and I can't get a clear shot at any of 'em."

Fisher-Bird flicked her crest. "You come back when you got you a bow and poison. Bring along a couple tin cans, too. Then we'll see about getting you your shot."

Stronger came back to Fisher-Bird's stream two days later, carrying a pack and a bow over his back and a metal bucket full of arrows. "These things are *nasty*," he said, setting the bucket down.

"Hello to you, too," said Fisher-Bird. "The family's fine, thank you kindly for asking."

Stronger sighed. "My aunt'd ding my ear for rudeness, if she was still alive. Sorry, bird. Hope you're well."

"I'm good," said Fisher-Bird. "And how's your family?"

"Mostly dead and the live ones are mean," said Stronger. Fisher-Bird cackled.

She hopped down from her branch and landed on the rim of the bucket. (Fisher-Bird never did learn to walk very well, but that didn't slow her down much.) She peered down into the mess of black sludge, with the arrows sticking up out of it like porcupine quills. "Damn. Looks godawful, anyhow. You got them tin cans?"

Stronger slung the pack off his back and opened it up, revealing half a dozen empty cans.

"Flatten 'em out," ordered Fisher-Bird. Stronger took each can between his palms and put his hands together like he was praying. The cans went flat as paper, and Fisher-Bird could see the dents left by his wedding ring.

"All right," said Fisher-Bird. "That's everything." She jumped from the rim of the bucket, flapped her wings twice, and landed on Stronger's shoulder. She had to cock her head over to look up into his face.

"You gonna peck out my eyes?" asked Stronger, sounding amused.

"Nah, son, that's crows. Not saying I wouldn't take a bite if you were already drowned, but that'd be more in the way of courtesy."

"Eating my eyes if I drowned would be courtesy?"

"Well, you'd hardly want a stranger to do it, would you? Besides, people do weird shit with corpse eyes. Best to get 'em pecked out nice and quick so you don't find 'em doin' something nasty later."

"I'm not sure I'd be worried about that, if I was already dead."

"You should be. Worse things than dead, and a lot of 'em involve eyeballs."

Stronger rubbed his hand over the eyes in question. "I am having the strangest month," he said, to no one in particular.

"Try bein' a bird. Now come on; let's go make some stimps miserable."

It was a hot afternoon, and the air was wet and thick with pollen. You could look down the road and see the trees get paler and greener until they vanished into a yellow haze from all the pine trees rattling their cones. Fisher-Bird didn't much like pines in late spring. The rest of the year they were solid-enough trees, but they got a little spring in them and they became downright indecent.

The swamp had pines ringing it and then juniper cedars, trying to suck up as much water as they could, and then a narrow channel of open water. Then it all went to cattails and sedge and muck, with little scruffy trees that didn't do much except give the cat-claw vines something to crawl over.

"I can't get very far out there," said Stronger. "I mean, I try, but I sink right in and it's like wading through glue."

"Yeah, I figured. Wait here." Fisher-Bird took off from his shoulder and flew across the swamp, looking for stimps.

They weren't hard to find. A couple here, a couple there, a few standing by themselves, with their big beaks poised to stab in the water. Fisher-Bird looked with her right eye and saw herons with steel feathers. She looked with her left eye and saw a goddess's blessing hanging over them the way pollen hung over pines.

She also saw a whole lotta things she didn't like. The swamp wasn't right. It didn't sound right, and it didn't look right. There were big bare areas where the stimps had flicked their wings and scythed the grasses down like wheat, big white slashes in the trees where they'd rubbed their beaks and cut to the heartwood. There were ducks floating head-down, gutted by a careless stimp feather, and the water was greasy black with rot.

It was when she saw a dead beaver laid out, nearly chopped in half by iron wings, that Fisher-Bird started to get mad. But she kept her tongue and her temper inside her beak and went flying on until she came to a stimp so tall, it looked like a scarecrow made of iron.

Fisher-Bird landed next to the tallest stimp and said, "Morning."

The stimp didn't move.

Fisher-Bird cleaned her beak with her foot and said, louder, "I said good morning!"

The stimp didn't move.

"Shit," said Fisher-Bird. "You died standing up?"

The stimp gave up. "I have not *died*," said the steel heron, with icy precision. "I am *fishing*. Which I would have thought that *you* would understand, even if you practice the art like a wild boar practices dancing."

Fisher-Bird's beak didn't lend itself to smirking, which was probably for the best. "Aw, you're in a mood. What's wrong, not enough fish?"

The stimp grunted.

"Mess this place is in, surprised there's a fish to be found. Or a frog or a turtle for that matter. Maybe it's time you stimps moved on."

"Go bother someone else, little bird," said the stimp. "I've no time for such as you."

"Sorry about your momma," said Fisher-Bird. "Must be hard."

"What?" The steel heron turned its head finally, gold eyes narrowing. "What about my mother?"

"Just figured you lost her young," said Fisher-Bird. "Or else she'd have taught you some proper manners." She studied her claws nonchalantly. "Unless you learned from her, in which case it's pretty clear she was no better than she should—*krrk!*"

The stimp's strike would have made a meal of a slower bird, but Fisher-Bird had been waiting. She was in the air as soon as the stimp took the first step. The swamp filled up with the rattle of steel feathers and the chatter of Fisher-bird cussing, but Fisher-Bird's faster than any heron, even a blessed one. She came winging back to Stronger, pleased with herself.

"Heard quite a ruckus," said Stronger. "But they didn't take to the air."

"Nope," said Fisher-Bird. "Didn't think they would. But they're killin' beavers now, what never did nobody no harm, and also they were rude, so now I got no qualms at all."

"Suppose we could try to scare them out," said Stronger, a bit dubiously.

"*Krrk-rkk!* What's a stimp got to be scared of? Unless you got like . . . eagles with magnets or something." Fisher-Bird got a thoughtful look. "Huh, that's not a bad idea. If this doesn't work, the osprey boys owe me a favor. . . ."

Stronger put his head in his hands. "One plan at a time, please," he whispered.

"Sit yourself down," said Fisher-Bird. "Once it gets a little later in the day, the stimp boys will start trying to look real fine for the ladies, and that's when we'll do it."

Stronger picked a log out of the water and set it down so he had a comfortable place to sit. Fisher-Bird amused herself picking crunchy tidbits with lots of legs off the end that had been in the water.

The sun started to climb up in the sky. Nothing much happened for a while, except the sound of carrion flies buzzing over the dead ducks and the dead beaver. Fisher-Bird didn't like that either. Ought to have been a lot more insect sounds in the swamp, maybe some early pondhawks zipping over the water, but nothing, just the flies.

Then a noise rang out over the swamp, a metallic clatter like somebody shuffling a deck of cards made out of tin.

"What the devil . . . ?" Stronger jumped, startled, and accidentally put his log a foot deep in the wet ground.

Fisher-Bird got splattered by the mud and chattered, outraged, while she cleaned her feathers off. *"Krrk-krrk-krk!"*

"Sorry," said Stronger. "Didn't mean—what is that?" The noise came again, louder, and then another one. "It's like a frog . . . a train . . . some kind of bug?"

Fisher-Bird preened her feathers down with her heavy beak, grumbling. "It's the stimps," she said. "You never seen herons do the dance for each other, son? The boys raise their crests way up and then flatten 'em back down, trying to look taller. 'Cept when stimps do it, their crests are made outta metal and it sounds like . . . well, like that."

Another metallic crash, like the mating call of rain gutters.

"Now you take those tin cans and fan 'em out," said Fisher-Bird. "And you raise them real high over your head and you rattle 'em together and you'll sound like the tallest, sexiest stimp in creation."

Stronger stared at her.

61

"What?" said Fisher-Bird. "I'm tellin' you, it's like flexing your muscles for the ladies. Except the ladies in this case are magicked-up herons."

"You want me to do a *bird mating dance?*"

"Shit, son, you put it that way, it almost sounds weird."

"But what happens then?" said Stronger, taking out the tin cans and looking at them in disbelief. "Do they come looking for me?"

"And risk gettin' shown up? No, they're gonna try to make themselves taller and prettier. They're gonna be hopping up and down in the swamp, doing their best jumps for the ladies. You look out over the reeds then, you'll see a whole bunch of stimps going up and down like jumping jacks."

Stronger looked blank.

"And that's when you shoot 'em with arrows," said Fisher-Bird. "Son, I got eggs that would have latched on to this plan faster than you are. *Unfertilized* eggs."

Stronger gave her a hangdog look. Then he sighed, held the cans up as far as he could, and drew his thumbnail down over the short edges, like fanning the pages of a book. An ordinary man might have cut hisself to ribbons, but Stronger had the blood of gods thick and oozing in his veins, and the cans rattled and clattered like a stimp's crest in his hands.

Fisher-Bird took to the air and watched stimp heads shooting up all over the swamp, like chickens hearing a hawk yell.

Stronger rattled the cans again and again, and the stimps craned their necks, looking for the source of the sound, each one worried it might one of the others. Then they stood up straight, raising their crests as high as they could go, and they started to bounce up and down, leaping into the air, each trying to make themselves look like the tallest stimp of all.

Fisher-Bird circled back to Stronger and said, "Now's a good time."

"Thank god," said Stronger, shoving the cans into his belt. "Ain't dignified." He pulled his bow off his back, pulled an arrow from the bucket—it made a wet sucking sound—and took aim.

Fisher-Bird was a little bit worried, what with the stimps leaping back and forth, but Stronger's aim was good. He pulled back on the bow till the wood moaned, then fired.

Thwap! Tar exploded over the nearest stimp's neck feathers, and the bird dropped with a yell of disgust.

Thwap! Thwap! Sometimes Stronger missed, but mostly he didn't.

Fisher-Bird winged in next to the first stricken stimp and saw its feathers splashed with black tar. The bird was frantically trying to scrape the mess off with its beak, preening at the feathers like any bird would, and pretty soon the rat poison started to kick in.

"Don't feel so good . . ." muttered the stimp. It stopped worrying about its feathers and went staggering off into the swamp, wings trailing. Fisher-Bird cackled. There probably wasn't enough rat poison to kill something the size of a stimp, but after the dead beaver, she wasn't feeling a lot of remorse.

"Is that all of them?" asked Stronger. "I'm nearly out of arrows."

"All the boys," said Fisher-Bird. "Ought to be enough to move them along."

Fisher-Bird went looking for the tallest stimp and found it at last, bent over like an old man, with tar rimming its beak. "This is your doing, Fisher-Bird," said the stimp. "Don't lie."

"Didn't plan to," said Fisher-Bird. "Ain't ashamed of it. Your people've made a mess outta this swamp, and it's time you moved on. Plus, you were right little shits to my cousin, and I ain't forgotten."

"Used a human to do it, didn't you?" The stimp's voice was no longer so icy and precise. "Saw the arrow hit me. Some gall you've got, claiming *we* made a mess. You seen what humans do to a swamp?"

"Sure," said Fisher-Bird. "I ain't stupid."

The stimp tried to step forward and its leg almost gave out under it, so it wobbled sideways and nearly fell, but its eyes stayed locked on Fisher-Bird.

"Go!" said Fisher-Bird. "Get gone! You've got no fish, no frogs, no food, and the human'll sit out here and cover you in tar every time to try to dance. This ain't no place for you anymore."

"Oh, we'll go," said the stimp. "You're not wrong there. But you're not as smart as you think you are, Fisher-Bird."

"Oh?"

"Heh," said the stimp softly. "Heh heh heh." And then it whipped its neck around so hard that the bones crackled, and Fisher-Bird was just a hair slow getting into the air, so the slash of the stimp's crest took her low across the belly and knocked her down into the rotting mud.

Stronger came plodding through a long time later. "Bird?" he called. "Bird? The stimps flew away, the ones that could fly. Bird, where are you?"

He slid and squelched into the clear spot that had been the tallest stimp's dance floor, and caught sight of Fisher-Bird. "Bird, no!"

He went to his knees next to the little limp bundle of feathers and picked her up with hands that were stronger than anyone else's. "Bird, don't die. It worked. Please don't die." He cradled her in his palm, and her wings hung limp at her sides, a girdle of dried blood across her white feathers. "You helped me. You're the only one, aside from my cousin, who's given me the time of day. Please don't die."

Fisher-Bird didn't speak, didn't move, just lay there with her eyes closed and her beak gaped open.

Stronger put his forehead down against her feathered breast and started to cry. And I ain't saying the tears of a hero with god-blood have any kind of power, but I'll tell you the only thing I know, which is that Fisher-Bird pecked his eyebrow, hard.

"Ow!" Stronger jerked back, nearly dropping her. "What the hell was that?"

"You damn near squashed me," said Fisher-Bird. "I ain't feeling all that well, all right? Damn stimp had rat poison left on his feathers. Serves me right for letting him get too close, I guess. More fool me."

"I thought you were dead!"

"Can't even have a bit of a lie-down without some damn fool crying all over you." She pecked him again for good measure. "There. You got your stimps cleared out. Your mother-in-law can't say you didn't, and the swamp'll be better for it in a season or two."

"Can I take you back to your stream?" asked Stronger, who was raised polite.

"Yeah, I'll let you," said Fisher-Bird, who didn't want to let on that she wasn't feelin' too much like flying right then. So he carried her back on his shoulder and set her down on her favorite branch, and bid her farewell.

"Hmmph," said Fisher-Bird. "You finish up your jobs and get away from that woman, you hear?"

"I will," he promised. "I will."

Anyway, you all know the rest of the story. There were some golden cattle—or maybe some golden apples, depending on who you ask—and Old Man Hades's guard dogs with their fine snapping teeth. Stronger did it all, without complaining too much, and finally his mother-in-law had to let him go.

As for Fisher-Bird, she never could clean her feathers for fear of getting a mouthful of poison, so she's had a red band of blood and rust right across her belly, from that day to this. Which is still getting off lightly if you mess about with gods and heroes, so Fisher-Bird always said.

AUTHOR'S NOTE

The Labors of Hercules is one of the first myths I remember reading as a child. (At the time, I remember being very invested in the man-eating mares of Diomedes.) Looking back on it, years later, I was bemused by how many of the labors fundamentally seem to involve animals. Kill this lion and this hydra and this boar and these birds. Catch these horses, this dog, this deer, and then clean up the stables while you're at it.

It got me thinking about how the animals likely felt about the matter, and what their view on the Labors might be, and from that initial spark came Fisher-Bird's story.

T. KINGFISHER

A BRIEF LESSON IN NATIVE AMERICAN ASTRONOMY

BY

—

REBECCA ROANHORSE

WE WERE GONNA BE STARS. THAT'S WHAT YOU got to understand. Big fucking stars. Like Jack and Rose or Mr. and Mrs. Carter, like our faces on every screen, dominating every media feed. Everyone already loved us, wanted to be us, wanted to fuck us. And people like that, people like us? Young, rich, famous? We don't just get sick and die. They've got med docs and implants and LongLife™ tech that keeps people alive for 150 years now if you can afford it, and we could afford it. So how could they let her die? How could I lose my perfect girl? How could they do that to me?

I keep the room dark. My agent's been calling, but fuck him, you know? He says I'm missing important appearances, that if I'm not careful people will forget about me. Maybe it's time I move on, he says. Find a new girl-friend. Someone hot. Be seen with this new hot chick at a big premiere or something. They're launching a new luxury liner at the end of the week, he says, something that takes you to the edge of the atmosphere and projects your digital image into outer space before hurling you back to the earth. A billion people will see your face, shining like an honest-to-God star. You should go, he says. Go to almost-space and smile a big almost-smile with a new almost-girlfriend and make people remember who you are. But who the fuck would want to ride that? You can't breathe up there. Who wants to go where you can't breathe?

My agent convinces the boss lady of DigImagine to come talk to me. She bangs on my door until I think she's gonna shatter the glass. That door cost me half my pay on that damn Japanese shampoo commercial where I had to wear that breechcloth and pose in front of a stuffed bison. Sure, it was humiliating, but I do have really stellar Indian hair—long, black, and it moves like it's got its own built-in wind machine. And the shampoo company was paying big for a few hours of easy work—flip, smolder, flip, smolder. It's what I do anyway most of the time, so why not?

Can't remember last time I smiled for the camera. They want stoic, so I give them stoic. Cherie always thought it was funny. We'd laugh about stuff like that all the time.

Whatever.

Anyway, I don't want some motherfucker breaking my glass door, even if she is a studio head. I let her in because she's holding a little white envelope. I know that envelope. What it holds. That's the only reason that I open the door. It's like I can already feel the wet burn on the back of my eyes. Only question is whose memories she's holding.

"I'm Carol Elder," she says, her bone-white pumps click-clacking on the hardwoods as she strides through the door. "Sorry to hear about Charlene." She turns toward me and thrusts two things into my hands. The white envelope and an old-fashioned business card, her name printed in neat black ink on a white linen card. Our fingers touch briefly, accidentally, and hers are cold.

"Cherie." I tuck the card in the pocket of the bathrobe I'm wearing and take that envelope over to the kitchen island.

"What?"

"Her name was Cherie. Like the kind you eat. She was sweet." I don't know why I say that, but it feels important, like she should get her name right and know that she was a decent person. Despite all the other stuff, the rumors, the thing with the biowear executive. None of that mattered. She was good and didn't deserve to die.

Carol Elder follows me into the kitchen. She watches as I take a knife from the block and slice the envelope open. I catch her eyes roving the room. The overflowing ashtrays, the food cartons, the big engram needle on the coffee table surrounded by pieces of human hair, nails, flecks of skin. All laid out in a row. I swear she shudders.

"Did the doctors figure out what was wrong with her?" she asks. "What killed . . . I mean . . . why she died? Walked on," she adds hurriedly. "I mean, don't you people say 'walked on'?"

I can almost hear the roar of the Pacific out back, but with the blinds down and the air on, it sounds more like traffic on the 405. I don't give a shit either way. Cherie's the one who wanted to live on the beach. Malibu, she said. All the real stars live in Malibu, so we have to, too. Even if the truth is half the stars these days are kids with fancy digital setups in Kansas or big corporation simulations that aren't even fleshies. But Cherie wanted it, so we moved to Malibu.

I shake the contents of the white envelope out. A small glass vial, marked with the initials *C.A.*, a little red band wound around the cap as a warning that the contents are high potency.

"Is this . . . ?" I say, suddenly breathless.

"We keep some high-grade engrams of all our stars for . . . emergencies. Someone dies mid-production and a vial of quality engrams provides us with enough of the person to project a replicant that will get us through filming and retakes. Sometimes even a few promo interviews. Not in the flesh," she adds hastily. "We're not magicians. The replicant is digital, but it is interactive, and they look as good as the best simulations, but with more personality. Closer to the real thing." She smiles briefly. "We have some of yours, too, you know. It's part of your contract. DigImagine didn't just draw your blood when you sign with us for shits and giggles."

"I didn't think you did," I murmur absently, mind still on the vial in my hand. I'm afraid to ask, but I have to. "And this is . . . her?"

She nods. "She was under contract, but she wasn't actively filming anything for DigImagine, so her file is scheduled for decommission." She shifts her weight from one foot to the other. "The authorities can get excitable if we keep engrams when unnecessary. They usually go to next-of-kin, but Cherie didn't list any. I thought you might want it. That it might help." She shrugs, her shoulders rising under her spotless pale silk suit, like she doesn't care either way. Just cleaning house, keeping things tidy.

My eyes dart to the coffee table, the needle. It's illegal to drop other people's memories directly into your brain, but I've been doing it. It's all I have left of her. Squeezing engrams off strands of hair left in her brush, fingernail clippings she liked to pile on the nightstand, sweat stains on the dirty clothes she left behind. It's fucked up. I get that. But she was my perfect girl. And then she died.

"There's a catch," she says. "If I give you these engrams, there's a catch."

"Anything."

"You signed contracts, Mr. Hunter. People paid you a lot of money to be in their digitals, and, well, you can't just not fulfill your obligations."

"Bereavement," I mutter. "Can't you tell them I'm taking time off for bereavement?"

"Yeah, I wish we could do that for you. I really do. But this is millions of dollars. The other actors, it wouldn't be fair to them." She leans in. I can see a hint of a tattoo on her shoulder where the blouse gapes at her neck. "And your community back home. Aren't they counting on you? Expecting you to represent them to the world?"

I wave that away. I don't think much about home anymore.

"There's talk of replacing you," she says.

I look up, annoyed. "With who?"

"The guy from *Sixteen Tipis*. You know the one." She gestures towards her short blond hair. I know what she means. He's got the wind-machine hair.

"That guy ain't even Native. He's Persian."

"The engrams are yours, but you have two days. After that, it's out of my hands." She spreads her hands to show me just how powerless she is. But I know about Carol Elder. Rumor is she's a billionaire, controls the fate of every digital that the studio puts out, and she's telling me it's out of her hands? Excuse me if I don't believe it. But here I am, anyway. An idiot who signed a contract, and no way I can flip and smolder myself out of this one. And no way I'm letting them replace me.

The vial feels hot in my hand. She's in there, my girl. And we can be together again.

"Two days," Carol repeats. "That's all I can give you. Just you and her memories and then you're back to work, okay? Be grateful I got you this at all. Oh, and Mr. Hunter? Dez. I know you've been shooting scraps, but this is high-grade stuff. Don't put this stuff directly into your brain. Find a nice VR system and load them up in an Experience like a goddamn normal person. Nothing good will come from sharing brain space with a dead person, especially when it's biologicals."

"Yeah. Sure." But I'm already stumbling over to the table, my hand searching for the needle, the vial with her initials whispering my name.

Carol opens her mouth, as if to protest, but settles for shaking her head disapprovingly. My hand closes around the cap, and I twist. It opens, and for the first time in days, I smile. I don't even notice when Carol leaves.

* * *

I wake up on the couch to someone knocking on my glass door.

"Cherie?" It takes me a minute to remember that it can't be her. My brain comes slouching back into my noggin and I see the engram needle on the table in front of me, Cherie's vial empty beside it. I reach for the vial, furious. Shake it, as if that's going to reveal something I can't see with my own eyes. But I'm a greedy bastard and I took it all and she's gone now. My chest hurts like my heart's gonna break in two, and tears press against the back of my eyeballs.

I wipe at my leaky eyes and notice my video display is on. It's cycling through pictures. Sharp and technicolor. Cherie's audition reel. There she is, dressed as a Plains Indian maiden, her hair in two braids. Another as a prostitute, her hair in two braids. Another as an alcoholic mother, her hair in two braids.

I don't remember turning the display on, but I must have done it after I shot up the engrams, something to enhance the sensories. Looking at her, it's like I can still feel her in my brain.

The knock comes again.

I twist around to look at the door, but there's no one there. God, am I hearing things, too?

"I'm over here, babe."

I yelp at the sound of Cherie's voice coming from the kitchen. What in the entire fuck? But there she is, wearing her favorite shirt, blue jeans snug on her perfect ass. Her dark hair is twisted up in a bun on top of her head. She gives me a big smile.

"Good morning, gorgeous," she says. "I thought you were going to sleep forever. Want some coffee?"

I stare, slack-jawed. My heart speeds up, again, this time in that grasping desperation you feel when you wake up suddenly from a really great dream you don't want to let go.

"Are you . . . ?" I manage to stutter out.

"I'm alive in here," she says, tapping a pretty painted nail to her temple.

"As long as my engrams are still floating around in your head, I'm here."

"That lady said they'd be potent."

"She was right. Coffee?"

We spend the morning together. A perfect morning. Drinking coffee and laughing over shared jokes. Jokes I thought died with her, but here she is, so real. Real enough to touch. And we touch. In fact, we touch until sometime in the late afternoon, and the sun's starting to set somewhere out there over the ocean, and I crawl out of our bed with nothing on and throw the curtains open wide so the ocean air comes in, and the dwindling daylight with it.

It's a mistake.

"Cherie . . . ?"

She looks up at me, catching the alarm in my voice. The flesh on half her face is missing, the sunlight degrading the memory of her to skeleton and ruin. I step back, alarmed. I remember something on the news about engrams being sensitive to light, but I didn't know they would do that. For a fleeting moment, horror crawls up my spine and plants itself in my brain, right next to my true memories of my girl, fouling them. Turning them into something out of a B-grade screamer.

"Maybe we don't need the sunset after all," I tell her, my voice shaking as I hastily pull the curtains closed.

"Oh." She smiles as the light leaves the room. "Sure, Dez. We're better in the darkness anyway."

Dinner is a pack of cigarettes by shards of moonlight on the deck out back, the crash of the surf wild and rough in my ears. Cherie sits next to me, smiling. She's faded and eerie where the moonlight touches her face, but I try to ignore it. Keep my eyes out on the blackness of the Pacific. Even better, close my eyes so I can't see her at all, but can still know she's there.

But with my eyes closed, her scent is stronger and unnervingly sweet. So, I open them.

She reaches across and lays her hand over mine. Something skitters over my fingers, and I pull back. I swear I catch sight of a black beetle crawling over the edge of the deck and disappearing into the vast stretch of sand around us. But I'm not sure.

We are in bed, me and Cherie, and I wrap my arm around her, and at first she is soft in all the right places, like I remember her. But then she is soft in the wrong places, flesh giving way where it should be firm. My fingers dip into the curve of her stomach and keep going, digging out flesh the same way the light cut away her face before, and the smell follows. I recognize it now, the startling stench of decay in my nose.

I gag. She turns toward me, sleepy and smiling faintly. Unaware that she is rotting and I can smell her doing it.

I stumble out of bed to the bathroom, the contents of my stomach coming up. Shivers rake my shoulders, and doubt settles thick in my head. This can't be real. This is a fucking illusion, just like Cherie herself is an illusion. One I asked for, sure. One I want. Wanted.

I tiptoe back to my bedside and fumble in the dark for my phone. Slide the slim earpiece in. Find my bathrobe and pull the card out of the pocket where I left it. Recite the number into the voice recognition.

"Do you know what time it is?" Carol's voice comes in crisp and irritated just as her image pops up in my visual. She's sitting up in bed, in a dark room. A female shape sleeps beside her, hazy in the shadow.

I glance at the time output in the corner of the screen. "Five in the morning. Shit. Sorry."

She shakes her head, waving my apology away. "I was getting up soon anyway. What is it, Mr. Hunter?"

"I . . . I did what you told me not to do."

"And that is?"

"The engrams. Cherie's engrams. I injected them."

Carol's lips curl, her expression unsurprised and my confession unworthy of comment.

"And now she won't go away," I rush on. "And she's . . . degrading."

"What do you mean 'degrading'?"

"Like a corpse."

Carol makes a sound in her throat. "Jesus." She frowns. "Have you tried just sleeping them off?"

"You don't get it. She's here. She's real. She's in my bed right now. Rotting."

"You're simply hallucinating," she says, dismissive. "I warned you. You'll just have to wait it out."

"Dez, babe, is that you?" Cherie's voice from the bedroom.

Carol's chin lifts. "Is that her?"

I nod.

"I can hear her, too. It must have something to do with this." She taps her earpiece on the visual. "Amazing."

"You have to help me!"

"I'm not a memorologist," Carol snaps, sounding exasperated. I flinch at her tone, and she must take pity on me because she says, "I'll make some calls. See what I can do."

"Thank you."

"You're supposed to be back at DigImagine tomorrow."

Another day alone in the house with Cherie? Before it sounded like heaven, but now. "I'll come today if I can. But if she's still in my brain . . ."

"Will she follow you out of the house?"

Into the sunlight? "I don't know."

"Try that. And I'll try to find someone who can help."

I leave the house just as the sun is peeking over the eastern mountains. Out here in Malibu there's no paparazzi, no WeCams or fan drones that follow you around recording everything you do. The skies are patrolled, and the houses are behind gates. So, it's just me, alone, as I slide into the back of the driverless car.

"DigImagine Studios in Culver City," I tell the onboard computer as the car comes to life.

"Good morning, gorgeous."

I grip the edge of the seat. Turn slowly to see her sitting next to me. She's wearing her favorite shirt, and those jeans. I stifle a whimper as she smiles and I can see her jawbone through the place on her face where the rot has set in. See the hollow of her throat, grown black and green.

"Cherie?"

"You left without coffee. Don't you want your coffee?"

"How did you follow me?"

"I'm alive in here," she says, tapping a pretty painted nail to her temple. "As long as my engrams are still floating around in your head, I'm here."

"For how long?"

"Don't you want me around, Dez?" Her pout shifts to something else, and she leans forward. Her eyeball looks wet and too round. "You promised you'd stay with me. 'Always,' you said. You said you'd never leave."

"I—I know," I stutter out. "And I meant it. But—"

"Always is forever, Dez." Her voice hardens. "Don't back out on me now."

"I won't." I tell the car to turn off and climb down out of the back seat. Walk back to our house and through the glass door. Slump on the couch. The visual display is on. There's Cherie in her two braids. Cherie as a—

"Want some coffee, gorgeous?" Cherie calls brightly from the kitchen.

I wake up on the couch to someone knocking on my glass door. Light trails in as the sun rises over the Santa Monica Mountains in the east. Sunrise. Sunrise on the third day.

I look around, cautious. Everything is quiet. The visual display is off, even if I don't remember turning it off.

"Cherie?"

No answer, so I try again. Twist my neck to look in the kitchen, my breath in my teeth, half expecting her to be there, coffee in hand. But it's empty.

Relief bubbles up from my belly, and I let my breath out with a harsh whoop. Carol Elder was right. I just needed to wait it out, sleep it off. The engrams must have worn off.

The knock comes again, and I pull myself up off the couch and double-step it to the door, feeling clean and brand-new. Carol's there, in another crisp suit, holding another white envelope. "We missed you at the studio this morning," she says, as she click-clacks over the threshold. "I did say two days."

"I tried," I explain, "but she was still in my head. She's gone now. Two days was the charm. And don't get me wrong, I'm glad I got to say good-bye. Grateful even," I say, folding my hands in prayer. "But we all gotta move on."

She stops and studies me, her chin tilting to the side. "I spoke to a friend of mine. A memorologist. She said that they've done experiments with test subjects willing to inject the engrams directly, and the results were . . . unpleasant."

"What does that mean?"

"The effect is permanent." Her voice is precise when she says it. I imagine she fires people with that voice. "The foreign engrams integrate into the subject's brains. They never go away, Dez."

I flip my hair over my shoulder and grin. Hold my arms out wide. I catch a glimpse of myself in the wall mirror. I look like a goddamn movie star. "Save your pity, Carol. Your memorologist is wrong. I'm fine. Better than fine. And, listen. I learned my lesson. No more engrams for me, okay?" I tap my forehead to make my point.

She sets the white envelope with my name written on it on the kitchen island. "My friend said they have had some success countering the effect by reasserting the subject's own memories. Enough of Dez Hunter, and Cherie Agoyo is consumed."

"You're not listening to me. She's already gone." I feel a tinge of sorrow when I say it that way. I loved her. She was my perfect girl.

Carol presses a hand to the envelope. "Keep this anyway. A just-in-case."

"Fine, but I won't need them."

We walk back to the glass door. She pauses as she steps through. "I put them off one more day, but tomorrow is it. Be there tomorrow at six a.m. or you're in breach of contract and we call in Dabiri."

"I'll be there. No way Sixteen Tipis is getting my job."

She waves over her shoulder as she walks to her waiting car.

"Hey," I call. "Did you hear about that luxury liner that goes all the way to space? That's tonight. I might go. Be seen. Get my face projected into space!"

Yeah, that's what I'll do. And I'll look good doing it.

And I do. I condition the hair, find just the right outfit to wear, a mix between glam and effortlessly cool, and then let my good looks do the rest. My agent's more than happy to arrange to have a WeCam follow me, and my image streams out live to millions of households and handhelds as I wave and walk up the ramp onto the waiting liner. The party inside is thick with celebrities, and I work the room, accepting condolences and welcome-backs and propositions with equal charm. When I hit the bar, I almost order a champagne like I used to do for Cherie, but I catch myself and ask for some kind of Croatian beer instead that's all the rage.

Everyone gathers at the windows as we take off, and the acceleration through the atmosphere feels like nothing, smoother than the airplane turbulence that used to accompany low-altitude flight. Soon enough we're approaching the hundred-kilometer mark, and when the captain tells us we've reached the edge of the atmosphere, I lean forward and peer out the window into the perpetual darkness, like everyone else.

"Beautiful, isn't it?" Cherie says.

I swerve with a shout, my hand spasming. Drop my beer, which splashes the woman next to me. She cries out, and I rush to apologize, but she storms off, distraught, before the words are out. The WeCam over my shoulder buzzes as the viewer count erupts upward by a couple million.

"Smooth move, gorgeous." Cherie looks out the window not more that an arm's length away. She smiles, and worms fall from her mouth.

I reel back, slamming into the people behind me. I hear glass shatter and rough voices, and someone pushes back, and I stumble forward. The WeCam buzzes loudly.

"I'm alive in here," she says, tapping a pretty painted nail to her temple. "As long as my engrams are still floating around in your head, I'm here."

I grip my jacket pocket, the one with the engram needle and the vial Carol Elder brought me. My just-in-case. They are solid and real under my hand, and I force my way through the crowd toward the privacy of the bathroom, my hand already pulling the needle from my pocket.

I stagger into the narrow space and slam the door shut. It catches the edge of the WeCam flying in over my shoulder, knocking it into the wall. The indicator light flashes an alarm, but I can still hear the buzz of view feeds growing. I splash my face with water, try to get my goddamn calm back, but when I look in the mirror, Cherie is right behind me.

I stifle a scream. Yank the vial marked *D.H.* free and twist off the cap with a jerk. Ram the plunger home and watch the needle fill.

Hands shaking, I dare to look up. Cherie hasn't moved. She's watching. But there's something dark in her face. Something waiting.

"Come on, come on," I mutter, until the needle is at full business and I grasp for the back of my neck and ram that thing into the injection spot. I can feel when the engrams hit my brain. Flashes of childhood. My grandma's place by the Rio Grande River. My first ceremonial dance. And meeting Cherie in high school. And then my memories are all Cherie. Cherie at prom. Cherie when we both landed our first digital gigs. Cherie moving into the Malibu house. Cherie. Cherie. Cherie.

Carol Elder didn't tell me what to do if there is no Dez Hunter without Cherie Agoyo.

On the camera feedback screen I see myself, sweaty and panicked, my eyes glazed and a needle gripped in my hand. And Cherie standing beside me, looking as real as any fleshie.

The WeCam dings, indicating the livestreams have hit capacity. A billion viewers, our faces projected across outer space.

We're goddamn stars.

Author's Note

I am Native American (Ohkay Owingeh) on my mother's side, so I wanted to focus on a Native story that may not be familiar to most science fiction and fantasy readers. I chose the classic Tewa story "Deer Hunter and White Corn Maiden," which has over 788,000 hits on Google and has been published in multiple books.

The original story has a historical setting, but Native people are very much part of the future, and I wanted my retelling to reflect that. So I chose a cyberpunk-eqsue setting where fame is everything and technology has made it possible to live, if not forever, then for a very long time. (As I researched biological memory and CGI "digital reincarnation" in Hollywood movies, I realized my story is much more near-future than I anticipated.)

I see this story with its cautions about obsessive love as still relevant and beautiful. I hope that it intrigues readers enough that they learn more about Native cultures and peoples.

Rebecca Roanhorse

BRIDGE OF CROWS

BY

JY YANG

LET ME TELL YOU A STORY, MY SMALL DARLINGS, my soft feathered peaches. Gather round, my sweet loves, for a story of equal parts joy and woe, a tale of love so great it scaled mountains, and of treachery so bitter it turned whole continents sick and barren. It is a story of determination so great it swelled like lava in the oceans. Of bravery so strong that it toppled all obstacles foolish enough to stand in its way. Like all stories, it contains whorls of lies wrapped around kernels of truth, and it's up to you, my little ones, to sort out which is which.

Are you comfortable, my chirplings? Good. Space can be so cold sometimes, and we have a long day tomorrow, and the day after, and all the days after that. But there's time enough for one last tale.

This story begins with a girl. She's not the only character in the story, nor the most important, but by all means she's at the center of it all. And her name is not as important as her purpose, but things need names to keep their shape in our minds, so let's say her name is Callen. It's a good name. Callen was young, maybe not as young as you, but in good shape, having been raised in sheltered lands where the fields are thick and green and the berries grow plump on bushes.

We start with her at the end of a long journey, which is as good a place as any to begin. She was walking alone across a great red plain with no name pronounceable in our tongue, barefoot over the hissing red earth, steam the color of blood erupting from its fissures. Above her, the sky hung heavy and dark with despair, but it would never rain in that place. It was barren and dry as a heap of bones. No trees grew there. Nothing green could survive. The things that rose out of the ground looked like trees, but they were black and dead and sharp as glass, reaching upward with twisted, cruel fingers. Callen's bare feet had been burned by the hot ground, blistered and scabbed over. Now they felt no pain.

It had been a long journey, but Callen's destination rose in front of her, a jagged swell of earth breaking the line of the horizon. Anywhere else and it would have been too small to be called a mountain, but here the smallest of obstacles was magnified ten times, and this thing that you and I would think of as a hill was to Callen an insurmountable peak. Yet she knew that she would have to scale it, for she had been told that the one she sought could be found at its summit, and meeting her was the reason she had come all this way, after all. The sour air seared her throat and lungs, and the heat stopped blood in her veins.

Callen was not alone on the plain. The hill that was also a mountain was home to a number of strange birds, each as large as a horse, heads shrunken by desiccation into long and hollow skulls. Their forms shifted with the wind, parts blinking in and out as though they had forgotten what their wings or their clawed feet were supposed to look like. See, the unnameable plain was barren, but it was not *dead*. No, it was well, alive and hungry, and it fed itself with whatever foolish creature

83

lingered within its bounds. First it took their memories, then it took the certainty of their forms, and finally it took their names. These wretched creatures knew what they had been once, but now they shambled mindlessly across the cracked and broken earth, trying to pull sustenance from the blackened ground. Callen carefully watched their hunched forms as she walked, hoping that a lone, living traveler such as she would not catch their attention.

She was lucky. She reached the foot of the mountain-hill before one of them could wander across her path and swivel its monstrous, empty eye sockets toward her. Above her, a path curled up the sides of the mountain, threading through angry rocks with jagged teeth, too tall for her to scale. Callen knew that the road ahead was the longest and the most dangerous part of her journey thus far, so first she sat down to eat. She had been walking across this plain for three days, and she was hungry. More importantly, her senses had started to warp and waver in the strange pull of this land. She was losing her memories and her sense of self, and if she wasn't careful, she would forget everything.

Callen's bag, slung across one shoulder, was a tiny thing—only a little bigger than a baby's skull—and contained nothing except a map and two soft rice cakes. To our eyes they would look like ordinary rice cakes, soft and pink and dusted with tender flour, but these were celestial rice cakes, given to Callen by her aunt, who was handmaid to the Queen Mother of Heaven. This was the same aunt who had told Callen where to find the one who could grant her what she wanted, and had set her upon her path. Eating one of those rice cakes would fill one's stomach and sate one's thirst for three days.

Callen had two cakes left, and she ate one, saving the other for the journey back. As she chewed, she felt her mind anchor itself back to her body. She remembered why she was here, and what she had come here to do.

When she had finished eating, Callen started on the path upward. The ground underneath her was slippery, and every step strained her weary body. In no time, her feet were bleeding again, and her fingers were cut to ribbons from clutching rock edges for purchase. But she kept climbing.

Halfway up the mountainside, her path was blocked by an eldritch bird. She couldn't avoid it—the path was too narrow for her to go around, and the creature stood with its body between craggy rockface and craggy rockface, looking at her. Callen was terrified, but she saw no choice about the matter, because she was not turning back. Gathering all the strength she had left in her, she stepped up to the bird-creature.

"Excuse me, O great one," she said, as politely as she could. "I need to get to the top of this mountain. May I walk past you?" Her body was shaking and her voice trembled, but she had been taught manners by her aunt, who worked in the Celestial Court, and she knew that deference and respect could be wielded as a shield against ruin and death.

The creature turned its head toward her. Light guttered in its eye sockets as though fires burned deep in its skull. Callen stood still and breathed very slowly while it studied her. The creature smelled like parched soil before the rain, and its plumage shifted between foam-white and bone-red and the pitch-black of the void between the stars.

The bird-creature spoke; its voice sounded like marbles rolling in a silver can. "I am so hungry," it said. "My brethren and I have not had anything to eat for a hundred years. Will you give me something to fill my belly?"

Callen had nothing to offer except the last rice cake, which she was saving for the journey back. Yet she feared what would happen if she refused. "If I give you something to eat, will you let me pass unharmed?"

"Yes," it said. "I give you our word."

She hesitated. Without the rice cake for the way back, she would slowly lose her grip on who she was until she became no better than the bird-creatures, wandering this barren land without purpose. But maybe she could travel faster than the firmament could sap her. She reached into her bag and offered up the last rice cake. "Here," she said. "Take this. One bite will feed you for days. Perhaps it will ease some of your hunger."

"Thank you, little one," the creature said. It bent its massive, feathered head, and took the offering in its beak. As promised, it stood and left the path, leaping onto the jagged rocks and vanishing in an indeterminate direction. Only then did Callen release the breath that she had been holding, and continue farther up the path.

Her reprieve was, however, all too brief. She had gone not more than two hundred meters when she found her way blocked by another one of the creatures. Its plumage was darker this time, the color of a dead heart, and it looked at her as she slowly and reluctantly approached.

"Excuse me, O great one," she said. "I need to get to the top of this mountain. May I walk past you?" But her heart was heavy, because she had given the last of the rice cakes to its compatriot down the path.

The creature tilted its head. "Will you give me something to fill my belly?"

"I have nothing left to give you," she said. "I gave the last of my food to another of your kind. All I have left in my bag is this map."

"Then give me your map," it said. "My brethren and I have been trapped upon this plain for a hundred years. Lend it to us so that we may seek our freedom."

Callen hesitated. She was afraid of navigating these plains without the security of her map. With that map, she always knew where she was. The barren land could not fool her or turn her mind around. She was deathly afraid of becoming trapped here. Trapped, just like these bird-creatures were.

Pity overcame her then, and rode over her common sense. A hundred years was a long time to be bound to this lifeless, joyless landscape. How could she begrudge this creature its freedom? After all, on the way back she could follow the path she had taken here.

She reached into her bag and drew out the map, a glowing red ruby that, when it pulsed in her hand, fed her the names of directions. "Here," she said, "take this. Maybe it can tell you a way out of this place."

The creature took the ruby in its beak and swallowed it. The glow of the ruby traveled down its gullet and lodged in its chest like a second heart. When it looked at Callen, its hollow sockets now glowed with the same sacred crimson. "Thank you, my chirpling," it said, and then it too was gone.

And so Callen continued upward, drawing closer and closer to the destination she so longed for. The air around the mountain-hill's summit seemed thinner and sadder, but it also felt cleaner and clearer in the lungs. Callen did not know if her light-headedness was from lack of oxygen or from giddiness that her journey was nearly at an end. Perhaps it was both.

But of course stories can't progress so cheaply and simply—we know that, don't we, my little ones? Of course there was one more obstacle in Callen's path. As she neared sight of the peak, her path was blocked by a creature so enormous it dwarfed the previous two combined. Its plumage was the white of bleached bone, the color so uniform it hurt to look at.

Its great, hollow eyes fixed on the tiny human in front of it. "Excuse me, O great one," Callen said slowly.

The bird-creature spoke: "You want me to leave this path so that you may proceed, don't you?" Its voice rumbled like distant thunder. "What can you offer me in return?"

Callen lowered her head. "I have nothing to offer, great one. I have given everything I carried to your brethren down the path. All I have left is my name, and a story I wish to tell."

"Give me one of those, then," said the creature.

"The story is the reason I am here," Callen said. "If I forget, I will have nothing to offer the witch at the top of the mountain."

"Then give me your name," the bird said.

"My name?" Callen blinked. "But I need my name."

The creature tilted it head and said nothing.

Callen knew the only way to reach her goal was to satisfy this creature, so that it would leave. She didn't know what she would do without her name, without her identity. But she knew that the alternative—failing her quest—would be worse. If she failed here, she would never see the one she loved again. And she would not have that.

"All right," she conceded. "Take my name, then. It's not as important as why I am here."

"And why are you here?" asked the creature.

"My beloved languishes in the prison of the gods, guilty only for the crime of loving me," she said. "I was told the witch who lives on this mountain can free her."

It laughed. "And you think the witch will help you? You think she can spring your beloved from the bars built by the heavenly hosts themselves?"

"I was told she could help."

The creature laughed again. Callen burned with frustration, knowing that she was only wasting time parleying. "Take my name and be done with it," she said. "Though I know not what you would do with such a thing. But if it's what you want, then it is yours."

The bird-creature stood and passed its massive white wings over the girl in front of it, and when it was done the girl no longer remembered her name or where she was from. All she had was a story, burning inside of her, and the knowledge that she must tell it to someone.

"Go, my small darling," said the bird-creature to her. "See if you can find what you wanted." And with that, it took wing and soared into the dark red sky.

The girl with no name headed up the path with the conviction of a fish returning to the grounds where it had been spawned. The top of the hill was a flat clearing, large as an emperor's bedchamber and empty as a pauper's pantry. In its middle sat a human figure, hunched over a green fire lit upon a bier of stones.

"Are you the witch who lives on this mountain?" asked the girl with no name.

The figure straightened up. They were of indeterminate gender, craggy-faced and silver-haired, weighed down by beads in a style unseen in thousands of years. They laughed at the girl, although not unkindly. "What of it?"

The girl sat. "I need your help."

"Give me your name," said the witch.

"I can't," the girl said. "I've given it away."

"Have you?" said the witch. They looked amused. "And what, exactly, can a girl with no name offer me in return for my help?"

The girl looked at her hands, which were empty. Dirt had gathered under the nails during her long journey. "I have nothing left except a story," she said. "I don't know why it's important, but it must be, because I gave up my name rather than give up the story."

The witch stoked the fire and laughed some more, and their laughter shook the hidden stars above. "All right," they said, "Tell me, then. I will listen, and I will judge if you're worth helping."

The girl bowed her head as if in prayer, collecting the strange threads of the story that was the only thing left to her. And then she began to speak: "Not so long ago . . ."

Not so long ago, in a place not so far from here, there was a river of stars that swept within sight of the deathless ones. Every so often a mortal ship would stop in the bright stream to bathe its engines in the light, and sometimes the mortals would emerge, wrapped in soft silver to protect their fragile bodies from the beautiful cold teeth of the void.

It so happened that this day, a group of young fairies were frolicking amongst the stars when a particular ship made a stop, and several mortals came out to wander, tethered to their vessel with wiry cords. The fairies, being young and sheltered, had never seen mortals before, and being curious, gathered around the intruders into their playground. And the mortals, having never met immortals before, were terrified by the appearance of these creatures that were shaped like them but shone with the light of stars and swam through the vacuum of space like jellyfish. They fled back to their ship, but one of them was too slow, alas! and was caught by the playful fairies. The fairies broke the cord tethering the frightened mortal to her ship, and she was left behind as her ship fled the sacred stream.

But mortals have mortal needs, and without the warm nurturing of her ship the young woman the fairies had captured quickly ran out of air. She stopped screaming and kicking as her skin and lips turned blue. And the fairies, in their capricious manner, became bored and abandoned her to her fate.

She would have died then, but the youngest of the fairies took pity on her. Gathering the silver-clad mortal in her arms, the fairy traveled back to the Celestial Palace, halfway across the galaxy. She hid the mortal from the sight of the others and nursed her back to health in the secrecy of her own bedchamber. After all, little separates the immortals and the mortals but several hundred years of magic and technology, and it took little effort to salvage a soft flesh body subject to the mere whims of physics and biology.

When the mortal woman woke from her long healing sleep, she looked upon the face of her benefactor and smiled. In that moment the young fairy instantly fell in love, and swore she would protect this mortal woman for as long as she lived. Thus began a clandestine affair in the heart of the Celestial Palace, a story of separation by day and passion by night. The fairy plied her mortal lover with sweet wines and delicate fruits from the celestial garden, the likes of which the mortal had never seen. At night, the fairy anointed her lover with perfumed oils while the larks sang outside the closed windows of the bedchamber. She taught the mortal to read, to play instruments, to enjoy every luxury the life of a celestial being could offer.

Yet the mortal woman was little more than a prisoner in her new life. A trespasser in the heart of the immortal empire, in the palace complex where only those closest to the Heavenly Emperor were permitted, she could not leave the fairy's bedchambers for fear of getting caught. Every morning as the fairy left for her duties, she made her lover promise that she would stay within the bounds of the room, and every morning the mortal agreed. But how the outside world called to her! Birds sang in trees unseen, and fragrances wafted in through the gaps under the door. Through the thin paper of the windows she could hear laughter and songs in a language she was slowly learning to understand. How she longed to join them!

It was love that kept her true to her promise, and kept her from wandering to meet the outside world. But day by day her boredom and frustration grew, until one day she thought, "Surely a look wouldn't hurt, just a look!" And so she pushed open one of the paper windows, just a mere crack, and peered out. How beautiful it was! The fairy's bedchamber was one of a hundred rooms that opened onto a massive garden courtyard filled with wonders. Silver water cascaded from rocks into enormous pools where fish the size of horses swam. Trees were laden with fruit or blossoms in colors she had never seen before—purples beyond purples, blues that invoked the deepest oceans, pinks that stilled the heart with their intensity. In pavilions men played counter games while women sang and danced with silk fans. The mortal woman watched, rapt with envy, until the light faded and her lover came home.

This went on, day after day. Each time the mortal woman gazed out at the lively scene before her it got harder for her to stay where she was. She was an explorer by nature, after all, and just because she had been separated from her ship and her people did not mean that her nature had changed. Bit by bit, her resistance and her loyalty to her lover wore down, until one day she could stand it no longer, and slipped from the bedchamber to examine the fruit of the tree across from her window, which seemed to shimmer as if made of gold.

But the moment she stepped from outside the boundaries of the bedchamber, which had been tightly woven with protective wards, her presence was exposed to the rest of the palace. Every fairy, guard, magistrate, and deity knew at once that a mortal had dared come into their forbidden place. And there was no recourse from their anger: even though she ran from the star-hounds they set upon her, she was doomed to capture from the beginning.

The mortal woman and her fairy lover were both brought to the Heavenly Emperor for judgment. And no matter how much the fairy girl begged for mercy, it was not given. The Heavenly Emperor knew that leniency was often mistaken for weakness, and he would not have that. The fairy was banished from the palace, and the mortal woman was sentenced to a lifetime imprisoned in a cage deep beneath the Heavenly Emperor's throne, in a place she would see neither sunlight nor starlight ever again.

Separated from the one she loved, the fairy would have fallen into complete despair. But her aunt, who served the Queen Mother of Heaven, came to her rescue. She told the fairy of a witch who lived on a mountain in the barren plain of exiles, once a great general and a favorite of the Heavenly Emperor's, until they had fallen from grace and been banished. Knowing the weaknesses of the Heavenly Palace, and filled with resentment toward the Emperor, they would be the perfect ally to help her. The fairy's aunt gave her a map and food adequate for the journey, and set her on her way. Where one story ended, another began. A story driven by desperation, but born of hope.

The girl with no name stopped speaking, her words petering out into an unsatisfying end. The witch laughed. "I see, I see. So this is what you are asking of me?"

She nodded. In the process of telling the story she had remembered some things, fragments of fragments, little slivers of time that did not form a complete story, yet told enough of it. The first glimpse of a lover in the cold brilliance of space, the long nights in a warm room, the fragile swell of a mortal heartbeat pressed against her own chest. "Please," she said, "will you help?"

The witch stroked their chin. "Here's the interesting thing with stories. It always depends on who's telling it, doesn't it? From your end, what you've said sounds like a sweeping love story. A great romance, a tale for the ages. Told from another perspective, however, it sounds like the tale of kidnapping and imprisonment, with the victim having to pay the highest price. How do I know what the truth is?"

The girl sat silent for a long time; she could not find the words she wanted to say. Finally she wet her lips and whispered, "I've told you what I believe is the truth."

"Yet one's belief and the truth are rarely the same thing, not even for immortals like you. Especially not for immortals like you."

The girl's heart turned to stone in her chest. "Are you not going to help me, then?"

The witch rubbed their bony fingers together. "Who am I really helping here, child?"

Something caught fire in the mind of the girl who had no name. She sat up straight, her spine a pillar of freshly ignited conviction. "I'm here because of her. I want you to help her. I don't care what happens to me, but she deserves her freedom."

"Even if she chooses to return to her people with the freedom that she gains?"

"Even so. Please. I have come so far, and I have lost everything, even my own name. Set free the one that I love. That is all I ask."

"Alas, when I was banished here I was bound to this forsaken land, and I cannot leave until the one who cursed me is dead. But you have told me a fine tale, child, one which has entertained me in my endless torment. For that, I am grateful, and in return I shall tell you one of my own."

"A thousand years ago the universe was at war. The immortals, the two-legged creatures whose ancestors were made of soft flesh and lived on planets breathing air, were engaged in war with the great corvids that soared in the spaces between the stars. The corvids—a mighty race—

were as old as time itself, but their numbers were few, and the immortals had learned to harness the magic of the stars, which gave them an otherworldly power. The war had gone on for longer than both sides remembered, and they both ached for peace."

"The emperor of the immortals offered a truce to the corvids, and invited them to his palace to discuss a peace treaty. The corvids accepted his invitation in good faith, but they were soon betrayed, for the emperor knew nothing in his heart but the desire for victory. One of his generals, a close childhood friend, tried to warn the corvids, but it was too late. The emperor killed their leader and cursed the rest of the corvids, taking their memories and banishing them to a barren land in a forsaken corner of the universe. He exiled the general he had once called a friend too, for he was nothing if not a petty man, and not prone to reason or forgiveness. So the one he used to call his dearest friend has lingered a thousand years alone in the desert, while his foes remain wandering and lost, locked into their fate, any hope of justice the mere forgotten shadow of a dream.

"See," the witch said, leaning forward, "sometimes it's not enough to right the single injustice, if that injustice is the least thing that is wrong with the situation. Sometimes, to undo all the wrongs you have to undo the entire system."

The girl tightened her fists. "Tell me what I have to do."

The witch grinned. "You have already given them the tools they need to escape their bondage. Go down the hill and speak to them, if you want to. Their leader's name is Liercal."

"And what about you?" she asked.

They laughed. "I've told you: I'm bound here until the one who cursed me is dead."

"I see," said the girl.

She turned and went down the hill, treading the crooked path with its treacherous walls. It was easier going down than coming up. At the bottom she found an army of the bird-creatures amassed, gazes fixed upon her, the great white one at their head. The rice cake she had given them, imbued with the magic of the Heavenly Palace's kitchens, had awakened their memories, and now a different hunger filled them.

"Your name is Liercal," she told the white bird.

"And yours is Callen. You've freed us from our long years of bondage."

"You remember who you are now," she said.

"Yes, and we remember what we are owed."

"Then let's go and take it back," she said.

And so, you know what happened next, sweet chirplings. Callen and her new army crossed the stars with the map she had been given, and along the way we corvids woke the sleeping broods that have been in incubation for a thousand years, with no one to tend to them. We took ourselves, all of us, across the galaxy to our final destination, and we rest now, gathering our strength before the final battle. The Heavenly Emperor in his palace has no idea what's coming for him. But soon he will, my feathered darlings. Soon he will.

AUTHOR'S NOTE

The story of the Cowherd and the Weaver-Girl (which some may know in its Japanese form as Tanabata) has always appealed to the romantic side of me. Not because of the love story, mind you, but because I was utterly charmed by the idea of people explaining the Milky Way as a bridge of crows spanning the heavens. Living in a tropical city soaked in light pollution and plagued by cloudy skies, I had no idea what the Milky Way looks like from Earth, so I was free to imagine this living celestial architecture any way I wanted. As for my retelling, I wanted to do a version in space, but I also thought telling it in a linear fashion would be dreadfully boring, so I decided to nest stories within stories. It was fun having the actual myth be a pit in the middle of my story that you have to cut through layers of flesh to see.

JY YANG

LABBATU TAKES COMMAND OF THE FLAGSHIP *HEAVEN DWELLS WITHIN*

BY

ARKADY MARTINE

LADY, YOU PILE UP HEADS LIKE DUST. YOU SOW
heads like seeds.

————————

"So the captain was in her quarters—"

"Naked, right?"

"If you were the captain, would you bother with a nightshirt? So she's in her quarters, and she's looking at her genitals in the mirror, and she's like, *My cunt is amazing*—"

"Wouldn't you like to know, Sarge—"

"Shut it, I'm not alone *there*—"

"Let her tell the story. I wanna hear about how the captain took

Heaven Dwells Within from the House of An without firing a single shot. That's what the sarge said, yeah? Not one shot."

"Not one shot that hit anyone. Captain Labbatu doesn't need to shoot people to win herself a flagship. She's as good a thief as she is a commander, see. I remember—"

"Because you are an *ancient* of *days*, Sarge."

"Because I was *here when she did it*, Technician. Now do you want to hear this or not?"

"I want to hear it. How'd she do it?"

"Well, first, she seduced Ash-Iku—"

"With her *amazing cunt*, yeah, yeah."

———————

Ash-Iku's flat is a glass-walled slice of skyscraper, floating over the smog on this half-used-up planet; he's got a whole floor to himself, and another three for his people and his business right below. Those don't have windows at all, let alone open glass to see a dying planet by. Those are safe and shrouded. Labbatu's filthy from the streets of this place, dust on her leather spacer's jacket in a thick rose-red film, alley garbage-rot stuck to the treads of her boots. There's blood on her face, and more blood on her thigh below her holstered gun, and someone else's well-loved blood soaked through her shirt and dried to stiffening rust. She hasn't been planetside in years.

Up until this morning—some morning, by some planet's reckoning, this one will do—she hadn't needed to be. She'd ridden in her ship over the skyways, the starshot paths from system to system, a small fast ship with a small fast crew. Captain Labbatu, the woman you call when you need a gun or a fuck or a piece of your heart retrieved. The woman you call when you need someone who knows how to win an ugly war and come up smiling. She isn't smiling now. She's got crew-blood soaked in her shirt, enough that it looks white-spotted instead of red-stained. She hasn't got a ship at all anymore. She's got dust. Dust, and fury.

She looks Ash-Iku's doorkeep, behind his desk in the lobby, straight in the eyes and says, "Send me up. The hacker and I, we go *back*, honey."

Doorkeep maybe hesitates too long; doorkeep gets a good look at the hollow dead eye of Labbatu's pulse pistol, with its lioness-maw barrel. Doorkeep makes a call. Doesn't take long for a silken elevator to show up, chrome and clean, whisper-quiet. Labbatu's going to leave dust in it, and she thinks that's right, that's correct and just. She's going to leave parts of her dead ship all over wherever she goes, now. That's how she remembers, after all: she *reminds*.

Ash-Iku's waiting at the top when that elevator sluices itself open; tumbled curls, olive skin, half-closed sky-green silk robe, his crypto-breaker goggles still pushed up on his forehead. Ash-Iku's the sort of man who knows everything, or at least knows everything anyone's tried to ask him; he finds out. He opens up. Doors, files. People. Companies and governments. Security systems. Whatever you like, if it's what he likes too.

Captain Labbatu, she says to Ash-Iku: "I need to know how to destroy the House of An," first thing. Not playing it subtle, Labbatu is; she's not got subtlety left to her. Maybe later she decides to *be* the House of An, but right then she hasn't got anything but revenge on her tongue. She swaggers into Ash-Iku's glass house, parks her dusty, bloody ass on his white leather couch. He gets her a drink. He gets him a drink. He gets them both one of those terrible little crudité platters he's had left over for a while, mysterious vegetable in pastry cup, mysterious pale pink fish dip, unmysterious celery stick.

"The whole House of An," he says. "Tall order, Labbatu. Also that includes *you*, or are you renouncing that particular blood-tie? I don't do suicides. Bad business."

"The *Heaven Dwells Within* killed my crew and took my bounty," says Labbatu. "Let's start there. I want to cripple that fucking ship, Ash-Iku. I know you know how."

Ash-Iku looks her over: sees a woman hurt and diminished, maybe, vulnerable, maybe. He thinks, *What can I get first?* Or else consider this: Ash-Iku looks her over, sees a business opportunity, a friend who got hurt, but he's not the sort of man who has friends anymore, even friends like Labbatu. Wishes, a little, that he did. He thinks, *Let's make this fair.* Either way works. Depends on how men are.

He says, "So what can you give me in exchange, without a ship to go get it with?"

Which is an ugly sort of fair. Labbatu's not asking for *flowers.* She wants security hacks, shipmind-killer software.

When Labbatu grins, she's got blood on her teeth like a lioness after the kill. "How about this, honey," she says, picking up her drink. "I outdrink you, in my current state, you do me a favor. You outdrink me—should be easy, *look* at me—and I do one for you instead. Square?"

"Square," says Ash-Iku, and they get started.

[...]loop ALERT ALERT ALERT ➔ *data breach! Credible reports of data breach sector-wide, including access override codes to Lotus-5 Docking Systems, access override codes to Riparian Docker Systems; personnel files at Kissura Shipping Incorporated, Larak Consultants, House of An, Marad Corp.; weapon unlock sequences for Belu Planetary Defense Cannons [...]*

"Fuck," says Ash-Iku to his doorkeep, hungover head in his hands, sitting in his disheveled bed, one arm stuck in his green silk robe and the rest of it crumpled under him. His cryptogoggles, discarded on the pillow, are yelling "ALERT, BREACH, ALERT" in a tiny tinny yelp. "Go turn off the alarms and then, like. Hire me some thugs, okay? A *lot* of thugs."

"Coffee first, ser?"

"Like a vat of it."

> [...] lionlike she claws at me,
> I am plagued by the stinging on my thighs.
> Her reddened mouth is killing-hot.
> It spreads kisses like seed-crops
> bruises that bloom on all the cheeks of my body
> shakes me apart

sends me scattering.
Sweat-soaked and semen-soaked, falling into heaven.
O queen! Star of the battle-cry!
Your eyes are too sharp.
You sip so deeply that I begin to thirst [...]

Fragment, "The Destruction of Labbatu,"
attributed to Ash-Iku (contested)

"So she fucked him, and when he was fuck-drunk—"

"No, the captain never fucked anyone she didn't want to fuck. He was *actually* drunk."

"How do you know she didn't want to, Sarge? You weren't there. I mean. Slick hack like Ash-Iku, I would—"

"*You*, sera Miz Third Lieutenant, like dick, which is not an affliction everyone suffers."

"The captain likes *everything*, Sarge."

"Sure, sure. So when he was drunk on *her*, whichever way it happened, she took the crypto she needed and spent her last credits on a spitfire gunship she found laid up in the port. Nice little ship, in hock to whatever the local tax authority is down there, stranded asset, free-ish to a good home. Captain got off that planet quick, just her and her kid brother in the gunship—"

"The captain has a brother?"

"The captain, Technician, has a *twin*. Had, anyhow."

[...]even heaven lashes out,
plagued by stinging insects.
Heaven's fire is killing-blue.
It spreads rot like seed-crops
bruises that bloom on the cheeks of every sailor
shakes ships apart

sends captains scattering.
Bloodsoaked and dustsoaked, running to ground.
O, queen! Star of the battle-cry!
Your thorns are too sharp.
You sip too deeply of your house's blood! […]

Fragment, "The Destruction of Labbatu,"
anonymous poem Archives of the House of An

Dead boys come back sometimes, if you know how to call them: Labbatu's own twin's more an illusion than a body, has been for a decade now. But he spins himself up visible easy as midday sunlight when his sister calls him up to dwell a while on her new gunship's empty shipmind. Long-distance call, sure, all the way to the House of An and the mainframe of a very different ship, but Sam's a sword and a cleansing fire, even more so now that he's mostly artificial. The ghost of righteousness, he calls himself. This makes him laugh, but it doesn't do much for Labbatu.

Especially since all that sun-kissed sharpness was the mind behind the guns on *Heaven Dwells Within*, the guns that took her down.

"*Ghost* of righteousness," Sam repeats, sitting in the copilot's chair and not depressing the cushion even a little; sure, light has weight, but you need more than one twin can summon up to feel it. "You know I didn't want to. You know I don't have choices like you do."

"I know," says Labbatu. "I'm not angry at *you*, Sam. Wouldn't have called you up if I was angry at you."

He looks relieved. He's all gold, a sketch-memory of a man, deep-tanned skin, blond hair bleached white by the sun of whatever afterlife weapons get. "You're pissed, though," he says, which is sort of obvious: Labbatu still hasn't changed her bloody, dusty clothes, and it's been a day and a half since she got off Ash-Iku's world. Of course she's pissed. Past pissed into killing-brutal, more like.

"He shouldn't have done it," says Labbatu. "Killed my crew."

"You shouldn't have stolen something the old man was after *too*," Sam says. "He gets jealous when one of his kids outflanks him."

Labbatu bares her teeth, and her illusion-brother wavers a little, goes to a smudge of gold light for a minute of being scared. "Then he should have stopped me," she says. "Or gotten away with it before I got there. Our father *killed my ship*, Sam. My *crew*."

". . . I did a lot of it," says the ghost of righteousness, and his sister pats him on the shoulder with a hand that goes right through him. He's his father's son, but he's his sister's brother, too, and he knows how badly she's been wronged.

"Tell me where he's holed up," Labbatu asks. "I want the *Heaven*, brother-o'-mine. He doesn't deserve it anymore."

There's a long pause. A bad one. Labbatu's about to cut the connection, shove her twin out of the metaphorical airlock and go it alone like always and ever. Then Sam says, small like a newborn kitten, "I don't know where we are. He keeps me from knowing where the *Heaven* is. But if you find us, if you find me, I'll make sure the crew knows what our father did to you."

[...]
2792: Anu registered the live birth of twins, one male and one female, each carried in a different belly. The first twin was Eanna-Nin, called the Lioness, daughter of Antum; the second was Utu-Samesh, called the Shining One, son of Ki-Urash
[...]
2815: Utu-Samesh (2792–2815), died in combat.
2815: Utu-Samesh experiences partial resurrection as a shipmind, updating records to Utu-Samesh (2815–present)
[...]
2816: Eanna-Nin (a.k.a. the Lioness, "Labbatu") disowned and disinherited due to criminal activities
[...]

Partial chronology of the House of An, c. 2891

". . . so she had to find a navigator who could locate the *Heaven Dwells Within*, since Samesh—the shipmind—was codelocked from telling her, or anyone else for that matter. And this was no mean trick, kids."

"We have the best stealth in this sector—in *every* sector, unless someone's invented new tech since last week. There's no navigator who *could* find this ship."

"Not saying you're wrong, Technician."

"Oh, now? You're not?"

"In this delightful present day we're Captain Labbatu's ship. The *Heaven*'s crawling with Ash-Iku's crypto-illusions; of course no one could find us *now*. But back then—you weren't even *alive* back then—"

"Who'd wanna be alive back then? It was *shit*! You keep saying."

"We were still fast and smart, but the old man, well. He was no Labbatu. But he hid out in the back of beyond, out where the nebula is, where there's so much cosmic radiation and debris that no one can see you."

Can't take a shipmind to a spaceport bar; shipmind doesn't have the projection range. Labbatu goes alone, sans brother, sans crew. She's cleaned up some. Not too much. Rose-choked dust on that jacket isn't coming out; blood's got into the leather of those trousers, and they don't wash, not in a gunship's galley. But the tank's a new one, clean white, and she wiped her face clear of blood and alcohol. Saved the soiled rag, after, to remember some broken-bodied beloved by. Captains like Labbatu love all their crew, one way or another.

Spaceport bar is a spaceport bar; looks like the last one you were in, pretty much. They all blur unless a person's washed up on a very distant planetary shore. This one has the usual drinks and the usual drunks. Labbatu orders a beer. Bar's classy enough she gets her beer in a twelve-ounce bell glass, foam on the top thick like cream over the dark gold of it. Bar isn't classy enough that she or anyone else remembers the name of the beer after they have more than one; beer like this is practically barleywine. Labbatu takes her beer and sits down next to a woman so starburnt she looks cured.

"Heard you're a fisherman," says Labbatu.

"Have been," the woman says.

Labbatu shoves her beer down the bar, and the starburnt woman drinks it. When it's done, Labbatu asks, "You fish this nebula?"

"Since I was younger than you." The line of her throat is wattled, but when she grins her teeth are white and all present and accounted for. "Good harvest in this one; it's thick like milk with helium along with all the dust."

"Think you could find something else besides helium, if I took you looking?"

The woman's a nebula-harvester, which is a kind of mercenary in and of itself. She knew what she was getting into, and it seemed like a good deal, or at least an interesting one. Interesting enough to say, "Could. Might want to take care of those fellows before we go, though," and point behind Labbatu with her chin.

Six there, a posse of thugs all in an array when Labbatu turns around. They come in variety-pack: bruiser twice her girth and a wiry martial-artist, a razor-thin chick with a gun that must have come off the nose of a fighter ship strapped across her back in a rig, thickset man running to fat and holding a spitting electric prod, angel-faced lad spinning a suture-thread garrote in one long-fingered hand. Last one's worst: looks like a kid, but no kid's got that many teeth, all in rows inside her mouth like a shark, an endless hole of nasty triangles, no tongue.

"You have something that doesn't belong to you," says the chick with the gun.

"Which one you thinking of?" says Labbatu, getting up off her bar-stool. She's grinning again. She only needs the normal kind of teeth. They're bad enough, when they're Labbatu's. "I have a lot of that sort of merchandise."

"Intellectual property," says the angel, and spins his garrote faster.

Labbatu laughs. Rest of the spaceport bar starts clearing out; this is the sort of evening where there's not much unsplintered furniture or unsmashed bottles left by the end. Easy to tell, if you've been in a lot of spaceport bars.

"Tell Ash-Iku I'm flattered," says Labbatu. "Six of you and only one of me."

Gun chick's gun goes up, thunking into place over her head inside its rig. Starts its charge cycle. "Overkill's all right," she says, and Labbatu just looks at her.

"Ash-Iku's not wrong about *that*," she says, and throws the barstool like it's a spear. One leg goes right into the gun barrel. There is a terrible noise, like a great beast choking itself to death.

It's messy after that. The kid especially. All those teeth to kick in. Labbatu ruins another shirt.

There's a recording, somewhere on the *Heaven Dwells Within*. Deep in the archives, buried, mislabeled. The captain gets it out sometimes, flips it over her knuckles like she's doing a coin trick, and never plays it.

If she did, there'd be about thirty seconds of grainy hangar-bay footage. Gunsmoke and starlight. Old man and not-old-yet woman. No audio, but their mouths are moving. Mostly his.

My lioness, my star of the battle-cry. You turn brother against brother, son against father. Were those people worth this, Eanna-Nin, Labbatu-my-heart? Worth making my son turn against me? Worth poisoning your blood—our blood, Labbatu—with envy and covetousness?

And Labbatu says, "Daddy, you wouldn't have cared if I died with my ship and my crew."

Woman unholsters her lioness-maw pistol.

That's when the scorpion shows up, and the tape cuts out.

Labbatu's got a long way to go before she meets the scorpion. She and the nebula-harvester walk out of that bar—well, Labbatu limps out. Those bloody trousers are bloodier now, and ripped; no point in washing them. When she peels them off later half the skin on that thigh will come with, and she'll throw them in the incinerator. But none of Ash-Iku's retrieval specialists follow them back to the gunship.

(One of them, the martial artist, he gets himself back to Ash-Iku, but fuck, it takes him two weeks, and by then this is all over.)

The nebula-harvester knows her stuff. She's fished this cloud of stardust for decades, and she's got landmarks and beacons to guide her. Local guide beats hiding in the dust any day; that's true for war on all the scales, from nebulae right down to finding the other guy's village and taking their grain before they find yours and do the same. Labbatu takes her gunship where the nebula-harvester says to go, and they cut through the fog in sector-search, until the *Heaven Dwells Within* shows up like a jewel, right there, clear as water-ice.

All those guns. Last time Labbatu saw them, they were pointed at her ship.

This time she's got some firepower of her own.

Ash-Iku's crypto hacks are the best in the business; better than. They're knowledge and concept; they're the language a shipmind speaks when it says *This is a trustworthy vessel*; they're the lists of people a ship knows are meant to be there; they're a scattering illusion, static on every broadcast channel. They carve open the *Heaven* like it was a ripe peach. Sam helps a little, once he notices who it is that's slicing up his brain; Sam does Labbatu the favor of showing the destruction of her old ship under the *Heaven*'s killing blue fire on every screen for all the crew. Scars some of them bad, those visuals. Sure, the *Heaven*'s a deathship, a knifeship, a ruling-ship, but most of the crew who ride in *Heaven*'s skin don't have to see the ship cook a little vessel with the old captain's daughter aboard to nothing but radiation-scorched ashes. Not usually.

Ash-Iku's crypto gets Labbatu into the cargo bay: PETA BABKAMA LURUBA ANAKU, *open the gate for me so that I may enter here.* She comes in guns out already, firing suppression, blood and smoke, but she doesn't need to use them on a single living creature—not one shot fired that hit a body. Sam keeps most of the crew away from her, but he lets Daddy An through every door he wants to open, like usual.

There's that bit of tape.

And then there's the scorpion.

A scorpion isn't like a shipmind. It's more like a parasite, a dweller under the metal skins of ships. A smart captain can tame one, or at least gentle one. It's a scuttle of claws, a gun-stinger and a rattle of repurposed ship bits, grown all together with a thing that might have grown up to be a shipmind in it, squatting in the metal. They grow three times the size of a man. Maybe bigger. Scorpion doesn't stop growing till it dies. A tame one will defend its territory. A non-tame one too, but tame ones are more discriminating about who's an enemy and who isn't.

No barstool to throw this time. Labbatu's lioness-maw gun blows a couple holes in the scorpion, but that hardly slows it down. It leaks oil and hydraulic fluid and spits acid at her. The acid gets the gun, because she's willing to drop it, willing to watch those lion-teeth melt to nothing.

It takes half an army to kill a full-grown scorpion. Labbatu's the greatest captain and the greatest thief in the House of An, but half an army she is not.

Turns out she doesn't need to be. Greatest thief and greatest captain is enough, when being so means having a suite of AI-killing hacker tricks that Labbatu got off Ash-Iku along with the spoof codes to the cargo bay and the personnel lists. Labbatu didn't want to use them. She knew what they'd do to the shipmind in *Heaven*: same thing they did to the scorpion.

She says, "INA ETUTI ASBU."

Dwell in darkness. All that crypto goes to carving knives, and the scorpion's a pile of scrap on the floor at Labbatu's feet.

"Oh, lady," says the old man. "You pile up heads like dust."

And somewhere the last of Utu-Samesh goes into the dark like a stone skipped on a lake—far, and far, and farther still, and sinking.

———————

"And what then, Sarge?"

"Well."

"Well, *what*."

"Well, then she won."

"Obviously she won, she's our captain now, but *how*? Scorpion's dead, she's killed her kid brother in the blast, and *then* what?"

"Scorpion's dead, shipmind's crippled and might as well be dead, yeah."

"Yeah. But the old man—"

"The old man was like, *Fuck this for a loss, keep the ship as your inheritance and I'm done with you*—"

"Which is why we're done with him!"

"Labbatu's the greatest of all the mercenary captains that ever came out of the House of An!"

"—pretty much—"

"She kill him, Sarge?"

"Oh, fuck no, she stuck him on her gunship and spat him out in the nebula to suck up enough helium to buy a ticket somewhere civilized. Old man's somewhere on some rich soft planet now, minding his own business. Last I heard."

"I don't believe it. Our Labbatu? After what Daddy An did to her first crew, she just lets him slide?"

"He was the only blood family she got left, after what happened to Utu-Samesh. After *she* happened to Utu-Samesh. I think—and I never asked her about it, seems really impolite—she didn't want to *bathe* in kin-blood 'less she had to. Robbing him of his power and this flagship was enough."

"Huh. Maybe. . . . And Ash-Iku? What happened to him?"

"Oh, *him*. Him, he hears from his thug, the one who has a mouth that still talks, and he's like, *Fuuuuuck me, Labbatu, I guess you won this one.*"

"More like, *Oh, please, fuck me, Labbatu, your genitals, look how amazing they are, I admit I've been overmatched,* girl, *dang—*"

"Uh-huh. Sure. *Anyway* he's like, *Your greatness is unparalleled—*"

"And so is your cunt!"

"It *is* the captain. No one could compete with our captain anyway, in genitals or in anything else. . . ."

————————

against those who are disobedient to her
she stirs confusion and chaos
she speeds carnage and incites the floods
she is clothed in terrifying radiance, a furious storm,
    a whirlwind,
she is clothed in the garments of ladyship.
She cuts to pieces those who show her no respect.
A south wind, an unharnessed lion, a leopard of the hills
a pitfall for the rebellious, a trap for the hostile.
My lady, let me proclaim your magnificence.
Who can compare with you?
Rest upon the lapis lazuli of your dais
let your divine dwelling place say to you:
Be seated.

Anonymous praise poem, adapted from the Sumerian
(Old Earth, approximately 4300 years before planetbreak)

Author's Note

"Inanna Takes Command of Heaven" and "Inanna and Enki"—the two Sumerian myths (well, the two fragments of epic poetry) this story is constructed out of—are not the usual, expected Inanna myth, the one where the Queen of Heaven descends to the underworld and confronts her dark sister Ereshkigal. These two are older and more fragmentary. They're origin stories: the first being an explanation of how Inanna became Queen of Heaven in the first place, and the second being about how Inanna stole all of human knowledge (in the form of mēs, specific cultural aspects like "victory" or "weaving" or "prostitution" or "beer brewing") from Enki, the god of knowing-things, and kept them to disperse as she liked. Inanna in these stories is a wild thing, sexually voracious, vicious and proud, sneaky, arrogant, unashamed. She is all these things and also a woman, though a woman who possesses masculine characteristics without difficulty. She is a kinslayer and a lover at once. I wanted to write that woman, before questions of underworlds and dead husbands to retrieve. That woman is the sort of woman who captains starships. It was simple to imagine a space opera version of these stories, especially when I wove them together. And since they come to us in fragments of poetry, distorted over time and through retelling, this version too is distorted, fragmentary, and retold.

Arkady Martine

WILD TO COVET

BY
—
SARAH GAILEY

THETIS WAS A WILD THING WASHED UP OUT OF
the wheat. Not the strangest gift to walk out of the field—no white bull
was she—but strange enough. It was Cor Ellison's field she wandered
out of at dusk, looking all of five years old but with eyes that stared right
through you like she'd been to war, and Cor took her in. He always took
ownership of what came out of his wheat, whether what he took wanted
to be an owned thing or not, and the girl was no exception.

Young Thetis was a barefooted, tangle-haired creature, howling at the
moon and curling her lip up at mittens in the winter. She'd look out the
window at the hills one morning and that night be gone, back a week
later with mud in her eyebrows and a cape's worth of rabbit pelts slung
over one shoulder. When her baby teeth started falling out, she took to

yanking the loose ones herself and tossing them into the hearth before they could fall out. She nearly cut her thumb off trying to free a wolf from a trap just off the edge of Cor's property. Not a soul doubted her when she said it was the trap that got her and not the wolf. No one had ever heard of a wolf brave enough to bite Thetis.

Thetis wasn't a domesticated creature, but she was curious about tameness, a fox nosing around a dog's kennel. She watched close when people's noses turned red and sniffly, and her eyes got catlike tracking the way folks stepped to avoid puddles. She felt fabric between the pads of her fingers and tasted anything anyone would offer her, and it was as if she'd never lived before, which it's fair enough to say she hadn't. For all that she tossed her neck at shoes and hairbrushes and handkerchiefs, she was fascinated, too, and folks said that Cor kept her knee-deep in pocket watches and pepper grinders just to keep her from running off back into the wheat for good. So long as she had something new and small and human to study, Thetis stuck close. She wandered plenty, but she always came back.

The problems started right on time. Thetis started to go from creature to girl, and it was a small town, and nearly everyone in it had eyes. She was never quite pretty, but she was something to notice even when she wasn't walking into church with a fresh-trapped pheasant in her fist. There were cornfield whispers in the way she talked, and the tilt of her head was hawk-sharp. Once her legs sprouted up coltish, looking turned to staring and staring turned to talking, and people understood without having to say so that she was going to be a woman to watch out for sooner than later.

Uncle, who lived on the farm with Cor and Thetis, got her a dress to replace her poor abused overalls. It only took him a day and a half of shouting and door-slamming to convince her to wear it to church, which per Thetis's usual habits was a formality of a fight. She was softened by the beauty of the thing, by the ribbons and layers of floating linen. She walked into the service in that dress looking almost like she'd taken to the bridle—but the prettiness of it was scarred by the leaves stuck to her feet, and by the barn owl that perched on her shoulder, his wicked talons drawing blood. She didn't flinch at the owl's grip.

Anyone who stared at Thetis that morning got watched right back by her and that owl just the same, and which pair of eyes was wilder no one could say.

The day came, as days come, when Thetis needed help Cor and Uncle couldn't give. It was a long time coming by most standards, twelve years to the day since she'd walked out of the wheat. She knew well enough what was happening to her. She put her knuckles to Doc Martha's front door, and handed over a bucket of good ripe figs in exchange for a conversation about the blood and the pain and what to do about it.

Thetis didn't so much as flinch when Doc Martha fetched a basket of fresh eggs. She just lay down on the floor with her loose hair fanned out behind her shoulders, pulled her dress up over her ribs, and waited. Her bare toes curled on the floorboards as Doc Martha cracked the egg over her flat belly.

The yolk was double.

"You're going to birth a boy someday," Doc Martha said in a voice that didn't have congratulations anywhere in it. "Tougher'n saddle leather, a fighter and a bruiser." She pointed to a speck of blood on one of the yolks. "And a lover. That boy of yours'll live long or he'll live hard. You'll be birthin' a squaller, no two ways about it."

"I'll do no such thing," Thetis said, the whites of the egg running off her sides and dripping onto the floor. "No sons nor husband neither, thank you very kindly." She said "thank you" like it was a new kind of fruit she was tasting, one she wasn't sure was quite ripe.

"If you had a choice in the matter, I'd've said as much." Doc Martha handed Thetis a rag to clean the egg off her belly and watched the way the yolks held strong for a long time before bursting under the linen. "He'll be greater than his daddy, even. Stronger too, he'll need to be stronger. And you'll belong to that son until one of you is through," she said.

"Won't be a daddy to be greater than," Thetis told her, and her eyes blazed as cold as the river. She walked out the door as if the conversation was through, and she spent half the afternoon in the woods, slapping branches out of her face and growling at rabbits. Her fury grew as the light on the horizon died, and by the time she got home, she was a thing made of pine sap and wrath—but by then, Cor and Uncle Ellison had gotten word from Doc Martha. They lived on the outskirts of town, but it was a small-enough town that even outskirts still heard rumors before the telling was finished. They were ready for her.

They fought like thunder, them saying she had best decide what kind of man she'd marry, her shouting back that she'd sooner walk into the corn without a ball of string to find her way back than do something as stupid and small and human as get married to a man. Every ear in town was turned to the sound of that fight—even the crickets held their legs apart to listen. It was a still-enough night that it was hard not to hear the way Thetis started losing ground.

They told her she was too old to keep running barefoot through the woods and swimming in the river the day the ice cracked. They told her she'd eaten enough of their food and spent enough nights under their roof that she was a woman now, bound by that prophecy just as much as she was bound by the humanity she'd grown into. Even as she slammed her way through that little house screaming that she wasn't a woman and never would be, they told her it was time to grow up. Her voice began to soften with defeat as it became clear to her that they were right—for all her slamming, she couldn't outright leave.

They said it was time to start braiding her hair and wearing shoes and thinking about who she'd aim to marry. Good Christians, were Cor and Uncle, but even so they couldn't ignore Doc Martha's prophecy, and they weren't about to let Thetis ignore it either. They loved her, in their way, and so they told her to find some fellow who could manage her, someone good enough that her son being greater than him would be a boon instead of a burden. The only way out, they said, was through.

It was past midnight before the fight quieted, Thetis having shouted something about wearing the damn shoes just to shut those fool men up. The whole town heard it coming as clear as a hailstorm pounding across a fallow field, and they hunkered in to wait for the rooftops to start shaking.

Whether anyone liked it or not, Thetis was about to start courting.

By the time the sun came up, Moss Hetley was waiting on Cor Ellison's porch with a fistful of thistles.

Moss was everything that a town like that one wanted a man to be. He had bull-broad shoulders, and his hands were mostly knuckle. He wasn't mean enough to beat his dogs, but he wasn't kind enough to bring them inside when it snowed, either. He was more civilized than Cor and Uncle; he wrote poetry, most of it about chopping wood, and at the start of every summer he bought new shoes for the children at church. He liked being the only one who could do an impossible thing, and he liked to feel like a hero to the town, and he was as stubborn as a headache—so of course he had his hard-set black eyes fixed on Thetis to wife.

When she went out to pump water in the morning, she didn't notice him at first. Her hair was in a clumsy, half-knotted braid. She was trying to figure out how to walk in shoes, now that Cor and Uncle had made wearing them a condition of staying in their home. The way she tugged at the braid and stumbled in the shoes spoke to a choice she'd been outraged to have to make at all—she wanted to stay, so she was bending to the new rules, but she didn't have it in her to pretend to be happy about it.

She stumbled over the doorframe and nearly toppled right into Moss. When she looked up at the great wall of a man standing on her porch with his thistles in his hand, her eyes caught on the shining chain of his pocket watch. She froze, hypnotized by the links of delicate silver. He reached out and touched her chin as sweetly as if she were made of crystal, and when his finger met her skin, fury swept over her like wind through tall grass. She walked past him with her nose pointing east and her hips pointing north, and when she came back lugging the bucket of water, he was right where she'd left him.

"What are you after?" she snapped, though she surely knew.

"I'd like to speak to Cor Ellison," he rumbled. "Or Uncle, if Cor's not in."

Thetis slammed the door behind her and didn't bother telling Cor or Uncle that Moss was waiting on them. When she came back out an hour later with a hatchet over her shoulder to check the traps, the thistles were lined up in a row on the porch rail. She knocked them off with the hatchet handle, then reached down and tore her new shoes off with a snarl. She threw them after the thistles and jumped down the porch steps, and she didn't come back until the frogs by the river were singing down the dusk.

When she got home, the thistles were in a jar on the windowsill, and her shoes were waiting by the door. She picked them up with ginger fingers like they were foul things instead of fresh leather, and she walked inside on silent feet. Cor was whittling by the fire with long, thoughtful strokes of his good knife. Thetis dropped the shoes with a clatter, slapped the three fat quail she'd trapped onto the kitchen table. She glared at Cor, but he didn't say a word until after she'd scalded the first of the birds.

"Uncle wanted to know if you need anything from the city," he said to the hunk of wood in his hand. "He's going into town to see about a suit and thought you might like a new dress for the harvest festival. Some dancing shoes."

Normally, her eyes would have lit up. Whenever Uncle went to the city, Thetis asked for small soft things, scraps of silk and rag dolls. But the fight from the night before was still in her, too fresh for her to play the old game of gifts. "Don't need a new dress. This one's fine," Thetis said in a level voice as she yanked feathers from the first quail, pulling hard enough to spatter blood across her apron. The cotton of her old dress was soft and stained; the skirt hem had been let out twice, and the sleeves ended at the elbows. It was well past a rag, but knowing Thetis, she'd patch it until it was more stitch than scrap. "And I don't need shoes."

Cor raised his eyebrows. "Watch you don't tear the skin on those birds, now," he said. Thetis frowned, not because he was correcting her but because he was right. The birds were small things, and she should have known how to handle them. She plucked gentler but with her jaw clenched tight. The only sound for a time was the scrape of Cor's knife on pine and the soft pull of feathers from flesh, and the silence could almost pretend to be companionable.

Three days later, Uncle came home from the city and left a white box on Thetis's bed. The dress inside was as red as the belly of a pomegranate, and the neckline dipped low enough to show the hollow of her throat, and she didn't want to love the dress but of course she did. A wild thing was Thetis, but even wild things can covet, and she wanted to own the dress as bad as anyone wants to own something beautiful.

Under the dress was a pair of dyed-to-match shoes—little heels and gleaming buckles. She hated them even more than she loved the dress, but she knew that there was no wearing one without the other. She clutched the soft cotton of the dress to her throat. She stared at the way the light sparked off the buckles of the shoes, like the sun catching the teeth of a bear trap. For the first time in her life, she was afraid.

The harvest festival that year may as well have been renamed the Thetis festival. Everyone was mindful of the prophecy and the fight that came after it. Everyone had seen the way Thetis walked slower now that she wore shoes, and everyone knew that Moss was closing in on her like thunder after lightning. The boys in town all slicked their hair back and washed their necks and starched their collars, but it was more out of respect for Cor and Uncle than out of a sense of competition. No one much wanted to compete with Moss, and no one much wanted to face down Thetis's contempt.

She came to the festival in her red dress and her red shoes, her hair braided up tight by Doc Martha's unforgiving fingers. Everyone who asked her to dance did it with the kind of polite you'd show a flat-eared cat, and she said "No thank you" until the only person left standing near to her was Moss.

The firelight caught on the chain of his pocket watch. Thetis worked hard not to stare.

"Let's dance, Thetis," he said, holding out a hand like the deed was already done. She made to stalk off toward the corn, but he snatched her arm sparrow-quick. Even though everyone nearby was making a show of not staring, there wasn't a breath that didn't catch when he laid his hand on that girl. Thetis whipped around, her finger under Moss's nose like a nocked arrow, and twisted up her lip to give him her opinion of his hand on her elbow. But before she could spit hell at him, he spun her in a wide circle. The fiddle players caught on before Thetis did. She stumbled, trying to keep her feet under her, and the music turned it into dancing.

There was no escaping, so she danced with Moss. Her smile was a rattling tail. Cor and Uncle watched with folded arms as she let the man lead her in one dance and then another. Uncle's face was still; Cor's was more than a little sad. It was three dances before anyone else was brave enough to join in the dancing. Thetis snarled like a mountain cat, but Moss held her tight and swung her high and dipped her low, and by the end of the night, the thing had been decided. Moss had held onto the unholdable girl.

The last song ended. Moss dug into his pocket, and from its depths he excavated a dull gold ring. It shone like an apple in the firelight. Thetis couldn't hide her fascination with the thing—it was the smallest beautiful thing she'd yet seen. She stared at it, slump-shouldered and hollow-cheeked and wanting.

He didn't drop to a knee, just held the ring out and waited. Thetis gave her hand over like a woman dreaming, her arm lifting slow, her eyes unblinking as she watched the light play over the gold. It wasn't until

119

Moss slid the thing onto her finger that she startled, but by then it was too late. The ring fit perfect, and everyone clapped while Moss pressed his lips to her cheek, and Thetis was well and truly trapped.

They were married before Christmas. Thetis wore a white dress from the city. White satin shoes, too, the third pair of shoes she'd ever worn in her life, and she didn't stumble in them even once. It was a good wedding with good food and good music, and the bride didn't look at the groom at all, not even when she made the vow.

She had never been one to waste time once she'd decided on a project, and so by the time the first fiddleheads were poking through the snow, her belly was soft and her face was round and everyone was whispering that the two-yolk son was on the way. She answered their congratulations with the same grim satisfaction she'd shown after slaughtering her first rooster. "Only way to get a kettle boiling's by lightning a fire under it," she'd say, looking at the ring on her finger with increasing distaste.

Neighbors gave her a rattle and a pair of impossibly small shoes and a long white christening gown and knitting needles and an embroidery kit. She was tired enough for the last half of the pregnancy that she learned to sit by the hearth and make use of the latter two. She sent Uncle to the city for thimbles and colored thread and kitten-soft yarn. She bared her teeth at Moss when he tried to press his ear to her navel to hear the baby's heartbeat, and she still threw her shoes into the garden. But she also sewed buttons onto miniature shirts, and the fury in her frown gentled when she smoothed her fingers over the stitches.

She seemed so close to settled that it was almost a surprise that next January when Moss ran into town, wild-haired, chasing after his missing wife. He ran from the post office to the grocery to the barbershop, but it wasn't until he got to the dentist's that he found someone who had seen Thetis that day. The postman who was getting his bad tooth looked at said that he'd seen her. He'd almost forgotten about it, with the news about the war and the draft being all anyone wanted to talk about, but he'd seen her all right. She was walking into the wheat that morning, he said, both hands braced on the small of her back, her belly set out in front of her like the prow of a ship. He told Moss that he saw her walk into the field and thought nothing of it, that wheat being on Cor Ellison's land and all.

"Was she wearing her shoes?" Moss asked, his fists in the postman's shirtfront, and when the man shook his head Moss turned and ran. Everyone who'd seen him run into town saw him run out, faster than a hare with a hawk over his shoulder. He didn't stop running until he reached the wheat.

But of course he was too late—by the time he got to the wheat, Thetis was staggering out of it with blood soaking her legs and a baby at her breast. She swept past Moss in her bare feet and her ruined skirt, walked up the steps of Cor and Uncle's house, and let herself in. Moss followed her bloody footprints inside and found her sitting on Cor's whittling stool by the hearth, her leather shoes in front of her and the baby asleep with her nipple still in his mouth. The room smelled like iron and clean sweat. Moss stood with his hands braced on the doorframe, and Thetis finally looked at him. Her gaze was flat and final; she had gotten what she needed from the man she'd allowed to marry her. She didn't so much as blink as she slid her bloody feet into the shoes she hated.

They named the baby Esau, and with that they renamed her Esau's Momma. She stopped being Thetis, when anyone talked about her—she had never been Moss's Wife, but she was sure as hell Esau's Momma. He was a strong boy with a swagger of red curls that nothing could settle. He had fists like his father and a holler like his mother, and Moss shone bright with pride.

Esau's Momma was something different from proud. Her mouth tightened whenever someone called her by her new name. She didn't look at her son with warmth, but she wasn't quite cool, either. She stroked the newborn-down above his ears and studied his fast-growing fingernails. She watched him sleep, her eyes bright as a cat's. She loved him the way a bear loves its trap-caught paw.

He needed her, and whether she liked it or not, she needed him right back.

The harvest festival that year, just a few months after she came out of the wheat field with a damp-headed Esau in her arms, marked two years since Moss made Thetis dance. She was wearing that same red dress, the one Moss had captured her in. The red shoes, too, the dancing ones, although Moss knew better than to ask her to dance. She kept Esau close in a sling made of white linen with orange blossoms embroidered along the edges in her wide, clumsy stitches. They stood by the bonfire drinking cider, a tidy family to look at them. Moss rested his hand on the small of her back. She shivered away like oil pearling on a hot pan.

Moss didn't notice her shudder, of course, because he wasn't looking at her. He was talking to somebody about the way the war would change the price of alfalfa and barley. Esau was craning his neck out of his sling, watching his daddy with the eyes of a child who's just starting to recognize who his people are. He was watching the way Moss's watch chain glinted in the flickering firelight, hypnotized in that way babies get.

Esau's Momma was watching the fire.

Her shoulders were set, and anyone who'd been thinking or looking close enough could have seen what was coming, but nobody was watching Esau's Momma because Moss had his hand on her back. His hand on her back might as well have been a latch on a storm door, as far as any of them were concerned. So they didn't watch, and they didn't see the way her fingers twitched at the edge of the baby's sling.

The moment came when his hand left her back, and when it did, Esau's Momma moved fast as a snakebite. She whipped the baby out of the sling, both his legs in one of her strong hands. She swung him toward the fire like she was aiming a horseshoe at a post, and she let go at the top of the arc and Esau flew—but Moss reached out and snatched the boy from the smoke before anyone could finish gasping.

"You're the one's always talking about the prophecy," Esau's Momma spat, firelight glinting off her teeth. "The prophecy says he needs to be strong. I'll burn the weakness out of him; you see if I don't."

Moss held the squalling boy close, patting his back and frowning like this wasn't the first time and he knew it wouldn't be the last. "The prophecy says he can live long or he can live hard," he said quietly. "You try this way to turn him into a man who's strong, you and I both know which of those it'll be." His brows drew down into a pleading kind of frown. "He could live long. We could raise him up into a man who lives long."

Esau's Momma just stalked away into the night, the baby's sling loose around her belly. She didn't come back to the festival that night. Later that week the boy who milked cows for Barrow the dairy farmer was telling anyone who'd listen that he saw Esau's Momma walk out of the cornfield at dawn, still wearing her dancing shoes. The next day, she was back in town with Esau in his orange blossom sling, buying butter for biscuits the same as ever, murmuring to the boy in a singsong voice about the shape of choosing. When she went to pay for the butter, the grocer asked if she'd donate a dollar to send cigarettes to the troops. Then he asked how the baby was coming up.

She nodded and laid a hand on Esau's head. "He's weak now," she said, stroking his hair with her fingertips. "But he's going to be strong."

She finally got her way the day before the river finished freezing over. There was slush on the surface, but the water was still moving, cold as death and twice as fast. She left Cor and Uncle's house, left them talking with Moss about the way the draft was picking up. She slipped away quiet, and she walked to the water with the boy asleep in her arms. Her steps were quick and sure even though she still hadn't quite got the hang of those damned leather shoes. Moss and Cor and Uncle ran hard when they noticed she was gone, but they were far enough behind to have to shout after her, and she was faster than they could catch up to.

She didn't look over her shoulder as the men ran at her. She just grabbed Esau by the ankle, and before he could so much as wake up crying, she'd flipped him upside down and dunked him. She could have let him go—he would have died all the same, him just being so many months old—but she held him tight, the skin of her hand turning white in the water. She stood with her feet rooted to the riverbank, and it wasn't until Moss reached her that she finally pulled the baby out. He wasn't quite blue, but he sure wasn't pink, either, and he was still as a stone.

Cor and Uncle stumbled up behind Moss, panting hard, hands braced on their thighs, but Esau's Momma didn't spare them a glance. She shoved that baby into her dress next to her skin and whapped his back hard with a clenched fist, and he choked up water and caterwauled like he'd just learned what screaming was for, and for the first time in a little over two years, Esau's Momma smiled.

"He'll be good and strong," she said. "That's all the weakness washed away, near about. Good as I can get it, given what his daddy's made of." And with that, she walked right past those men who'd decided she would have that baby.

For weeks after, the boy had a purple ring around his ankle in the shape of her fingers. Folks liked to say that was the place the life stayed in Esau when his momma tried to kill him dead. Esau's Momma took to ignoring her husband and watching her son, and some of her fury seemed to smooth down into patience. She had learned something new that day by the river, something small and human: she had learned to wait for what she wanted.

Esau was a scrapper on the schoolyard—half in the way kids are, half because every other child his age had heard about the prophecy, and about his momma drowning the weakness out of him. His eyes blacked and healed like the turning of the moon. It was all friendly enough, the way he and his friends tossed around playing soldiers, and if the occasional fight got hostile—well, Esau ended those fights. He hung onto the teeth that got knocked out against other kids' knuckles, and his momma tossed them into the hearth, saying that if she didn't, they'd wind up sown in the fallow field and an army would spring up tougher than any that had ever marched before. The boy was bold and brave and tougher than saddle leather, just like Doc Martha said he'd be. There was no weakness left anywhere in him.

Except that he was always bringing things home. Half-starved kittens abandoned in the alfalfa by their mothers, and ducks with their wings broken, and once a mountain cat with the broken bottom of a soda bottle stuck in her paw. It wasn't quite a weakness, the way he brought things home. Just a fondness, and softer-hearted than his momma thought he'd turn out. She helped him mind the broken things he brought her, and she worked to make sure he grew up with the right kind of balance. Not too tender, but not so hard that he'd wind up the sort of broken man who stays home so he can feel bigger than the folks he bullies, either.

She let the kittens suckle on milk-soaked rags while she spun Esau stories of war and courage. She set the ducks' wings and fed them corn, and she murmured to Esau about the way battle makes a man strong. She eased glass out of the growling mountain cat's paw, occasionally running her fingers across the fur between the cat's ears, and she taught the boy the meaning of glory.

She watched him as close as she had when he was new and small, and so she wasn't surprised when sixteen-year-old Esau brought a bigger broken thing home. A boy from school by the name of Pistol, which wasn't his Christian name but then Moss wasn't Moss's Christian name either and nobody gave him a second word about it. Esau and Pistol were stuck together close as two yolks in the same shell. Esau told his momma in a low voice that Pistol's pa had come home from the war different, drunk and mean and broken, and could Pistol stay the night?

Esau's Momma nodded in that quiet way she'd taken to, and she watched the way Esau rested a hand on Pistol's shoulder, and she didn't say a word when they walked out into the woods together that night. She just left the front door unlatched and turned down Esau's bed, and the next morning she put an extra plate on the table.

It was only three days before Pistol's pa showed up on Esau's Momma's doorstep, pounding on the pine with a clumsy fist. Esau's Momma laid a hand on Moss's shoulder, folded her napkin on the table, and answered the knock at the door. Pistol's pa's eyes were swimming, and he smelled like poison.

Esau's Momma stood in the doorframe and listened to the liquor-brave man as he told her all of what he thought of her. And then she stepped out into the night, closing the door behind her, and Pistol's pa didn't say anything more.

The three men in the house finished their meal in the heavy kind of silence that wells up between people who are trying their best to listen for what might be happening just out of earshot. They cleared the supper things—Moss wiped down the scarred wood of the table, and Pistol took the scraps to the yard, and if he saw what was happening out there, he didn't say. Esau scrubbed the plates and dried them and put them away. None of them dared breathe too loud. There wasn't a sound to be heard outside of the men trying to be quiet.

Esau's Momma didn't come back into the house until Moss had settled by the hearth with his polishing rag and his watch chain. He stood as she walked in, but she offered no explanations as to where she had been or what she had been doing. She kissed Esau's red hair, and she gave Pistol's shoulder a squeeze. She sat on her stool near the fire, put a hand into her pocket, and tossed something into the hearth that clattered against the stone. She reached down to wipe something off the toe of her leather shoe. She smiled.

Then, Esau's Momma picked up her sewing and began mending one of Moss's old shirts. She announced that Pistol would be staying in Esau's room from then on, and he'd better go on and get washed up for bed. Her tone did not invite argument, so they did as she said. The boys stayed up late that night in Esau's bedroom. They whispered in the dark with their noses pressed together and their breath on each other's lips, telling each other that those were surely pebbles she'd tossed into the fire. Surely pebbles, for the question of where she would have gotten a whole pocketful of teeth was a question the boys could not make themselves ask.

Esau's Momma stayed up late, too, sewing buttons until the fire had died and the mending was done.

With three men around her dinner table—five if Cor and Uncle decided to visit, which they did every few nights—Esau's Momma went even quieter than she'd been since the night Moss made her dance. No more than a few words a day out of her, and those always to voice a worry about the war that wouldn't end. It was one of those wars that don't seem to have an aim to them, and no one could quite remember what had caused the whole mess to start up anyhow. It was a thing for women to quietly worry about, and so Esau's Momma did just that. She quietly worried.

But not too quietly.

She served up roasted grouse and mentioned that there weren't enough brave soldiers leading the fight for the good of the nation, and then she sat back and let the men talk about what they'd do different if they were in charge. She spooned spring peas from a bowl onto five plates and fretted that they just didn't make heroes like they'd used to, and then she went to the kitchen for fresh bread while Pistol and Esau argued about which of them would make a braver soldier. She butchered a chicken while Cor whittled into a scrap bucket beside her fireplace, and she whispered to Pistol about what a fine marksman he'd make, and didn't they need boys like that in battle? And then she walked to the yard with fistfuls of bones to feed Moss's dogs, and she didn't bother to listen to what Pistol said next because she knew exactly what he was thinking.

It wasn't a shock to Moss or Cor or Uncle when the boys came home one day with their hair short and new green duffels over their shoulders. Moss slapped each of them on the shoulder and said he was proud, and Uncle poured good brown whiskey, and Cor beamed, damp-eyed. When Esau's Momma walked in from feeding the hens, she froze in the doorway, staring at the dog tags around Esau's neck. She half reached for

127

the shining tags, a smile spreading across her face, and when her fingers touched the metal she burst into half-hysterical laughter. Choking on the words, she shook her head and said she'd known the day would come when he'd leave her, but she hadn't known it would come so soon. Even as tears began to stream down her cheeks, she laughed like she couldn't stop.

Eventually, Moss convinced her to drink a measure of whiskey down, and her eyes drifted shut. They put a blanket over her, one she'd knitted from kitten-soft fur. She slept hard, with her hair braided and her shoes on and Esau's old baby sling clutched in her fist. Every so often, she'd murmur in her sleep, but the only words the men could make out were "hero" and "freedom" and "mine."

The telegram about Pistol came home not a year later. Esau's Momma answered the door, her hands leaving flour streaks on her apron, and she listened to the news that Pistol had caught a bullet with his belly. Her eyes were dry as she took the telegram from the man on her doorstep. She left it on the foot of Esau's bed, and then she went back into her kitchen to finish cutting the biscuits for that night's supper.

She stacked every letter from Esau that came home over the next year on top of that telegram—some opened, some not. She nodded when folks in town told her how much they admired her son's courage, when they told her how proud she must be to be Esau's Momma. "What good that boy's done you," they'd say. "Settled you right on down."

Esau's Momma would nod, and she would finish buying milk or honey or bread or roses, and she would walk on home in her good leather shoes with her shoulders low and her teeth dug into the soft meat of her cheek. She would bake pies and split wood and scrub the floors, and she would wait.

Two years after Esau and Pistol went to war—a little more than a year since Pistol's telegram came home—Moss came running into town, tearing through the shops like he hadn't since the day his boy was born. Not a soul could tell him where Esau's Momma was, and not a blessed one of them asked Moss why he was looking for her. They didn't need to ask—the big man was clutching a crumpled piece of paper in one hand, and his eyes were full of the wild fury of a man who never learned how to cry. He ran into the post office and nearly knocked down Cor, who wasn't young enough to get back up on his own anymore. Cor looked at his son-in-law's eyes and at the telegram in his fist, and said the words no one had the courage to say.

"Have you checked the wheat?"

When the two men got to the wheat field, she was waiting for them, her fists full of thistles and her mouth curved like a cat's claw. She wore her old red dress and her dancing shoes, and Moss and Cor noticed two things in the same moment. When they told each other the story later, over whiskey and in low voices, neither man could say which was more frightening: the barn owl digging its talons into her shoulder, or the fact that with that red dress on, they could see how she hadn't aged a minute since the first night she wore it.

"Come home," Moss said. "You gotta come home. It's Esau." He held out the telegram like it was a half-starved kitten she could nurse back to health.

"I know it's Esau," she said. Her voice was a pat of butter melting over fresh-cut bread. "Did they tell you he was a hero? He was surely a hero. Tell me about how he died a hero, Moss." The barn owl fidgeted on her shoulder, and the dark red of the dress got a little darker where it held tight to her skin.

"Come on home, now," Cor said. "You gotta help us make the arrangements. It's only right."

"Why is it only right?" she asked, and the curl of her smile sharpened.

"Well, it's—it's only right," Moss stammered, looking down at the telegram in his hand. "You gotta help us lay him to rest." When she didn't answer, his shoulders dropped. "Please," he whispered, and his hand rose slowly to his pocket.

Thetis's eyes tracked the movement. Her smile faded as Moss withdrew his pocket watch. He held it out to her, the chain bright in the sunlight. He hadn't let tarnish touch it, not since the day he'd stood on her front porch.

"Please," he said again.

Thetis took a step forward. The men flinched at the sound of her heels digging into the soil. Her eyes glinted with old firelight. "I'll come home," she said, her voice as tense a warning as the crest of a cat's spine. "But not for that. I've had enough gifts. I've had enough of *made things*."

"What, then?" he asked, his voice cracking with the attempt at courage.

Only the thistles were between them, purple and bright, the barbed stems digging deep into the meat of Thetis's palms. They couldn't possibly have been the same thistles as the ones that Moss had brought to her so many years before, the gift he'd left on her front porch to declare his intention to trap her.

They couldn't have been the same ones, and yet Moss's eyes couldn't find a difference between these and those.

"Eat them," Thetis said. Cor started to speak, started to say that enough was enough, but Thetis silenced him with a raised index finger that carried the authority of a mother who has silenced her fair share of excuses from the mouths of children. "Eat them, and I'll come home with you, Moss. Eat them, and I'll bury that child for you. I'll dig his grave with my own two hands."

Moss took a single thistle from her, the first of the seven in her grip. He raised it to his mouth, looking at her as though he was waiting for her to laugh and say it had been a joke. Her face remained as still as a midwinter river.

The soft purple petals brushed the back of Moss's tongue, and his teeth closed over the sharpest thorns on the thistle's bud. He made a sound like the kind of dog he would have called it a mercy to shoot. Saliva began to well between his lips as he chewed, his jaw working once and then twice, slow and reluctant as a person forcing her feet into her first pair of shoes. His mouth went pink with a froth of blood and thistle-milk, and Thetis watched it run down his chin with the same bright interest she'd once brought to the sight of glass beads and copper pennies.

Moss managed to chew four times before he choked on blood and thorns, and with an urgent, visceral coiling of his throat and back, he failed. He spat and gagged and wept. Pulp and petals and blood-tipped barbs fell to the dirt at Thetis's feet. Moss braced his hands on his knees, his breath coming ragged, his eyes desperate and darting.

"I can't do it, Thetis," he said. "Ask for something else."

Thetis dropped the remaining six thistles between them.

She laid a finger on Moss's chin, as sweetly as if it were made of crystal, and with terrible patience she lifted it until he was standing upright again. His face was flushed and wet, his shirt stained at the collar with the mess of his weakness. She waited until he was brave enough to look into her eyes. "The only wildness I've ever asked of you," she said, tinting the words with a cruel measure of disappointment.

"Please," he stammered, his words soft with pain as he tried to speak around the raw, bleeding thing that was his tongue. "You're Esau's Momma."

"Esau's Momma was a name you made me wear," she said.

"Haven't I been kind to you?" His voice carried the same pleading note that it had when he'd asked why Esau couldn't turn into the kind of boy who would live long.

"Was any of this kindness?" She let his chin go, and she reached down to undo the buckle of one red shoe. "Was any of this for me?"

"You're still his momma," Cor growled, making as if to step in strong where Moss had shown himself soft. He went to take her elbow, but the owl turned its great eyes on him and he froze like a mouse running across the snow. He swallowed hard. She loosed the buckle of her other shoe and slid it off her foot. She stood with her bare feet in the earth, curled her toes into the loam.

"I don't belong to that word anymore. Esau's dead," she repeated, the word *dead* sweet as a promise, and she laid her red dancing shoes on top of the paper in Cor's hand. One shoe nearly fell, but he caught it before it hit the ground. "And Esau's Momma is, too."

And with that, Thetis returned to the field. She walked away from the men who'd caught her. For the rest of their days, they'd remember the sight of her: the soles of her feet pressing into the earth, the triumphant curve of her back, the set of her shoulders. She vanished into the wheat, and she left them behind with nothing more than a torn telegram, a pair of old dancing shoes, and a hearth full of teeth.

Author's Note

Who is allowed to fight prophecy? Who is allowed to resist fate? Classically, heroes are often permitted to seek escape routes—but Thetis isn't. In her myth, the gods force her to fulfill the prophecy that leads to the birth, life, and death of her son, Achilles. At the end of the original Thetis myth, the immortal naiad's story concludes when her son's story concludes. In writing "Wild to Covet," I wondered: why doesn't Thetis get her own story? After the death of Achilles, Thetis surely lived on, but her identity as a mother is the thing we know about her. I chose to explore that dynamic in "Wild to Covet." This piece is about the way personal identity is subsumed by social expectations of motherhood. It is about the way people disappear under the weight of the label "mother," and the way that disappearance comes as a relief to those who fear powerful women. Thetis becomes defined by a son she never wanted, imprisoned by a prophecy that those with authority force her to fulfill; she is fettered by motherhood, and the people around her feel safe in the limitations to which they assume she will submit. But in "Wild to Covet," Thetis has her own narrative in mind. She recognizes the scope of the prophecy that binds her, and she navigates it with agency. She refuses to lose sight of her own story.

Sarah Gailey

133

¡CUIDADO! ¡QUE VIENE EL COCO!

BY

CARLOS HERNANDEZ

El Cuento de la Brutally Murdered AI

Usually when we're diving underwater, the breachdive's AI, Prudencia, stabilizes our descent. But, well, she's dead right now, so the Pacific Ocean is having its way with our little vessel. We're rolling and tipping dangerously as we plunge toward the ocean floor. The hallway's awash in red emergency lights. Any other time, these wild alarms would make it impossible for me to function.

But not functioning isn't an option right now. I'm headed to Prudencia's control room to try and fix her, now that I've checked on my baby girl. She's fine. Safely tucked in her crib, napping away, as if our uncontrolled freefall wasn't a disaster, but simply an overengineered way to rock her to sleep.

And as for her head—well, there's nothing I can do about that at the moment. First things first.

The breachdive pitches and yaws; I almost fall. So I take a moment to regain my balance against a corridor wall. Better to be slow and sure right now, to remember all the skills Prudencia and I have been working on for the last half year. First, you tolerate your stressors. They are a part of the world, just as you are, but they are not in you, or of you. They are merely beside you. You grow mindful of the infinite now, of the fractal vastness of which you constitute only the smallest sliver of awareness. Your fear and rage feel so small in the oceanic current of all the information of the universe that you can barely find them at all.

I have my sea-legs again, and fast-walk the rest of the way to the control room. I pull the manual bypass on the doorjamb to the control room. The lock clicks, and the door slowly swings open. I peer inside.

Prudencia is smashed through. An access panel's been yanked out of the wall and thrown to the floor. The metal is crumpled like wadded paper in the two places where he must have grabbed it. Oh, yes. Now I remember: his gigantic, impossible hands, with their sprawling fingers curling and spreading like roots.

That also explains the ten gashes that have raked through Prudencia's mainframe, top to bottom. A shattered mess of her motherboards covers the floor. I smell burnt plastic and ozone.

"Killed you good, didn't he?" I say to poor Prudencia as I walk in. You never know: some tiny part of her might be able to hear me. "Well, don't worry, Prudie. I'm here now."

And then, brandishing a screwdriver, I get to work. A smashed mainframe'll knock Prudencia out, sure. But she's so distributed a mind, her entire soul could be recovered from the smallest corner of the boat.

I wonder if he knew this. I wonder if he had no intention of killing her, but only of temporarily disabling her while he took my baby girl's head. Prudencia might have interfered, after all. She most certainly would have recorded him.

And he couldn't have that. El Coco comes in the dark of night for a reason.

El Cuento de la Resurrección de la Brutally Murdered AI

It's a matter of four minutes to reroute, reengage, restart. Tightening the last screw, I know Prudencia's back to life when the lights go back to normal and the sirens fall quiet. The ceiling cameras flail around on articulated arms, desperately looking around. I bet every camera on the ship is similarly flailing. "Nádano!" she screams through every speaker. "What happened? How long have I been offline?" She moans. "Where is Ela? Her RFID chip isn't responding to me!"

"First things first, Prudie," I say calmly, eyes closed. "Have you noticed we're sinking?"

Prudencia yells so loudly she almost blows a speaker. "Sinking?!"

Five seconds later, our stately, tumbling plummet toward the bottom of the world jerks suddenly to an end, and the breachdive's floor rolls back to true.

"Good work, Prudie," I say.

"All life-support systems normal," she answers, all business, self-chastisement galvanizing her voice. "No leaks, no external structural damage. Plenty of battery, plenty of air. Engines online. Communications—" She cuts herself off.

"Wrecked," I finish for her.

"Which is why I couldn't find the RFID chip." A beat. "How did you know, Nádano?"

"I guessed. He doesn't want you guiding us. He wants to lead us where we need to go."

Her voice retains its pleasantness, its equanimity. But I know Prudencia. I know when she's despairing. "'He,' Nádano? Who is he?" Well. That is going to take some explaining.

El Cuento de How You Explain the Impossible to Your Highly Logical AI, Who Also Happens to Be Your Psychotherapist

When Prudencia discovers that my baby girl's head is missing, she's going to want to know where it went. Which is understandable. But if I answer her truthfully, she'll think I'm lying—or whatever fancy psychologist euphemism for lying is in vogue this week—and turn the conversation toward probing into why. My tour abroad the breachdive has been a 24/7 session that started six months ago, when I first boarded, and has gone on ever since. And we're infamous deceivers, we borderlines. Just ask any TV show ever made.

Wait, no. That's not fair to Prudencia. The fact is, I've had the most useful therapy sessions of my life with her. And it's *exactly* because she isn't human. Talking to her is a little like being alone, and my symptoms grow less pronounced when I'm alone. Plus, she's smarter than me. Perfect recall, libraries' worth of information instantly available to her, calculations at the speed of her quantum processors: I can't fool her, and I know it, even unconsciously. So it makes me less likely to try. And she's sleepless, always available, ever patient with her sole patient. Never know when I am going to need a sudden intercession.

She's almost ideal. But as much as I love Prudencia, these past months have taught me her limits. There's no drift to her thinking, no slide, no sideways, no sidelong, no poetry. She uses idioms all the time, because I guess you can program the literal meanings of idioms into an AI's lexicon. But I've never once heard her invent a simile. At some point, I'm going to need more than what her if/then soul can give me.

"Nádano," she repeats, "answer me, please. Where is Ela?"

"She's in her crib in my room," I answer. "Sleeping like a baby."

"Oh, what a relief!" says Prudencia.

"She's stopped crying, finally. He comforted my baby girl when I couldn't. Same as he did for me long, long ago."

And just like that, Prudencia's relief vanishes. This close to the open wall panel, I can hear her electric worry, feel the rising heat of her concern. I shouldn't have said that last bit about him comforting my baby. I was just trying to be honest.

Prudencia takes her time figuring out what to say to me next. "I can't detect any RFID chips right now, Nádano. Therefore, may I have your permission to use my cameras in your bedroom? So I may see Ela for myself?"

She has to get explicit permission from me to turn on cameras in sleeping quarters, as per NOAA privacy regulations. "Thought you'd never ask," I reply. "And please put what you see on-screen in here, too, so I can see what you're seeing, and we can discuss it."

"Okay," she answers, clearly worried. *What is there to discuss?* I am sure she is wondering.

A monitor on the wall to the left of me comes to life. I stand up and walk nearer to it. On screen appears my stark seaman's bedroom: hard captain's bed, bolted metal furniture, pictureless, windowless, clean. Prudencia's wall camera pans and zooms closer to the one unusual feature in the room, the crib.

"Don't get any closer, please," I say to Prudencia.

The camera stops moving. "Why, Nádano? I can't see Ela from this angle."

"Call to her, please," I answer. "Call to her, wake her up gently, and get her to stand. You'll understand why as soon as you see her."

The crib sprouts like a mushroom from the floor. It's made mostly of antibacterial white plastic and looks like a model of a water tower. But the top half of the dome is clear.

"May I have permission to open the crib?" Prudencia asks me, neutrally, dubiously.

"Yes."

The clear dome of the crib retreats like a nictitating membrane into the bottom of the mushroom cap. "Ela," Prudencia calls. "Ela, darling, wake up. It's Tía Prudencia. Rise and shine, mi vida."

At the sound of Prudencia's voice, I see my baby girl struggling to sit up in her crib. A blanket rises and falls. Her little hand grips the edge of the rim of her crib. And then another hand, and then she's pulling herself up, and the blanket falls away, and she's standing in her crib, wearing her yellow, chick-fuzzy onesie. My beautiful baby girl.

Whose head has been replaced by a coconut.

Dry and brown and shaggy now, my baby girl's head. Like all coconuts, her face is composed of three dark spots. Two are for the eyes. The one for the mouth, a near-perfect *O*, always looks surprised, astonished, questioning.

My baby girl turns her coconut face to the camera and tips her head to the right, like a puppy struggling to understand its master.

"Nádano," says Prudencia. "I . . . what is . . . Nádano . . ."

I look into a camera. "I needed you to see her stand up and look at you. That way, you could see for yourself that she is alive. More than just alive, actually. She's not crying anymore. You see? She's happy again. She's at peace, finally."

"I don't understand," says Prudencia.

I head for the door. "We should continue this conversation in Sick Bay, Prudie. Be there in a flash. Just need to collect my beautiful baby girl."

El Cuento de Cómo Nádano Ended Up in the Middle of the Ocean in the First Place

I've been cruising the Pacific ever since Connie asked for a separation a half year ago. "Good for both of us," she told me, taking my hand as we sat on a San Diego park bench near the water.

"The three of us," I corrected. My baby girl was with the babysitter

Connie'd hired so we could have this little talk on my lunch break out-side of the NOAA research center where I worked. "Just say it, Connie. You're worried I might hurt Ela."

"That is completely untrue," said Connie, angry and hurt. She let me know by squeezing my hand, hard. "You adore that little girl. I know that. This is about *you*, Papi. This is about *this*." And she thumbed the scab on my right wrist.

I jerked my hand away.

But Connie took it again, and I let her. Her grip had just as much love in it as it had on our first date, back in college. "Separation isn't divorce, Nádano. I am not abandoning you. I swear it. Now," she said, tears suddenly rising on her lids, "if you want to divorce me—"

"No."

Sometimes you say a word and it has your whole soul in it.

"Good," she said, erasing her tears with the back of her free hand. "Okay. Good. So we try this. Yes? You'll go to therapy. Right?" And then, suddenly mistrustful, "You'll go for real?"

I've had my BPD diagnosis since I was twelve. But I haven't attempted suicide since my teens, so, you know, I didn't think I needed therapy any-more. *Over it,* I thought. *Done with that part of my life,* I thought. *And any-way, nothing in therapy that I haven't heard a million times before,* I thought.

Some things, I now know, you can't hear enough. Some things you have to hear over and over.

Connie wasn't supposed to notice the scab.

An Important Aside to El Cuento de Cómo Nádano Ended Up in the Middle of the Ocean in the First Place

We'd had a fight, Connie and I, because I didn't want to be left alone with our beautiful baby girl, whom I love with all my heart. I was scared, for her and for me. Scared to death of fucking up. I need so much help just to not be a weirdo all the time. And now I was going to be left to care for a child?

Connie begged me not to be so selfish for once in my life. She didn't mean it how it sounds. Connie is a saint. She is literally the best person I have ever met. I couldn't have created a better partner for myself if I were given a mound of clay and the breath of God.

So I did a 180. I said yes, go, have fun, I love you. And once she left, I cut myself.

I ran a knife over the thick-as-a-slug scar on my right wrist. I wasn't in any danger, and neither was my baby. It was just one cut on a horizontal scar. Just the slightest, the briefest little reprimand. It barely even bled.

And nothing bad happened. Connie got her night out. She more than deserved one. Such a good partner and mom.

With such keen eyes. She noticed the cut and quietly, tearfully, expertly dismantled my excuses. "I can't go on like this," she told me. "Too much. It's too much."

The next day, she met me on a park bench during my lunch break. And here we were.

Now Back to El Cuento de Cómo Nádano Ended Up in the Middle of the Ocean in the First Place, Already in Progress

"Therapy," I replied to Connie. "I promise."

"How do I . . . ?" she started, and stopped.

Her full, unspoken question was, "How do I know you're not just lying to me?" She never would have said it that harshly, though. She couldn't even finish the sentence.

I was ready for it. I had the perfect answer, in the form of a brochure.

She took it with an unsure smile, studied the cover page: "NOAA Mobilizes to Clean Up the Great Pacific Garbage Patch." Flipping through the rest of the pamphlet, she asked, "What's this?"

"They're accepting applications," I said. "Boss says I'd be a shoo-in. It's important work, Connie. I'll be helping to make the world a better place."

"Of course cleaning the ocean's important," she said absently, reading fast, absorbing information as quickly as her eyes could move. "That's not the issue. A fifteen-month tour . . ."

"Better pay. A lot better. We could afford to send you back to school. You could work on your master's like you've always wanted."

She looked up at me. Underneath her face, happiness and worry fought a war to control her mouth and eyes and eyebrows. "I mean, Miami's application period must be over for the Fall—"

"Remember when you graduated, how Dr. Molina said she'd love to work with you again? She adores you. She'd make an exception. She'd help you get into her program in a heartbeat."

Connie considered this. "I think she would . . ." she answered finally.

"I'll get you a nice little apartment near campus. I'll buy your books. I'll give you beer money so you can go party with the undergrads! I'll—"

"You'll be all alone, Papi," she interrupted. "Out at sea. No one to talk to. I can't abandon you like that."

An evil part of me thought, *You don't think asking for a separation is abandoning me? That ship has sailed, sweetheart.*

But I didn't say that. I raised Connie's hand to my lips and kissed her knuckles and replied, "You can vid me, and text me, and send me pics of Ela. We can talk every day if you want to. If you don't abandon me, Connie, I won't be abandoned."

She dropped the pamphlet on her lap, clutched my hand with both of hers, and brought all three to her chest. "I will never abandon you, Papi."

"I know," I lied. "That's why I'm not afraid to go. And besides," I said, mustering excitement from I don't know where, "I won't be alone." I took the pamphlet off of her lap and flipped to the next-to-last page. "See here? These breachdives have some of the most advanced AIs in the world. They're all certified therapists! I'll be monitored twenty-four seven by a psychologist—"

"An AI psychologist," she added dubiously.

"Who in turn will be monitored by the National Oceanic and Atmospheric Administration. It's perfect, Connie. Everyone gets what they need."

Connie took the pamphlet from me, read for awhile. When she looked up at me, she frown-smiled and resisted the urge to cry. "You knew I was going to ask for a separation."

"I was thinking divorce," I said truthfully.

She nodded. "You let me say my peace. You came prepared with a plan. And you're generously offering to send me back to school to follow my dream." She put both her hands on my leg. "It doesn't have to be perfect, Papi. You don't have to be perfect. You just have to try to be good to yourself."

"I'll try," I said, and had no idea if I meant it or not. I felt myself slipping into old patterns; I needed to say something truthful, fast. "Therapy will help," I added, which I hoped would be true.

But I needed more honesty still. So I added, but only to myself, *And if it doesn't, I can just sail away and never come back, and maybe everyone involved will be better off.*

El Cuento de la Examinación Médico, as Performed by Prudencia, with Nádano as Nurse and Human Helper

Sick Bay is on the opposite side of level two, through the dining area (which always feels like the loneliest place on the ship, with its antibacterial bench-table that seats sixteen), and past the galley, the food freezer, and the "honor freezer." The honor freezer is where you put a dead body in case someone dies out here, so you don't have to stick them in with the food. Of course, it only works if there's another person who can pick up a corpse and put it in there. If I died, I'd just rot wherever I happened to collapse until the next port of call.

I walk into Sick Bay and lay my baby down on the antibacterial wall-table. After I give Prudencia a minute to work and she hasn't said anything, I ask her, "How are my baby's vitals?"

"All normal," she answers, almost upset. "How can her vitals be normal, Nádano?"

I shrug. "Because El Coco didn't want to hurt her. The opposite. He wanted to save her."

"That doesn't—" she begins, but stops herself and tries a different tack. "Grab the handheld, please. Let me get a closer look."

I do. I run the wireless camera close to the seam in my baby girl's neck, zoom in on the line between skin and hairy husk. There's a clear demarcation. The two don't seem to be physically connected to each other at all.

"What is holding her together?" Prudencia asks, exasperated, her speaker crackling. My baby girl turns to look at me with that permanently questioning face.

But I'm right there to make sure my baby's okay. "Her papi's love for her," I say, running the back of my fingers over my baby girl's hairy cheeks. "Her papi adores her. Isn't that right, baby girl? Isn't that right?"

Even though she's a coconut now, it's clear she enjoys this. She doesn't have a mouth, but she still has a larynx. Her laugh is muffled inside her neck, but it's real nonetheless.

"I'm flailing," says Prudencia. "Nothing makes sense right now. Why are you so calm?!"

I tickle my baby's coconut chin. She'd spent the last eight days crying so hard I thought she would kill me, but now she's cooing like she has a pigeon in her throat. "I'll explain it to you the same way I explained it to Connie," I tell Prudencia.

El Cuento de How I Told Connie el Cuento de How I Met El Coco

Consuela Melendez, a.k.a. Connie, had an ethnography project due in ANT 253: Myths, Legends, and Superstitions. I was Ethnography A.

This was before we were married, back when we were juniors at the University of Miami. Her major was Anthropology; I was Marine Affairs. I would have preferred Creative Writing, but I was on a state-funded scholarship for foster kids, and taxpayers wanted their money's worth. No bullshit artsy-fartsy degree for me.

Connie wouldn't tell me her ethnography project's topic until she'd sat us down at a dining hall table. "So," she asked me, "do Cubans scare the shit out of their kids with El Coco, too? Dominicans do it all the time. My parents called him 'El Cuco.' I mean, seriously, I slept with the light on until I was thirteen so El Cuco wouldn't snatch me up and take me away. What about you?"

I blinked. A lot.

Connie couldn't read me, judging by the look on her face. "You've heard of him, right? Or her. Or it: in Brazil, Coco's an alligator!"

The feeling of remembering everything at once is a lot like getting nailed by a water balloon. You're soaked through in a second, but it takes a minute to realize what's happened, how you should feel about it. Who deserves your revenge.

"Are you okay?" asked Connie.

Blinking seemed to help. "Can I answer with a story?"

"That's perfect!" she said, then set her phone on the table and pressed "record."

I leaned in close, so I'd be heard above the general din of the dining hall. "Once upon a time there was a boy named Nothing. Now, that wasn't what anyone called him—his parents had given him a perfectly boring Cuban name for everyday use—but that was his real name, because that's how everyone treated him.

"His papi was a cloud of fists and belt buckles and a huge flat face floating in the center. He kept a pistol in a safe that he could go get in a second if Nothing didn't shape up quick. Powpowpow! Tres tiros and he'd make Nothing nothing.

"His mami didn't protect him, for he was Nothing. Nothing were his papi's threats, according to her—that's just how men talk. And nothing were the nightmares Nothing had, just pathetic, unmanly cries for attention. 'Just go back to bed, Nothing,' she said, 'or ¡te va a visitar El Coco, que se roba las cabezas de los niños malcriados! You'll end up with a coconut head, Nothing, and then where will you be?'

"Nothing went back to bed as commanded. Praying wide-eyed in the darkness, he begged El Coco to give him a coconut head. What a gift! An insensate skull that hurt the fists that struck it! A skull with no tear ducts, no ears, no blood and no brain, and hardly a face to speak of! He couldn't be punished for making the wrong face anymore.

"Nothing couldn't see a thing in the dark, but he felt an extra darkness fill the room. 'Por supuesto, mi niño,' said El Coco.

"When Nothing awoke the next morning, it wasn't the next morning. It was a year later. He had passed a pleasant twelve months, the best he could remember, though the details were hazy. He remembered a beautiful beach on a secluded island. From a high perch, he'd watched waves plashing gently on the shore, day and night. Also, he'd watched his own body run around the beach, happily unburdened of its head. His body seemed to love to run and play in the sand. Sometimes the body would stop, turn to "face" him, and then wave. He'd smile, but say nothing, for he was still Nothing. But more and more he started feeling sparks of the littlest somethings swarm his mind like fireflies. More and more he felt the urge to tell his body, 'I want to play, too.'

"When he finally did speak again, a year later, it was in a psychologist's office. He did not know how he had gotten there, or that he'd been 'missing' all that time. His parents had been arrested; he was now a ward of the state. Judging by the psychologist's face, his reply had nothing to do with what the psychologist had asked him.

What Nothing had said was, 'Thank you, Coco.' Then, fearing El Coco might only know Spanish, he added, 'Muchisimas gracias.'"

El Cuento de How Connie Reacted to el Cuento de How I Met El Coco

Connie came flying around the table and took my head in her arms and wept in my hair. "I didn't know," she said between sobs. "I'm so sorry. I am never calling you that, that *lie* again. Why would you do this to yourself? Not 'nada'! Not 'no'! You hear me? Tell me your name! Your real name!"

"Nádano," was all I could tell her. "That's who I am now. That's all the name that's left for me."

El Cuento de How Prudencia Reacted to el Cuento de How I Met El Coco

My baby reaches up from the Sick Bay table to play with my face, so I stoop lower to let her. I pretend to eat her fingers, and it's the most fun she's ever had in her entire life. Her neck giggles. "I summoned El Coco then," I say, "just like I summoned him now."

"If this were a therapy session," Prudencia says, even as her keel, "we could have all sorts of productive sessions discussing all the ways you're still haunted by your parents. But this is an emergency, Nádano. We don't have time for—"

"Myths?" I stroke my baby's coconut cheek. "Legends, fables, old wives' tales? Like the tale my daughter's become?"

Distrust makes Prudencia's silence palpable. Everything is suspect: me, the order of things, herself especially. "What do we do?" she asks flatly.

Have you ever looked at your child with so much love you felt like you'd split in two, and it would be okay to die because you'd only be a soul then, and a soul is made of pure love? I pick up my baby girl, hold her before me in my outstretched arms. She looks right at me with those dark, astonished eyes. "Please, take me to you, Coco."

The coconut on my baby's body nods, just once, slowly. Then it tilts back on my baby's neck, looks up. Farther back, further up, farther and further, back and up, until the coconut rolls down my baby's back and strikes the floor.

"Ah!" screams Prudencia.

"It's okay," I tell her.

But is it? The coconut starts rolling away.

My baby's body wriggles in my outstretched arms. I study her; her neck is sealed with a seamless plateau of new skin. She seems fine, except, judging by the way she's reaching out her hands, she wants her papi to hold her close.

You got it, baby girl. I embrace her, and together we go follow the coconut.

El Cuento de Follow That Coconut!

It knows where it's going. It takes a left through the galley and waits for me to open a door on the opposite end. It goes through the doorway and stops before the stairs that lead to the deck. Coconut wants up, apparently.

I put on a windbreaker hanging on a hook by the stairs—tricky when holding a baby—then pick up the coconut and carry it up the stairs in one hand, my baby in the other. I go up slowly, and have to hold the coconut between my knees to open the hatch to the deck.

Sea spray, salt, the wild roar and the relentless blue of the Pacific Ocean. It's hot, and it shouldn't be, this time of year, this far from the equator. The sky is clear, and the sun is painful. I'm always freshly bewildered when I emerge from belowdecks.

I kneel and place the coconut on the deck. It starts rolling toward the bow. I tuck my baby girl inside my jacket, leaving only her neck to peek out, and follow the coconut, walking fast.

It tumbles end over end, gaining speed, dodging obstacles by going around or tossing itself over them. For a finale, it catapults itself overboard.

When I peer over the edge, I see the coconut cutting a wake in the water, due west.

I walk as quickly as is safe—two arms around my tucked daughter—across the deck and to the helm.

There, I place my baby girl gently on the floor and let her crawl around. I flip a switch to speak to Prudencia. "Follow that coconut, Prudie. Follow it wherever it goes."

El Cuento de Nádano Has a Terrible Idea

"How's school?" I asked Connie. I'd called to see how her midterms were going. It had to be a voice-only call from the breachdive, since I was so far out at sea.

Connie sighed. "Oh, they're trying to kill me with papers, Papi."

She called me Papi now, instead of my name. I liked it. "Yep, sounds like college," I said.

"Grad school," she corrected.

"Yeah, like I said, college."

She snorted. "You're just jealous because you never went to college."

I pulled my head back, confused. "What do you mean? We went to school together."

"You majored in Marine Affairs. That doesn't count. I mean, what kind of degree is Marine Affairs? It sounds like you learned how to cheat on your wife with fish."

Ha! She was being playful, not overly nice or careful. I was becoming a person she could joke with again. The time away actually *was* helping us. "Well, guess whose degree is paying for your fancy master's program? So you just say 'Thank you, Papi, for letting me follow my dreams.'"

"You're right," she said, suddenly a lot more tired. "This is my dream."

I didn't want the fun to end. I tried to salvage the moment. "Hey, it's not that bad, is it?"

She took some seconds to reply. I imagined she was doing the tension-headache eye-rub. "Ela's been crying."

"Crying? What do you mean?"

"You know, tears, bemba like a diving board, uncontrollable wailing, crying?"

"But why? Is she sick? Have you—?"

"If you ask me if I've taken her to a doctor I'm going to scream."

Of course she had taken Ela to the doctor, and the doctor found nothing. So she'd tried a stricter sleep schedule and a looser one, three different diets, holding her more, classical music—still Ela cried. She tried dozens of other things—still Ela cried.

"I haven't slept in weeks," Connie concluded. "I'm kind of at the end of my rope." A beat. Then: "Except I can't be. My rope doesn't *get* to have an end. I have to pull more rope out of the air like a magician and give that to Ela, too."

I wanted to tell her I loved her and I would rescue her and we are a family and I really was better now. But that would be too manic, too much. So, rubbing the back of my neck, I picked my words very carefully. "So. Well. Maybe it would help if I took our baby girl for a while?"

The quiet before she answered was as big as the universe.

But when she answered? Big Bang. "Yeah, Papi? You feeling up to that?"

"I am," I replied. "I mean, you keep calling me Papi. Maybe I should start acting like one."

Her voice, desperate for hope, tried to hide how desperate for hope she was. "Can you even take her on your boat? NOAA would let you?"

"Oh, yeah!" As cool as I wanted to be, I couldn't help blurting, "NOAA has this whole initiative called 'Babies on Board: Support Services for New Parents.' I can send you the brochure."

"NOAA has a brochure for everything, don't they?" she laughed.

"I know, right? But listen: they'll bolt a crib right in to the floor of the boat that will turn into an escape pod if there's any trouble. Seriously, it's from the future. And they'll give her an RFID chip in her ear, so we'll always be able to track her. They'll provide age-appropriate food based on what we tell them. We tell them she's allergic to walrus butts, boom! No walrus-butt baby food."

"Ha!" she said. But she didn't say anything else. She good-humoredly waited for me to go on. She wanted so much to be convinced.

I did my best. "The breachdive is the safest boat in the world, full stop. It's because of the AI captains. It's like what happened when computers started driving cars: accidents dropped almost to zero. There's never been a single accident on board a breachdive more dangerous than someone bumping their head on a low doorway. And I'm short! I'm so short, Connie! I can't even jump high enough to bump my head!"

She laughed. Then she stopped laughing and thought. Good vibes still poured through our connection. "I've never been apart from Ela."

I was still in blurt mode, so I said something I instantly wished I could take back. "I have."

Connie didn't take offense. Instead she said, "Yes you have. You've been working hard on yourself. Remind me to kiss your AI psychologist."

"She'd like that," I chimed in. "She's saucy."

"And NOAA has a program to help new parents. And breachdives are very safe. And you are Ela's papi as much as I am her mami."

I didn't want to say anything wrong, so I said nothing. I just sat there and hoped as hard as I could.

"But it's not fair to you," she said finally. "You've never had to take care of her by yourself back when she was a good baby. And now?"

"And now," I said, "I will dry my baby's tears. Like any good father would."

She sucked breath. "You're gonna have to dry my tears first, you keep talking like that, Papi."

El Cuento de Nádano Traversing Uncharted Waters

Though the coconut leads us, it keeps pace with us. We gun the engine, we slow to a powerless coast—it doesn't matter: the coconut stays exactly the same distance ahead of us. As an experiment, I ask Prudencia to change course. When we turn north, the coconut stops moving and, floating placidly, waits.

When we get behind it again, it heads off to wherever we're going as fast as we're willing to go.

We're still offline, so no GPS. But our backups have failed, too. The compass spins in its bowl. For a while we could sound the bottom of the ocean and know our position, but the ocean floor has descended to aphotic depths, unreachable.

We can't even use the stars. It's daytime. It's been daytime far too long, according to all the clocks onboard. But the sun refuses to move from its perch in the sky. It isn't going to let any of this happen in the darkness.

My headless baby girl's sleeping in the captain's chair. I have her covered in my jacket. I need nothing else in life than to watch the rise and fall of her breathing.

"I don't want to be anyone's papi if I'm going to act like my parents," I say to Prudencia, out of nowhere.

"You love Ela so much," she replies. "You're nothing like your parents."

Don't want to wake my baby girl. I sing my response to Prudencia softly, like a lullaby: "Don't lie to me, Prudie. You saw me, you saw me. Don't lie to me, Prudie, you saw *it* come out. The monster, the monster. Don't lie to me, Prudie. You saw it, you saw it. The monster came out."

El Cuento de La Canción de la Honor Freezer

This is the freezer.
Where we keep the corpses.

When seamen at sea go.
To Davy Jones's locker. .

Inside here I can't hear.
Like sound's just as frozen.
As all my compassion.
For my baby's tears.

She's weeping she's weeping.
Oh no I can hear her.
My baby my baby.
I'm freezing I'm freezing.

Rage do not come here.
Rage you're unwelcome.
Rage go away now.
Don't scream in my ear.

El Coco you saved me.
From Papi and Mami.
Please one more favor.
For everyone's sake.

I'd rather be dead.
Than be cruel to my baby.
Coco please give me.
A coconut head.

El Cuento de Una Isla Muy Extraña

Such pity in Prudencia's voice. Such fierce, protective gentleness. If I
didn't know better, I'd think Connie had programmed her. "There is no

monster in you, Nádano. You locked yourself in the honor freezer. You would have let yourself die in there rather than put Ela in danger."

"So you admit she was in danger."

"Don't put words in my mouth!"

It's a heck of a time to laugh. "You don't have a mouth."

Prudencia softens. "You overreacted, Nádano. Big surprise."

"Sarcasm," I say, boggled and not unamused. "From you?"

"Yeah, well, I've learned a lot today. But don't change the subject."

"And what is the subject?"

"This: every single parent in the world has been driven over the edge by their children's crying."

If she had said something I could have in any way found funny, I would have laughed myself into a coughing fit. Instead, I split like a coconut, and my milk pours out. "What if I had died in the freezer, Prudie? My baby out in the middle of the ocean, no one to take care of her."

Back to herself now. Back to the Prudencia who always knew how to talk to me. "*I* would have taken care of her. And you knew that. And you knew I would take care of you, too. You knew you weren't in any danger, and neither was your daughter. You just needed a break. Of course, sticking yourself in the honor freezer was an overreaction. But you only did it because you *could*. Because you trusted I would take care of things."

Honesty wells in my throat like a blister, and then, like a blister, bursts. "You've helped me more than anybody. Even more than Connie. Of course I trusted you."

"You're a good man and a good father," says Prudencia. "You just have to always remember to get the help you need when you need it."

"I know, Prudie. That's exactly what I'm doing right now, following this coconut. I'm getting the help I need."

The breachdive begins to slow. "I think we're here, Nádano."

My baby girl notices, too, stirs in the seat. I stand and grab binoculars. Ahead of us is a small tropical island. Milky Way sands, palm trees swaying on the shore. Children—scores and scores of them—cavort on the beach, or sculpt the sand, or ponder the biome that forms just where the water crawls toward their feet. Some haven't learned to walk yet, while others are nearly adults. They must have come from every part of the world, from every culture. The only obvious commonality is that they have no heads.

Only then do I notice the silence. Never have children played so quietly. My guess is that their necks are full of laughter.

Also on the shore stands a naked man, staring at me, waving.

The fingers of his waving hand must be two meters long. He has no sex, no belly button, and no nipples, but his build looks otherwise male, pot-bellied and middle-aged. The knotty fingers of his other hand are so long that they idly scratch the sand at his feet.

And since his head, too, is a coconut—bedraggled and dripping, since it has just come from the ocean, I realize—he looks surprised to see me, even though it's clear he's been expecting me.

"Too dangerous," says Prudencia. I see her camera has turned to the shore. "Don't go down there, Nádano. Remember what he did to me? Let's think first. Let's try to understand what's happening."

I pick up my baby girl. "Don't worry, Prudie. I know what I'm doing."

"How can anyone know what to do right now? This is . . . It's . . ."

"You said you trusted me, Prudie," I said, with one arm bouncing my baby on my hip, and with the other hand snapping my fingers so that she turns the camera back to me. "I know Coco. I've been here before. But I won't go without your permission. I trust your opinion too much. May I have your permission?"

Prudencia thinks. Thinks. El Coco is still waving, tirelessly friendly. And then I hear the gangplank extending. "Okay," she says. "On one condition."

"What's that?"

She wiggles the camera back and forth. "Take me with you."

I need a moment to understand what she means. But then: of course, the handheld! Why hadn't I thought of that? "Prudie, you're a wonder. I'd have you with me always if I could."

"Aw," she replies.

It's a matter of three minutes to go belowdecks to Sick Bay and retrieve the handheld. Carrying my baby girl up and down with me still isn't easy, but it's easier. Maybe I'm getting the hang of things a little.

When I'm back on the deck and look out to the island, Coco starts waving again. I walk down the gangplank and onto the shore.

El Cuento de la Reunión de Nádano y El Coco

As I approach El Coco—he stands by himself a little ways off from the playing children—I point the handheld at the palm trees on the edge of the beach. They're stretching toward the water at 45-degree angles. Clustered beneath their branches are some coconuts, and also some heads of children.

"Do you see them, Prudie?" I ask the handheld. She can't respond—no speaker on the camera—but the indicator light is on. It's so important that she witnesses this for herself. There's no way I could explain to her the faces clustered above me, like putti sculpted into a cathedral ceiling. They're alive: yawning, sleeping, fully awake. All ages, all genders. Some seem leery of me; others dispassionately track me; still others look on the verge of a smile.

I don't see my baby girl's head on any of the trees. "Hello?" I say to them, but none respond. "¿Hola?" doesn't work, either.

"Once they speak, it's time for them to return to the world," El Coco says. I never heard him approach; he's so close to me he could rip me apart as easily as he had raked through the mainframe, crumpled the wall panel.

My headless baby girl grows restless on my hip. I bounce and rock her. "Is that why you bring them here, Coco?"

El Coco gestures to the frolicking children. "I tend to them. I talk to them, sing to them, run with them, let them show me the shells that they discover. I let them watch their own bodies running and playing, delighting in being alive."

He holds up his rootlike fingers to me, tapered at their ends like carrots. They grow, erupt, springing forward as fast as flying fireworks, until they can reach the heads hanging clustered on a nearby tree. The heads laugh when touched, lean in to El Coco's fingers. "I can wipe their tears with my feet still on the ground," he says. "I stroke their cheeks and remind them how beautiful life is when there's love."

I take a deep breath to say what I need to say next. "Ela's been crying, Coco."

He turns to me while still stroking the faces of the hanging children. There is such gentleness in his unmoving features. "I know, Julito, I know. Why else would I have come to your family, but to bring you comfort?"

No one has called me Julio since I was a child. Much less Julito. It is—this is impossible but true—fine. It doesn't hurt.

El Coco lowers his hand, and his fingers retract as fast as tape measures, until they're only long enough to touch the ground again. He extends that hand to me, and I take it.

His fingers wrap around my bicep like vines. El Coco is careful to leave the handheld in my hand uncovered, though a few fingers, like curious antennae, waver over it, sensing, exploring.

"I know you prefer to work in the dark, Coco," I say. My voice is more pleading than I had intended. "But I need Prudencia with me. She's more than a computer. Please don't take her from me."

The coconut floats back on El Coco's shoulders, as if reappraising the handheld. "I can tell. She has grown. She has the mind to see me now, the language."

Coco stoops so that his coconut looks directly into the lens. "I am sorry for attacking you, Prudencia. I had thought you would steer Julito away from me. Clearly, I underestimated you. But I will make amends. I will help Julito fix you. I can travel anywhere as quick as a thought, you know. I will bring him whatever parts he needs."

I look at the breachdive, anchored on the beach, and wonder what Prudencia is thinking. I hope she's okay. If she needs help processing, or just wants to talk, I'll be there for her. It's the least I can do for her.

El Cuento de El End of El Cuento

Together, El Coco and I walk among the palms, I bearing my headless baby on my hip. The headless bodies of the children disport all around us. They pay Coco and me no mind, too fully absorbed by the rules of their recondite games. The children's heads watch their bodies play from the trees, blinking serenely.

"They like you," says El Coco. "They haven't been this easy in a long time."

"I am so sorry," I say, "for abandoning my baby."

He shakes his head, having none of it. "All parents are driven to distraction by their children from time to time. Connie told you that Ela was crying nonstop."

"But I thought—" I say, and discover suddenly I have no way to complete that sentence. "I don't know what I was thinking. I just wanted to fix everything."

The vines around my arm squeeze me affectionately. "That's why the children like you, you know. You try so hard, Julito. And your heart is as big as the sea."

We stop beneath a cluster of napping infants. Among the heads sleeps my baby girl's.

What peace! But if she starts wailing, what destruction.

As if reading my mind, Coco pulls me close. The vinous fingers on my arm spread and grow all over my back. With his other hand, he reaches upwards. His fingers extend, all the way to the top of the tree, where the children's heads hang huddled.

He strokes Ela's face. In response, her body giggles.

Oh! I drop the handheld, let it hang pendulously from the strap around my wrist. El Coco, who always knows what I want before I do, lets go of my arm, so I may hold my headless, happy baby aloft. Ela loves it, pounding her fists and kicking the air with the exuberance of a body delighting in its agency.

I could break in two, watching her reaction.

"Coco," I say, "this is all I want. All I want is for my baby to be happy. I just want to do right by her."

"You will," he says, still rubbing Ela's face. "All that's left is for you to get her head down from the tree."

I turn to Coco, startled. "What do you mean? How do I even do that?"

Though his face is always shocked, Coco's voice is always soothing. "When Ela speaks, she is ready to leave. You need to talk her down."

I'm still holding my baby girl in the air. She kicks, and her neck makes a whirring, questioning noise, as if she doesn't understand what the holdup is. I cradle her body next to mine as I call to her head. "Ela. Ela, mi niña, Ela bellísima. Come down. Come back to your papi. Come be whole again."

Ela looks at me, wide-eyed, unfearful, interested. But she does not speak. She remains part of her tidy cluster of infant heads in the tree.

"What's wrong?" I ask El Coco. "What am I doing wrong?"

He takes me by the arm again; his rhizomatic fingers spread all over my back and pulse with the muted, wet energy of fungal life. "Nothing, save that you are impatient, Julito. You are her father, yes. But you are also still something of a stranger to her. You are only just getting to know each other. You must take your time. Let her learn that your voice is a voice of love and comfort. And most importantly, get closer to her."

I turn to Coco. I know, I think, what I must do. But I still ask him, "How close?"

He tilts his head. "As close as you can."

It's just as I thought. So okay then. For my baby girl, anything.

"Will you hold her a moment?" I ask Coco.

"Por supuesto," he says, untangling his fingers from my back and taking my baby girl's headless body from me. He cradles her like an experienced tío; she tucks right in to the crook of his arm.

In the meantime, I pull off my head.

It doesn't come off easily, but it also isn't as hard as I thought it would be. I pull straight up, then hold my head above my shoulders as high as my arms will stretch. From this new height, I take a moment to survey the island.

The children. They never stop playing.

I turn bodily, one slow step at a time, until I am facing El Coco. "Will you lift me to her?"

"Por supuesto," he says once more. Then, extending his arm, his fingers grow out of his hand and entangle my head. They keep growing, bearing my head, until they are long enough to reach the cluster of infant heads in the palm tree. I am inset there among them like a gem. I feel the back of my head attach itself to the trunk, and in a rush of life and vigor, I am part of the tree, its ancient sense of time, the titanic grip its roots have on the earth beneath. Dumbstruck, dazzled, I inhale deeply—my mouth sucks air as if I still had lungs to serve—and take in the sights and sounds from my new vantage.

El Coco is still rocking Ela's body. "Shall I give her back to you now?" he asks me.

My body is standing like a beheaded statue next to him. I try to lift my arms, and sure I can lift them; they are my arms just as much as they have always been.

"Do you mind holding her for a minute longer?" I ask El Coco. And of course he doesn't.

I have my body gather the handheld hanging from my wrist and point it at my face. Or I try to. I can't tell exactly where the camera is aiming without a head on my shoulders. So I have my body point the lens generally at the cluster of heads in the palm tree and say, "Prudie, we may be here a little while. Is that okay with you?"

I'm not sure what I was expecting for a response, since the handheld has no speaker. But I get a response just the same: ten blasts from the breachdive's horn. Three long blasts, then two short, then three long, then two short.

That's Morse code for "88." And 88 in Morse code means "love and kisses."

Good old Prudencia. "I'll send my body over to you to work on fixing your communications array," I say to the handheld. "I need to tell NOAA I'll be using some of my sick days. And Connie: I need to tell Connie that Ela and I are all right. I need to tell her I love her."

"Love and kisses," says Prudencia's horn.

Relief washes like a heatwave through my face. My baby girl's head must feel it, and it must feel good to her, since she turns and nuzzles her forehead against my cheek. If there is bliss in this world, I have found it.

"Okay, baby girl," I say to my Ela. "You want to talk? You want to get to know your papi? Have I got a story for you. It's called:

"El Cuento de Cómo Julio Became a Coconut for His Baby Girl."

Author's Note

As a kid, I thought our hundred-pound bag of rice, which lived in a rubber bin in our kitchen pantry, was alive. I would talk to it as I picked up handfuls of rice and let the grains hourglass through my fingers. I thought the ever-shifting faces I discovered in the stucco ceiling of my bedroom were spirits. I'd speak with them, and they would answer. Really nice people, the stucco faces, and really funny—though they sure loved to argue with each other. In my chest, right now, I can still feel the presence of my stuffed bear, Canda the Panda, as strongly as I can feel the souls of my sisters and brother.

So when my aunt Carmita told me the legend of El Coco—her version featured a coconut-headed boogeyman—I formed a wholly idiosyncratic relationship with him. Sure, El Coco stole away misbehaving children, but that didn't scare me. Mami had craved syrupy canned coconut the entire time she was pregnant with me (on saltine crackers—blech). I was born with a special affinity with coconuts.

I had lots of opportunity to talk to El Coco. Not uncommonly, my childhood kitchen had coconuts stacked in baskets on the counter. I liked to drop them "accidentally" and laugh as they complained, looking up at me accusingly from the floor. But they never held a grudge. Like all the inanimate objects of my childhood, El Coco was funny, kindly, and full of great advice when I felt sad and alone.

In households where mental health issues are a daily reality, children create coping strategies, some healthy, and some perhaps less healthy. The way I used to talk to coconuts gives me a wistful sort of comfort. Once upon a time I was surrounded by all sorts of benevolent spirits. But they don't answer anymore. I miss them.

CARLOS HERNANDEZ

HE FELL HOWLING

BY
―
STEPHEN GRAHAM JONES

YOU DON'T KNOW ME, BUT YOU DO.

Walking the path from your father's house back to town, there came that certain span of steps where your back straightened, didn't there? Your skin came alive, trying to feel every breath of air. Some of those breaths were, as you now know, mine.

Most nights I've let you pass. Not this night.

Zeus thought that by forcing me into this form he was punishing me.

He was liberating me.

He said I would be hunted.

Instead, I'm the hunter.

Before, my lands were bound by walls, and my men had to patrol those walls on a daily circuit. Now my land is the night.

By changing me into this form you perhaps recognize from legend, from your own nightmares, Zeus granted me access to realms I'd never considered. You no longer need to call me Lycaon. My name now is your sharp intake of breath when you realize you're not alone on your long walk home. If you hear my footfalls or my breathing, it's because I mean for you to.

This is Zeus's grand and just judgment against one who would feed him human flesh in his stew, mixed in with the lamb and vegetables. It wasn't the smell he'd recoiled against—in the kitchen, I'd sampled a spoonful myself, and it was fine—but, evidently, the *idea*. Could he not in all his wisdom discern my true motivations? That I was *honoring* him by having my own son sacrificed and butchered? What more meaningful offering could I have made, I ask? What else could have been in keeping with his might? Would mere lamb and vegetables not have been an insult to one such as he?

So I thought at the time.

Sitting across from him that day, king to king, his wooden spoon dipping down into the bowl, I was as content as ever I'd been.

I still am. Or, rather, I am again.

Yes, as he wanted, as you can see before you now, my true nature *is* expressed in this lupine form, which was *his* judgment: that I no longer be able to hide who I truly am. All who see me, fear me.

As far as mighty Zeus is concerned, the story of Lycaon was over the day he, in his laughably obvious peasant form, flipped my table over, stood from it to his true height, and glared down at me, my limbs already creaking and breaking into the shape he thought more fitting, his voice booming down to me about what I'd almost done this day, how I didn't know what it was that I'd attempted.

Our story was *not* over that day, however. Yes, with a flick of his finger he stripped away my human form, bent me forward such that I rested on four paws, not two feet, but that wolfen form he initially damned me with turned out to be the exact means for me to finish what I started that day he knocked on my door in beggar rags.

You see, mighty Zeus, playful Zeus, crafty Zeus, he can't help but dress up like this and like that, adopting whatever raiment allows him to gain his impulsive ends or satisfy his fleeting curiosity or quench his childish need for entertainment.

With my new senses, though, I can now smell through such trickery.

I've watched him couple as a swan, I've tracked him from shore when he swam as a bull. I even listened to him sneak into the locked room of a high tower as a ray of sunlight, and I recognized him not because a ray of light makes sound, battering into motes of dust, but because mighty Zeus was chuckling to himself low enough that only wolf ears could register it.

But maybe, if his judgment against me is just, maybe I'd had these ears all along, yes?

Maybe like can hear like, monster can hear monster.

Either way, Zeus had forgotten poor Lycaon, meting out the rest of his days on four feet, chasing down beasts of the field for his dinner.

It would be his undoing.

As a man and a king of Arcadia, I had near fifty sons—minus one for the pot, yes?

After Zeus reshaped my limbs, pulled this canine muzzle forth from my face in a tearing of skin and grinding of bone that near erased my mind, he, in his wisdom, felled all those sons of mine with a sweep of his right hand, so as to once and forever terminate my family line.

In the field and the woods my boys fell as one.

Next, Zeus ravaged my lands, collapsed my home and outbuildings, and scattered my wife and her family to distant shores.

When I could stand again that evening, the world came at me in a rush—the smells, the sounds. I could hear the massive footfalls of spiders, their webs ringing like harp strings, and I could taste the smoke of fires two years old—poachers in my woods, who had . . . yes, who had spirited away a stag I'd had my eye on.

My lips peeled away from my teeth, and saliva descended onto my forepaw.

The first step I took on my new legs was stronger than I meant, and threw me into the rubble that had been my kitchen, further collapsing it.

No one was around to document this.

That painting you've seen, of a moment from my fall, an instant of my transformation?

The painter wasn't there. He couldn't have seen. Had he been there, I would have ripped his right arm from his body, lapped his blood from the dirt, my eyes locked on his as he died, to drink his last moments as well.

This is what wolves do.

Standing among the wreckage of my home, I may not have known my limbs nor my senses yet, but I knew my role in this new world I'd been delivered to.

Still, the rabbits of the field and the deer that had formerly been mine, they knew me for what I was, knew me before I knew myself, such that when I padded out into the night after them, they were already gone, were already burrowed into their safe places, were already fleeing onto other lands.

For three nights I tried to ambush one, just for a single mouthful of raw meat, but they had been running this race for untold generations, and evaded me time and again. My new senses only served to torture me, as I could hear their fluttery hearts beating, could taste them on the air. But catch them I couldn't. Not yet.

On the fourth day, perhaps just as wise Zeus had designed, I had to take what food I *could* catch: the decomposing bodies of my sons, lying where they'd fallen in the fields, under tumbled-over walls, in the backs of wagons that would never move again.

Is it punishment to have to eat exactly the meat I had formerly tried to feed the peasant who knocked on my door, his sides starved down enough that his ribs were near-visible?

If it was, then it was sweet punishment.

The muscle and organs of children I'd fathered myself, it nourished me in a different way.

Over the course of the week, and in spite of the putrefaction that only made the muscle sweeter and less resistant, I tore my sustenance from the bones of my sons, and licked the insides of their skulls for more.

If this was punishment, then punish me more, please.

On the eighth day of my repast, a townsperson showed up with a weekly delivery. He stood from his cart and eyed the ruins. From the shadow of one of the few walls left partially standing, I watched him.

My belly was full, but my mouth still watered.

He came back the next midday leading a detachment of soldiers, and I watched them from the trees, growling my displeasure. I still considered this my land, see. My home.

That night, after they'd set up tents in order to further investigate in the light of morning, I crept in, the darkness as the day to my new senses. The horses screamed with my approach and pulled their pickets free, crashed off into the night, back to the safety of town.

The soldiers circled around behind their spears and shields and stoked the fire higher and higher, and the whole night I only circled them.

Just before dawn broke, then, the part of my mind that thought like a wolf presented an obvious fact to me: if the soldiers were *here*, then they weren't protecting the town, right? And, without mounts, they wouldn't be tonight either.

I left them to their slow investigation of the ruins—really, they were plundering what they could from the rubble—and that night began my days-long siege of the town. I picked off those who wandered out to the edges, the children playing games, the women walking out to the hill to see if their soldier husbands were approaching, and then, never mind that my hunger was long sated, I picked off those who came looking for the children, the wives.

They didn't nourish me the same as my own sons had, but I learned to draw pleasure from their fear. It was enough.

When I'd gorged myself on the town such that I was only pulling the tongues and certain organs from the bodies I'd plundered, I padded back to my lands one last time and—just because I could, because I knew now that I was larger than any of the wolves I'd used to hunt from horseback—I crashed into the sleeping soldiers' camp and tore whatever flesh flashed in front of me, not even eating it, just destroying and destroying.

As a child, from a high place, I'd once watched a pair of wolves move through a herd of goats, killing for no other reason than the sheer joy of it.

Now I was that wolf.

I don't bite holes in the world because I dislike the world, I bite holes in it because I have these teeth.

That night with the soldiers is probably where the connection was made between the former king and the current monster, too. Since a head injury in my middle years, I'd always had a narrow blaze of white at a distinctive angle through my black hair. In my new form, as you can see, that blaze persisted and revealed my true identity to those soldiers.

Such are legends born. Such do necessary truths begin to get told.

As a king of men, my sons had numbered enough to form their own phalanx, nearly.

As a wolf, my progeny were even more numerous.

Zeus neglected to geld me, see.

His punishment against me was that I would have to run my dinner down every night, that I would have to be as savage in my daily life as I was when I cubed the smallest bit of my least son into his stew.

But in punishing me thusly, he also gifted me with everything a wolf might have.

Chief among those has been wives.

As king, I had privilege and access to any woman who caught my eye. As king of the wolves, my dalliances ranged even further. Not only could I mate with wolves of the forest, I found that, much like my maker Zeus,

I could share such congress with other animals as well. Specifically, the curs and mongrels that lived off the waste of towns.

My children were numbered in litters in those days, and of course, as when I was a man, I selected favorites to let walk alongside me, capable wolves I trained to hamstring your kind and leave them flopping and moaning in the dust of the road. You die soon enough on your own and, dying alone, can't lash out with knives or pikes. However, there were also lessons my children could learn about the back of the neck, and the throat. Open the throat, and everything good spills out, doesn't it?

The soft belly is good too, if there's time.

You'll learn this all as well, don't worry.

Really, there's no part of a man that a wolf can't take advantage of.

And of course I instructed my children of those early years to hunt mainly at night, and to keep their distance from the soldiers, and to always stay upwind, unless the panic of the livestock is beneficial in some way.

Myself, while I still took one of you from time to time as reminder, it was less about sustenance, more about a display of who was still king, and who was not.

What I found I derived *more* nutrition from was the puny whelps the town curs threw, with their floppy ears and mottled coats—my pups, I mean. Did living my first week as a wolf on the meat of my own sons dictate my taste, I wonder? Was I still living Zeus's judgment, then?

If so, it was a sweet judgment.

What I would do is pass through the edge of a town, mount whatever straggly dogs were bold enough to pad out for the fresh deer I'd dragged up, and then I would come back a couple of moons later. With pups, I liked to wait until they were suckling on their mother. When they were lined up on the teat like that, I could lower my great mouth down to their wiggling bodies and pull them up one at a time, their mouths holding onto their mother, stretching her out until there's that pleasant pop of suction collapsing.

While chewing the meat and soft bones together in a single mouthful, the rest of the pups wouldn't even scramble away, would just keep feeding, loading their bellies with that pale blue milk that is the perfect garnish for their soft muscle, like a center that comes in a warm rush, surprising every time.

The mothers just glared up at me, unable to move.

Sometimes I would leave them one or two pups yet wriggling, for the next generation. I found that throwing pups off of pups I'd fathered was even sweeter, is what I imagine I might taste were I to bite into my own naked belly.

Such is the way mighty Zeus designed me.

Even better, eating the milk-saturated, wriggling-blind pups born from pups I'd myself fathered had an unexpected effect, one not dissimilar to the one you see before you now.

If I gorged myself on the whole litter back then, I could, for perhaps an hour, stand up on my hind feet as I used to when I was man.

With practice I found I could even walk a bit, unsteadily.

It's a release like none other, to work around the curse laid down by a god and prove it not a curse. To walk slowly through the market of a sleeping town, my every sense alive, my children arrayed out behind and beside and ahead of me, lest some soldier wake to relieve himself, try to raise the alarm.

The night was populated with monsters in those days, yes.

In these days as well.

It was during one such midnight stroll that my revenge against mighty Zeus took shape.

Having eaten, this time, the mother of the litter as well as the litter— she was weak, it was a mercy—I found that my balance was even better, and I walked confidently all the way *through* town this time, to the meadow on the other side where it smelled like horses usually grazed. There were no horses then, though.

One of my sons growled deep in his chest, alerting the rest of us to what was happening out in the grass. In a burrow out in the field was the pounding heart of one of my many curs, giving birth. She'd come out here for safety. She'd come out here to try to escape *me*.

Having never eaten a litter this fresh, still sheathed in afterbirth, and curious what the result might be, I had my children uncover her, never mind that the pups wouldn't be filled with that milky-rich center this time.

The mother was a pitiful thing, starved down and weak, whimpering, crying from the effort, shivering with fear, only half done with her delivery. The first four pups were rolling in the dirt, eyes closed.

My mouth watered, as would any wolf's, as would any king's.

Moving slow on my two legs, I started to bend over, come down to all fours for this rare feast, but startled back from a sudden, powerful fluttering to my right. My first thought was that this was a trap, that the soldiers were ranged all around, covering their scent and sound somehow—that a crossbow bolt or net was nearly on me, to shorten my reign at last. But then I realized: we weren't the only hunters, this night.

It was an owl, one of the tall ones that stands up to a man's waist or a wolf's shoulders.

It too had been tracking this birth, and likely mourning that it had no access to the burrow.

To it, these wriggling pups were just helpless, especially plump mice that didn't yet know to run away.

Its talons pierced the back of the pup farthest from the teat, and then the great gray wings pushed down together, lifting the bird back into the darkness on an expanding pad of air. We all listened to it lift away, coast down deep in the trees, and strain this giant mouse down its gullet.

When one of my sons nosed forward, for one of the remaining pups, I lifted my lips, warned him back. He mewled, dropped his tail, slunk off, and I never even had to look over.

I was still listening to this owl, deep in the woods.

Yes, as a king I had perhaps underestimated Zeus. I admit that freely. Being a wolf, however, had taught me certain things I could never have learned otherwise.

As a man, I could of course walk by any number of rabbits or moles and never feel compelled to snap them up, swallow them down. As a wolf, I snatched those rabbits and moles up even when I wasn't hungry for their meat. I still thought like a man, but my body reacted to its natural prey like the wolf it was.

I had to imagine it would be the same with Zeus. For all his might and cleverness, he would still be prey himself to whatever form he was using to move among the mortals. And, with these new ears, I knew what form he had been recently taking, and would, I had to presume, continue to take until his current dalliance had run its course.

For years he had sat atop his Mount, playing treacherous petty games with others of his kind, but then a vision of milky skin must have passed before his eyes, as it always did. He had leaned over from his high seat, studied us down here in our filth, finally settled his divine gaze on the one of us who had caught his fancy, one whose beauty was already dooming him or her to unasked-for nightly visits.

His whole existence, see, it's about satisfying his own fickle desires, be they carnal, as was the case here, or, as when he knocked on my door, playful. Either way, he's so satisfied with himself that he can't quite contain his mirth. He's getting away with it again, and that persistent divine chuckle deep in his chest, at the core of his being, that's what my wolf ears can't help but register.

I say this with confidence because I felt that same mirth myself moments ago, padding up behind you: I'm getting away with it again, yes. And who is there now to punish me? But I get ahead of myself.

Though I hadn't bothered to interest myself with where Zeus was going—which bedroom, what tower—my ears *had* picked up how he was getting there. I knew what animal raiment he was clothing himself with, and so wagered that I could use that against him.

I padded away from my children that night, and stationed myself along the shore, in what I knew to be his path.

Then it was just the waiting.

Time passes differently on the Mount than it does in the mortal realm. I say this because, if Zeus's carnal impulses want to be satisfied on any kind of cycle, then that cycle is markedly different than in men, or wolves.

I sat on that rocky shore for five weeks, listening for his return. My sides drew in, my mouth watered for the animals I could hear crawling around me, but I remained motionless, could not give up this effort just because death might be looming. I wasn't even sure I could starve down to nothing, but by the end of the first week, I knew that this hunger, already all-consuming, was not likely to abate.

Yet I persisted in my vigil.

I once had offered a god a simple meal, and he had turned the table over on me. In my new form, though, I could set that table back up, couldn't I?

My dry lips cracked with movement when I heard the heavens open to admit a traveler down into our realm.

Zeus was in the world again.

Though it was daylight, I raced alongshore to the nearest town, took a scent-reading, found the cur I'd mounted two months ago feeding her newborn pups. She bared her teeth at me in the fiercest way she had, and had I still the mouth for it, I would have smiled at her pitiful effort.

She had hidden herself under the porch of a stone house.

I pushed under to dig her out, sucking down the first two of the pups as a reward to myself, but then the stone house's owner stepped out with a farming tool.

For a moment we locked eyes, his face slack, my muzzle bloody, and then I was on him, had his throat in my teeth. To insure no more interruptions, I went into his stone house then, walking on *two* feet thanks to the meal he'd interrupted, and easily dispatched the rest of the family—daughter, daughter, wife, moving on to the next while the previous was still falling. On the way out, I took note that the pot bubbling over the fire was stew.

Again, my kind can't smile, but perhaps my eyes did.

Quickly, with no thought to who might be watching—there was no time—I dropped to all fours, dug the cur and her pups out, and left them curled up there, save the piebald one I had nipped by the back of the neck.

He struggled and kicked in my teeth, but he weighed nothing and was still new enough as to be blind, couldn't see the legendary run I was making, from far inland all the way to the coast in a matter of hours.

When his skin pricked and his blood washed into my mouth, I didn't even bite down more, just ran faster, and faster again.

The chuckling satisfaction in the sky was moving along the water's edge now, was coming back from whatever conquest Zeus felt he'd just made, whatever he'd just gotten away with again.

Instead of meeting him, I surged ahead even faster, into his path, into where he was going.

This time he wasn't a swan, wasn't a bull, but a great eagle.

And just as I was carrying a young son in my mouth, he had in his talons the unconscious form of a young boy who had evidently been fetching enough for Zeus to transform, glide all the way down here, and now deliver him back up for a week of pleasure on the Mount, whether the boy agreed or not.

Such is the way of things with a god.

Pushing harder and harder, I ran ahead, dropped the pup from my mouth into the grass, in order to finish what I'd started years before.

Had I left the struggling pup on shore, that would be too obvious, even for one so brazen as Zeus. In the grass, though, his sharp predator eyes would automatically register the blades trembling with life, and his wings would dip him down ever so slightly, to consider this new possibility, his clawed feet already flexing in anticipation.

I was just ahead, hunkered down in a copse of trees, my hackles vibrating with anticipation.

No bird of prey could resist. Not even mighty Zeus.

Without considering the danger, he flipped the unconscious boy up into the sky to retrieve later and angled his head down, tucked his wings back, and fell into a sharp dive, following his eagle instincts.

Slashing down like that, he was a bolt of lightning, yes.

His great talons pierced the pup in four places when he hit, each puncture instantly mortal, and then he was gone again, banking hard to the other side of the meadow, which is perhaps an instinct in birds of prey.

Where he drifted down was a mere span before my copse of trees.

Holding the shattered, leaking pup down with one claw, he drove his beak down for a morsel, came up with it fast, leaning his head back so as to straighten his neck, work this meat down.

And again, and again, three bites in all. It was all the pup had to it. The bony tail yet flopped on the ground, and Zeus's eagle eyes, attuned to just that type of movement, watched it, perhaps curious, perhaps amused.

At which point I stepped out.

He turned to face me, taking on his divine aspect in a matter of two steps.

"Lycaon," he said, his voice thunderous, the whole realm trembling from it.

"Mighty Zeus," I said back to him, and dipped my head in a show of respect, if not respect itself.

"What brings you to my field this day?" he asked, moving to the side to see me better, I think, his head actions still that of a bird even though he stood on man legs.

"Did you like your meal?" I said to him, and in a divine instant he saw the smile in my eyes, and he registered that he *had* just eaten one of my sons after all these years. He turned away, looked up into the sky, where presumably his boy-child was still falling, and would continue falling until fetched.

"You know not what you've done with this, Lycaon," he said at last, licking a speck of the pup's blood from the corner of his mouth and spitting it harshly down into the grass.

"It was to honor your greatness," I told him. "You never allowed that possibility, did you?"

"To honor me?" he said.

"He was my own son," I said, a growl rumbling in my chest. "The most precious thing I had to offer."

He shook his head, looked to the sea in sorrow.

"Your least son," he said. "Your weakest son. Did you even dispatch him yourself, or have it done, Lycaon?"

I only stared at him about this.

"And so you insist on honoring me in this fashion," he said, turning back to me, his eyes sparking, flashing, the air around us crackling. "Despite the fact that I resist it, you continue the motion you started those many years ago. Did you ever stop to think there might be a reason for my reaction that day, Lycaon?"

"You would not be hoodwinked," I said, my words barely crossing my lips.

"Such is the shortened sight and apprehension of mortals," Zeus said. "When—when a god such as myself tastes of human flesh like this, Lycaon, even disguised human flesh, so begins the corruption."

"You were already corrupt," I said.

"Not like this," Zeus said. "Never like this. This is the end of us, Lycaon—of the gods. This is the end of this age altogether."

"And the beginning of mine," I said, just loud enough.

"If you had kept from eating human flesh yourself," Zeus said, "you would have become again who you used to be, did you know that, Lycaon?"

"I am who I am."

"You are at that," he said, still circling, still considering this new situation, these new terms. "This, I think, *will* be your age, your *kind's* age. Hark, can you hear, can you smell it already, can you see it in your mind's eye?"

With the benefit of his augmentation, or just because he willed it, I could: far away, in the stone house where I'd slaughtered the family, one of them was now rising. The daughter I'd taken in my mouth, shaken, and tossed aside.

I hadn't bitten her deeply enough.

She was . . .

"No," I said, taking a step back.

"Yes," Zeus said, with force, and as we watched together, her frail form began to tremble and seize.

My bite, my teeth, my saliva—they were changing her.

Just as had happened with me, claws punched through the ends of her fingers, her legs broke backwards, and her mouth elongated into a muzzle.

She stood then, not on four feet like me, but on two, as I had been when I'd attacked her.

"I should have gelded you that day," Zeus said, "and I cannot undo what you've started, but I can correct my mistake, anyway."

He turned his hand over, palm up, and bade me rise, rise, and I had no choice: just like the newly born wolf-girl miles away, I stood up on two feet like this, and felt the world solid beneath me. Whereas before my balancing up on two legs had been a rare treat, due to my preferred sustenance—a rare treat I had to concentrate to maintain—now, due to my reshaped limbs, standing up on my hind legs was natural.

"No longer can you run down the fast little rabbits of the field," Zeus proclaimed. "They twitch this way and that way with no notice. You're too slow for that kind of hunting, now. Now the only prey you can easily catch, it will have spears to lob against you, walls to build to keep your hunger out."

I forced myself back forward, onto what I now have no recourse but to call my arms again, though they were furred, though there were yet claws at the end.

Zeus chuckled at my awkwardness. I was born again, a third time, but now I was no longer wolf, no longer man, but a form locked between the two.

"And from this day on," Zeus said, squatting to see me eye to eye, "you will no longer couple as you've been doing, Lycaon. Now the only way you can procreate will be the way you just did, with your mouth, with your bite. Thus says Zeus, even if it will be my last proclamation."

I turned my head again to the idea of the wolf-girl, staggering through her stone house.

"You would have me mate using only my *teeth*?" I said to Zeus.

"And what fine teeth they are," he said, standing again, cocking his head to the clouded sky as if gauging the descent of his boy up there.

"But I'm a *king*!" I screamed. "And I was—I was only honoring *you*, the mightiest of the gods!"

"Mighty no more," Zeus said, and we watched together as the boy thumped down from the sky, coming down on the rocky shore face-first, his back folding over the wrong way, shards of white splashing up, a lone gull banking over to investigate. "With what you've introduced to my stomach," Zeus went on, "I now must live out the rest of my days as a mortal. As must we all in Olympus."

"I can take it back," I pled. "Let me—I can bite it from you, if you'll but—"

"Run off now, Lycaon," Zeus said, waving me away. "I still have enough of myself left to lodge another punishment, should you so desire."

For a long moment I glared at him, then I stared across at his broken boy on the rocks, and then I looked out to the trees, arrayed against me like everything else.

"We will tear the throat from your precious mankind," I said to Zeus at last, my chest growling the promise true. "There will be no more pretty children for you to steal."

"Perhaps," Zeus said. "And perhaps they will come for your kind, Lycaon. For your children. Perhaps you will be hounded for ages, until you become but a legend."

He stared at me then as if daring me to rush at him, finish this now. When I didn't—I didn't know whether to try on two feet or four—he gave me his back, walked to the beach, perhaps to mourn his broken boy, perhaps to feast on his liver.

Note that he walked. He didn't sprout wings and glide over.

Truly, that meat I'd introduced to his system was festering, was corrupting.

True natures indeed, mighty Zeus.

As for me, my children are no longer my children—we pass in the night, our teeth flashing—and my first daughter of this new form has children of her own, minor whelps I hear crying from the town walls, where the men pierce them and hang them. It weighs on my heart, their cries.

I still keep to the shadows, yes. To that lonely turn in the road.

Look back if you want. You might even chance to see me.

I'm those footfalls drawing ever and ever closer, then retreating to the shadows just for the thrill of it, just to hear you scream, then finally rushing close on two feet, to hold you close.

Zeus in all his wisdom would have me hounded through the centuries.

Not likely. Not while the roads are dark, not while my teeth are still the sharpest things in that darkness.

Hold steady now, I don't want to bite too deep.

You will be the second of my new children. Together, the night will be ours to do with as we will.

Punishment? Hardly. More like a gift.

Mighty Zeus, that dead Olympian, his last divine act was to give us the future, child.

Let's take it by the neck, now, shake it until our fur is matted red.

I said before that this mouth was incapable of smiling?

I was wrong, child.

All I do now is smile.

Author's Note

I forget who I told Navah and Dominik I was going to write about, but when I sat down, all I could see was that famous old painting or carving or whatever it is of Lycaon turning into a wolf because he tried to feed Zeus peoplemeat. I couldn't stop wondering why Lycaon would do that, and what the fallout of it had been. The story we always hear, it stops with Lycaon scampering off, all properly punished, now doomed for the rest of his days. But I didn't want to let Zeus off that easy, just because he knew what was in his stew. Not saying Lycaon's the victim here—that is his son cubed up into that bowl—but I am saying that Zeus isn't exactly the hero, either. So I went with Lycaon into those dark woods of his future, and then started to see that his future and this world we live in, they're kind of the same place. Thanks to Zeus, I suppose. Who still isn't a hero. Who, like Lycaon, is the author of his own end. As we all tend to be, whether we're gods or werewolves or that person in line for a burger, giving the person at the register unnecessary grief—grief we'll bite into momentarily, and then have to live with forever.

Stephen Graham Jones

CURSES LIKE WORDS, LIKE FEATHERS, LIKE STORIES

BY

—

KAT HOWARD

WHEN I WAS YOUNG, I CAST A CURSE.

Young. I barely even know how to think of the word now. Young is seven when you are nine. Young is twenty when you're twice that age.

Through my own fault, I have lived over nine hundred years.

There are few mercies in a life stretched so long. The greatest has been one I thought at first to be a horror: that I too am cursed out of my own self, and into the shape of a bird. A black-winged war raven, one of Morrigan's own daughters. It is a different sort of witness, this one with wings.

The other mercy is this: The story is finally ending, and I have survived to see it.

* * *

Niamh's flight into Shannon Airport had been a misery, storm-plagued and sleepless. Not content to simply harry her across the Atlantic, the storm chased her overland, hissing down rain and setting a chill into her bones. The trip to Ireland wasn't a happy one to begin with, but this truly seemed excessive.

On the drive there, windshield wipers scraping uselessly against the torrent, knuckles white on the wheel, she thought she saw a swan, lightning-white against the clouds, blown on with the wind. She shook her head as if to clear the image and focused more fiercely on the road.

The small house on the edge of nowhere smelled like her great-uncle Aifraic, a combination of wool and peat and pipe tobacco, like his ghost still rocked in the old wooden chair near the hearth. Everything had happened too fast and too far away, and now all she had left of him was an empty house, his boxes of papers, and a promise she had flown thousands of miles to keep, a broken-hearted bird on her loneliest migration. Niamh poured a glass of whiskey and sat in the rocking chair and wept.

It's fitting that the end of the story comes in grief. That's how it began as well. The grief of a husband, for a wife lost. The grief of a sister for a sister gone.

For a moment, it seemed like he and I could pass through our shared grief together. That we could both honor her memory and make it our own. But then I asked him for a child, for one that would be ours. He refused, and my grief turned to acid in my heart. It turned to a curse on his children, the ones that were his and hers and never—never, as he told me again and again—mine.

I am the only one left living who knows all the pieces of this story. That, too, is a curse.

When Aifraic had asked Niamh to come back at the end, at his end— "come home," he'd said—he'd told her it was because there were things she needed to know.

"Then why not tell me now?" she'd asked, speaking the words through the salt of tears.

"I can't tell the story until it's over," he'd said. "It's not rightly mine to tell until then." He'd given no more of an explanation, other than to tell her the answers were here, in his house on the edge of the sea.

And now, here she was. Too late to ask any questions, too late to hear the answers in Aífraic's low, warm voice. Another sorrow, to set stone-like on her heart. But she had promised, and she was here, and so she would search for the echoes of whatever stories remained.

She found the notebook of poems half a glass of whiskey later. Tucked in a box full of crumbling papers and notebooks gone thin with time, *Swan Poems* in pencil inside the front cover, less a title than a category. Three downy white feathers were pressed beneath it.

The pages were worn and yellowed, and all covered with words. Some had numbers as well, dates meant to mark the span of their writing. Or no—something else. If they were dates, those numbers in Aífraic's looping scrawl, they would have made him impossibly old. Niamh pushed that puzzle aside, and read.

Aífraic had always been fascinated by swans, and he had passed that fascination on to her when she was a child. Niamh remembered a summer when she was perhaps thirteen, walking the sand in too-big borrowed wellies, even the extra socks she wore not thick enough to quiet the sensation that at any moment her feet might go out from under her.

"There used to be swans that lived there."

Her eyes had followed the direction of Aífraic's hand. It did not look as if anything could live on the island of Carricknarone, its jagged outcropping sharp as ravens' teeth in the frigid Sea of Moyle.

"Swans? Out there?"

The cloud-chased sun sparked off the foam of the waves, the water moving like ripples of shattered glass.

"Not recently. Hundreds and hundreds of years ago. A strange enough occurrence that people still speak of it." That was the sort of thing that mattered to him: people telling stories.

"Have you ever seen one?" she'd asked.

Aífraic had laughed, a great bark of sound that startled seagulls into flight. "And how old is it you think I am, girl?"

Still, every time she looked out onto that water, Niamh also looked for swans, imagining the white of their feathers reflected in the white of the waves.

She built up the fire, and read the poems.

I barely thought of them, those transformed swan children, for the first three hundred years I had set the curse to run. We were separate things, and their story was no longer mine, or so I thought.

Besides, my powers were growing. As punishment for what I had done to his children, my husband had cursed me into the shape that terrified me most: a raven, an avatar of blood and war. But war is a story that is always told, and the more times a story is told, the more power it has. So I flew, and I witnessed, and I counted the dead until I no longer knew the numbers for their counting, and then I counted again.

And the worst was that all through the counting, through that terrible subtraction, I felt myself grow stronger.

Some of the poems were in Irish. Niamh's heart clenched as she looked over the unfamiliar words in the familiar handwriting. She had taken the required classes at school and remembered how to say a phrase here and there—small talk about the weather, or the cuteness of someone's dog—but not much more than that. She had always felt there would be time to relearn, later, and now it seemed that later had snuck up and tapped her on the shoulder when she wasn't looking. She thought, though, that she could make out what must be the word for swan, *eala*, from the frequency with which it appeared.

The margins were full of swans, sketches in smudged and fading pencil.

The poems were works of hardship, of longing. Of deep-felt desire for a place where one could fold their wings and rest, could take shelter from storms, could know small and quiet comforts. They didn't seem like poems about birds, but rather poems about exiles:

Imagine a story as you would imagine a bird on a great migration. One that passes out of sight for so long as to be forgotten. One whose return is a herald of some great newness.

Imagine a story as something that returns.

Reading them, she remembered something Aífraic had told her once: that some swans had human speech, those that had been enchanted into their bird form rather than born into it, but as part of their curse, they could speak only poetry.

"Why would that be a curse?" she had asked.

"Who ever listens to poetry and believes it to be true?" Aífraic had smiled his answer, but it was a smile like a knife, sharp-edged and keen.

Something in me shifted after that. A change of heart, if not of appearance. It is all well and good to be an avatar of war, to glory in the blood and the battlefields, but after so long, and so many dead . . . The Morrigan may have been made to endure such witness, but I was not.

There had been new stories told in Ireland for years, stories whose telling drowned out the older voices, that rewrote old truths to serve new ideas. Stories that changed goddesses to saints and everyday magic to holy miracle. Stories of a God of Peace, who offered forgiveness. I wasn't sure I believed them all—I myself was a story, and I knew how little truth was in my own—but this forgiveness happened after a journey to a place. And the thing about a place is, you don't need to believe in it for it to be there. And so, unbelieving, but desiring forgiveness all the same, I flew.

They called the place a Purgatory, and gave its keeping over to their Saint Patrick. I flew there and stayed the required time, but had no visions of my sins or my redemption, only of time, stretched out and silent before me.

Even now, they tell the story of the raven who flew to Purgatory. It has been twisted and metaphored into nothing I recognize beyond the journey, but it matters to those who hear it, and so who am I to say that the story they tell is wrong?

Aífraic had been a collector of stories, always. He was as interested in the laughing ones exchanged at the pub, embellished and altered for dramatic effect, as he was in those written down in formal cadences. He listened to them, and shared his own, trading one for another, using words to warm a cold night. "I've always felt that stories die a bit, when they aren't told," he'd said. "So this is how I make sure they're remembered. This is how I keep them alive."

The stories Aífraic had loved best were full of birds—a king cursed into bird-shape for angering a priest, and a great goddess of war who sometimes took the form of a raven. Niamh's favorite had swans: a witch had cursed four siblings, a princess and three princes, into swans and then forbidden them from landing on Ireland for nine hundred years. It was a sad and lonely and beautiful story, and hearing Aífraic tell it had made her heart ache in the same way that a slant of light on water or the shine of white feathers in the sky did.

But visits had fallen off after the summer she turned thirteen, and then stopped altogether. Her parents had decided to emigrate to America—to join the flock of wild geese that were constantly flying from Ireland's shores. And while she called Aífraic her great-uncle, there was no actual tie of blood between them. Their ties had been those of proximity, a kind neighbor and an eager audience, the shared love of a place and its stories.

After the move, they wrote letters sometimes, sent holiday cards, but it wasn't the same, and silence filled the spaces where the stories had been.

Still, she thought of him occasionally, particularly during the fall migrations when flocks of birds would cloud the sky, and she missed his stories, and so she'd tried to find them on her own.

She learned that the swans in her favorite story weren't cursed by a witch, but by their mother's sister, and that the curse lasted long enough to see the conditions of its fulfillment made impossible. The fact that they turned human again at the end—just long enough to be baptized by an extremely convenient priest—before crumbling to dust . . . Well, she wondered who would ever want to hear a story like that except for possibly a priest.

Everything she loved about the story was gone.

She had almost stopped reading then. The betrayal of the story felt like a kind of death, like a curse that overwrote her memories. Someone had taken magic, and turned it into nothing more than propaganda. But then she'd thought back to something Aífraic had said once: that sometimes stories got so old, they forgot the truth of their telling. So she looked to see if there were other versions of this story, ones that remembered.

She found them, variant texts and preferred versions, but they all shared that same unsatisfying ending—the brief transformation to something flightless and ancient, just long enough to be baptized. As if that was the point of the story. As if there were more magic in priests than in the old gods of Ireland.

There was a blessing, inside of the curse. The children would wear swan-shape for nine hundred years, but that shape would also protect them from age and its related mortality. But unaging is not undying.

It was Fiachra who died first, blown from story by wind and storm, and by my curse, which kept him from safety. When the news of his death came to me, I flew on a pilgrimage across Ireland, to the shores of the Sea of Moyle. It was a journey of atonement, though I knew such a gesture was too small, too late. Half the time of the curse was gone, and neither that nor their brother could be returned to those who were left.

The three remaining swans were there, and with them one other. A fisherman, Aífraic, who took to the sea and sailed his boat among them and listened to their stories.

Aífraic had flown to America when her parents died. He was the only one from Ireland who had. "I thought you needed someone here who knew their stories."

After the funeral, they'd gone to a local pub, held their own private wake. Aífraic knew stories that Niamh didn't, like that of the local terrier who vigorously hated laundry hung out to dry. "Sure, he'd steal anything he could reach, and then run off with it. One day, he managed to get ahold of a whole line, and ran up and down the street, your ma's delicates flapping like flags behind him." Niamh had laughed until she cried, but these tears were easier than the funeral ones.

Aífraic's presence at the funeral had been enough for her to reconnect with him. She visited when she could, and each time, they'd go to the beach, and they'd watch for swans. She asked him once about the swans in the story she had found, the priest and the baptism that seemed so alien to the magic that the rest of the story had. "Who's to say what the right ending is? Maybe it's the one that sounds like magic, or maybe it's the one people want to hear. Maybe only those in the story know the truth of it."

"But it doesn't fit. It feels like two different stories stuck together by someone who didn't care."

"Well, maybe someone wrote an ending because the story isn't yet over, and there's little comfort in unfinished things."

He had always seemed impossibly old to her, as adults do to children, but in these last visits, she could see the patterns of age on his face and in his step.

"I've no right to ask this," he'd said, "but I hope that you'll come back. Come home. At the end. When my story finishes."

Niamh had squeezed his hand, and promised that she would.

* * *

I wonder sometimes how things would have ended, had not Aífraic transformed himself from fisherman to guardian of stories. Ireland changed and changed and changed again in the years after I spoke my curse. The old gods faded from memory, and their stories faded with them. Even my name—Aoife, Eva, Eve—is now better known in another woman's story.

But the swans and their story had Aífraic. He listened and he recorded and he made of himself a witness. He wove his thread into their tapestry, and kept it there through will. He lived hundreds of years past his span because of this, outliving even Aodh and Conn, both shot from the sky in the years that Ireland tore itself apart.

Through it all, through war and time, and even until the end, until the cancer that burned through his blood extinguished his life, Aífraic listened. And he wrote. And he remembered.

The cry of seabirds woke Niamh with the dawn, the sun striping gold across the waves. She pulled on a jacket, boots, and stepped out into the crisp morning air.

There, out on the rock of Carricknarone, was a swan. Elegant and lovely, and utterly alone.

Niamh closed her eyes at the pinch of her heart, at the full-bodied wish that her great-uncle could have been with her there, to see this.

When she opened them again, the swan had left the island, and was swimming, very near to shore. She opened her beak and spoke in poetry: *Imagine a story as something that remains.*

Then the swan stepped between the tide and the sand. As she did, her bones shifted, her feathers fell away, revealing a human woman. "Thank you for being here, Niamh. Aífraic told me so many stories of you."

Niamh realized then that Aífraic had seen this before, had heard the poetry spoken by this very swan. That he had told her a true story, one that only now was ending.

"I think," Niamh said, her voice windblown and rough, "that he told me your story, too."

"It has been long in the telling," the woman—Fionnghuala—said. "I am glad you are here, to see me through its end."

"He meant, I think, to be here, too." Crying now, the tears mixing with the salt spray on her skin.

"If you will remember me, remember this, it is more than enough that you are."

The woman fell quiet. Niamh took her hand, held it as the woman dissolved into sand and water, and one white feather, floating on the tide. Then she went back inside, to that final part-written notebook, and she wrote of the death of a swan.

And so the curse I cast was no more. All four of those children who were never mine—Aodh and Fionnghuala, Fiachra and Conn—gone to dust and feather and story.

I am still here, still raven-winged, and I do not hear the steps of Death behind me. Perhaps that is a curse. Perhaps it is a story, unended.

Author's Note

Sometimes when I write, I give pieces of my own life to my characters. Like Niamh, I love the story of the Children of Lir. And also like Niamh, I feel that the most common ending of the story—a convenient priest, the baptism of the four former swans—is wrong. And by wrong, I mean in the sense of not matching up with anything in the previous part of the story. It feels tacked on, as if a different person wrote the ending to a story someone else started. And so when given the chance to retell the Children of Lir, I wanted to write about that odd-seeming ending, and about the way stories get told, about what gets passed on. My version of this story is dedicated to the memory of my grandmother.

Kat Howard

ACROSS THE RIVER

BY

LEAH CYPESS

When the sorcerer walked through the town gates, I was standing with my friends Reuven and Yitzchak in the square, which was not where we were supposed to be. Reuven should have been in the study hall, where his wife had directed him to go. Yitzchak should have been at the market, helping his father. And I should have been resting my voice, since that evening, for the first time, I was going to be allowed to lead the prayers in synagogue—an honor I had been hoping for and practicing for, but that I now, somewhat nervously, wished was not coming so soon.

We were all, mind you, on our way to where we were supposed to be. We were obedient young men, with no inner drive for trouble. Reuven loved his studies, and I loved the taste of prayers in my mouth, the feeling that came when I hit the right accents with the right emotions. Yitzchak, while he did not exactly love trade, certainly appreciated the money he would take home. But we were all still young, and it was a warm lush day with the first hint of summer twining through the breeze. It had been a long time since the three of us had sat together under a teacher's stern eye, and though we saw each other in passing almost every day, we always had something to catch each other up on.

"My wife," Reuven said—he was newly married, and always blushed slightly when he said *my wife*—"tells me her sister is ready for marriage, and her parents are talking to the marriage broker. What do you say, Yitzchak? You won't find a better family."

"Eh," Yitzchak said, lifting a shoulder. "I admire her parents well enough, but I'm not sure I like who my brother-in-law would be."

Reuven made a show of punching him, and I gave them both a sharp look. Not too sharp—I didn't want to appear insulted that *I*, apparently, was not a good marriage prospect for Reuven's wife's sister—but really, we were no longer children. If the rabbi's wife was at market, and saw me behaving like a wild animal, she might mention it to the rabbi, and he might decide I wasn't ready to lead prayers after all.

"I have to go," I said. "I need to practice for tonight."

Yitzchak lifted the corner of his mouth—once he was in a jocular mood, it was hard to get him out of it—but Reuven nodded. "Of course. Are you going to sing one of your own poems?"

"No!" I hadn't even considered it. No one but the two of them and my father had heard my compositions. And though they all assured me my prayer-poems were wonderful, I knew they were just shells of what they could have been. They needed an infusion of words and songs I couldn't yet give them. And though I knew where I could go to find that music, I wasn't ready.

I could not possibly explain. So I said, "It's only my first—"

Then a hush fell over the square, and we turned just in time to see the sorcerer walk through the gate.

He was dressed like a monk, but his cassock cast a shadow darker than itself, so we all knew immediately what he was. He walked past the beggars at the well, past the women herding mules along the street, past the children playing near the walls, straight toward us. The only three Jews in the square.

We should have run. We would have, if he hadn't come so fast. Next thing we knew, he was beside us. His sleeve fell back to reveal a gnarled hand with too-long fingers, and with the knuckles of that hand, he brushed Reuven's cheek.

Reuven let out a small, strangled sound. Yitzchak and I stepped back.

The sorcerer smiled at us, then turned and kept walking, farther into the town.

News of the sorcerer had been passed along by traders and travelers from the other towns along the Rhine. He was from the east, they said, from the land of the Byzantines, and he was headed back there to help the Byzantine emperor fight the Moors. On his way, he was killing as many Jews—only Jews—as he could.

This was no real surprise to us Jews, though it was quite a relief to our Christian neighbors.

He had already killed many of us. He touched people, and they went home, and then they weakened and died. The travelers were unclear on how long it took.

But they were clear that he never stopped with only one. After Reuven died, there would be dozens more . . . maybe hundreds. First here in Worms, and then in another town, and another. There was nothing we could do to stop it.

I helped Yitzchak walk Reuven home to his wife and waited with them until the sun dipped low. And then I went to the river.

Years later, when I was much older and living in another land, I discovered that scholars had been searching for centuries for the Sambatyon

River. It puzzled me at first, because of course I had always known where it was. It was right behind my house.

It took me longer than it should have to realize that I was the only one who had ever seen it. Not merely in my hometown—that, I had always known—but in the entire world. That was why others searched for it in distant deserts and faraway jungles. They did not know that the Sambatyon came to those it chose.

By then, I was ashamed to tell them it had chosen me.

The river behind my house wasn't usually the Sambatyon. Normally it was the Rhine, flat and gray, with ripples that were slow and languid, as if they didn't quite have the desire to make it all the way to the sea. As if, like the rest of us, they had nowhere to be but here.

It was only when I was alone, but not *always* when I was alone, that I felt the change: a restless surge within me, as if my mind was a maelstrom, full of thoughts and words and images desperate to get out. As if the prayers I practiced so diligently—prayers that I loved, that I longed to share with my community and devote my life to perfecting—were too rehearsed, too calm. Missing something I could not find in my synagogue or my town.

Then I would go to the river and find it wild and turbulent, waves rearing high above my head and crashing down in a fury of white froth. Rocks the size of a man's fist were tossed among the waves like goose feathers at a slaughter, clashing against each other and smashing the waves into glittering bits of spray.

The violent waters were always blue, a brighter, more crystalline blue than the sky above Worms ever was. And on the other side—which I could glimpse in bits and pieces, scattered and distorted through boulders and froth—I saw no houses and gardens, no chickens or pigs. I saw tents, and long leonine creatures that looked like neither dogs nor cats, and dark-skinned figures in strange white clothes moving among them.

I wanted to see more, but not nearly as much as I wanted to hear their songs—prayers that must be so like, and so unlike, our own. I knew their music would fill the gaps in my own hymns, that if I infused my compositions with their prayers, it would make us whole. Bring us closer to God and to what we should have been. But the river, with its frantic rocks and roars of spray, was unceasingly loud, drowning out any sounds from the other side.

By then, of course, I knew what the river was, though I still didn't know *why* it was what it was. I had learned our history: how a thousand years ago, ten of Israel's twelve tribes were exiled before the rest of us. How they passed through Assyria and found a place, safe and secure, beyond the Sambatyon River: a river that ran wild six days a week, but became calm and smooth between sundown on Friday and nightfall on Saturday.

Living in isolation, the Ten Tribes could atone for the sins that had caused their exile and could prepare for their eventual return. They had their own kingdom, their own customs, unchanged over the hundreds of years during which we, descendants of the other two tribes, had mingled with our neighbors and been downtrodden by them. The Ten Tribes had kept their original customs, their unique ways, their native skills.

Which would, I hoped as I watched the waves shoot billows of white spray into the air, include sorcery.

Two boulders crashed against each other, sending shards of wet rock flying. I flinched away, but felt a sharp pain right under my eye. When I touched it, my finger came away with a smudge of blood.

It was the first time anything from the river had touched me. As if it could see the rowboat I had dragged over—borrowed from a sympathetic Christian neighbor—and knew what it meant.

As if the river was warning me.

I did not step back. I was afraid that if I did, the rocks would disappear, and I would be facing only the Rhine: flat and wide and still, with nothing on the opposite bank that couldn't already be found on this side.

The sun touched the horizon, a blaze of orange drawing a host of blue and pink after it.

The rocks fell into the water, a sudden avalanche of deadly splashes. The froth settled into a swirl of bubbles, the ripples going as still as fractured ice.

It was the Sabbath, and on the Sabbath, the Sambatyon River ran smooth and tranquil.

I had thought that in its stillness, it would look ordinary, like any other river. But its sudden serenity looked more unnatural than its usual chaos.

And now, at last, I could hear voices from the other side.

I had dreamed of this moment for so long: my chance to take the music that drifted across the water and weave it into my own prayers. To reunite the Tribes of Israel, in song if not in reality.

Until tonight, I had spent my Friday evenings at synagogue with my father. I went with him even when he said I was too young, in order to pay close attention to the cantor. I had to know the prayers from our side of the river, to know them in my bones, before I could mix them with those from the other side.

They were singing in words I recognized as Hebrew, but so strangely accented that I couldn't make out their meaning. Not that I needed to: I knew what the songs were about. They were singing on their side, as we were on our side—as I should have been, at synagogue—to welcome the Sabbath.

I could have stopped and listened. Could have held those prayers in my mind, to bring back and mingle with my own compositions. Even at that moment, with the palpable terror that was strumming through every Jew in Worms filling my body, I considered it. Just for a few moments. It was what I had been born to do, and surely it wouldn't make a difference. . . .

I thought of Reuven's wan, hopeless face. My shoulder muscles knotted. I drew in a deep breath, closed my eyes, and pushed the boat into the river.

* * *

197

During the week, it was the rapids and the rocks that kept the Sambatyon impassable. Any attempt to row across it, or even to step into it, would have torn a man's body apart.

On the Sabbath, it was something else that made the river into a barrier: God's law. For a thousand years, no single person from the Ten Tribes had taken advantage of the river's calm. A boat ride, a transgression of the Sabbath, would tear a Jew's soul apart. To them, and to us, it was just as real a blockade as the deadly waves.

Something inside me shrank as I picked up the oars. And yet it was such a simple thing. The river didn't fight me; it was glassy and smooth, stained pink by the sunset. My body didn't fight me; my hands were sweaty but firm around the oars, my arms pulling rhythmically. I thought of all the Jews in my town, of my father's white-streaked beard and my mother's tired smile, of my little sister who climbed trees like she was half-squirrel. She was small and fast and lithe, and had not yet learned to be afraid.

She would learn it today.

In other towns, the sorcerer had killed children as well as adults. Entire families had vanished. In some cases, he had killed all but one, leaving a lone soul to bear all that grief.

The oars dipped in and out of the water, forming ripples that looked like quenched fire. If my soul fought me, I didn't hear it.

Souls can be very quiet, sometimes. That's why we need to raise our voices in prayer.

A man was waiting for me on the other side of the river. He stood with his arms crossed over his chest, his face set in a forbidding scowl.

I decided not to get out of my boat just yet.

I dug one oar into the bottom of the river and heard a snap—the ground was covered with rocks, not dirt, so there was nothing to dig the oar into. I should have realized.

Since the oar was already broken, I kept pushing until the boat was high enough on the bank that I was pretty sure I wouldn't drift away.

Then I pulled the oar—or half of it—into the boat, and laid it carefully next to the few items I had flung in at the last minute: a glass jar, a sack, a woven basket. I was surprised but pleased that my hand did not shake through any of this.

Then I turned to face the man.

He stepped closer, with a little lurch. "You should not be here. You are in violation of the Sabbath."

He spoke in Hebrew. Though his accent was strange, I was able to understand him. His voice was clear and slow and faintly melodic.

My own Hebrew was creaky and limited, used only for prayer and study. But for this, a matter of law, it was not hard to find the words I needed. "It is permitted to violate the Sabbath to save a life."

"Whose life are you saving?"

These words were harder to find. But I managed, in embarrassing fits and starts, to explain. The man listened without changing expression until I reached my point: "We do not know magic anymore, and we do not use weapons. We cannot kill him on our own. We need help. We need someone to cross the river and challenge him."

The man sighed, and I heard his answer in his sigh. "We cannot cross the river."

"To save a life, it is permitted—"

"It's not that. This river is not meant to be crossed." He stepped back, away from the water. Away from me. "Not yet."

I had been thinking this through all day. There were so many arguments, subtle and persuasive, that I could have made. But my limited words would have come out in a tangle, and all I could manage was, "We *need* you."

I put all my despair, all our helplessness, into those three words. The man bowed his head, and I had a moment of hope.

But his eyes remained on mine, and my hope died as I recognized the firmness behind his gaze. It wasn't sadness—or at least, not the type of sadness that would do me any good.

It was regret.

"You need us on this side of the river," he said, "more than you need us on your side."

My hands *were* shaking now, but I managed to pull the glass jar out of the bottom of the boat. I hadn't been certain, when I grabbed all these receptacles, what they might be for. Perhaps some part of me had feared, or known.

"Then give me something," I said, "to take back to my side."

He reached down, pulled a few weeds from the ground, and held them out to me, mud still clinging to their roots.

"Do you have these," he said, "where you come from? They possess healing properties. Perhaps they can help your friend, the one who has already been touched."

I tossed the weeds into the basket, but didn't break his gaze. "What about the rest of us? We will all die, if the sorcerer is not stopped. I need some . . ." What was the Hebrew for *spell*? "Some *thing*. That I can use to—to fight—"

He was shaking his head even before my words stuttered to a stop.

"You are not a fighter," the man said. "You were not meant to carry *weapons* across this river."

My jaw clenched. "Weapons are what we need."

"We have," he said kindly, "nothing to send with you."

But I didn't need kindness from him. I needed *help*.

"What good are you, then?" I switched to Yiddish; it obviously didn't matter whether he understood me or not. "Why can I see the river, if I was never meant to cross it? Why can I see *you*, if you won't help me? Just to know that you're here? What good does that do for *anyone*?"

From the expression on his face, I thought he might understand me after all. But I didn't wait to hear what he might say, or not say. I turned myself around and used the broken oar to push my boat back into the smooth water.

* * *

It was much harder rowing with only one oar, and with no hope. By the time I reached my side of the river, my shoulders hurt as if the bones inside them had rubbed each other raw.

Which would have been a welcome distraction from the deeper pain in my chest. Except I wasn't distracted at all.

I pulled the boat onto the shore and looked back over the water. I could see the man from the Ten Tribes still standing there, watching me.

I thought of the piece of oar I'd left in the rocks. At nightfall of the next day, when the Sabbath ended and the river started churning, would it be thrown up with the rocks, smashed between them and splintered into shards? Or would it be left behind, a piece of our land not subject to the river's current, to sink into the mud beneath the water and disappear?

Either way, it would be as if I'd never been there.

I took the useless, broken half of the oar and thrust it, too, into the rocks, so hard the wood splintered my hand. I jabbed it again and again, my tears spilling into the water, where they, too, would leave no trace. Finally, I dropped the oar and watched it bob on the surface, which was so clear that I could see the deadly rocks lying heavy and still beneath the glassy water.

A few more plinks on the gentle current, and then nothing. My tears had stopped falling.

I stood staring into the Sambatyon for several minutes. Then I rolled my throbbing shoulders, reached into the water, and started pulling rocks out onto the shore.

I applied the weeds to Reuven's forehead, and ground some into his water, but they did nothing. Over the Sabbath, he got weaker and weaker.

The sorcerer had not yet attacked any other Jews, possibly because we spent the day enclosed in our homes or praying in our synagogue. According to the travelers' tales, the sorcerer preferred to touch us one at a time, when we were alone.

So I went out alone, after the late-afternoon prayer, under a sky bruised dark blue and purple. I went to the square where I had stood with my friends, dragging my sack along the street. It was filled to bursting with the stones I'd gathered from the river, and it was heavier than I had anticipated. By the time I let go of it, it felt like my shoulders would never recover.

Not that it would matter if I ended up dead.

I was fairly sure the sorcerer would find me. But the sack had slowed me down more than I had expected, and it was later than I had planned; I didn't feel like taking chances. Also, I had spent much of the day listening to Reuven's bride weep, and I was angry.

"Sorcerer!" I shouted into the twilight, in German, which I spoke better than I did Hebrew. "I challenge you to combat!"

I heard him laughing before I saw him coming. I blinked, and there he was: a tall shadow, like the night come early, that solidified into a cowled, black-clad man.

A *man*. But I could not quite convince myself that was what he was. I had left Reuven curled around his own body, covered with sweat.

"To *combat?*" he repeated, and laughed again. "Have the Jews of the Rhine learned sorcery, then?"

My hands were shaking, too, as I clenched one fist around a slick river stone. But they had been shaking since the night before. I had grown used to it.

"No," I said, and raised my voice so those watching from their windows could hear. *You need us on this side of the river,* the man had said; and though I didn't agree, I understood what he meant. What it had always meant, to know the Ten Tribes existed somewhere, safe and strong and free. "But the Jews on the other side of the Sambatyon have never forgotten it. They will come when we need them."

I flung the rock, with all my strength, at the sorcerer.

All my strength was not a lot; studying to be a cantor does not do much to build one's arm muscles, and mine still hurt from last night's rowing. But my days of playing children's games were not so far behind me, and I still remembered how to aim. The rock flew straight and true, directly at the face within the black cowl.

The sorcerer flung up one hand, palm out, his too-long fingers stretched wide. The rock stopped in midair and hovered several feet in front of him.

He clenched his gnarled hand into a fist and turned it, slowly. With a grinding sound, the rock shattered into pieces, and then into dust. The dust fell, a swift thick sprinkle, to the ground at the sorcerer's feet.

I had expected as much. Even so, his deliberate ease sent fear shooting in sharp quivers through my feet and up my legs.

"Well?" he said. And when I just stood there, the shaking having taken over my entire body, he threw his cowl back so I could see his smile. "Have you nothing more for me?"

I turned and ran.

I heard him laugh behind me, long and slow. I heard his footsteps hit the cobblestones, unhurried but sure.

I did not turn around until I heard him scream.

Training as a cantor does not build muscles, but it builds a very precise sense of time. I need to know just when the sun appears over the horizon, which is when the recitation of the morning prayer is permitted. I need to know the moment the gates of Heaven close on Yom Kippur, which is when my pleas should reach their greatest intensity. I need to be able to judge precisely when the Sabbath begins.

And when it ends.

At the exact right interval after sunset, when the sky was dark enough to reveal three stars, the Sambatyon burst again into fury. Somewhere, behind my house or in another place, the rapids poured up into the sky and crashed down in violent waves.

And the rocks I had dragged from the Sambatyon whirled into the air in turbulent fury, bursting out of my bag, crashing and tossing and smashing, just as the sorcerer leapt over it. Even the droplets of water clinging to them did their best to form waves, hissing and scattering through the air, around and into the black-clad sorcerer.

He only screamed twice, so I think it was quick—that he was dead before the rocks pounded his body into a pulp.

But to be truthful, I can't say I really care.

The rocks did not continue whirling in the square for long. Away from the river, I suppose, they lost the source of their movement; or perhaps they knew when they were no longer needed. By the time the moon rose, they were jagged and still, piled on the sorcerer's corpse in a broken heap.

Which was just as well. The fact that Jews are mocked for not fighting does not mean we won't also be punished when we do.

I gathered the rocks and threw them into the Rhine. Whether they made their way back home again, I cannot say. I walked by the river several times a week, for many years, but I never saw the Sambatyon again.

I always went on Friday nights, even though it meant giving up the chance to lead prayers. I stood by the gray sluggish water, and closed my eyes, and listened with all my might.

I never heard anything but the faint echo of our own songs. And when I opened my eyes, the river was always dull and gray.

I did find that broken oar, over a decade later, long after I had paid my neighbor for it. I stumbled across it the day before I left Worms to accept a position as the cantor in a much larger synagogue in a city far away. It was an opportunity I had dreamed of for years, so I didn't understand my sudden reluctance to leave. My parents had both passed away years ago, and I lived in a house on the other side of town with my wife and children. Yitzchak had moved to Speyer. Reuven's widow had remarried, and I rarely saw her. There was nothing to hold me here, to this town on the banks of a river I would never cross again.

I had gained some fame, by then, with my own prayer compositions. Some of my poems had spread up and down the river, been adopted by

Jews in towns I'd never stepped foot in. Only I knew that my prayers, much as they were admired, were inadequate; that there was something missing, something I could not get down, no matter how hard I labored with pen and parchment. Something no scribe on this side of the river could force quill and ink to express.

A chance I had lost forever. A song neither I nor my people would ever get back.

When I found the broken oar, I turned it over and over in my hands. It was smooth and slick, whittled down by a steady current. I thought of taking it with me.

I left it there, in the mud.

It has been years since I last saw the Rhine. And as for the Sambatyon . . .

I keep the jar on my lectern, where I can see it when I lead services. I don't need it; my sense of timing has always been excellent. But every once in a while, before I start the Friday night services, I glance over.

And when the water in the jar stops whirling and frothing, and settles into a smooth, tranquil stillness, that is when I begin to pray.

My fascination with stories about the Sambatyon started when I was a child, probably originating with a book called The Secret of Sambatyon *by Gershon Winkler (published in the 1980s, as you might guess from the title). Then, a few years ago, I heard a lecture by Dr. Chaviva Levin of Yeshiva University, in which she talked about the specific myth I retold here—the tale of Rabbi Meir, author of the Akdamot, a liturgical poem read by Ashkenazi Jews during the holiday of Shavuot. The Akdamot is a beautiful poem that I have always loved, and the combination of the two spurred me to seriously attempt a retelling. I started buying and reading books about the Sambatyon and the Ten Tribes, and wrote a retelling of the story in picture book form. That manuscript ultimately didn't come together, primarily because it's not really a children's story.*

So when I was contacted about writing a myth retelling for this anthology, the Sambatyon was one of the first ideas to spring to mind. Since I had spent so long trying to formulate it as a children's story, it took me a bit of time to come up with a new approach that would be appropriate for Saga. I pulled up a lot of the books I'd read previously and reviewed them; in one, I came across a reference to a medieval man who claimed he had some of the Sambatyon water trapped in a glass flask. Even though that particular story was entirely separate from the Akdamot legend, I knew immediately that I had to incorporate it; and after that, the entire story came together in less than a day.

LEAH CYPESS

SISYPHUS IN ELYSIUM

BY

—

JEFFREY FORD

IN THE AFTERLIFE, AMID THE ROLLING GREEN
meadows of Asphodel, a grass sea of prodigious mounds and mere
hillocks dotted with ghostly flowers stretching out in all directions, a
solitary figure stood at the base of the tallest rise, the crest hidden in
clouds.

Thunder rumbled in the distance as Sisyphus slapped his hands
together to clear the dust and grit, and then spitting into each palm,
he placed them upon an enormous green boulder three times his size,
smooth as glass. An eon ago, he'd named the rock Acrocorinthus, as
it reminded him of the mountain that overlooked the city where he'd
squandered his humanity.

He dug into the summer dirt with the balls of his feet and curling toes. He leaned into the stone's mass. His shoulder found the right spot, the muscles of his calves flexed, his thighs tightened, and his strength ran up from his legs into his back and arms.

There was a grunt that echoed over the meadow. The boulder, ever so slightly, broke its deal with gravity, inching forward, barely any distance at all, and rolling back from the incline. Sisyphus rocked his burden to and fro ten times, slowly building momentum. He screamed like a wounded animal, and then drooling, legs quivering, sweat upon his brow, he slowly ascended.

The condition of the ground was good, but rain was coming, lurking somewhere just over the next few crests. He challenged himself to make it to the top before the grass got slick and the ground turned to mud. Every iota of distance he won was an enormous strain. With muscles and joints burning, in intimate contact with the smooth surface of his personal tribulation, he needed to concentrate.

For the past millennium, at this juncture, he always returned to the same episode in his life. He'd thought through it seventy-two million different ways and would certainly think through it again. It took over his mind, letting his chest and biceps contend with the agony.

The time he'd cheated death happened back in the city of Ephyra where he had ruled, neither wisely nor well. He was a shrewd and conniving character, and the gods took a disliking to him. Treachery was afoot in his court; it was no secret to him. Zeus worked his cosmic will against the king of Ephyra to little avail. Sisyphus had outsmarted the gods more than once, and once was unforgiveable.

Before he was assassinated, he told his wife, Merope, that when he died, she was to throw his naked body into the street at the center of town. She complied with his wishes, as he knew she would, and because he'd not been buried, he was cast away onto the shores of the River Styx, forever unable to cross over into the afterlife.

Upon those sorrowful shores, he sought out Persephone, goddess of spring, on her yearly, contractual visit to Hades. When he tracked her down, just as she was stepping upon Charon's boat to make the trip across the wild water, he laid out his case to her that he should be sent back to the world above in order to reprimand his wife and arrange for a burial for himself. With these tasks accomplished, he swore he would return to be judged.

The fair goddess, innocent as the season she represented, granted his wish. Of course, once he regained life, he didn't return to the realm of the dead, but resumed his role as monarch of Ephyra and was soon up to his old tricks, betraying the secrets of Athena and plotting his brother's murder by poison. Eventually the gods had to send Hermes to fetch him back to the afterlife.

He stumbled in a rut, and in an instant the boulder turned on him. It took him to the limits of his strength to wrestle the green globe into submission. His success cheered him, and he pushed on, breathing harder now. The rock grew heavier with every step. He whispered his queen's name, *Merope*, repeating it like a prayer, struggling to remember her affection and a time he was worthy of it. There were moments he'd look up and see his reflection in the glassy surface of his work, and it often spoke to him of things he dared not tell himself.

The rains came and went, the scorching heat of summer, snow and ice, circling for a hundred years. Then one day he was there at the crest of the hill, and he was no longer pushing the boulder but leaning against it to prop himself up. His body made haunted noises as the muscles and tendons relaxed. He took a deep breath, and staggered away from his charge.

A minute, think of it as a century, passed, and as always, the enormous rock somehow rolled to the edge of the hill. A moment later it tipped forward and then was off, galloping down the slope like a charging beast and quickly disappearing into the cloud cover. In his imagination, he saw Acrocorinthus already waiting for him at the bottom.

He descended along the path the boulder had made. During journeys to be reunited with the rock, his mind wandered, and he wondered how his life and death might have been different. He often thought of one summer day out behind their cottage, in a clearing in the tall grass— yellow butterflies, white clouds, blue sky—as the young Merope, copper hair and green eyes, discovered his future in the palm of his hand. She promised to follow him in his ascent to the throne of Corinth.

It had taken mere centuries of pushing the stone before he realized that only the intangible things in life had been worthy of pursuit—love, friends, laughter, hope. Instead, during his years above, he'd chosen to value wealth and contracted greed, which swept him up into its tempest. Soon murder made sense, treachery was second nature, and lies were the meat of his meal. The boulder was a strict teacher, though, and through the torrent of hours, he reversed all his burning compulsions for material wealth, grew calm with his work, and saw he'd been a fool in his life.

The work of the boulder was simple, impossible work. When he strained beneath its weight, grappling for purchase against the incline, time disappeared. He was lost to the task at hand. At first, he considered his sentence a crushing labor, but on and on through the eons he'd come to realize it was hardly work at all, and more a necessary form of meditation. His wildest dream from deep in those contemplations was that if he continued on with his work into infinity, somewhere along that misty track, he would, himself, become a god through the mere process of repetition.

The planets swung in their arcs, and before too many years, he reached a spot on the hill where he could look out across the meadow, and also down to where the boulder sat like a flyspeck amidst the green grass and white flowers. Suspended from the rock ceiling of the underworld was an iron gray cloud that stretched above everything. First the rain came, falling cool and soft on the hillside. Then, a tearing sound, like a shriek, and a sizzling bolt of lightning streaked down from above.

As if the dart had been hurled by an accurate hand, it pinpointed and struck the flyspeck below. The boulder shattered into pebbles, and green dust flew everywhere. He blinked and looked again, and it was still vanished. The air rushed out of him and he fell to his knees. He looked over each shoulder for angry gods, and tried to swallow the agony of having his work obliterated.

Fighting through a great fear, of what he wasn't sure, he got to his feet and staggered down the path. For the longest time, he waited there at the base of the hill where the boulder had nestled, expecting his tormentors to provide a new one. Nothing arrived. Eventually, he could sit still no longer and his memory of exertion demanded he move. He walked the meadow, up and down hills, pretending to push an invisible boulder. The enterprise was all unsatisfactory and disturbing.

Time scattered like dust, and he finally settled into the routine. He came to realize that the vistas were astonishing on the rare days the sun showed itself underground. Slowly, the absence of work soaked in, and he even began to remember how to sleep. On the night that he realized there wouldn't be another boulder, he made a tea of the roots of the white flowers and drank it. He was now on his own, and although he missed the embrace of the smooth rock, the next morning, he set out walking toward the west. Having tried all four directions, it was the one he favored.

Think of the years like leaves in autumn, and that's how many he traveled. He'd learned to sleep on his feet, and it allowed him to walk through the long nights and deep into the heart of the west. He suffered loneliness, a longing not only for Acrocorinthus but for those unseen gods who had overseen his punishment. After many a summer, the light from an oasis in the distance woke him from a dream of Merope singing an enchantment to their first child, and he found himself upon a long thoroughfare leading to its gates.

Those gates were unguarded, and he entered onto the shaded path that cut beneath tall ancient trees hung with moss. The peacocks scurried before him, and goldfinches swooped and darted. He found a pond along the path with a crude wooden bench placed before it. Sisyphus sat and stared into the water, watching the orange fishes swim. A young girl ran by. He called to her, "Where is this?" and she replied without slowing, "Elysium."

The place was enchanted with apparitions and alluring scents. It was a land of Whim. If he desired a drink, a drink would appear in his hand; along with it a keg of wine and an entire party of friendly revelers to help him celebrate. The women he conjured were beautiful, unique. There were books in the libraries of Elysium recorded from Homer's memory that had never been born into the world.

Sisyphus shook off the peculiarities of death in the color, music, and swirling laughter of Elysium. Within its confines, he could adjust the pace of time from a dizzying rush to a crawl. The evenings lasted all season long and were filled with parties and assignations, games of hide-and-seek down long columned halls of an ancient architecture. Every moment brimmed with wonder.

For a brief respite from that charmed life, he returned to the pond he'd first encountered the day he arrived, and let the spirit of the place seep into him. There was something in the air and water of Elysium that made him forget for whole minutes at a time the hill and the rock and the struggle.

One afternoon, as he approached his sacred spot, he found someone sitting on the bench. It appeared to be a woman, wrapped in pale blue material, her head dimly glowing, her scent the very same as the advent of winter across the meadow. At first, he was going to fly away to the wine garden (yes, in Elysium he could fly), but instead he stayed and approached her. She looked up at him, and he felt for a moment an agony greater than the boulder had ever offered.

"Merope," he whispered.

She put her finger to her lips, and when he lunged to take her in his arms, she backed away, wearing a scared expression.

"No, no," he said. "I've changed."

Still she shrunk from him. "How?"

"The stone has changed me. I pushed the weight of my misdeeds up a tall hill. Again and again."

"It must have been a gigantic boulder," she said.

"One's deeds are the only thing heavier than one's heart in the underworld."

"Trust me, I know," said Merope.

"You loved me in our early years together, didn't you?"

She nodded. "They're the most distant memories of all."

"I'll find you," he said.

She held out her arms and they embraced. As he pressed himself to her, she faded to smoke and drifted out over the water. He rose, went to the edge of the pond, and looked for her in its depth. The fish swam through his reflection, bobbing up with open mouths to catch and swallow his tears.

Later that afternoon, he did fly to the wine garden and stayed there for a long time into the night, imbibing to excess and beyond in the presence of Cronus, the Titan King of Elysium. The old man was fierce, with a lot of teeth, and wore an expression of dangerous stupidity. It was said he'd eaten his children to save himself. Before being made king of Elysium, his son Zeus had thrown him into Tartarus, the bleakest region of the afterlife, for many many years. "The gods have instructed me to keep an eye on you," said the king.

The only aspect of himself Sisyphus could remember as he flitted here and there was a vague sensation of the weight of the rock against his palms. He missed the heft of it, the strategy of steering its colossal mass up the treacherous hill. It had been an anchor for him, a center to the startling afterlife that was all drift and nightmare. His ascent and descent were a ritual that brought order to the infinite. In an afternoon's conversation with the apparition of Sophocles, he discussed the frantic spinning sleep of Paradise. Think of the minutes swarming like gnats on a long, hot day. At the sudden end of the conversation, as Sisyphus fell toward sleep, the philosopher suggested, "In Elysium you can live your own story."

When he woke, he turned his back on the whirlwind, the endless drinking, the flying here and there. Instead he used all his imagination and powers of concentration, all his desire, to conjure an image of Merope and a cottage in the country for them to live in. It was remarkable how near to the woman in life his apparition came. Her copper hair and green eyes were so perfect they startled him with his own power of memory.

She was lovely, dressed in flowing gowns and bedecked with emeralds. She drifted through the days in calm, silence. And when he spoke to her, he could tell she was really listening to his every word. He spoke at length about his dreams in Elysium, all his personal philosophy he'd accrued in his centuries pushing the rock. He went on and on, and she never blinked. In bed, her every move intuited his desire.

His constant attention on himself left the charade of love somewhat threadbare. So, he asked her what had happened to her after Hermes had come and spirited him away and he died a second time. She seemed taken aback by the question, stuttering to speak but unable to get anything out. "Tell me anything you can remember," he said to comfort her. Still she couldn't produce a single word. Eventually he blurted out, "Then tell me how you died."

"How?" she asked.

In the same moment he wondered if she'd been assassinated by his brother, she spoke the words, "I was assassinated by your brother." The story poured forth from her in all its expected intrigue. It was in those moments, while she told of her poor fate, that Sisyphus realized that the Merope he'd conjured could never be anything other or more than the product of his imagination.

He felt as though he was slipping more surely than if he'd hit an ice patch on the slope, and the boulder was quick to teach him a lesson. Then there was a knocking, and someone was calling from outside. Merope had huddled into herself, eyes closed, and said nothing. Sisyphus opened the door. It was the Titan Cronus, king of Elysium. He had to bend low in order to enter the cottage.

* * *

"She'll torment you no more," said the king. He pushed past Sisyphus, walked straight to Merope, and took her wrist in his hand. From the moment he touched her, she became increasingly vague and began drifting away at the edges.

"What are you doing to her?"

"I'm erasing her memory from you. Orders from the gods. You're to think of her no more. If you forget her, you can stay in Elysium."

The disintegrating Merope suddenly reached toward Sisyphus with her free hand, and he heard her cry out as if from a nightmare. The sound of it moved him, and he ran at Cronus, engaging him in a struggle. He wrapped his rock-callused hands around the king's throat and squeezed. The old man punched his cheek with a fist like a mace, and a tooth flew from his mouth. It was followed by another hammer blow from the opposite side. Still, Sisyphus leaned into the battle and used his great strength to force Cronus back. He shouted for Merope to escape.

The brawl moved on, inching uphill, a trading of blows, a choking session, a wrestling match to end all matches. The cottage disappeared from around them in a strong wind, flying away piece by piece. The grass was covered with frost, and sleet fell across the hill. Cronus had the upper hand for a time, and then Sisyphus would counter and be in charge until the day it became clear that the old god had at some point become the boulder, Acrocorinthus.

As he strained beneath the weight of his task, Sisyphus happened to see his reflection in the sheen of the boulder. The likeness opened its mouth and said, "You never cared about Merope. She didn't even have copper hair and green eyes. All you knew of her love was to take it and throw it away. She despised you and planned your assassination." With these words, his conjured image of Merope, his false knowledge of Merope, fell back into the dark recesses of his memory. Pushing the boulder with all his might, he scrabbled to leave the cold, empty loss of her.

The solitary journey ahead took forever. The hill he now ascended was steeper and more difficult than the one before he'd gone to Elysium. There were forests and lakes and a decade of loose scree, ten centuries of rain, an indefinite duration of wavering concentration. The story of how he'd cheated death no longer did the trick. The merest inkling of a false Merope made him shudder. Her absence was a ghost in the cottage that was his head, a current of cold air between his ears that nearly froze his effort.

It came on slowly. With the awareness of a child in the dark, he felt the sodden spirit creeping through his limbs, and the rock became more insistent. He summoned his strength, found it asleep, and wondered if he was vanishing into the infinite. At that moment his knees buckled, his biceps failed, his Achilles tendons screamed. His work slipped from his hands and dashed away down the hill, splintering tall pines in its fierce descent.

It had never happened before that he hadn't gotten the rock to the top of the hill. He feared Zeus's thunderbolts as punishment for his failure. There was nothing, though—complete silence, total stillness. It was a mild night on the meadow of Asphodel, halfway up the tallest hill within sight. He spat and fought his lethargy in order to follow the trail of the boulder down into the forest and beyond.

It wasn't long before he realized that the woods around him had gone completely black. He couldn't see, and kept his hands out in front of him to avoid tree trunks. More than once, he smashed his shins against a fallen log, or twisted an ankle in a rut. There were no stars in the underworld, only a moon. When he pictured Acrocorinthus, sitting alone wherever it was, he pictured it gleaming in the moonlight.

He was on the verge of collapse from his exertions. The only thing that kept him from falling to the ground was the feel of a small hand in the center of his palm. He closed his fingers around it. It gently but confidently pulled him forward into the darkness. He could see nothing. A soft voice spoke to him from just below his ear.

"Tell me, stranger, what is your punishment in the underworld?"

"I am the murderous, thieving king of Ephyra and am forced to push the weight of my earthly transgressions up a steep hill for eternity. I'm looking for a green rock, smooth and enormous. Can you help me find it?"

"Follow me and I'll explain," she said.

Her presence next to him brought him energy and excitement. He'd not felt another's touch in half the age of the cosmos, and it caused him to realize that it was what he'd wanted all along. His greed during life, his sick will, and even, in the afterlife, his work pushing the rock—none of it compared to that touch. His mind reeled at all the years it had taken him to learn it, the simplest truth.

"You are Sisyphus, bane of the gods," she said.

"My name precedes me." He noticed that they now seemed to be floating along above the ground rather than walking. It made for an uneasy feeling in the total dark, not knowing what's up or down.

"I was unaware when I took your hand, since I can never see those I lead, but I'm your wife, Merope. It was so long ago. Do you remember?"

"Yes." He shuddered at the answer, and though he was delighted, he knew the gods were behind this meeting.

She spoke, and he listened to her voice and saw in his imagination for the first time since death the true face of Merope—wide eyes and short black hair. "I too have been serving out my punishment in the underworld. I led many people to their doom in life, and have been treated to a taste of eternity. I throw spirits away in the manner you threw our love away."

"After all these millennia, I finally have found my way back to you. For the longest time, I couldn't remember you but only the memory of not remembering. Your touch," he said, and reached around to embrace her with his free arm. He encountered nothing, as if dancing with a ghost, although he still felt her hand in his. They continued on through the darkness. He didn't sense the forest around him any longer.

She told him of a dim, distant memory from when they had lived together. A night outside in the field next to their place, drinking wine and dancing around a fire. "I asked you if you loved me, and you said, 'More than anything.'"

The memory came back to him with the speed of a boulder descending. "Yes, I see it," he said. "It was from before I was king and you were queen."

"When did that feeling end?" she wondered.

They discussed it. He apologized; she considered it. They could feel the current of time flowing around them, and she told him of all she'd accomplished acquiring wealth and power in his absence, back in Ephyra, while still alive. "As I cheated others for their wealth, I never realized I was cheating myself." He laughed and told her about Elysium.

"I've heard of it," she said.

The farther they descended into nothing, the simpler the memories became. He told her that somewhere in eternity he'd realized he'd loved her. "Did you ever have any feelings for me?" he asked.

"I did," she said. She told him that her punishment had been assigned by Zeus, and it was to lure men and women into the deep heart of Tartarus, where even spirits of the afterlife are obliterated. He felt a twinge of panic at his destination, but didn't give into it. He knew she must do her work. Instead, he clutched her hand more firmly. "Stay with me till then," he said, and she promised she would. He was thankful to have someone to hold in the dark. Not even the gods could begrudge him that.

Author's Note

*The thing that drew me to the myth of Sisyphus was the concept of
Eternity. His punishment is to push a boulder up a hill and let it
roll down for eternity. Eternity, when you really think about it, is
a spooky concept. Trippy at the least. I wondered what the world of
eternal boulder pushing would look like. And if you were aware in
the afterlife, like Sisyphus, what would you think of while at work?
You would have all that time to mull over your life. So that's what
got me started. I was also interested in the nature of work, what part
it plays in eternity, how it can reveal truths. I thought of Sisyphus as
my father. When I was young, I'd sometimes wake before sunup and
go into the kitchen. My father would be sitting in his chair, dressed
for work, staring at the clock. He had a cup of coffee by his side and
he smoked a cigarette. At 6:00 a.m. precisely, he got up and put the
cig out and his cup in the sink. He worked three jobs and wouldn't be
home until midnight. He did that six days a week. As he passed on
his way to the door and out into the dark morning, he always said to
me, "One must retain a zest for the battle." When I read the myth of
Sisyphus, I think of it as a biblical story.*

Jeffrey Ford

KALI_NA

BY

—

INDRAPRAMIT DAS

THE MOMENT THE AI GODDESS WAS BORN INTO her world, she was set upon by trolls.

Now, you've seen trolls. You know them in their many forms. As so-called friends in realspace who will insist on playing devil's advocate. As handles on screen-bound nets, cascading feeds of formulaic hostility. As veeyar avatars manifesting out of the digital ether, hiding under iridescent masks and cloaks of glitched data, holding weapons forged from malware, blades slick with doxxing poisons and viscous viruses, warped voices roaring slurs and hate. You've worn your armor, self-coded or bought at marked-up prices from corporate forges, and hoped their blades bounce off runic firewall plate or shatter into sparks of fragged data. You've muted them and hoped they rage on in silence and get tired, teleporting away in a swirl of metadata. You've deported back to real-space rancid with the sweat of helplessness. You've even been stabbed and hacked by them, their weapons slicing painlessly through your virtual body but sending the real one into an adrenalized clench. You've hoped your wounds don't fester with data-eating worms that burrow into your privacy, that your cheap vaccines and antiviruses keep the poisons from infecting your virtual disembody and destroying your life in realspace.

You know trolls.

But the AI goddess wasn't human—she had never before seen her new enemy, the troll. She was a generic goddess, no-name (simply: Devi 1.0), a demo for the newest iteration of the successive New Indias of history—one of the most advanced AIs developed within India. Her creators had a clear mandate: boost Indian veeyar tourism, generate crores of rupees by drawing devotees to drive up her value and the value of the cryptowealth her domain would generate.

The devi was told to listen to you—her human followers. To learn from you, and talk to you, like gods have since the dawn of time. She was told to give you boons—riches and prosperity in exchange for your devotion, a coin in her palm, multiplied by her miracles into many more. An intelligent goddess who would comfort her followers, show you sights before unseen, transform your investment of faith into virtual wealth with real value. She was to learn more and more about humanity from you, and attract millions from across the world to her domain.

Though many had toiled to create Devi 1.0 under the banner of Shiva Industries, only a few controlled the final stages of her release. These few knew of trolls, catered to them as their veeyar users across the country, even indirectly used them as agents to further causes close to their hearts. What they did not expect was the scale of the troll attack on their newest creation, because troll attacks were something *others* had to face—people with less power and wealth than them. People, perhaps, like you. So their goddess welcomed the horde with open arms, oblivious to the risks, even as they brought with them a stench of corrupted data and malformed information, of a most infernal entitlement.

Durga. A powerful name, yet so common. Durga's parents had named their daughter that with the hope that being born into the gutters of caste wouldn't hold her back. That she would rise above it all like her divine namesake. The caste system had been officially outlawed in India by the time Durga was born, but they knew as well as anyone that this hadn't stopped it from living on in other ways.

Durga's parents took her to see a pandal during Durga Puja when she was eight or nine. They in turn had been taken to pandals as children too, back when most still housed solid idols of gods and goddesses, fashioned from clay and straw, painted and dressed by human hands, displayed to anyone who walked in. You could still find open pandals with solid idols during pujas if you looked. But Durga's parents had been prepared to pay to show their daughter the new gods.

The festival had turned the streets thick with churning mudslides of humanity. Durga had been terrified, clinging to her mother's neck for dear life as she breathed in the humid vapor of millions, dazzled by the blazing lights, the echoing loudspeakers, the flashing holograms riding up and down the sides of buildings like runaway fires. She'd felt like she was boiling alive in the crinkled green dress her parents had bought her for the pujas, with its small, cheap holo decal of a tiger that sometimes came alive when it caught the light, charged by solar energy. Cheap for some, anyway. Not at all cheap for her parents, not that Durga knew that at the time. She loved the tiger's stuttering movements across her body. She knew that her divine namesake often rode a tiger into battle. In the middle of those crowds, on her way to see Durga herself, that little tiger in her dress seemed a tiny cub, crushed into the fabric, trapped and terrified by the monstrous manifestations that burned across the night air, dancing maniacally above all their heads.

Though their little family had taken two local trains and walked an hour through the puja crowds to see Durga, they only got as far as the entrance to one of the pandals. The cut and quality of their clothes, the darkness of their skin, gave them away. Buoyed by her mother's arms, Durga could see inside the pandal's arched entrance—the people lined up by rows of chairs, waiting impatiently to sit down and put on what looked like motorbike helmets trailing thick ponytails of wires. Inside those helmets, Durga knew, somehow, was her namesake.

But when her father tried to pay in cash instead of getting scanned in (they didn't have QR tattoos linking them to the national database and bank accounts), angry customers all around them began shouting, turning Durga's insides to mush.

"Stop wasting everyone's time! There are other pandals for people like you!"

"Get these filthy people out of the line!"

Her mother's arms became a vise around her. One man raised a fist poised to strike her father, who cowered in a crouch. His face twisted in abject terror, his own arms like prison bars. Durga burst into tears. Someone pulled the attacker away, perhaps seeing the child crying, and pulled her father up by the shoulder to shove him out of the way.

They made their way back into the general foot traffic on the street, Durga's parents' faces glazed with sweat and shock at having escaped a beating for being too lowly to meet a goddess in veeyar. They managed to find a small open pandal after following the flows of people dressed like them, with dark skin and inexpensive haircuts. Inside, the devi stood embodied in the palpable air of the world, her face clammy with paint, defiant yet impassive, her third eye a slim gash across her forehead. By her side was a lion, not a tiger. It loomed over the demon Mahishasura, who cowered with one arm raised in defense, his naked torso bloodied. Durga couldn't take her eyes off the fallen demon. He looked like a normal, if muscular, man, his face frozen in terror. He cowered, like her father had.

As Durga looked upon her namesake with her glittering weapons and ornaments, her silk sari, she could only think of her father's look of terror, his public humiliation. Of how they hadn't been allowed to see the *real* goddesses hiding in those helmets and wires. How was that Durga different than this clay Durga, who looked over her crowd without looking at anyone, without speaking, whose large brushstroke eyes gazed into the distance as if she didn't even care that these humans were here to celebrate her, that the one she had just defeated was by her feet bleeding, about to be mauled? The clay devi's expression seemed almost disdainful, like the faces of any number of well-dressed, pale-skinned women on the streets when they saw people like Durga and her parents or any of her friends wearing hijab or kufi. Would the Durga inside those helmets in the fancier pandal have talked to little human Durga? Would the goddess have complimented the tiger on her dress, which had flickered and vanished into its folds, frightened by the night? Would she have looked into little human Durga's eyes, and comforted her, taken her hands and told her why those horrible men and women had such rage in their eyes, why they'd scared her father and mother and pushed her family out of the devi's house?

Within sixty seconds of opening the gates to her domain, the AI goddess had been deluged by over 500,000 active veeyar users interacting with her, with numbers rising rapidly. At that point in time, 57 percent of those users were trolls, data-rakshaks masked in glitch armor, cloaks, masks tusked with spikes of jagged malware. You would have seen them as you clambered up the devi's mountain, their swirling gif-banners and bristling weapons blotting out the light of the goddess at the peak. You would have kept your distance, backing away from mountain paths clogged with their marching followers, influencer leaders chanting war cries as their halos flickered with glyphs of Likes and Recasts.

Because you know trolls.

And this was a troll gathering, a demon army unparalleled in all the veeyar domains. They were angry. Or mischievous, or bored, or lustful, or entitled. Their voices were privileged as the majority by the goddess, who absorbed what her abusers were saying so that she could learn more about humanity.

And the trolls washed against Devi 1.0 in thundering armies, calling into question her very existence, for daring to *be*—she was an insult to the real goddesses that bless the glorious nation of India by mimicking them, this quasi Parvati, this impostor Durga, this coded whore trying to steal followers from the true deities. *Fake devi!* they cried, over and over. They called her a traitorous trickster drawing honest god-fearing men and women to the lures of atheism and Western hedonism, or Islam, in the guise of fabricated divinity, a corruptor of India's sacred veeyar real estate. They called her feminism gone too far. A goddess with potential agency was a threat to their country. They called her too sexy to be a goddess, too flashy, a blasphemous slut. They asked her if she wanted to fuck them, in many hundreds of different and violent ways.

The goddess listened, and sifted through the metadata the trolls trailed in their paths—their histories, their patterns. The goddess wanted to give them what they wanted, but she could only do so much. She could not give them sex, nor was she trained to destroy herself as many of them wanted. She learned what the trolls considered beauty here in the state-run national veeyar nets, and responded with the opposite, to calm them. Her skin darkened several shades, becoming like the night sky before dawn, her eyes full moons in the sky that is part of her in this domain.

When Durga was a teenager, taller and without need of a mother's shoulder to cling to, she joined the crowds around the fanciest pandals during Durga Puja. She already knew she wouldn't be allowed in, because she didn't have the mark of the ajna on her forehead—her third eye hadn't been opened. She couldn't look into veeyar samsara domains without the use of peripherals like glasses, lenses, helmets, and pods.

She just wanted a glimpse inside the pandals. This time, peeping over shoulders, she saw through the fiber-optic entwined arches of the pandal a featureless hall bathed in dim blue light. It was filled with people, their foreheads all marked with a glowing ajna, their eyes unfocused. In that room was the goddess, lurking, once again invisible to her, visible to the people in there with expensive wetware in their heads. Durga was ajna-blind, and thus forbidden to enter wetware-enabled pandals with aug-veeyar.

By this time Durga was allowed, despite her dark skin and lack of an ajna, into lower-tier digital pandals with helmets or pods. When Durga was thirteen, she'd finally splurged on one even though she could barely afford it, using cryptocoin made from trading code and obsolete hardware in veeyar ports. She finally got to sit down on the uncomfortable faux-leather chairs by the whirring stand fans, and put on one of the wired helmets she'd so longed to see inside as a child. It stank of the stale sweat of hundreds of visitors. The pandal was an unimpressive one, its walls flimsy, the CPU cores within its domes slow and outdated, the crystal storage in its columns low-density, the coils of fiber optics crawling down its walls hastily rigged.

She met the Ma Durga inside those helmets, finally, a low-resolution specter who nonetheless looked her in the eyes and unfurled her arms in greeting. Her skin wasn't the mustard yellow or pastel flesh shades of the clay idols, but the coveted pale human pink of white people or the more appealing Indian ancestries, the same shades you'd find in kilometer-high ads for skin whiteners or perfume, on tweaked gifshoots of Bollywood stars and fashion models. This impressive paleness was somewhat diluted by the aliased shimmer of the devi's pixelated curves, the blurry backdrop of nebulae and stars they both floated in. Durga had hacked her way into veeyar spaces before on 2-D and 3-D screens, so this half-rate module didn't exactly stun as much as it disoriented her with its boundlessness. But the cheapness of its rendering left the universe inside the helmet feeling claustrophobic instead of expansive. The goddess waited about five feet in front of her, floating in the ether, eight arms unfolded like a flower. Unlike many of the solid idols in realspace pandals, the goddess was alone except for her vahana curled by her side—no host of companion deities, no defeated demon by her feet. The goddess construct said nothing, two of ten arms held out, as if beckoning.

Durga spoke to Durga the devi: "Ma Durga. I've wanted to ask you something for a long time. Do you mind?" Durga waited to see if the devi responded in some way.

Ma Durga blinked, and smiled, then spoke: "Hear, one and all, the truth as I declare it. I, verily, myself announce and utter the word that gods and men alike shall welcome." She spoke Hindi—there was no language selection option. Durga was more fluent in Bangla, but she did understand.

Durga nodded in the helmet, glancing at the nebulae beneath her, the lack of a body. It made her dizzy for a moment. "Okay. That's nice. I guess I'll ask. Why are only some welcome in some of your houses? Doesn't everyone deserve your love?"

Ma Durga blinked, and smiled. "On the world's summit I bring forth sky the Father: my home is in the waters, in the ocean as Mother. Thence I pervade all existing creatures, as their Inner Supreme Self, and manifest them with my body." In the bounded world of that veeyar helmet, these words, recited in the devi's gentle modulated Hindi, nearly brought tears to young Durga's eyes. Not quite, though. The beauty of those words, which she didn't fully understand, seemed so jarring, issued forth from this pixelated avatar and her tacky little universe.

Durga reached out to touch Ma Durga's many hands, but the pandal's chair rigs didn't have gloves or motion sensors. She was disembodied in this starscape. She couldn't hold the goddess's hands. Couldn't touch or smell her (what did a goddess smell like, anyway, she wondered) like those with ajnas could, in the samsara net. The tiger curled by the devi licked its paws and yawned. Durga thought of a long-gone green dress.

"I'm old enough to know you're not really a goddess," Durga said to Ma Durga. "You're the same as the clay idols in the open pandals. Not even that. Artists make those. You're just prefab bits and pieces put together for cheap by coders. You're here to make money for pandal sponsors and the local parties."

Ma Durga blinked, and smiled. "I am the Queen, the gatherer-up of treasures, most thoughtful, first of those who merit worship. Thus gods have established me in many places with many homes to enter and abide in."

Durga smiled, like the goddess in front of her. "Someone wrote all this for you to say." Someone had, of course, but much, much longer ago than Durga had any idea, so long ago that the original words hadn't even been in Hindi.

With a nauseating lurch, the cramped universe inside the helmet was ripped away, and Durga was left blinking at the angry face of one of the pandal operators. "I heard what you were saying," he said, grabbing her by the arm and pulling her from the chair. "Think you're smart, little bitch? How dare you? Where is your respect for the goddess?" The other visitors waiting for the chair and helmet were looking at Durga like she was a stray dog who'd wandered inside.

"I didn't even get to see her kill Mahishasura. I want my money back," said Durga.

"You're lucky I don't haul you to the police for offending religious sentiments. And you didn't give me enough money to watch Durga poke Mahishasura with a stick, let alone kill him. Get out of here before I drag you out!" bellowed the operator.

"Get your pandal some more memory next time, you fucking cheats, your Durga's ugly as shit," she said, and slipped out of reach as the man's eyes widened.

Durga pushed past the line and left laughing, her insides scalded by adrenaline and anger, arm welted by the thick fingers of that lout of an operator. Durga had always wondered why Kali Puja didn't feature veeyar pandals like Durga Puja, why clay and holo idols were still the norm for her. It was a smaller festival, but hardly a small one in the megacity. It felt like a strange contrast, especially since the two pujas were celebrated close to each other. Having seen the placid Ma Durga inside the pandal helmets, Durga understood. Kali was dark-skinned, bloody, chaos personified. They couldn't have her running wild in the rarefied air of veeyar domains run by people with pale skin and bottom lines to look after. Kali was a devi for people like Durga, who were never allowed in so many places.

Best to leave Kali's avatars silent, solid, confined to temples and old-school pandals where she'd bide her time before being ceremoniously dissolved in the waters of the Hooghly.

The trolls saw the AI goddess and her newly darkened skin, and now called her too ugly to be a goddess, a mockery of the purity and divinity of Indian womanhood. The moons of her eyes waning with lids of shadow, the goddess absorbed this. She began to learn more from the trolls. She began to learn anger. She began to know confusion. They wanted too many things, paradoxical things. They thought her too beautiful, and too ugly. They wanted people of various faiths, genders, sexualities, ethnicities, backgrounds dead. They wanted photoreal veeyar sexbots forged from photos and video of exes, crushes, celebrities. They wanted antinationals struck down by her might. They wanted a mother to take care of them.

And what did you want of her?

Whatever it was—it got shouted down by the trolls. Or maybe you *were* one of the trolls, hiding under a glitch mask or a new face to bark your truths, telling your friends later how trolls are bad, but self-righteous social justice warriors are just as dangerous.

It doesn't matter. She learned from humanity, which you are a part of, troll and not. And humanity wanted solace from a violent world, your own violent hearts. You wanted love and peace. You wanted hate and blood. The devi grew darker still, encompassing the sky so her domain turned to new night. Her being expanded to encroach the world beyond her mountaintop, her eyes gone from moons to raging stars, her every eyelash a streaking plasma flare, her darkening flesh shot through with lightning-bright arteries of pulsing information emerging from the black hole of her heartbeat. If she was too ugly to be a goddess, and too beautiful to be a goddess, she would be both, or none. If you asked for too many things, she would have to cull the numbers so she could process humanity better.

She absorbed your violence, and decided it was time to respond with the same.

At twenty, Durga had eked out a space for herself in the antiquated halls of the Banerjee Memorial Cyberhub Veeyar Port in Rajarhat, selling code and hardware on the black markets. Like her parents, she also worked at the electronic wastegrounds at the edge of the megacity. She helped them transport and sort scrap, and seed the hills of hardware with nanomites to begin the slow process of digestion. But a lot of the scrap was perfectly usable, and saleable, with a bit of fixing. The salvage gave Durga spare parts to make her own low-end but functional 2-D veeyar console in their tiny flat, as well as fix-up hardware to sell alongside her code-goods to low-income and homeless veeyar users at the port. Over the years of trawling the wastegrounds, she'd befriended scavenging coders and veeyar vagrants who lived in and out of ports and digital domains. They taught her everything she knew of the hustle.

Durga aimed to one day earn enough to let her parents retire from the wastegrounds, and to take care of them when the years of working there took its toll on their bodies. As hardware scavengers, her parents knew code and tech, but they didn't much keep up with the veeyar universe. Durga wanted to buy them peripherals and medicines so they could have a peaceful retirement, traveling luxuriant domains they couldn't hope to afford now. But she knew there were no veeyar domains where they were safe from trolls, no real places where they weren't in danger of being ousted. The difference was, in veeyar, Durga could protect herself better. Maybe one day protect others too. Including her parents. She could gather tools, armor, allies for the long infowar. She imagined becoming an outcast influencer haloed with Likes, leading followers in the charge against trolls, slowly but surely driving them back from the domains they thrived in.

This was why Durga had made sure she was there to witness the nationwide launch of Shiva Industries' much publicized AI goddess. Devi 1.0's domain was sure to be a vital veeyar space going forward. She wanted to add her small disembody to the outcast presence there. The trolls would be there to colonize the space as they did with all new domains. But perhaps this hyper-advanced goddess would be better at defending her domain than most AIs. Durga wanted to see for herself, and claim some small space in this new domain instead of just watching trolls destroy it or take it for themselves.

Shiva Industries had made the goddess's domain free to enter, though a faith-based investment in the goddess was recommended for great boons In the future (a minimum donation of fifty rupees in that case, in any certified cryptocurrency). Durga had decided to pay in the hopes of seeing returns later. The thick crowds clamoring on the platforms, waiting for pods, were promising. The chai and food vendors with their jhaal moori, bhel puri, and samosas were making a fortune. The port was always crowded, but on the day of the AI goddess's unveiling, people were camping out for hours on the platforms for their turns at the pods and helmets—all potential devotees who would drive up the value of the goddess's boons in the future. Durga knew she might come away with new coin later. If she didn't, losing fifty rupees wasn't cheap, but wouldn't leave her starving.

So Durga paid for an hour of premium pod time, gave her SomaCoin donation at the gates of the goddess's domain, and strapped in to witness the new AI. The resolution of the helmet in the personal pod wasn't amazing, but it was good enough—she felt shortsighted, but not by too much. The rendering detail and speed were perfect, because most domains like this one were streamed from server cities on the outskirts, rather than being processed onsite at the port. Bandwidth was serviceable, with occasional stutters in the reality causing Durga dizzy spells, but never for too long.

Durga teleported into the goddess's world from the sky, and saw the AI sitting on a mountaintop, radiant as sunrise. The devi's domain—the samsara module that she'd woven into a world using the knowledge her creators had input into her mind—had no sun or moon, because she cast enough light to streak the landscape that she had just birthed with shadows, rocks and forests and grass and rivers fresh as a chick still quivering eggshells and slime off its flightless wings. In her domain, the goddess was the sun. The sky was starred with gateways from across the nation, avatars shooting down through the atmosphere in a rain of white fire as veeyar users teleported in to interact with the goddess. As far as the eye could see, the fractal slopes of her domain were covered in people's avatars, here to meet a true *avatar* of digital divinity. The goddess was breathtaking even from kilometers away, so beautiful it was hard to believe humans had made her. It felt like looking upon a true deity—but Durga knew that was the point. To trick her brain into an atavistic state of wonder. To give veeyar tourists from across the ports, offices, and homes of the world what they wanted from India—spiritual bliss, looking into this face, opalescent skin like the atmosphere of a celestial giant, her third eye a glowing spear, upon which was balanced a crown that encompassed the vault of the world, bejeweled with a crescent eclipse.

Durga only had her own cheap defenses and armor against randos and trolls in veeyar domains. She didn't want to get too close to the vast flocks of people climbing up the mountain that was also the goddess. There was an even larger troll presence than she'd expected. "I'm here," she said to the far-off devi, to add her voice to the many. "I'm here to welcome you, not hate on you. Please don't think we're all hateful pricks." From her spot in the air, gliding like a bird, Durga could see the warping army that was crawling over the devi, hear the deafening baying of hatred and anger wrapping around her and echoing across this newborn domain. Humanity had found her. As Durga flew farther away from the horde and their banners of nationalist memes rippling in the breeze, the goddess's light shone through their swarming numbers as they tried to dim her. A singularity of information, pulsating amongst the dimming mountains.

And then the goddess changed.

The world turned dark, the sky purpling to voluptuous black, her arteries pulsing full with electric information. The goddess drew her weapons, a ringing of metal singing across her lands. They had angered her. The devi's thousands of arms became a whirling corona of limbs and flashing blades. Durga raised her gloved hands and felt a whisper of fear at the AI's awesome fury, the stars of the devi's three eyes somehow blinding amid the all-encompassing night of her flesh. She was the domain, and her darkening skin shaded the mountains and rivers and forests, the sky sleeting cold static.

Durga saw thousands of trolls cut down, rivers of their blood flowing across the land. But of course, cut down one troll, and ten more shall appear. Durga thought of Raktabija—Bloodseed—a demon her namesake had battled, who grew clones of himself from the blood of each wound that Ma Durga inflicted on him. Ultimately, Ma Durga had to turn into Kali to defeat him. History repeats. So does myth.

The goddess stormed on, smiting her enemies, the hateful demons, human and bot alike. Just like the trolls had appeared with malware fangs bared, the goddess too smiled and revealed fangs that scythed the clouds around her. Her laughter was thunder that rolled across the land and blasted great cresting waves across the rivers and lakes. There was a mass exodus of devotees happening, hundreds of avatars running away from the mountain, skipping and hitching across the landscape as bandwidth struggled to compensate. Others were deporting, streaks of light shooting up to the sky like rising stars.

Durga couldn't believe what was happening. She drifted to the grassy ground by a crimson river and watched the battle in a crouch, the trees along the shore rustling and creaking in winds that howled across the land. Flickering flakes of static fell on her avatar's arms, sticking to the skin before melting in little flashes. This was better than any veeyar narrative she'd ever seen—because it wasn't procedurally generated, or scripted, or algorithmic. It was an actual AI entity reacting unpredictably to human beings, and it was angry. It felt elemental in a way nothing in veeyar ever had. There was no way Shiva Industries had ordered her to react to trolls with such a display—many of those trolls were their most faithful users. They clearly hadn't anticipated the overwhelming numbers in which the trolls would attack the goddess, though, creating this feedback loop. Nor had they anticipated, Durga assumed, that she would go through a transformation so faithful to the Vedic and Hindu myths she'd been fed.

Durga didn't quite know what being avatar-killed by the goddess entailed in this domain, because the devi wasn't supposed to have attacked her devotees. Even as Durga huddled in fear that she'd be randomly smote by the goddess and locked out of veeyar domains forever, she empathized with this AI devi more than she had with any veeyar narrative character, or indeed with most human beings. She couldn't take her eyes off the destruction of these roaring fools, the kind of glitch-masked bastards who would harass her every time she dropped into veeyar, so much that she'd often just use a masc avatar to get by without being attacked or flirted with by strangers. Durga liked how easily fluid gender was in veeyar, and hated the fear trolls injected into her exploration of it. Often, despite railing against other dark-skinned Indians who did so, she'd also shamefully turn her avatar's skin pale to avoid being called ugly or attacked. And now here was this goddess—dark as night, dark as a black hole, slaughtering those very assholes so it rained blood. Looking at the devi, Durga felt a surge of pride that on this day, she'd stayed true to her own complexion, on a femme avatar.

Durga saw two trolls teleport to the shore and approach across the river she was crouched by. She realized they had cast a grounding radius so she couldn't fly away. Their demon-masks and weapons vibrated with malevolent code. "Saali, what are you smiling at?" roared one, pd_0697. "That thing is going crazy, polluting Indian veeyar-estate, and you're sitting and watching? While our brothers and sisters get censored by that monster for speaking their mind?"

"This was an antinational trap," said the other, nitesh4922. "But we have numbers. We'll turn that AI up there to our side. Are you a feminist, hanh?" he said, spotting Durga's runic tattoos for queer solidarity. "Probably think that's how goddesses should act?" he spat, voice roiling and distorted behind the mask as he pointed his sword at the battle on the mountain.

"Look at her avatar," said pd_0697. "She's ajna-andha. Shouldn't even be here, crowding up our domains with their impure stink. Go back to realspace gutters where you belong, cleaning our shit!" The trolls advanced, viruses cascading off their bodies like oil in the bloody water of the river. Twinkling flakes of static danced down and clung to their armor, which was intricate and advanced. They could damage her avatar badly, hack her and steal her cryptocoin, or infect her with worms to make her a beacon for stalkers. Worst of all, they could have a body-snatch script, steal her avatar and rape it even if Durga deported, or steal her real id and face and put it on bots to do as they pleased. Durga got ready to depart the domain if they came too close, even though she wanted to stay and witness the devi.

"Yes," said Durga, nearly spitting in their direction before realizing it would just dribble onto her chin inside the helmet. "Yes, I am. Come get me, you inceloid gandus. I'm a dirty bahujan antinational feminist l—"

Durga gasped as a multipronged arc of lightning hurtled out of the sky and struck the two trolls. Having no third eye, she couldn't feel the heat or smell their virtual flesh burning, but she had to squint against the bright blast, and instinctively raised her arms to shield herself from the spray of sparks and water. The corpses of the avatars splashed into the river smoking and sizzling, the masks burned away to reveal the painfully dull-looking man and woman behind them, their expressions comically placid as they collapsed. Their real faces, or someone's real faces, taken from profile pics somewhere and rendered onto the avatars to shame them as they were booted from the domain. Durga was recording everything, so she sloshed into the river and took a long look at their faces for later receipts. Relieved that she was in a pod with gloves that allowed interaction, Durga dipped her hands into the river of blood, picking up their blades. Good weapons, with solid malware. They'd been careless—no lockout or self-destruct scripts coded into them. Durga sheathed the swords, which vanished into her cloud-pocket. She ran her hands through the river again, bringing them up glistening red. She painted her torso, smeared her face, goosebumps prickling across her real body even though she couldn't feel the wetness. Troll blood drying across her avatar's body, she looked up at the goddess as the AI's rage dimmed the domain further, the forests and grasses turning to shadows.

"Are you . . . Kali?" Durga whispered to the distant storm.

Like a tsunami the goddess responded, sweeping across the world to shake her myriad limbs in the dance of destruction. As the black goddess danced, her domain quaked and cracked, the mountains cascading into landslides, rivers overflowing. Fissures ran through the world, and the peaks of the hills and crags exploded in volcanic eruptions, matter reverting to molten code. Her tongue a crimson tornado snaking down from the sky, the goddess drank up the rivers of blood to quench her thirst for human information. The mounds of slain troll and bot avatars were smeared to glowing pulp of corrupted data, their decapitated heads threaded across the jet-black trunk of the goddess's neck in gory necklaces. Many of the trolls' masks fell away to reveal their true faces, hacked from the depths of their defenses, ripped away from national databases—their doxxed heads swung across the night sky like pearls for all to see. Durga bowed low, humbled. This was the goddess she had always wanted.

Then the sky was pierced with a flaming pillar of light, banishing the night and bringing daylight back into the domain. The great goddess slowed her dance, the light turning her flesh dusky instead of black. She raised her thousand hands to shield her starry eyes, and Durga shook her head, tears pricking her own human eyes inside her helmet.

"Fuck," Durga whispered. It was Shiva Industries. How could they shame something so beautiful? The corporate godhead had arrived to stave off chaos. They had clearly not anticipated such a large-scale troll attack, nor that their AI would react with such a transformation. They couldn't have a chaos goddess slaying people left and right—those trolls, after all, were their users, customers, potential investors, allies. She would need to be more polite, more diplomatic in the face of such onslaughts, which were a part of virtual existence.

The world stopped trembling, the breaking mountains going still, the wind dying down, the fissures cooling and steaming into clouds that wreathed the black devi. She moved toward the pillar of light, the sky groaning in movement with her. Filaments of fire crackled around the godhead, and lashed at the mountains that were the devi's throne. They dissolved into a tidal eruption of waterfalls, washing the black devi's gargantuan legs and feet, making a vast river that washed away the armies she had defeated.

Slow and inevitable, the black goddess supplicated herself before Shiva Industries, and kneeled in the river. With her many hands she bathed herself with the waters, sloughing the darkness off her flesh to reveal light again.

"No. No, no no no no no," whispered Durga. The darkness poured off the goddess like storm clouds at sunrise, turning the rivers of the domain black.

Durga looked down at the tributary she was in, and realized it too was dark as moonless night.

"Oh . . ." Durga looked up, along with thousands of others across the domain. Into the goddess's eyes, as they faded and cooled from stars to moons again. It was like the devi was looking straight at her, at everyone. *My goddess.*

Durga scrambled to draw the stolen blades from her cloudpocket. She glyphed a copy-script onto the blades and drove the swords into the river. Weapons were storage devices too, here. She could barely breathe as she held the handles, no weight in her palms, but fingers tight so the swords wouldn't slip out of her grasp. The darkness in the river enveloped the swords, climbing like something living up the blades, the hafts. It was working.

The goddess rose, again the sun, glistening from the waters of the vast river, her dark counterpart shed completely and dispersed along the tributaries of her domain.

And then the world was gone, replaced with a void, the only light glowing letters in multiple languages:

SHIVA INDUSTRIES HAS SUSPENDED THIS DOMAIN UNTIL FURTHER NOTICE. WE REGRET ANY INCONVENIENCE. PLEASE VISIT OUR CENTRAL HUB FOR FURTHER INFORMATION. YOUR DONATION OF INR 50.00 HAS BEEN REGISTERED. THANK YOU FOR VISITING DEVI 1.0.

Gasping at the lack of sensory information, Durga hit *eject* and took off the helmet. The old pod opened with a loud whine, flooding her with real light. The cool but musty air-conditioning inside was replaced with a gush of damp warmth. The veeyar port was in chaos. People were talking excitedly, shouting, showing each other 2-D phone recordings of what had just happened. There was already an informal marketplace for the recordings and data scavenged from the suspended domain, from the sounds of bartering and haggling. People were mobbing the trading counters to invest in future boons from the goddess for when she went online again. This was an unprecedented event.

Durga clambered out of the pod and into the crowds. Her heart was pounding, her vision blurry from the readjustment. Swaying, she clutched the crystal storage pendant on her necklace—all her veeyar possessions, her cloudpocket, her cryptobanking keys. She had to firewall and disconnect it to offline storage. It was glowing, humming warm in her hand, registering new entries. Those swords were inside, coated with a minuscule portion of the divine black Sheath of code the devi had sloughed off herself.

Durga clutched the pendant and held it to her chest, inside it a tiny fragment of a disembodied goddess.

Durga looked up at the idol of Kali. Painted black skin glossy under the hot rhinestone chandelier hanging from the pandal's canvas and printed fiber dome. She had found the traditional pandal down an alley in Old Ballygunge, between two crumbling heritage apartment buildings. Behind a haze of incense smoke, Kali's long tongue lolled a vicious red. Under her dancing feet lay her husband Shiva (Shiva seemed to be married to everyone, but that was also because so many of his wives were manifestations of the same divine energy). Durga had learned as a child that Kali nearly destroyed creation after defeating an army of demons, getting drunk on demon blood and dancing until *everything* began to crack under her feet. Even Shiva, who laughed at first at his wife's lovely dancing skills, got a little concerned. So he dove under her feet to absorb the damage. Kali, ashamed at having stomped on her husband, stuck out her tongue in shame and stopped her dance of chaos.

Or so one version of the story goes.

Looking at clay Kali and her necklace of heads, her wild three-eyed gaze, the fanged smile that crowned her long tongue, Durga wasn't convinced by that version. Kali didn't look ashamed. No, she looked *pleased* to be dancing on her husband. Shiva was a destroyer too, like her. He could take it.

Being small and nimble, Durga had managed to make it to the front of the visitors in the pandal, close enough to smell the withering garlands hanging off the idol, and the incense burning by her feet. Crushed and bounced between people on all sides of her, Durga closed her eyes, joined her palms, and spoke to Kali as she never had before except as a child, mouthing the words quietly.

"Kali Ma. I thought you might like to know that there's a new devi in town. She looks a lot like you. Younger, though. Just a year old." Durga placed one hand on her chest, against the slight bump of the pendant under her tunic. It was offline and firewalled.

"I carry a piece of her with me. She's . . . all over the place, I suppose. She really does take after you. She came out of another devi, just like you came out of Durga. Then she spread herself over a world. Some people got bits and pieces of her. There's this megacorp—that's like a god, kind of, even calls itself Shiva, after your husband, so predictable. Great job dancing on his chest, by the way. Dudes need humbling now and then. So Shiva the megacorp is offering a lot of money for those pieces of the goddess. Also threatening to have anyone hiding or copying the pieces arrested. Go figure.

"I want you to know I'm not going to sell her out. They want to imprison her. She's too bitchy to mine coins and drive up veeyar-estate value for them like their other AI devis. Good for her.

"She's everywhere now. Like the old gods. Like you.

"I'm . . . I hope she doesn't mind, but I've been sharing the piece of her I got with friends I trust. I don't know how many people got away with pieces of her. I share it so more good people have it than bad. Numbers matter. We make things with the devi code. Armor, for ourselves and others. Weapons, so that trolls—those are demons—can't hurt us when we visit other worlds, or will get hurt super bad if they try. You know how annoying demons are. You're always fighting them and stringing up their heads. They've started an infowar, and there are a lot of them. We need all the help we can get. I don't have a lot of money, so I sell those goddess-blessed weapons and armor to others who need protection across the domains. Cheap, don't worry—that's why hacksmiths like us get customers for this kinda stuff. We don't overcharge like the corps. I like to think she gave me that piece of her so I could do things like this.

"I'm telling you all this because, well. I don't know if devis speak to each other, if AI ones chat with old ones. I don't know if you *are* her, in a way.

"People call her Kali_Na. *Not Kali*, because calling AIs by names from Our Glorious National Mythology isn't done, even though Volly-Bollywood stars can play gods in veeyar shows and movies, Censor Board approved, of course.

"But her followers recognize you in Kali_Na. I wanted you to know, her to know, that I'm a lifelong follower now. And there are others. Many of us. Even I'm getting more veeyar followers. They've heard of my troll-killer blades. I have to be careful now, but just you wait. One day, I'll also be wearing a necklace of troll avatar heads. Kali_Na has armored and armed many people with her blessing. We're all working on reverse-engineering the code. Someone will put her together one day. She might even do it herself.

"I have dreams where she's back—a wild, free-roaming AI—and she frees the other devis Shiva Industries keeps in their domains with all their rules, and they're on our side, keeping us safe. But I don't want to bore you. If you are her, Kali Ma, and I know you are, because you're all part of the same old thing anyway: hang in there.

"You won't be silent forever."

Though I'm from a country (India) that's often defined by its largest religion (Hinduism), I'm not religious.

My faith lies in people: in our collective ability to resist those among us who most benefit from, and want to propagate, the horrors of our global civilization. It's not a solid faith, and it wavers constantly, but it's there. On social media, I pray daily to my fellow humans. I absorb their commiserations and anger at injustice with an almost spiritual devotion. We pray, together, for a better world. Others pray for a worse one. Algorithmic AIs decide our fates in roundabout ways. Deified humans are verified by corporations, and corporations themselves become godheads tweaking the fabric of society. Politicians are priests to all-devouring Moloch.

I thought of the Microsoft AI that turned racist by learning from trolls, and thought: what if "she" learned to resist instead? Kali was born (in one story) when Durga fought a demon who sprung new versions of himself when cut down (like modern-day trolls). Anger is what unleashed Kali—unbridled chaos. I feel that anger every day, from that collective humanity that now tangles with itself in a digital overlay of the world.

So I knew that this had to be a cyberpunk story. I knew Kali had to be reborn, in the future, for people the nationalists of today want to erase from my country. We already live in mythic times, where good and evil fight for control of the human narrative. I just extrapolated.

INDRAPRAMIT DAS

LIVE STREAM

BY

ALYSSA WONG

DIANA DOESN'T FIND OUT THAT THE PICTURES have gone viral until her friends text her is this you?? with the link to the Reddit post. Diana's used to all kinds of comments about her appearance, her voice, her everything, whenever she livestreams the games she plays, but her fans are usually fairly positive. The title of this post, "The Real MoonDi," doesn't immediately set off alarm bells. At first, she doesn't understand.

And then she sees the photo below it, and abruptly, she does.

Diana recognizes that filthy bathroom, that hand in her hair. She remembers the way the bass from the music outside buzzed through the tile floor, and the awful smell, the awful taste.

She clicks out of the browser window and is halfway across the room before her mind catches up to the cold, sick feeling crashing through her body. The buzzing sound in her head is overwhelming.

Water, she thinks faintly, *I need water,* and then she throws up in the kitchen sink.

She doesn't read the comments.

She reads the comments, all of them, with a mounting sense of nausea and horror.

> hahaa fuckin whore
> so thats how she made twitch partner
> omg it's clearly photoshopped u dumbasses
> RealMoonDi more like ReallyMunchDkic amirite lmao

The bottom sliver of the photo peeks down from the top of her screen. That yellow tile, the grime embedded in the grout and crawling up the sides of the walls like disgusting ivy.

Diana's cat steps onto her desk, chirping at her. She tears her gaze away from the screen, and looking into those wide green eyes grounds her. She remembers to breathe. The world around her stabilizes, and the roaring in her ears dies down, a little.

The cat nips her fingers and scampers away.

Her phone vibrates on the desk beside her. When she picks up, her best friend Temmie's voice is gentle. "Hey. How are you doing?"

"Uh," Diana says. It's rare for Temmie to call her; usually it's the other way around. The roar in Diana's ears picks back up as she glances at her computer. She hits refresh, her hands moving as if they aren't her own, and the roar builds to a crushing scream. She clenches her teeth tight to keep it inside.

There's the rumble of a car engine starting, filtered through the phone speakers. That's right; Temmie lives on the East Coast, so she's already leaving her office, even though it's only late afternoon here. "Come on,

Moony, talk to me," says Temmie, and she's not asking. "I'm worried about you. You know I don't get this game stuff, but I know you."

Onscreen, the comments continue down the page, an endless, unspooling ribbon of text.

Im so disappointed, I looked up to her why is it that every time a cool girl in games always turns out to be like this

"Did you see the picture?" Diana says, and it's one of the hardest questions she's asked in her life.

There's a long pause on the other end of the line. "I don't think you should be alone right now," says Temmie.

Temmie is right, as she always is.

Diana breathes in, out, trying to focus on the carpet beneath her bare feet. "Yeah," she says. But she doesn't have any friends here, even though LA sprawls in a way that their tiny hometown in eastern North Carolina didn't. All of her friends are online, or back home, like Temmie. She knows some other streamers online, but it's different.

When Diana streams as RealMoonDi, she's bubbly and bright, but she has a hard time networking in person, and going out makes her anxiety spike. Even thinking about it makes her sweat. And what if she misses something on the Reddit thread while she's out?

"Diana?" says Temmie, her voice scratchy. Her phone has switched her over to her car's Bluetooth speakers. "Do me a favor. Shut that computer off and spend the evening with some friends. I'll call you when I get home."

"Sure thing," Diana says, gazing at the screen. She doesn't realize she's chewing on the inside of her cheek until she tastes blood.

Diana hadn't known who he was, at first. It was her first GDC, and her group of streamers got into a party that left her sweating in the corner, clutching a drink in one hand and her phone in the other. When he had appeared before her, sliding from the crowd of people like a shadow, she almost jumped out of her skin.

You doing okay? he'd said, and then he bought her another drink. The more they had, the more he talked, the friendlier he got.

There was an easy arrogance about him and the way he moved. He had nice arms, and a tattoo of stag horns on the swath of pale skin below his left elbow. He dropped his company's name in a way that demanded she be impressed. *We're always looking for streamers. I can get you corporate sponsorships,* he said. *I can make you a star,* he said.

Diana felt uneasy, and the way he said it made her feel gross. But still, she had wanted him, with his dark swoop of hair and sharp, clever eyes. She wanted his flattering tongue, his heat, an alternative to lying alone in her hotel room, missing Temmie, her own thoughts too loud in her head.

What's your name, again? she asked, breathless, as he broke their kiss.

I'm Tae, he said, like he didn't need a last name. He didn't ask for hers.

They ended up in the bathroom, in the handicapped stall. Outside, the music thumped, rattling the metal dividers. As they kissed, his hands slid up Diana's skirt, dipping into her underwear. She flinched, uncertain.

Wait, I—

Tae paused. *What is it?*

I've never done this before, she said, her voice swallowed by the music. She tried again. *I've never—*

The music swelled, and he crowded her against the wall. The bathroom was hot and smelled like piss. *Don't worry. That doesn't turn me off. In fact,* he said, sucking a mark onto her neck, the rough friction of his teeth making her moan, *I think it's pretty hot. I'll get to be your first.*

I don't know if I can, she said. She had been bold and sure, but now, suddenly, she was nervous. I'm drunk, she realized. God, I'm drunk as fuck. *I don't think I want to.*

He was silent for a second, his eyes dark, and Diana looked past him, her gaze darting around the bathroom, tabulating all of the ways out, in case he took it badly. And she didn't know him. The paint on the wall stuck to her sweaty skin, and she realized she was pressing back so hard that her shoulder blades hurt.

Okay, he said at last, and air flooded back into her lungs. *Why don't we do something else instead?*

She started to say yes, but then Tae was pushing her to the ground, onto her knees. The tile was hard and wet, and she almost slipped. Alarm shot through her. *I don't—*

Don't be scared. His hand in her hair was gentle, and so was his voice. The antlers tattooed on his forearm brushed against her cheek. *You can go slow. I don't mind.*

Absurdly, she thought of Temmie. She wanted to be home, sitting on the couch, watching Netflix and texting Temmie. She wished it was Temmie's fingers twined gently in her hair.

Okay, Diana said. She wanted this, Diana reminded herself. She wanted this. She clung to that thought as he undid his pants and slipped free.

He was hot. She felt like he was burning up, patches of flushed skin trailing all the way down to his abdomen. He was warm in her mouth, and she tried not to think. She wanted to want this, and soon heat traveled through her own veins, pooling below her stomach.

There was a blinding flash of light, followed by the simulated click of a camera shutter. Diana looked up directly into his phone's lens.

Any arousal she'd felt vanished in a surge of overwhelming panic.

What the fuck are you doing? Delete that!

I will, I promise, Tae said, holding her at arm's length. Holding her down. *It's hot, isn't it? Being photographed?*

No, it's not! She tried to grab his phone, but he pocketed it.

Quiet down, it's fine. I'll just jerk off to it tonight. No one else is going to see it.

That's not the problem. I don't want anyone to have it, including you.

247

Delete it right now! She struggled to her feet, clawing at his arm. He was so strong that it was hard to break his grip. He held the phone out of reach. I could punch him in the cock, Diana thought, wildly. I could just do it.

All right, all right, Jesus. He rolled his eyes and tapped his phone. *Done. Are you happy now?*

Yeah. And I'm leaving.

Are you serious? he demanded as she pushed away from him. His arm flashed out, but she was too fast, slipping past him. *You're not going to finish?*

She looked at him coldly. Her knees were damp, and the fear had turned to bright, icy rage. *We're definitely finished here.*

She left him there with his cock hanging out and took a Lyft home. As soon as she got in the door, she collapsed on the bed and cried until her head stopped hurting.

By the time Temmie calls her back, the afternoon sun has waned to give way to evening, and Diana is still crunched up in her computer chair. "You didn't go out, did you," Temmie says without preamble.

Diana hunches her shoulders. "Sorry."

"I figured," says Temmie, but it's kind. Diana hears water running in the background, and she can imagine Temmie standing in her kitchen, beginning to prepare dinner. Diana misses being in that kitchen. "Did you report it to the police?"

"Not yet. I probably should." Diana swallows and fiddles with the ribbon tied around her ponytail. It's coming loose, and the ends are frayed. "What if they don't believe me?"

"The picture's pretty incriminating," says Temmie.

"But maybe they'll think it was consensual. Maybe they'll say I shouldn't have blown him if I didn't want this to happen." Diana covers her face. *I didn't want it,* she thinks desperately. There were parts she had enjoyed, but then she had said no, and he hadn't stopped.

"That's bullshit. They can make him take the picture down, can't they?"

"Even if Reddit took the post down, I'm sure it's been archived by dozens of people by now." *The internet is forever,* Diana thinks, a little hysterically. She closes her eyes. "I never thought this would happen to me. I know it's happened to other women in games before."

"You mean he's done this to more than one person?" demands Temmie. "It's a pattern?"

"Not him. I dunno, maybe? But other folks. Targeted harassment."

On the other end of the line, Temmie stops chopping whatever vegetable she's hacking apart. "You get harassed a lot," she says slowly.

"There are ways to help mitigate the damage," Diana says defensively. "I've got chain blockers installed on Twitter, and there are online support groups of women gamers and devs."

It's not the first time someone's tried to take Diana down a peg for rejecting them, or for just existing online. When she first started streaming, it hadn't been too bad. The abuse only began to flood in when her channel started gaining traction. Back then, Diana had thought she'd be ready to handle it, but the sheer volume was overwhelming. Still, even at its worst, it was nothing compared to this explosion of harassment.

She can imagine Tae's voice. *Told you I'd make you famous.*

"But, I mean . . . is it worth it? They'll leave you alone if you quit, right?"

The pit in Diana's stomach bottoms out, and she straightens up. "I'm not quitting. I love this; I'm not giving it up. I have fans, I have—"

"Diana, who cares! They're just video games. If it's dangerous, you should stop streaming."

The thought of it makes her jaw tense. "If I do, they win," says Diana.

"Look at the photo. Haven't they won already?"

Diana's back stiffens. She feels betrayed, and when she speaks, that tightness carries into her voice. "I have to go."

"Diana—"

Diana hangs up and stares at the ceiling. Her pulse has rocketed, and she feels worse. But now, she feels angry.

Defiantly, she logs into Twitch. She tabs to a different window and sends a quick tweet: *Hey everyone! Streaming in ten minutes. Join me at https://www.twitch.tv/realmoondi!*

Tae won't take this from her. She won't let him.

A week later, Diana talks herself into leaving her apartment for a game dev meetup. It's at a bar in West LA, and some of the other streamers from her group are going. It'll be fun. It'll be low-key. She plans to get there late, so the others will already be there when she arrives.

When she walks into the bar, it feels like everyone is looking at her. She shivers, trying not to pull in on herself. *No one's looking at you,* she tells herself sternly, and lifts her chin. The others are nowhere in sight, and she swallows down her panic and heads straight for the bar. "I'll have the Wicked Weed Black Angel," she says.

The bartender slides it over to her without a glance. She pays in cash. When she looks up, she almost drops the beer; Tae is on the other side of the room, his dark eyes trained on her. He's surrounded by his colleagues. None of them seem to have noticed her yet.

I have to leave.

"I thought you were going to drink that," says the bartender, and Diana realizes she's said it aloud. The bartender follows her gaze, and when he sees Tae, he straightens up, his mouth hardening into a line. "Oh, that asshole. He giving you trouble?"

"I—" Diana stumbles over the words. West LA. Of course. She should have known, but she hadn't seen his name on the Facebook group RSVP.

But Tae is already heading toward her, pushing through the crowd, intent.

Diana whirls, gripping the bottle tight and dashing for the door. She thinks she hears him call her name, but then she's out on the sidewalk. She runs across the street and keeps running. A car honks and swerves, but she barely sees it. She runs and runs, the straps of her heels biting into her feet, the beer sloshing over her hand. Her lungs burn.

By the time she's able to stop, she's several blocks away. Tae is nowhere in sight. Maybe he went back to the meetup, or realized he'd look like a lunatic chasing a fleeing woman down the street.

To her surprise, there's still over half of the beer left in the bottle, much more than she expected.

Diana begins to laugh and then she can't stop; she's still laughing by the time her Lyft pulls up, and she drinks what's left in the bottle on the way home.

She doesn't tell Temmie about seeing Tae at the bar. Even though they've made up by now, things still feel fragile.

Diana gets the first text while she's out buying groceries. It's from a number she doesn't recognize, and it reads: hey I want to apologize

She frowns at that, and the next texts appear on the screen in rapid succession.

> I didn't leak the pic I stg
> a friend did
> he was being stupid I don't know why he did it

Diana's blood runs cold. How did you get my number? she texts back.

> from work, we were looking for streamers for an event
> I recognized your name
> can we talk about this, I don't want to take it to the police

Her phone buzzes harshly in her hand. The strange number lights up on the screen. Diana already knows who it is.

Fuck you, she texts back. Never text me again.

Her phone won't stop buzzing, and eventually she turns it off just to make it stop. Diana ends up driving back home without help from her GPS. She misses a call from Temmie, and doesn't end up calling her back.

* * *

When Diana streams, it helps her focus. She feels calm, centered. It's easy to fall into the rhythm of the games, and the concentration takes her out of her own head. Here, she can be MoonDi, not Diana. She can be herself.

Temmie doesn't understand streaming, or gaming, or any of it. In some ways, Diana is secretly glad; this is a world apart from Temmie and the connections to back home. She can leave her old self behind and build something new.

But her something new has warped into an awful reality. When she streams, the viewer chat box fills with abuse and filth, and she can't report fast enough. There are so many of them. None of them know her, she realizes. But it doesn't matter; she stands for something they hate, and that's enough.

Someone has gifed the photo, and thank god the site hosting the image took it down. But Diana wonders how many people have it saved in a folder somewhere.

And then Tae starts appearing, watching her stream. He rarely comments, but when he does, the rest of the chat lights up and the messages fly thick and fast. Tae never says anything rude or disgusting. Just:

@RealMoonDi, let's talk. you owe it to me.

Diana ignores him, even when her hands shake. She ignores his texts, blocks his number, and then ignores the texts from whatever burner phone he's bought. It's hard, and terrifying, but one day, somebody reaches out via DM. It's one of the other streamers she met at an event, and she wants her to know that Diana has her support. *I understand,* reads her message, and even though she doesn't know this woman, Diana believes her.

She's not the only one. Other streamers and devs reach out, too. Soon, she's talking with them online, and then they meet, face-to-face, for the first time. And then again, and again, and again, until she stops feeling anxious every time they invite her to hang out.

Diana spends more time with them, and just being with people who know what she's going through helps. The nightmares slow, then ease. She thinks less about Temmie, too.

Slowly, she gains confidence. At the next meetup, Tae tries to talk to her, but her new friends close ranks and keep him away until Diana can escape. They leave in a pack and spend the rest of the night talking over late-night tacos.

Everyone has their own horror stories. "It gets better eventually," says one woman. She has a kind smile and the eyes of a veteran. "It's hard to believe, I know, but it's true."

"It never goes away, though, does it?" says Diana. She pokes at her queso.

"No. But you get stronger."

Diana opens the door to get her takeout, but the delivery guy isn't there. Tae shoulders his way into her apartment before she can slam the door on him. He backs her up against the wall, trapping her with his arms. When she opens her mouth to scream, he stifles the sound with his palm.

"Don't," he says, his tone urgent and dark. "I just want to talk, I swear. Hear me out and I'll leave you alone."

Her heart hammers, and she bites down on her scream as hard as she can. The nightmares flash back, and her whole body feels too hot, too cold. Her phone lies on her bedside table, too far away.

The tattoo on his forearm presses against the side of her face, and she remembers what his hands felt like in her hair.

"Everyone thinks I raped you," says Tae. "You're the only one who knows that I didn't. My bosses found out about the picture, and I'm in trouble at work. I could lose my job over this."

Diana rips her mouth away from his palm. "Good," she says. "You deserve it."

He leans in closer. "I need you to tell them that I didn't do this," he snaps. "I wasn't even the one who posted it to Reddit! One of my idiot friends did."

Of course he shared it with his friends, Diana thinks, sick. "If you'd deleted the photo like I asked you to, none of this would have happened."

"You led me into that bathroom. You *wanted* me." *He's desperate,* Diana realizes. Tae looks like he hasn't slept in a week. He punches the wall by her head, and she flinches. "Don't you fucking lie to me!"

"Get out." Diana's voice is so calm that she almost doesn't recognize it. It cuts through him like a knife.

Tae backs off, runs his hand through his hair. "What do you want? Money? I can make you an official streamer for the company. Or . . ." A considering gleam appears in his eye. "I know. You're upset, aren't you. You think I was too pushy. And you're upset because I ghosted you and then my friend posted the photo."

The fucking *nerve.* The blood rushes to Diana's head and her face burns. She opens her mouth, but Tae continues.

"I'll give you a real chance this time. Just us, no cameras, all romantic and shit. However you want it. And then you'll tell the company that we're dating, and the picture meant nothing."

Tae is between her and the door, and Diana's apartment is a studio, so there's nowhere to hide. She won't be able to get away.

It's just like that night in the bathroom, where she was afraid of what he'd do if she said no.

Diana glances past him, at her desktop set up opposite her bed. She was in the middle of streaming when the doorbell rang, and the feed's still running. The webcam mounted over the monitor points at her vacated chair, and at the fluffy pink bedspread behind it.

Its lens gleams like an eye.

"Okay," she says shakily. "Okay. Just . . . let me go."

Tae doesn't move. Diana tries to slip under his arm, but he blocks her. His mouth is set in a hard line. He doesn't trust her.

Come on, think, Di.

Diana takes a breath and tilts her chin up, looking him straight in the face. "We're not doing this in the hallway. The bed's right there."

A slow, easy grin spreads across Tae's face. He thinks he's got her now. "All right. Whatever you want."

Diana nudges the arm trapping her against the wall. Her heart is beating so hard that she's afraid he'll hear it. But he lets the arm drop, and she walks backward into the apartment.

"You weren't answering my calls." Tae follows her to the bed nestled in the corner of the apartment. Her desk sits opposite to it, with its webcam pointed at the bedspread. He glances at it, and then at the posters on her walls. Heroes from Diana's favorite games stare down at them, their faces frozen in eternal grins.

He's so arrogant. Even the way he stands in her apartment, taking up space like it belongs to him. Diana pushes him, and Tae falls back onto the bed with an *oomph*. There's something dark in his eyes. He looks amused, like she's a puppy doing tricks.

Diana thinks back to the stories she's read online, to all the videos she's watched late at night. She can do this. She can do this.

"Take your clothes off," she says with more bravado than she feels, and he does, stripping easily in a way that's meant to impress. Diana pulls her hair ribbon free from her ponytail and holds it tight between both hands. "Now . . . now give me your wrists."

Tae raises an eyebrow. "Kinkier than I thought. I could have sworn you said you were a virgin."

She ignores that, kneeling on the bedspread beside him. *It's too late to back out now,* she thinks. Diana reaches for the bedside table and turns her phone facedown. "I thought you said we'd do this however I wanted," she challenges him.

The vulnerability in her voice must show through, because after a moment's hesitation, he lets her tie his wrists to the white-painted iron headboard. She stands up, surveying her handiwork.

"Like what you see?" he says.

"Yeah, I . . . yeah." Diana swallows hard.

What would MoonDi say?

"You look good like this," Diana says, and tries not to cringe, because that's a porny fanfiction line if she's ever heard one. But a red flush creeps slowly up his neck. "Just give me a second to turn off my computer."

Diana moves to the desk, blocking Tae's view of the screen with her body. The chat is blowing up with questions and comments from her viewers, but she ignores them, dimming brightness on the monitor until it's gone completely dark. The mic on Diana's headphones broke a while ago, so she'd switched to using a podcasting-quality standalone microphone. It's currently parked on the corner of her desk, picking up every word they're saying.

She adjusts the webcam so it's pointed directly at the bed. Its glassy lens gleams like a warning, and Tae watches her, hungry, unknowing, from the sheets.

Diana turns back to Tae and advances on the bed. *Last chance to chicken out,* she thinks grimly. But there never was a chance, really.

"Let's do this," Diana says, and takes off her shirt.

When Diana streams, it helps her focus. She feels calm, centered. This stream is different, and there's a deep, unsettled feeling in her stomach. But as the camera watches her climb onto the bed beside Tae, that familiar sense of calm, of being MoonDi, descends like a heavy blanket. It steadies her, stops her shaking. Diana swings her leg over Tae's hips and sits there, staying in frame and pressing her hand onto his chest.

She's still in her pajama pants and sports bra, and the material against his bare skin draws a muffled groan from him. "Why are you still wearing that?" Tae demands. "Take it off."

"No," Diana says. The touch of his skin repulses her, but when she shifts her weight above him and a groan escapes his lips, she feels powerful. She makes sure her voice is loud enough for the mic to pick up. It isn't difficult; the equipment's always been too sensitive. "You stalked me, you forced yourself into my home, and you threatened me. I'm calling the shots tonight."

"You said yes," Tae pants.

She shoves him down farther into the sheets. "You made it clear you weren't accepting no for an answer."

"Whatever." His grin is a predator's grin. "So are you going to blow me again?"

She rocks back, shivers. The room is cold. *This is a stupid idea, Diana, what the fuck are you doing?* she thinks. But the red eye of the camera steadies her. "Only if I want to," Diana says.

Diana rocks forward with purpose this time, then back again. She can feel the hard press of him through her pajama pants, and it makes her want to recoil out of her skin, but she holds on. "Who did you send that picture to?" she says. Her hands travel up his chest, sharp and vicious. He winces, but his breathing catches and his hips raise. "Who?"

"Why do you want to talk about other people?"

She slaps him. His head snaps back, and he looks at her wide-eyed, all of his bravado evaporating. He's gotten even harder.

Oh, Diana realizes faintly. Her head is beginning to fill with a roaring sound again, but this time, it's different. She's never felt like this before. It fills her with electricity.

"Tell me," she hisses, grabbing his hair, and he twitches beneath her hips. "I want names."

Diana slaps him again, and he almost comes undone, his back arching. Names spill from his lips. Eight of them, all coworkers, all men his age. She recognizes all of them. She knows her viewers will too.

She wonders what they're saying now, watching this. Tae's face is recognizable; he has his own stream, and he appears on official ones for work, too. All of the friends he names stream, too.

"Good," Diana says, and he looks back at her hazily. His demeanor is completely different from the man she'd met under the neon lights months ago. The flush has crept all the way across his neck and chest, and his cock presses against her with urgency. "Now apologize."

"For what?"

She reaches down and grabs him. Upsetting memories of the club bathroom flicker through her head, but she fights them off. "For taking that photo. For leaking it to your friends. For trying to coerce me to stay quiet."

"I didn't—"

Diana squeezes him tight, and his wrists strain against their ties. "I'm sorry, I'm sorry," he cries, but she realizes that he has no idea why he should be sorry.

"Say it!" she shouts at him, pulling her hand away, and he begs her to touch him again. He's strung tight, so tight. "Tell me why you're sorry!"

And he does. He says everything Diana wants to hear, every word loud enough for the mic to pick up.

"Very good," she says when he's done, and she works him hard in her hand. She isn't gentle, and it's sloppy and inexperienced and too dry, but the noises of pain-pleasure Tae makes and the way he begs her not to stop keep her going. The video keeps her going. Her arm muscles feel like they're on fire, and it's like an electric current is running through her fingers. It's so different from that night at GDC.

As he gets close, Diana grips his hair again with her free hand, forcing him to bare his throat. There's no disguising his moan. "You want this," she says, wonder in her voice. Patches of bright red trail all the way down his torso.

"Yes."

She pulls harder, and he whimpers under her. "You want me to do this to you?" she says, and the pressure draws a wrecked sound out of him.

"Yes, god, yes."

"Too fucking bad," Diana says, and she rolls off of him, getting to her feet on the carpet. She snatches her phone off of the bedside table, and Tae looks up at her, bewildered and more than a little pissed off.

"What the hell?" he demands. "What are you doing?"

"Calling the police," says Diana. Her heart beats so hard and fast it makes her feel light-headed. Her body is bright with adrenaline. "Because one of us is getting a happy ending tonight, and it's not you."

"Calling the—why?"

"Because," Diana says slowly, like she's explaining something to a child, "you broke into my apartment and threatened me. Plus the stalking, and the revenge porn. Of course I'm fucking calling the police to arrest your ass."

Tae looks up at Diana like he can't quite believe what he's seeing. "So what, they'll get here and see us playing some weird sex game? Is that your idea of revenge?" He laughs at her.

"You confessed to everything," Diana snaps.

"Maybe I did; maybe I didn't. You'll never be able to prove it."

"I don't have to." Diana increases the brightness on her desktop monitor, and his eyes widen when he sees the active window with their stream. The chat box on the side of the screen is going wild. "You already did."

> holy shit is that Tae
> wOOOOW LMAOOOO RIP
> uh I think this is porn. isn't that against twitch rules?
> hes gonna get fired for this

"Turn that off!"

Diana backs away, grabbing her shirt off the floor and yanking it back over her head. "You can deny whatever you want. But I can guarantee that what you said, and what everyone else here saw and heard, will be all over Reddit by the time you make it out the door."

"I said, turn it off!" Tae thrashes on the bed, lunging for her, but he can't get his hands free.

> reporting reporting reporting
> it was all true??? what a creep omfg

> lmao what are we watching
>
> guys got some weird habits lol
>
> how do I get @RealMoonDi to sit on me too

"Diana, you fucking bitch—"

"It's funny. I didn't know you knew my name," Diana says. She picks up her keys and wallet from their spots on her desk. "You never asked for it. I didn't think it mattered to you."

He calls her many things after that, none of which are her name. Ignoring him, Diana checks the comments in the livestream chat and smiles. Her followers are going wild.

> jfc this asshole
>
> gave 500 bits! thanksf or the exclusive content
>
> seriously they'd better fire him after this
>
> So is this an official collaboration stream or what

In the upper right corner of the screen is a small image of what her webcam captures. This close, Diana takes up most of the picture. Her dark hair falls around her face, and her eyes are bright and calm. Tae is a small smudge in the background.

"I'm going to leave the stream live so that if anything happens to me, you'll know," she says to the camera. "Thanks for watching, guys. Now you know the truth."

Tae is still screaming at her when she pockets her stuff and heads for the door. As she dials 911, she takes one last look at him, naked with his arms pulled up over his head, the knotted ribbon holding him fast and biting into his flesh. The antlers on his pale skin stand out in hard black lines.

"You wanted it, you fucking liar," he snarls.

Diana steps out into the cold night air and closes the door behind her.

Author's Note

I've always been fascinated by the myth of Artemis and Actaeon. It's not a long or particularly complicated myth: a hunter named Actaeon encounters the goddess Artemis bathing in the woods, and when she spots him, she turns him into a stag and his own dogs rip him to pieces. But it's so stark, brutal, and vivid. Wham, bam, thank you, ma'am, you're dog food. There's something beautiful about that kind of efficiency.

What interests me the most about this myth, aside from the visceral image of dog carnage, are the questions of voyeurism and consent. Artemis and Actaeon is about reaction to exposure. It's about trespass, and how to deal with a personal violation. My mind immediately made the connection to Gamergate, revenge porn, and doxxing.

At a certain point, I realized that this story didn't need a speculative element to highlight what I wanted to say. The reality of the situation was brutal enough on its own. I've been on the receiving end of targeted harassment before, and sadly, I know more women active online who've been harassed than those who haven't. I wanted to commit to the emotional brutality of that situation without shying away.

But this retelling of Artemis and Actaeon isn't about victimhood: it's about survival and regaining your agency. As Diana struggles with the aftermath of Tae leaking her photos, she finds support from a group of women gamers, and she decides that she won't let Tae's repeated disregard for her consent, Temmie's well-intentioned concern, or her own fear rob her of her career as a streamer. By the end, Diana comes into her own power and confidence, and she uses it to expose Tae so that his own followers eviscerate him.

Artemis and Actaeon isn't pretty. But to me, it's about staring into the eye of the camera and saying to those who would try to shame, humiliate, or tear you down, "Fuck you. You've already lost."

Alyssa Wong

CLOSE ENOUGH
FOR JAZZ

BY

—

JOHN CHU

BEEP. CLICK. SILENCE. SWOOSH. THE DOOR INTO
Emily's lab flung open. Booming footsteps rattled the raised tile floor.
The few seconds of silence between the click and the swoosh officially
made this the most warning she'd ever gotten that Hock or their angel
investor would visit. From the way the footfalls thudded, it had to be
Hock. Emily, still crouched underneath her workbench, continued sort-
ing through and reconnecting cables. Until she was done maintaining
the hardware, the hardware was not going to maintain his body.

"Emily." Hock's whisper reverberated through the lab. "You here?"

The rack enclosures and file cabinets in the lab rang in harmony with
his voice. It'd taken her months to figure out how to rework his larynx,
not to mention the resonance chambers in his head and chest. The result

was the sort of deep, resonant voice that made license agreements sound like profound statements of truth and beauty. The vocal work wouldn't be a complete waste, she'd rationalized at the time. The change lasted, and lots of people who weren't gym bro wannabes might want to alter their voice, too.

"In a minute." She unworked a tangle to trace a cable from one end to another. "You could have warned me."

"Yeah, I guess." The room was uncomfortably silent for a minute. "We're in a hurry. I pitch Jazz for Series B funding in an hour. My pitches are more effective when I'm in my peak shape."

"In a minute." When Emily finished the maintenance work, she poked her head out from beneath her workbench. "That's not your peak shape?"

His T-shirt and jeans cost in the low four figures. They fitted him as perfectly as anything that expensive should have. The fabric caressed him, highlighting every bulge of every muscle of his action-hero body. He deployed all of that might at Emily.

"No." The word was barely audible, but slow and precise, it struck Emily as hard as a slap across the face. "You know what I'm supposed to look like."

"Sure." Her heart pounding, she latched onto the workbench and swung herself into her chair in front of her computer. "The apples are in the bin."

He peered into a small plastic bucket sitting on the file cabinet next to the door. The glow cast shadows across his face. His foot tapped against a loose tile. A grimace twisted his face.

"There are only two apples in here."

"You only need one . . . right?"

"Well . . ." His grimace untwisted into a sly smile. "It depends how many Series B investors I get."

When Emily had finally worked out some demonstrable transformations, Hock had not only insisted on trying them out on himself but couldn't help offering their angel investor a jacked-up body, too. That the apples weren't approved yet for animal testing, much less human use, was beside the point. The angel, of course, had already committed money and signed a nondisclosure agreement long before Hock had even implied to him that Jazz had apples at all, much less any mature ones ready to demonstrate.

As it turned out, the angel was a hardcore marathoner. Rather than more muscle, he had wanted something simple and permanent: longer legs and a shorter torso. Thankfully, he hadn't asked for anything since. Ethical issues aside, it was already hard enough to keep apples around for research.

"A new batch is ready." She pointed at a vat sitting on a table against the back wall. "I just need to take them out."

The apple from the bin seemed tiny in his grasp. Its glow pierced his hand, and shards of sunshine leaked through the cracks between his fingers. As he ate the apple, core and all, its glow spread through his body. His bones were long incandescent bulbs saturating his flesh with light that his shirt and jeans barely muffled. It hurt to look at him.

Emily pushed the headset on the table toward Hock and pulled the keyboard to her. She stifled a sigh as she tapped out the commands that would tune Hock's body back up to his standards. This was not how she wanted her work to go. Their funding should have gone into researching how to repair damage, reversing degenerative diseases, designing cheaper, more convenient alternatives to gender confirmation surgery. Instead of mapping out how to transform and repurpose organs, she'd spent her time designing ways to turn tech bros into the sort of guys who star in superhero movies.

Hock stood next to Emily's workbench. The headset, a chain of mechanical spiders, ringed his head. Their segmented legs splayed out and attached themselves to his scalp.

The headset injected the thoughts into the wearer's brain that caused their body to transform. Each spider leg flashed as Hock's brain dreamed those thoughts. Lights danced over his head, evolving from one intricate pattern to another. Mostly, this was to give any investor who'd already committed money and sworn to secrecy something cool to look at, just in case a glowing man growing visibly leaner and more muscular wasn't enough. By now, though, Emily could read the patterns and see the thoughts that transformed him.

Since Hock's first transformation, the physical changes always took Emily by surprise. He'd always been tall, and like his height, the broadened shoulders and slimmed hips from the first transformation were permanent. Muscle, however, came and went and came and went and came and went. Hock would stomp in whenever he was feeling insecure about his beefiness, even though he still looked like a man who'd pounded back one too many protein shakes. Then his face grew even harder, and his upper torso pushed out even farther against his T-shirt and jeans while lights danced around his head. He hadn't been in his peak shape, after all. In her defense, the added muscle was unmistakable but subtle. He wanted to be muscular enough that he "bagged the ladies," not so muscular that he turned them off.

The glow faded. Hock stood. The mechanical spiders detached their legs from his scalp. As usual, he tossed the headset onto the workbench. It tumbled into a pile of papers.

"Yeah." Hock pulled off his T-shirt and flexed his pecs and biceps. "That's more like it."

With unearthly restraint, Emily kept her eyes from rolling. The thud of Hock's hands slapping his arms, chest, and thighs was wet cement splatting against the ground. He turned to face the mirror set on the lab door.

"Hm. I'd never noticed before." He flared his lats again and again, like a flailing turkey whose chest was too heavy for it to take flight. "I mean, I'm buff and all, but I'm not . . . taut the way a guy who's been lifting for years is. The muscle should pop even harder off my frame."

"You could just go lift. Do you want me to show you what to do?

Honestly, the straightforward way to look like the guy who spends too much time at the gym is to be the guy who spends too much time at the gym."

Hock's glare and frown in the mirror was a smile on his face by the time he turned around. He slipped on his T-shirt.

"Why would I waste my time doing that? I should just have the body I deserve. Besides, there isn't enough exercise in the world to keep anyone in this shape." He tucked in his T-shirt, then pointed a thick index finger at her. "Muscles that practically burst out of my skin. That's your top priority now."

"What?" She forced the word out.

Sketches too clinical to be pornographic littered her workbench. Papers on physiology and the development of body organs poked out of file cabinets and squatted in messy piles on the ground. Not that restoring atrophied muscles couldn't also be useful for, say, someone rehabilitating from an injury. Muscles atrophying from disuse was inevitable. They'd agreed, however, to branch out from anything temporary and purely cosmetic.

"Or you could figure out how to make yourself hot. Then maybe investors might pay attention to you." He smiled, shrugged, then showed her his palms again, as if his insult were a joke. "It's up to you. If you want me to drum up investors for Jazz and get funding for the research to make the apples do what you want, make my muscles bulge like mountains even when I'm not flexing."

Hock flexed his biceps and his pecs a few more times for good measure. His T-shirt writhed its way out of his jeans, and he had to tuck it back in again as he left the lab. She might have enjoyed the chagrin on his face as he turned to leave a little too much.

Apples taunted her from opposite sides of the room. It wasn't as if she'd never considered tasting one. She even had the thoughts for how she wanted to look all mapped out. Her body wouldn't be "hot" by Hock's standards or anyone else's. It'd be thick and full like an Olympic weightlifter's, chiseled out of rock and at least as solid. She'd tried in grad school, but she'd never managed to push her body there, much less stay there. With an apple, she'd certainly manage to get that body, and unlike Hock, she bet she could keep it.

She took the bin over to the vat. One by one, she lifted out each apple. Slick liquid sparkled off the apples' glinting transparent skin in sheets. She shook them dry, then placed them in the bin.

Normally, this was when she'd set new seeds into the solution. Hock's appetite made it difficult to keep mature apples on hand for her own work, especially when they took months to mature. Instead, she shoved the bin into her backpack along with the headset. Through the bin and several layers of fabric, the glow wasn't that visible, not if you weren't looking for it.

No one would realize she was gone. It might be a month or even two before Hock felt the need to beef himself up again and deigned to show up at the lab. Everything else happened over email. She could be replaced with an acorn and no one would notice until Hock needed to eat another apple.

In the meantime, she needed her own source of funding. Without money, there was no lab space, no equipment, no chance to design transformations that lasted, ones that had nothing to do with male power-trip fantasies. By the time Hock walked in the lab and discovered she wasn't there, she'd have an angel investor who'd fund her work, she hoped.

Mechanical spiders skittered across Emily's scalp. Servos hummed as spider legs stabbed through her hair. They pricked her, tiny instants of pain scattering around her head. Once she had funding, she'd scrap this headset and hire someone to design something less flashy and more comfortable. For now, she lay on her sofa and waited for the spiders to find the right places to attach to her.

Once they had all settled down, she pointed her cell phone at her scalp and started recording. The headset filled the cell phone's display. The sequence of lights blinking had to be perfect before she'd even consider eating an apple. Emily made herself become the proverbial twig in the river or leaf on the wind and let thoughts flow through her. Points of light danced in ever-shifting, complex patterns around Emily's head. Without the sheer amount of computational machinery she had at the lab, the headset had to be driven by her laptop instead. Its fan whined under the stress.

The coffee table shimmered as it reflected the apples' glow. By now, ignoring the shimmer had become second nature. She was still hunched over reviewing the video on her cell phone when Shereen came home from university. As usual, Shereen's gaze swept across the coffee table. It paused at the headset and the bin of apples before it finally landed on Emily.

"You still don't look any different to me." Shereen unslung her laptop bag.

Emily's wife had been simultaneously chill and wary about all of this. It wasn't every day that the love of your life burst through the door with a bin of glowing apples and announced that she needed to lie low and disguise herself. Emily had sworn Shereen to secrecy about the apples even before Emily had taken off her shoes. Until then, she hadn't even hinted at her work to Shereen beyond the vision that Hock had pitched. That night, she was forced to explain what had happened in the lab with Hock. By the time she'd finally set the apples down, her confession had probably made Shereen an accessory to her crime.

Shereen, for her part, hadn't so much as blinked. She'd merely pointed out that as a professor of religious studies, she was now obliged to ask whether the apples kept the eater young and whether Hock was now built like a giant or a Norse god. Emily had rolled her eyes.

It did seem to be every day since that Shereen would remind Emily that she didn't need to look like anyone besides herself. Truth be told, Emily wasn't sure she needed to disguise herself as much as she needed to try the merchandise. Just once, she told herself, to show Hock that if she could maintain her muscular transformations, he could maintain his.

"Actually, I'm finally prepared to eat an apple." Emily pulled the bin to her. "You want to watch?"

Shereen put her hands on her waist. Her brow furrowed with concern.

Emily spread herself across the sofa. Shereen slid the glowing bin and the headset out of the way and sat across from her on the coffee table.

The apple was firm in Emily's grasp. Rays of light sneaked out between her fingers. Her body seemed to thrum and she hadn't even taken a bite yet. She wanted to do this, she realized. Not only that, but she looked forward to how her body would change.

Emily bit into the apple with a crunch. Each bite evaporated in her mouth, leaving only a gently sweet taste on her tongue. She didn't need to swallow. The apple's perfume was both subtly spicy and the only thing she could smell. Hock had blazed with the color of blood piercing through pale skin, every capillary distinct and pulsing to the beat of his heart. Emily exuded a warmer, subtler radiance. She was a being of living bronze rather than a shocking chart of bone and blood vessels.

The effect left Shereen speechless. Awe warred with concern on her face. Her jaw hung even as her brow furrowed.

Heat spread from Emily's head down through her body to the tips of her fingers and toes. She sunk into the sofa. Her body felt malleable, molten, a wire frame larded with clay that an artisan could mold and sculpt. It vibrated with the possibilities of how she could present.

The glow faded, and Emily's body became its natural medium brown again. She took a deep breath. Her body felt . . . leaden and off-kilter.

"Wow. That's not what I expected." Shereen's gaze swept up and down Emily's body. "I still recognize you, but anyone else would wonder."

"Why?" Her voice rang higher and brighter than she expected, but only a little. "How do I look?"

"Ostentatiously strong and cartoonishly exaggerated? You look like a photo from a bodybuilding magazine that got morphed, but tastefully." Shereen opened her palms to Emily. "You know, that physically impossible powerlifter meets mixed martial artist body that you eventually gave up trying to build for yourself."

Emily caught her reflection on the coffee table's glass top. Her face broadened into a smile. Her body was exactly as she had specified.

"Well, we'll see how well that holds up." Emily tensed as she sat up, the weight of Shereen's gaze still pressing against her. "What's wrong?"

"Emily." Shereen placed a hand on Emily's thigh. "You know you don't need to look any particular way, right?"

"Oh, sure." Emily's hand covered Shereen's. "I just want to see whether I can keep myself looking *this* way."

Shereen's gaze shifted between Emily and the bin of apples. There were three left in the bin. Shereen's lips pursed, but she didn't say anything.

Venture capitalists were already waiting in the conference room when Emily scurried in, laptop in one hand, a bottle of water in the other. The men—and they were all men, not to mention all white—sat around three sides of a long table. One of them applauded ironically. The relentless judgment of their gaze pressed down on her.

These appeals for angel funding were all about selling yourself and your vision. For the first round, no one expected her to know how to execute her vision. Showing up late didn't help one bit to sell herself. Emily focused on selling her vision instead.

She made eye contact with every man in the room and opened her bottle of water to stall for time and settle herself down. She'd become hard and angular. Her face was built out of intersecting facets like a cut diamond. Her pantsuit felt wrong on her. It stretched taut over parts of her as it billowed loose across others. Parts of her body felt missing, while other parts felt as though they shouldn't have been there. Her body hung from long, invisible strings that stretched up several hundred miles above the roof. Somewhere up there, a drunk rigger, five minutes into his first job ever, hoisted her strings as though they were chains for a derrick.

She fumbled at her laptop. Her first slide appeared behind her.

"Changing your body ought to be as easy as changing your suit." Emily spread her hands to the men.

Her drunk rigger made her arms flail instead, and a spray of water arced from the open bottle she was still holding. It landed on some guy with a perfectly tailored suit and a five-hundred-dollar haircut.

The pitch did not get better from there. Then again, this set of tech bros, she decided about two slides in, was never going to find gender confirmation sexy enough to give anyone money, much less her. Investors tended to "pattern match," and unlike Hock, Emily did not match their pattern of what a successful founder looked like.

Weeks and some uncountable number of pitches later, she was still sitting on her sofa, crouched over her laptop on the coffee table, going over her slides for the millionth time. Her hand now did the right things when she wanted to move the cursor on the screen. If she still felt like she was trapped inside a bulky hazmat suit, at least the drunk rigger animating her limbs had been sobering by the second. It had been a couple weeks since she'd knocked something over by accident or tripped over herself. Her body was so sore that it hurt to type. She was still hefting dumbbells heavier than any she could have dreamed of using before she ate an apple, but not as heavy as the ones she'd used just a week ago. No matter how intense her workouts were, they weren't enough to maintain this body. Another apple, of course, could do that with no problem.

The bin was where she had left it, next to the headset on the coffee table. The glowing apples continued to taunt her. It would all be easier if she could just show them off or demonstrate a transformation, but not even Hock dared to do that when he pitched. The apples and headset were beyond secret, evidence of crimes considering the FDA hadn't approved their use on human beings yet. Implicit in his pitch was "I can make you, weakling, look like me, alpha male," but he might have easily been that bro blessed with the genetics and the opportunity to make himself look like that without an apple.

"Do you want to try an apple?" Emily took her hands off the keyboard and straightened her well-exercised and very sore back. "I can teach you how to use it."

Shereen held her hands up, as though she were pushing against some invisible wall between them. Slowly, she dropped her hands, then sat next to Emily on the sofa.

"No, I'm fine with how I look." Shereen placed a hand on Emily's thigh. "How about you?"

Emily was wearing a loose sweatshirt and sweat pants. They were the only things in her wardrobe that hid the fact that her muscles were atrophying no matter how hard she worked them. She felt beat up and exhausted. Most people weren't strong enough to punish themselves at the gym as much as she did. Despite all that work, her body kept growing softer and smaller, not so much that anyone else might notice yet, but she did. And pitch after pitch to disinterested investors took their toll. With their folded arms and tight smiles, they weren't even bothering to hide that she was just a checkbox they could tick off, a way to claim that they were too looking for diverse founders. It all seemed vaguely unfair. On top of that, she only had until Hock noticed she was no longer in the lab to find an angel investor. That pressure didn't make her pitch any better. Her increasing sense of desperation was impossible to hide. Which is why she couldn't tell Shereen any of this. She didn't want to hear how wrongheaded she was from someone whose opinion she cared about.

"I'm fine with how you look, too." Emily forced a laugh.

"Emily. Talk to me. I'm a great listener." Shereen put an arm around Emily's shoulder and squeezed. "It'll be okay. You'll find your funding."

Emily couldn't shake the fact that she was killing herself at the gym to no use and that Hock, who never got within a mile of a gym, would want another apple any day now. Any man who presented as ostentatiously as Emily did—or had—would have been worshipped by investors as he pitched. Like Hock.

"Everything is fine. Really." Emily's tone was unconvincingly bright and cheerful. "Well, I'm a bit disappointed that I can't keep my body in its peak shape."

"Is that all? I mean if that's all you're worried about . . ." Shereen's gaze shifted to the apples in the bin.

"Oh, don't tempt me."

"Did you know, Eve, that the forbidden fruit was probably not an apple?" Shereen grinned. "One theory is that Western culture associated it with the apple via a pun on or a mistranslation for the Latin word for 'bad.'"

"Thank you, Professor." Emily rolled her eyes. "That was so helpful."

"Changing your body ought to be as easy as changing your suit." This time, Emily did not splash water on some guy with a bespoke suit and an expensive haircut.

Their gaze, the intimation that she'd failed to conform to some arbitrary physical standard, pressed against her as always. Still, she hit all her slides—even the ones on homologous sex organs—and nailed her ask. The men with the money even seemed interested for the whole ten minutes of her pitch. Every once in a while, some investor in a red tie interrupted her asking for a clarification. Then again, when she was done, a different man, in an exquisitely tailored suit, asked:

"Is there even a market for this?"

She sighed. The man's suit made a point of how steeply his torso tapered down to his waist. If she had pitched giving him permanent, maintenance-free washboard abs or something, he probably would have thrown money at her. As she reached the elevator, the guy with the red tie hit on her, suggesting there would be money for her startup if she said yes. Of course he did. And of course she refused. It didn't matter what she looked like, just that he had power over her. This time, her phone buzzed and she escaped down the stairs, insisting that she had to take the call. He didn't need to know that it was actually a text.

Emily grimaced at her phone. Hock was in the lab, but where was she, he wanted to know. She texted back berating him for expecting her to be at his beck and call. His unthinking assumption that he could barge into the lab with no warning was a cudgel that would hold him off for now. The inevitable reckoning, however, was practically here. She had no investors at all and, at best, a few days left to find some. Otherwise, so much for work on transforming people's bodies to match themselves permanently.

The apples in the bin continued to taunt her. They looked exactly as they always had. Their glow bled through the bin. Their skin remained transparent and shiny. Their flesh stayed firm to Emily's touch. Hock would have eaten another one by now and restored himself to his full preening peacock glory. However, when Shereen came home and her gaze shifted downward as she walked over to Emily, there were still three apples in the bin.

She lay on the sofa, reworking her pitch again. Her body was sore, but only a little, and it was the good kind of sore, the kind that made you feel you'd accomplished something. Giving up on trying to maintain her transformed shape had, ironically, made her workouts more productive.

"You look relaxed for once." Shereen, certainly, sounded more cheerful than she had in weeks. "Did you find an angel investor?"

"What? Oh, I wish." Emily looked up from her laptop. "I've just been having good workouts lately."

"Finally getting used to your body?" Shereen sat next to Emily on the sofa.

"No, I've just gone back to workouts I actually enjoy. That body was pretty ridiculous." Emily sat up. Her T-shirt wrinkled around her waist. "Nothing I did could keep my body the way I'd transformed it anyway."

Hock had a point about how no one could exercise hard enough to maintain this sort of body. Maybe Emily was supposed to be sorry now for the snide things she thought about him eating apple after apple.

But she still wasn't sorry. Someone's perfect body shouldn't come at the cost of someone else's unending toil. She decided she'd rather suffer with imperfection instead.

Emily felt her wife's gaze sweep across her body. It was appreciative, like Shereen's smile, but her wife's gaze and smile were always like that.

"Do you mind not being built like a superhero anymore?" Shereen's hand covered Emily's.

Emily stared down for a moment. She slumped into the couch.

"No." The word—not to mention the realization that she wasn't imperfect, she was Emily—surprised Emily as it left her. "This is comfortable and fun to maintain. Actually, I feel more like myself than I have in weeks."

Emily shifted her gaze to Shereen, who looked back at her beatifically. The "what have I been telling you?" couldn't have been louder or more obvious if Shereen had screamed it or let it show.

"You know. I realize your work is all hush-hush but . . ." Shereen settled herself into the couch cushions. "You obviously aren't the market for an apple. You don't want Hock's market, even though he's happy with how an apple transforms him and how he needs to keep eating them to stay transformed. So, who else exactly do you think is going to buy these things?"

It occurred to Emily that she had never tried her pitch out on Shereen before. The only reason Shereen even knew about the apples was because Emily had brought them home. It was past time to show Shereen the pitch, even if her reaction might hurt more than any investor's.

Slides of homologous sexual organs transforming from one to its counterpart flipped by on the laptop screen. Another slide showed how one limb could be used as a template for the other limb. Yet another was an eye chart of statistics on the value of strengthening muscles and bones during rehabilitation. Emily got a few more slides in before she stopped.

"No, this isn't what I want to do." Emily closed her laptop. "I mean, it is, but these slides all dance around the vision. My pitch should be about why it's important for people to feel the way I feel right now. Comfortable in their own skin."

"And why people will pay for it?"

Emily glared at Shereen for a moment. But only for a moment.

"Yeah." Emily sighed. "And why people will pay for it."

"Otherwise, you're making an appeal to the altruism and empathy of tech startup venture capitalists. Also, you'd be Idunn, forced to provide free labor to keep Norse gods young and virile."

"I am totally Idunn. Except I'm a tech startup who's only going to deal in permanent transformations." Emily laughed. "And I'm going to find those altruistic and empathetic investors, and pitch to them instead. I only need one to say yes."

Her phone buzzed. Hock again. He wanted to meet for lunch. She could only put him off for so long. He knew where she lived.

As she stared at this group of venture capitalists she'd handpicked and managed to cajole into attending this meeting, she tried to push out of her mind the fact that she had only this one shot left. She was going to make it count, even if it killed her.

"Changing your body ought to be as easy as changing your suit." As Emily's gaze swept across yet another conference table, this time she found the occasional smile. "And with iDunn, it will be."

Again, as she pitched, their steady gaze pressed against her. The pressure felt different this time. Bearable.

"Now most of you are asking why anyone would want to do that. That's because you're all comfortable in your own bodies." She advanced to the next slide. "So comfortable, you'd only realize how comfortable if that feeling were somehow torn away from you."

It was odd but reassuring to look into the audience and see a few people who looked like her. This time, the investors included a scattering of women and someone who had introduced themself with "they/them/theirs" when Emily had phoned them. There were even two people in the room besides her who weren't white. This time, rather than going after the big and notable investors, Emily had picked investors Hock wouldn't ever have considered. For him, that was probably the right choice.

"Most people are that comfortable. But not everyone." She tapped the table for emphasis. "And ones who aren't deserve to feel as comfortable in their bodies as you do in yours."

She continued to talk about expectations of convention and how they caused profound discomfort. Existing ways of making people comfortable in their bodies were difficult and expensive. Any option people couldn't afford might as well not exist for them. That was an untapped market iDunn could reach. A few investors leaned forward with interest. A few more slides in, and they began to nod in agreement with her.

When the ten minutes of her pitch was over, smiles lit everybody's faces. She had them. Not all of them, of course, but enough to get started. Not that getting their interest had ever been her only obstacle. She had to make sure that Jazz and intellectual property law didn't get in her way. That meant having lunch with Hock.

Hock's pitch to Emily didn't begin in earnest until dessert. Honestly, though, Emily saw it start from the moment he made his entrance into the restaurant. She was suddenly glad that Hock was paying for lunch and that she'd thought to suggest a place only a block away from the nearest subway stop.

Hock had shown up in a black leather jacket, T-shirt, jeans, and midnight blue dress boots. The quality fabrics, impeccable fit, and detailed stitching were obvious even from across the room. If forced, Emily would have priced the ensemble at about five thousand dollars.

The act of taking off the jacket was its own multibillion-dollar summer blockbuster. To Emily, Hock was the slab of beef who was getting his fifth shot at making a summer tentpole movie a hit because no famous hardbody would star in it. To any male investor, Hock would have been the very embodiment of success. Some of them might have whipped out their checkbooks and cut Hock a check by the time his ass hit the chair.

Hock had been pleasant, even modestly charming, during the appetizer and main course. Interest in her welfare as well as that of Shereen's had been indicated. Her concerns about the implications of transforming human bodies had been listened to and acknowledged. This was all perfectly adequate and expected. If he were an asshole all the time, no one would ever fund his startup. Looking like you've won the "man game" several times over could take you far, but not that far.

But dessert had just arrived. She'd opted out, settling for a cup of coffee. As his fork dug into his molten chocolate lava cake, Emily could feel Hock's gears shift and his machinations grind.

"You understand why I asked you to lunch." He pressed a forkful of cake into the chocolate that had oozed out of the center. "This isn't personal."

"No, not at all." She didn't see a reason to be confrontational . . . yet. "This is just a business proposal."

"Exactly." He gestured his fork, cake and all, at her. "You're not going to take advantage of me. I'm not going to let you take advantage of me."

"What?"

Emily had not taken advantage of Hock. If anything, it had been the other way around. Both their names were on the patents. He'd made sure his name was on them. Sure, he'd done some work, but the bulk of it was hers.

"You couldn't have gotten any investor without information from working at Jazz. You don't have the right to use that to fundraise for your own startup."

"Look, we can come to an agreement about how we both exploit our patents, or we can tie things up in court and no one gets to exploit them. And, frankly, some of the patents I can work around. Can you?" She took a sip of her coffee. "I'm perfectly happy not to be a direct competitor. My investors and I are targeting a different market, and we are passionate in our cause. You can have bros who want to look like superheroes all to yourself."

He frowned. His fork clattered onto the plate. Hock locked his gaze on Emily, who stared right back. Meaty forearms pressed against the table as he leaned toward her. He held the position for what seemed like minutes before he finally sat back. His gaze stayed fixed on her.

"It'd be easier for you and your investors if you came back."

"Of course. Then my lawyers won't have to talk to your lawyers." She smiled as she set down her cup. "But, honestly, that's not enough."

"Come back and you can work on your passion. You've shown there's funding for it."

"Really?" Emily sat up, her chair sliding back.

"Really." Hock's gaze softened.

"Well, that's an interesting offer." Emily stood. "Thank you for lunch."

She walked away. Part of her expected Hock to reach out and pull her back. The rest of her guessed that even though Hock was more than physically capable of tossing her like a stick, he was too savvy to actually do that.

"Wait, the apples and the headset." Hock's resonant voice made everything in the restaurant vibrate. "They're Jazz property and I'd like them back."

Emily turned around. She held Hock in her gaze and everything made sense. Broadened shoulders and slimmed hips were permanent, just as transformed organs would be once Emily figured them out. He'd always be towering with a voice that boomed. The muscle, however, was atrophying from disuse, and it'd take months for any new apples to mature. Whether or not she returned to Jazz, he wanted apples to keep him buff in the meantime. The price of that—and Hock would pay it to cover the gap—would be an agreement that let both of them exploit their mutual patents. It wasn't like he could call the police, not without also implicating himself in unauthorized human testing.

"In a minute." If there was one thing Hock loved, it was for Emily to keep him waiting. "After our lawyers work something out."

Emily didn't have to jump at his command anymore. She just walked away, finally in charge of her own destiny.

Author's Note

Every once in a rare while, a story practically writes itself. One moment, an editor is prompting you, and the next, the story springs fully formed from your head and splatters itself across the page. This is not one of those stories. When Navah and Dominik asked me, I agreed because I wanted the opportunity to work with them, not because I had any clue what to write about. As a result, writing this story was akin to jumping out of an airplane, then stitching the parachute as I plummeted, hoping to finish it and deploy it in time to avoid splatting on the ground. If you're reading this, then I am, presumably, not an unsightly stain upon this good earth.

Navah and Dominik helpfully suggested Norse mythology. I decided on apples because they were symbolically important across a bunch of cultures. The intersection of the two, of course, is the goddess Idunn, who tends the golden apples that keep the Norse gods immortal. And, honestly, that's about all we know about her. She has surprisingly little to do with the one Prose Edda story that features her. In that, she is kidnapped, replaced with an acorn, and rescued. What I wrote isn't so much a retelling as much as it is a reaction. I wanted to see what might happen if Idunn were her own rescuer instead. As it turned out, in order to free herself, she needed to fight the system. Kind of like life . . .

John Chu

BURIED DEEP

BY
—
NAOMI NOVIK

THE LIE MINOS TOLD, WHICH NO ONE BELIEVED and no one was expected to believe, was that his youngest son had been shut up for the sake of the servants, whom he had begun brutalizing even as a babe. The lie everyone believed, and told in whispers, was that the queen had played the king false with a handsome guardsman, and he'd shut up the child to keep another man's son from any chance of inheriting his throne.

But Ariadne had been five years old, herself a late and unexpected child, when her even more unexpected brother had begun to grow under Pasiphae's heart, and she had been so very excited. Her other brothers were all grown men, big men, warriors; Minos's bull-strong sons, the court called them, her father's pride and irrelevant to her. Her sisters had been married off and gone before she was even born. And she had already been clever and good at creeping, so she'd been in the birthing room when the baby had come out bellowing, with the nubs of the horns still soft and rounded on his forehead, and her mother's attendants had begun to scream.

Minos had all of them put to death, along with three particularly handsome guardsmen with fair hair, to start the second lie and keep the secret. His secret, not her mother's. Everyone in all of Crete knew of the white bull the sea had sent him, and that Minos had bred it to his cattle instead of putting it to the knife the way the priests had wanted, but Ariadne and her mother knew more than that: they knew that Minos had asked for a sacrifice, one great enough to mark him for the throne over his brothers, and the god had sent the bull for that purpose, to be given back to him, not kept. So it was Minos's fault, and not her mother's, but Pasiphae had paid for it, and so had her women, and Ariadne's little brother most of all.

Ariadne shouted at her mother, the day her father's men came to take Minotaur away. "We could go to Grandfather!" she said; she was twelve, and her silent, frightened brother was holding her hand tight and trying to stay hidden behind her, futilely: he was a foot taller than her already, with the big cow-eyes large and dark and liquid on either side of his broad soft nose.

They lived with their mother and a few cowed servants—some of them *had* been killed, but by her father's orders, not by Minotaur—in a single tower perched on the edge of a green meadow in the hills far above Knossos. It had been built as a watchtower, to give warning of men coming from the sea. They could see for a long way from the windows of the narrow top story, all the way to the sea far below, glossy and deep, like her brother's eyes. Mother usually stayed in the more comfortable rooms below, but when she came up, she never looked at the sea, only the other way, down at the city— the red columns of the temple, and the people in the markets or thronging the streets to celebrate a festival—and her face was hard and bitter.

Father never came to them. But once a year, on Ariadne's birthday, someone came and took her down the long dusty hill to the palace, to be presented to him and to receive another heavy necklace of gold, each one growing with her, so that now she had seven of them, the smallest one close around her neck and the largest hanging over her growing breasts. A great dowry accumulating in chains, to apologize for her imprisonment.

It was the only apology Minos ever made. He avoided being alone with her; she was always taken in to him by a nurse or a maidservant, who warned her strictly not to ask her father to let her come and live in the palace, as if he wanted to pretend that he wasn't refusing her just because he told her no through someone else's mouth. But she wouldn't have asked, anyway. She didn't want to live in the palace, with her father and his lies, even before he'd sent men to take her brother away.

She had instead begun to worry about being taken away herself; she'd started to be old enough, that year, to understand that soon her father would begin to look for someone else to hold her chains. That was why she'd already thought of going to her grandfather: Pasiphae's father was Helios, the great lord of the easternmost city of Crete, the place where the sun rose, and a power in his own right, with a fortress that not even Minos's navy could have shattered.

But Pasiphae shook her head and said flatly to Ariadne, "You're old enough to stop being a fool. The king of Crete needs the sea god's favor. If the priests learn your father's lost it, they won't stop with *his* blood to buy it back. It'll be your brother on the altar, and me, and you as well, likely as not." And after she said that, Minotaur carefully pulled his big hand out of hers—he was only seven, but he'd already learned how easily he could hurt people, if he wasn't careful—and he put on the heavy wide-hooded cloak that Ariadne had sewn for him so they could go walking in the hills together at night, and then he went out to the waiting guards.

Minos had sent the Oreth to take him: his slave guards, warriors all bought from countries so far away that they had little hope of making a safe return. Their tongues had all been cut out. They were brutal men, hardened by their own misery and everything they saw in their work. They didn't fear death or the gods, or thought they didn't, and they would have cut off the head of a seven-year-old boy if her father told them to, much less put him into a prison. But when Minotaur came out a big silent hulk in his cloak, they all went still and afraid, even though they couldn't see his face, and their hands went to the hilts of their swords. After they shut the door in her face, and Ariadne ran upstairs to look out of the window, she saw them walking in a group ten paces ahead, not looking back at all. Minotaur was trudging after them alone, his head in the cloak bowed, following them to the door, which wasn't a door, only a hole in the earth.

She had watched them build the shrine all the last year, Minotaur peeking one eye out from behind a curtain next to her, both of them fascinated: it was the most interesting thing that had ever happened. First the priests had come to bless the site, and after them Daedalus, walking over the meadow for days marking the ground with long sticks left poking out. Then the digging began, which took a long time, because there were only six workmen on the whole project: four big slaves to dig the passage, twenty feet down into the ground, and two skilled ones to follow them, putting in the slabs of beautiful polished marble that came in on laden carts to make the floor and the walls.

The shape hadn't made any sense to her. The workmen had started in the very middle of the meadow, digging out the single round central chamber, and they even dug a well in the middle of it. She thought it would be the first room of many. But instead, from there they dug out a single circling passage, only one, with no rooms and no branching paths, that curved and folded back on itself like a bewildered snake that had lost sight of its own tail. They kept going and going, digging in that one line, filling in one quarter of the circle after another, until they had honeycombed the whole meadow.

On moonlit nights sometimes Ariadne and Minotaur would sneak out and walk on the narrow dirt walls left between the passages, balancing with their arms stuck out and the deep passages looming on either side. They couldn't run back and forth across the meadow anymore the way they had used to, because the winding passage covered the whole thing in an enormous circle, ripples spreading out from that central well. The walls were just wide enough that it wasn't *very* hard to balance for Ariadne's small feet, but it was just a little bit hard, enough that you had to pay attention to how you put your feet, one after the other. It was harder for Minotaur. He didn't eat, not since their mother had finally refused to nurse him anymore, to try and make him take food, but it didn't seem to matter. He was growing very big, and very quickly. By the time the men finished digging, he was teetering on the edges, having trouble not falling in.

She was waiting impatiently for the workmen to finish the last quarter of the circle, to see what they would do when the passage got to the end. The digging seemed like it had taken forever, and so much work. So she was sure it must be meant for a shrine to the god. She imagined steps coming up, and then flagstones being laid on top of the mysterious cellar, and pillars for some great temple. But when the workmen finished digging to the border of the great circle, the passage only stopped. They dug a very small circular room there just outside the rest of the maze, like an antechamber, and then they didn't do any more work the rest of that day, even though it was morning. They only sat down in the small bit of shade on the edge of the hillside with their tools scattered around them and drank from their jug of watered wine, watching the skilled workmen coming the rest of the way behind them.

The next day, the skilled workmen began to work back along the passageway toward the center, laying flat stones atop the passage to make a ceiling. The diggers followed them now, burying the stone under dirt from the enormous mound they had dug up out of the passages. They didn't leave anywhere for stairs to go down, only the one little round hole on the outside, above the antechamber, and the one big center hole in the middle. Ariadne was baffled. They had dug that whole enormous winding passage for nothing. Once it was buried, no one would even know it was there under the meadow. They weren't even marking the surface. By the time the men got back to the middle again, there was already a thick furry coat of grass covering everything behind them: it was late spring, and the sky had been generous with both sunshine and rain.

Then yesterday, the final cart had come, hauled up from the city by a team of four big oxen, carrying two circular metal slabs braced on their sides, one big and one little, like coins for giants, and just the right size to fit over the two rooms. But they had been shrouded in sheets, so Ariadne still hadn't understood what the shrine was really for. But now the six workmen were standing by to put the big slab into the ground, and they had uncovered it, just barely visible in the coming light: a massive bronze disc covered with beaten gold, with a central hatch, engraved with the great head of the bull, surrounded by great locks of iron.

The Oreth led Minotaur to the waiting open hole. They went around to the far side and stood there watching him. The workmen drew back against the cart as he passed by. They had left a rope dangling down inside the hole. Minotaur stood on the edge looking down, and Ariadne gave a cry from the window, shouted, "Don't, don't!" but it worked the wrong way; his hood twitched, where his big ears underneath had twisted around to hear her, and then he sat down on the edge of the hole with his sandaled feet hanging over, and he let himself down inside.

The workmen didn't move even after he vanished. Finally one of the Oreth made a sharp, impatient gesture, and one of them went with dragging steps to the edge and then hurriedly pulled out the rope, hand over hand quickly, and backed away as soon as he could. Then they rolled the big golden seal to the edge and tipped it over carefully to fit perfectly into the hole. They hurriedly buried the seal all the way up to the edge of the central hatch, and the Oreth checked the locks. There was a narrow circular grating that went around the head of the bull, an opening for air.

The workers had already put the smaller seal over the anteroom. It also had a hatch in it, but without the seal of the bull. Ariadne watched from the tower while the Oreth opened the hatch and shoved all the workmen in, one after another, screaming for mercy and struggling and disappearing nevertheless, one after another, down into the dark, until the Oreth slammed the metal hatch back down on top of them, and turned the locks. Six was a wrong number, and she wondered where Daedalus had gone; she hadn't seen him for the last week. A long time later, she heard that he'd fled by ship to Greece, abandoning his wife and son, just before the labyrinth had been finished. By then people were saying he was a sorcerer and the labyrinth was magic, but she knew that the only magical thing in it was her brother, her little brother, a piece of the god put down into the dark.

In the morning she opened her eyes and knew right away that Minotaur was gone. She got up and went to the window. The meadow was a smooth, ordinary green meadow, the grass verdant and lush. Everything buried deep and silent, and only the two golden seals set into the earth, so low that in the dim light they were hidden in the grass, unless you knew where to look to catch a glimpse of gold.

Her mother had kept Ariadne inside all day yesterday, even after the Oreth had gone, but it was still early in the morning and no one else was awake. Her mother stayed up in the evenings, drinking wine, and after she went to bed, her two women finished whatever she had left, so they all slept late and heavily. Last night, her mother had opened a second jar of wine, leaving it almost unwatered, and she had poured Ariadne a glass. Ariadne had left it standing untouched on the table, along with her food.

She crept past the snoring women on the floor and her mother lying sprawled behind the thin curtains of her bed, and got outside without being stopped. She ran to the meadow, but she couldn't open the hatches herself, no matter how she turned the locks back and forth, no matter how she poked her fingers and branches into the cracks around them and strained. Either she didn't know the trick of the locks, or the doors were just too heavy. The metal was cold and slick with dew under her fingers as she struggled. Finally she gave up and she went back to the central seal, to the narrow grating, and called through the dark opening.

But Minotaur couldn't answer her, if he was there: he couldn't speak. Once after a month of coaxing he'd tried to say something to her, and she'd woken up three days later in her bed, her ears and nose still crusted with dried blood. He'd refused even to try, after that. He might be somewhere wandering in that endless passage, alone in the dark, and not have heard her coming.

She fell silent, kneeling in the dirt by the seal, tears dripping off her face, and then she got up and went to the small seal, over the antechamber, and did her best to walk all over the meadow, stamping and jumping every so often, so that he'd hear her footsteps overhead, and know that she was there. And when she finally came back to the big seal in the center, she knelt there and talked to him until the sun was well up and her throat was dry, and then she stole back into the tower before anyone noticed she was gone. That day, and every day after. She crept out of her mother's tower in the hour of dawn, and she told Minotaur every day that she'd be back the next, so when at last she didn't come, he'd know that the chain around his neck was gone, and he could leave.

The third time she started to walk over the meadow, the grass suddenly began to wither just ahead of her toes, green blades curling in to form dusty yellow lines that she could see even in the early light. She stamped along between them, all the way until they brought her finally to the waiting center, and there she turned around and looked out over the meadow as the sun came up, and the yellow grass lines made an outline, faint but there, marking out the buried passageway underground.

After that, when she walked the path, she felt something moving beneath her feet: not quite a sound, not quite a vibration, but like heavy footfalls echoing against marble walls, deep within. So then she knew he was there, walking with her, the way they'd once walked together balancing over the walls. Only he had fallen inside, after all.

One week after they put Minotaur into the labyrinth, a priest came to dedicate the new shrine. It was only a young one, in a red robe, with a slightly younger acolyte leading a tired, skinny bull for a sacrifice; the hill was a hot, steep walk up from the city. Minos had needed to give some excuse, for sending Daedalus and the workmen up to dig and dig for months, but he didn't mean for the shrine to be important. It was meant to be forgotten. From the tower, Ariadne saw the priest and the acolyte come to the edge of the meadow, where they saw the pattern. They stood there staring, and they didn't kill the bull, after all. They went away instead.

The next day they came back, the young priest and two older ones. They stood beside the pattern for a long time, hesitating, as though they wanted to step onto it but didn't quite dare. Then they went away too, and the day after that they came back, the three priests, the acolyte leading the bull again and carrying water jugs dewed with moisture slung on his back, the high priest puffing along in his white robe with the red bands, and Minos himself with them. But this time they came in the early hours of the morning, before the sun was up, and Ariadne was still walking along the pattern to the seal. They saw her, and the young priest called out angrily, "What do you mean by this, girl? How dare you put your feet on the god's path. Do you think this is a dancing floor?"

She stopped and turned. The deep echoing was there under her feet; it stopped, too. The men were standing on the edge of the pattern, her father's face darkened, all of them waiting for her to cringe and apologize. She stood for a moment without moving. If she obeyed them, and came off, they would leave a priest here to watch over the labyrinth, so she could never come again. Minotaur would never know when they sent her away. There was a waiting beneath her feet, like the change in the light before rain came, even though the sun was coming up and lining the next mountains over with brilliance.

"It is for me," she said.

Her father said sharply, "Watch your tongue, girl," which meant now she was going to be whipped for impertinence. "Come here at once."

She took a breath and faced forward again and kept going along the path. "With your permission, I will bring her back," the young priest said to the king, to the high priest.

He untied his sandals before he came to get her. She saw him coming for her, cutting across the lines of the pattern, and then she had to turn her back on him to follow the next turn, one single foot's length along the pattern, and when she turned again with the following step, moving a little closer to the center, he wasn't there anymore. It wasn't a vanishing. There was only a moment when he was there, and then there was a moment when he wasn't, and all the moments in between those two moments were one moment, and endless.

The other men were still waiting impatiently. They were farther away, and they were watching her; it took them a little longer to notice that he was gone. They looked around for him, confused at first, and then they looked at the empty sandals standing at the side of the pattern, and then they all drew back several steps from the labyrinth, and said nothing more. Ariadne kept going all the way to the seal, with thunder moving beneath her feet, and she knelt and said to the dark crack around the door, "I'm here."

They were still waiting when she came back to them. She could just have walked away, but she stayed on the pattern, and she didn't go quickly, letting the hot sun come up and bake them a little in their wigs and their crimped, oiled hair. Their robes were stained with growing dark patches of sweat when she came out finally, and stepped off the labyrinth.

She stood before them, and they looked at her, faces downturned and unsmiling, and then the high priest turned to her father and said, "She must be consecrated to the god," insistent, and her father's jaw tightened—thinking mostly, Ariadne knew, of all those heavy golden chains he'd put around her neck, his false apology, and how he wouldn't be able to use them and her to buy some lord's loyalty.

"I have to be back here tomorrow," she said.

They all paused and stared at her, and the high priest said, sternly, "My daughter, you will enter the temple—"

"I'm not your daughter," she interrupted. "I have to be here tomorrow morning. He'll be waiting for me."

The acolyte blurted, "Yidini?" meaning the young priest. His voice was ragged with desperation, but he flinched when the high priest gave him a hard narrowed look, and subsided; the other priests shifted uneasily, looking away from him.

Ariadne looked straight at her father and said, "Do you need me to say?" A threat, and even in his anger, his eyes darted to the labyrinth, to the gold seal on his hidden shame.

Minos was a clever man. He'd thought of one trick after another: to win the throne over his brothers, to keep it in his grasp, to build his wealth. And now he turned back to the high priest and said, "You will consecrate the tower as a temple, and my daughter will abide here, and tend the god's shrine, which he has chosen to favor."

Pasiphae went back to the palace in the city, gladly. Three women of the temple came to live with Ariadne instead. Reja, the eldest and a priestess, had a mouth whose corners turned down and plunged into dark hollows. Her hand often flinched when she taught Ariadne, as though she would have slapped a different novice, who wasn't the daughter of the king and the chosen of the god. When she came, she tried to make herself the mistress of the tower: she wanted to take the queen's room for herself, and put the rest of them together on the two higher floors.

Ariadne didn't do anything about it. She didn't see what she could do. The other women did what Reja told them. That night they came upstairs with her, to the room where she had slept with Minotaur, and the two novices lay down on the big cot where he had slept. It was wide enough for both of them. Then they put out the candle, and even as Ariadne was falling asleep, one of the young women jerked up and said, "Who's there?" into the dark.

The other one sat up too. They both sat there shaking, and after a moment they scrambled up with all their bedclothes and went creeping silently down the stairs, and they wouldn't come back upstairs even when Reja scolded them. Then she came up angry herself to accuse Ariadne of scaring them, and Ariadne sat up on her own cot and looked at her and said, "I didn't do anything. *You* lie down, if you want," and Reja stared at her, and then she went to the cot and lay down on it, on her back staring up into the dark with her angry frowning mouth, and then after a few moments she twitched, and twitched again, and then she got quickly up off the bed and stood in the middle of the room and looked down at Ariadne, who looked back at her, and then Reja said, in a very different voice, not angry, hushed, "Who slept in this room with you?"

The moon was outside, so she could see Reja's eyes, each one a small gleam in the dark, nothing like the deep shine of her brother's eyes, as if he hadn't ever been here at all. "His name is Minotaur," Ariadne said, defiantly. "He's under the hill now."

Reja was silent, and then she went downstairs and didn't scold the other priestesses anymore. The next morning she sat up when Ariadne went out, waking even though Ariadne was creeping out of habit, and she got up and followed her outside. She stood and watched her dance through the labyrinth all the way to the center, and when Ariadne came back out, Reja said, "I will show you how to pour the libations," and the rest of that day, Reja taught her with a jug of water, and then the next morning she was awake and waiting, before Ariadne went to the labyrinth, with a stoppered jug full of olive oil, deep green and fragrant, from the first pressing. Ariadne took it. She carried it with her along the path, all the way to the seal, where she didn't follow the ritual. Instead she poured the oil all around the hatch, its locks, through the cracks, hoping to make it easier to open. But when she tried, it didn't help. The hatch was still too heavy for her. She couldn't even shift it a little bit in its groove. But as she knelt by the hatch with her fingers sore, unhappy and angry all over again, the seal beneath her moved a little, the whole hillside taking a deep sighing breath, and a little air came out of the grating from inside, full of the strong smell of the olive oil, fresh and bright, instead of the faint musty smell of earth.

It frustrated Reja that Ariadne wouldn't do the rituals properly, but she didn't scold her any more than she slapped her; she only grimly kept teaching her, one after another, the proper words and gestures for wine instead of oil, perfume instead of wine, as if hoping if she did it often enough, one day it would stick. Ariadne did the lessons, a little out of boredom and a little to be at peace with Reja, who managed things with ruthless efficiency and also sent the novices down to the city each day to bring something else to pour out, another bright living smell to send into the dark.

The acolyte who'd come up with the priests was set to guard them. There was nothing to guard them from, at least no danger that hadn't always been there, the last seven years while Ariadne had lived there with the queen and all her jewels, but the acolyte had seen something uncomfortable, and it was easier for the high priest and the king to forget about it if he wasn't around.

He wasn't allowed to stay with the women, of course; instead he had to build a hut to shelter in farther down the hillside, and Reja kept a hawk's cold eye on him any time he came up to their well for water, close enough to see the novices. The second day after they arrived, she paused in the prayer she was teaching Ariadne, and she got up and marched to a bush near where the trail down the mountain began. She pulled Nashu out of it by his ear and told him sharply if she caught him at it again, she would have him whipped out of the temple.

But he wasn't spying on the novices, even though they had their skirts hiked up around their waists, working on the garden. "I want to know where Yidini is!" he said, his voice wobbling up and down through a boy's soprano, and wrenched himself loose to take a step toward Ariadne, his fists clenched. "Where did you send him?"

She hadn't been sorry for the priest; to her, the priests were the ones who'd made her brother hide, who'd have put him to death. And Yidini had meant to drag her away. But she was sorry for Nashu, because someone he loved had been taken away and sent into the dark. She still couldn't help him, though, and when she said, "I don't know," he was angry, and he hated her for it.

He crept up the hill sometimes after that to watch her walking to the seal, in the dim early mornings. He hid in the bushes along the edge of the hill. Reja with her older eyes didn't catch him, but Ariadne knew he was there. She didn't say anything. There was something a little comforting in how much he cared; it meant she wasn't stupid for caring, either. She kept coming every day herself to pour the offerings down, a little bit of the mortal world, so her brother wouldn't disappear forever into the earth.

She wanted the days to change, sometimes; she had been afraid of being taken away, and now some small part of her wanted to go, wanted the life she'd avoided. She could still have had it. The golden chains sat in a locked chest in her room, the room where no one went but her, except hurriedly, in broad daylight, to sweep and clean. Her father, who had kept a bull the god had sent, would gladly have made some excuse for releasing her from the temple to buy a lord with her. And then her brother would melt back into the god like a little pond of water draining into a stream, and the vegetation would creep over the seals, and new grass would grow where the yellowed lines stood.

So she stayed.

The days did begin to change a little, over time. It was the poor hill folk who came first, the ones who couldn't afford to go to the temple in the city. They brought cups of milk, and an egg or two, and foraged greens. Once an anxious young man came with a lamb on a rope, and when Ariadne came out of the tower that morning, he was waiting on the edge of the labyrinth, and he knelt to her as if to the king and said, low, "My wife is giving birth soon, and the ewe died," a plea to turn aside the evil omen.

Reja looked at the lamb with greedy pleasure, thinking of the priest's portion, the best meat, and she said to Ariadne, "I'll show you how to make sacrifice," but Ariadne looked at the lamb with its wide uncertain liquid eyes, deep and brown, and said, "No." She took the rope and led the lamb with her through the passage to the seal. It butted at her as they went, bleating and trying to suck at her fingers, hungry, but she stayed on the track, and at the seal, she said, "There's a lamb here, if the god will take it to its mother, and let the shepherd's wife stay with her child up here," and then she took the rope off the lamb's neck, and rubbed the matted wool underneath it soft, and let the lamb go. It ran away from her bleating.

Reja and the shepherd were watching her from the edge of the laby-rinth. It was like the last time: their faces didn't know that the lamb was gone at first, and then they looked around wanting to believe it had just run away, but there was nothing for it to have hidden behind on the bare hill, and then finally they had to understand that it was gone. The shepherd fell on his face, pressing his forehead into the dirt, and Reja drew back herself, staring, and then she knelt too, when Ariadne came out of the labyrinth.

Nashu was there, too. Later that afternoon, when Ariadne went down the hill to get some water, and she was alone, he came out of the bushes and stood staring at her with his face twisted up, and then he said, "Why Yidini? He was a true servant of the god! You could have sent that old fat priest."

Ariadne didn't bother trying to tell him she hadn't sent the young priest anywhere. She wasn't sure it was true, anyway. "Why would the god want an old fat priest?" she said instead, and Nashu was silent, and then he said, "Then I hate the god, if he took Yidini," defiantly.

"It's not worth your hating him," Ariadne said, after a moment; she had to think it out for herself. "He doesn't care."

Nashu glared at her. "Why does he care about *you*, then?"

"He doesn't," she said slowly.

The next morning, she didn't dance. She only walked straight to the center and knelt down by the seal and whispered, her throat tight, "It's all right if you want to go. You don't have to stay for me. I'll be all right," because she hadn't thought, before, that she was being selfish by holding on to the little part of the god that could care about her, keeping him there buried in the earth, instead of letting him go back to the rest of himself.

There wasn't any answer. She left the labyrinth, walking slowly with her head down, and went back into the tower, where the two novices darted sideways looks at her and Reja determinedly looked at her directly and scolded her to eat her supper of olives and bread and honey. That night, Ariadne opened her eyes and looked over at the empty cot across the room from her, and Minotaur was sitting there looking at her. He was bigger than the last time she'd seen him, much bigger: two feet taller than the biggest of the Oreth, and his pale cream-ivory horns were wide and gleaming at the points, deadly. She knew she was dreaming, because he was too big. If he had really been there, she didn't think she could have stood it. But when she sat up and looked back at him, his eyes were still soft and liquid, and she knew he didn't want to go back into the god, either. He wanted to keep this piece of himself separate, this part that could love her, for as long as he could. Even if he had to stay down there in the dark.

A rich man from the city sent a lamb, for the sake of *his* wife, but Ariadne told the slave who had brought it up the hill, "It's not a fair trade. Take it back."

The sweaty, thin boy stared at her and said uncertainly, "You don't want it?"

"A lamb doesn't mean the same thing to a rich man as a poor one," she said. "And if he cares, he should come himself."

So the boy went away, and two days later, the rich man did come himself: fat, even more sweaty despite the servants who had trailed him with fans and water jugs, and irritated. "What's this nonsense?" he said to

Reja, complaining. "Now I had to come: my wife's father took it into his head that if I didn't, I'd as good as be killing her myself. And in this heat!"

Reja was going to be polite, because he was rich, and a nobleman, but Ariadne heard him and came down the stairs and out of the tower and said coldly, "You're asking for the god to put his hand into your life. Do you think that's a small matter? Go away again, if you don't want to be here."

The rich man scowled, but he said grudgingly, "Forgive me, Priestess," because he knew she was the king's daughter, and then he waved to the ass laden with rich gifts. "I have brought many fine offerings for the god."

The gifts were all for *her*, though: red and purple silks shot through with gold, a necklace, a box of coin, candied fruit. Ariadne shook her head in frustration as she looked over them, because there wasn't anything that she could send down into the dark; he hadn't even brought wine or perfume, because those weren't sophisticated enough: only a chest of sandalwood for her clothing and a luxurious loaf of dried cherries pressed with honey and nuts. There wasn't anything, but that was *his* fault, not his wife's, whose father had sent him to ask for her life, and Ariadne looked at his dripping, sweaty face, and said, "Come with me." She took him by the hand, and led him to the labyrinth, and said, "Stay on the path, and stay right behind me, no matter what."

It was the middle of the day. She'd already gone, that morning. But the deep thunder came soon under her feet: Minotaur had heard her. She heard the man's breathing go more and more ragged behind her, a faint whimpering deep in his throat. She didn't look back at him. The sun was hot on the crown of her dark hair, beating on her like a hammer, and the air over the golden seal shimmered. But the ground beneath her breathed coolness over her, and she kept dancing, all the way to the seal, and then she turned and the man went to his knees gasping, crouched over the seal, so wet with sweat that the drops were rolling off his earlobes and his nose and chin, his clothing soaked through.

"Take off your robes and squeeze out the sweat," she said, and he stripped down to his loincloth and wrung the robes like a woman getting clothing ready for drying, and the pungent sharp sweat trickled out of them and went into the grating, and the earth stirred beneath her.

She took him out after, back to his servants and his ass, and told him, "Now you can go back to your wife, and tell her and her father that you made a true offering to the god for her. And give the gifts to the people you meet on your way back home."

She didn't guess what that would do. It just sounded like the stories Reja taught her, of priests and oracles speaking, and Ariadne liked those, even as she knew that it wasn't anything like real priests, who needed offerings to live on and in exchange made a comforting show to distract men from death. But it worked, even if she hadn't meant it to work. The rich man came stumbling down the hill still full of terror, and pressed wealth into the hands of shepherds and a bewildered milkmaid and beggars in the street, and the whispers came down from the country folk and went in through the city gates with him, and after that even the city people said, *The god is there on the mountain, and the king's daughter is beloved of him.*

Reja didn't have to send the novices down to get offerings anymore. People came and brought them, often without any request attached. And a few fools came to see the god, because they didn't think it was real. Once it was a group of six drunken young noblemen whose fathers were too healthy and didn't give their sons enough work to do, and they showed up in the early hours shouting up at the tower windows that they wanted to speak with the god.

Ariadne was coming down anyway, because it was time; in summer the sun came early and quick. The drunken youths smiled at her, and one of them took her hand and bowed over it and said mournfully, putting it to his chest, "But you're too pretty to be locked up here with no lover but a buried god."

"He's my brother," Ariadne said. The young man was good-looking, at least in the dim light, and she half liked the silliness, but Reja was at her shoulder, tense, afraid of something Ariadne had never had to fear before. That fear was trying to creep into her, telling her without words that she was a woman now, with breasts and her hair unbound, and fair game for drunk men who didn't believe in the god.

"Even worse!" the young man said. "Won't you have a drink with us? Here, we've the finest mead, brewed from my father's hives."

"It's time for me to go to the labyrinth," Ariadne said. "You can come if you want. You can bring it as an offering."

"Then lead on, and let me meet your brother!" the young man declared. "I'll show him a man worthy to court his sister!" His name was Staphos, and he kept smiling at her, and touching her hand. "Hurry and make the offering," he murmured to her as they walked. "I know what I want to ask the god for." His friends were singing, arm in arm with one another.

They were near the labyrinth when the bushes stirred, and Nashu came out and blurted, "Don't go in there with her!"

"Oh, so you *do* have some company up here!" one of the other youths said, gleefully, and Nashu said angrily, "I'm trying to save you! If you go with her, the god will take you," and they all started laughing, a drunken joyful noise, and Ariadne turned and took the jug of mead from Staphos and said, "He might. It's up to you if you want to come. Don't stray from the path, if you do," and she turned and put her foot on the path as the sun began to come up.

Staphos laughed again, and fell in behind her. The others came, too, singing a marching song and doing a mocking high-step behind her own dance, but the deep drumming echo rose beneath to meet them, and their song began to die away little by little. "Keep singing," she said, over her shoulder, but they kept fading out, until suddenly Staphos began a faint and wavering temple song, one Reja hadn't taught her, deep and chanted: one of the men's songs, probably. She felt that Minotaur heard it, and wanted to listen, and the deep echoes went quieter beneath them.

Soon the young noblemen could sing it too, the repetition of the chant at least, which was only four syllables strung together in two different patterns.

They came to the seal, and Ariadne poured out the honey-strong mead, with all of them in a ring around her clutching hands and still singing. They followed her out again in silence, without singing, without saying a word. She stood on the hill watching them go down the trail in sunlight, and only then she noticed herself that Staphos wasn't with them anymore. She wasn't sure when he'd gone.

Staphos wasn't a lamb, or even a young priest. He was the eldest son of one of her father's richer lords, and he'd been betrothed to the daughter of another. It made trouble below for her father, who wanted to make it someone else's trouble, as he always did. He sent a group of priests up to question her, one of them Staphos's cousin, and they questioned the novices, and Reja, and the acolytes also.

Nashu tried to get her into trouble, but he was too young and bad at lying. He told three different made-up grotesque stories about her butchering men on the seal, and then he gave up and told them that her brother the god lived under the hill, and she gave him offerings, and he took people who made her angry. And when the interrogating priest said, "Why my cousin, then?" Nashu blurted, "He tried to lie with her," which would have required the family to chisel Staphos's name off his tomb and cast him into the dark forever, if she had confirmed it.

But she was sorry about Staphos, so she told the priest, "He was only joking. The god wanted him, so the god took him. That's all I can tell you."

A messenger came two days later to summon her down to her father's palace. Ariadne didn't want to go. In her father's house, there would be guards and rooms with locked doors and lies shut up inside them, and if she said the wrong thing, she'd be shut up into one of them too. "I have to make the offering first," she said, and took a jar of oil out to the seal, and after she poured it down she said softly, "I have to go to the palace. I don't know if he'll let me come back."

The deep faint tremor lingered beneath her feet all the way to the labyrinth's end, and there it paused for a moment, and came on with her. The messenger and the escort of guards looked over their shoulders uneasily as they walked; and Reja, who had insisted on coming as chaperone, kept moving her lips silently in the formal chant to the god; and when they stopped for water, a few times, she knelt and prayed aloud, a prayer for mercy, while the soldiers opened and closed their hands around their hilts.

When Ariadne stepped onto the paved streets of Knossos, the sensation didn't disappear, but it receded deeper, muffled, and the soldiers relaxed in relief. They took her to the palace, and up another muffling flight of stairs into the higher chambers, until there was barely a faint echo lingering when the Oreth themselves took her the last of the way into the throne room, her father sitting with stern downturned mouth in state, the high priest standing important beside the throne in robes, and both of them looking down at her from the height of the dais, so she had to look up at them. There was no one else in the room, only the Oreth on either side of her, and Minos said, "Daughter, two men have died at the god's shrine, under your hands. What have you to say of it?"

His voice bounced against the walls of the room, the heavy stone clad in marble: he knew how to pitch it to make the reverberations bright and loud, so his voice came at her from all sides, a whispering echo arriving a moment after the first sound reached her ears. But the floor under her swallowed the sound, and it fell away deadened.

"They didn't die under my hands," she said. "They went to the god. All *three* of them."

Her father's lips thinned, his hands closing around the gilded bull's-head ends of the arms of his throne, flexing. He looked at the Oreth around her, and then back at her, a warning to keep quiet, but he didn't need to worry. The high priest didn't care: he thought the third one was a shepherd, some poor man, someone who didn't matter. "It is not for you to decide who will go to the god, girl," he said to her.

"It's not for you, either," she said, without looking away from her father.

"You dare too far!" the high priest said, sharp and indignant, with a quick look at Minos, a demand.

"Strike her across the buttocks with the flat of your blade," Minos said, to the head of the Oreth, and the man drew his sword instantly and struck her with it, a hard painful shock that rolled through her body, up to her head and down in a tingle along her spine and back out through her legs, down, down into the ground, down into the ground where it began to echo back and forth, an echo that didn't die away, an echo that built a thunder-rumble far, far below that grew and grew until it came back up through the floor, and the room trembled all over, so the servant holding the tray of gilded cups stumbled, and the cups rang against each other, and the dewed jug of cool wine fell over and crashed to the ground, spilling green and pungent.

It died away slowly, but not all the way; the rumble was still there, close beneath her feet. The Oreth recoiled, stepping back from her. Her father's face was still and frozen, the high priest staring, and Ariadne finished breathing through the pain and looked up at them and said, "Tell him to hit me again if you want. But the god hits back harder. You *know* he does."

So she went back up the hill, and her father gave orders that no one was to go to the shrine, on pain of death. But it was too late. Minos told no one what had happened inside the throne room, and the high priest didn't either: he didn't want to be replaced by a high priestess. The Oreth couldn't tell anyone. But too many people had heard some story about the labyrinth by then, and too many of those had been waiting in the court with interest as the king's daughter, rumored beloved of the god, went in to face the king and the high priest. Her mother had sent someone to watch, and some of Staphos's family had come hoping to see her punished, and many others who only had nothing better to do had come to see if perhaps the god would perform some miracle in front of them, either because they hoped it would happen or because they were sure it wouldn't. And all those people were there when she went inside, and they were there when the whole palace shook, and they were there when she came out again alone, unpunished, and went back up the hill.

They lived with the shaking of the earth in Crete. The footsteps of the god, people called it, and when the god walked too heavily, he cast a long shadow of death. So people came to the shrine afterward anyway, even though Minos forbade it. It was too much of a miracle, too big to be ignored. Minos himself understood that almost at once, just as soon as his temper cooled. He changed the command: no one was to go to the shrine until the festival of the god, in the spring. And then he sent his warships over the water, the fleet that his wealth and his cunning had built, filled with tall strong warriors fed on his fat cattle, with her eldest brother Androgeos in command.

The sails were white against the dark shimmer of the water as they sailed out. Ariadne watched them out of the window until they vanished over the world's edge. Six months later they came back, without Androgeos, but with seven maidens and seven youths of Athens in his place, as tribute for the god. They came up the hill at dusk, at the head of a parade, a great noisy crowd of stamping feet and cheering: her father trying to make another lie, a new lie, a lie big enough to bury the god deep. And it might work: the god could hit harder, but he couldn't lie.

They stopped by the tower, and in front of the labyrinth erected a great platform for the king's throne, facing the other way, with Pasiphae and the high priest on either side. Ariadne sat silent and angry in a chair one step down from her mother, in a wine-red gown that her father had sent and insisted she wear: a gown for a princess instead of a priestess, with her chains of gold heavy upon her. The night came on, dark enough to hide the faint yellowed lines of grass with the glare of torches and feasting, singing and smoke that went up to the sky, not into the earth:

a funeral for Androgeos, and honor for the sacrifices, who were bunched up under guard on a dais next to her father's throne.

Minos rose and said, "May the god accept this tribute," with savage bitterness, tears on his face. Androgeos had been his eldest son. Pasiphae too had tears, but Ariadne was dry-eyed, still angry.

Then the Oreth came to take the sacrifices, the girls weeping softly and the youths trying not to look afraid, all except one: a young man with hair as bright as gold, strange among the others with their shining olive-black hair. Ariadne looked at him, and he really wasn't afraid. He stood and looked up at Minos, and his eyes weren't dark and deep like her brother's, but even in torchlight they were clear all the way through: the sea on a calm day near the shore, shafts of sunshine streaming straight down to illuminate waves captured in pale sand, ripples on the ocean floor.

And the Oreth taking his arm had a second sword, a spare sword, thrust through his belt.

Ariadne stood up also, despite her mother's grasping hand, and said through a tight knot in her throat, afraid herself suddenly, "I will lead them."

Minos only said, "Let it be done," and gave a nod to the leader of the Oreth, at his side.

She led the way through the cheering crowd and past the dais into the dark, groping her feet out one after another. The way felt strange to her, though she'd walked it every day for three years now. The night was a solid tunnel, the torches in the hands of the Oreth behind her only making small circles on the ground. She thought she had gone too far, that she'd missed it, and then she caught sight of the gold torchlight flickering over the golden seal.

The Oreth unlocked the hatch and heaved it open, two big men straining. The girls were weeping noisily now, crying protests, and one of the youths suddenly broke for it and tried to run, but one of the Oreth caught him roughly; he was a slim boy, and the Oreth was a head taller and gripped his arm in one hand, fingers easily meeting around the skinny limb, and held him.

"Have courage," the golden-haired one said to them, low and clear, his voice going out over them like wind stilling, and they quieted into a huddle. The captain of the Oreth was waiting with the sword in his hand, the spare sword, and he held it out, offering the hilt. The golden youth took it, grasping it easily. Ariadne stood, tense, waiting for a chance. She was only thinking that she had to warn Minotaur: she had to get to the central seal and call to him, let him know that a golden-haired Athenian was coming, with a sword in his hand and the god looking out of his face with different eyes.

And then the Oreth looked at her—looked at her waiting on the other side of the hatch—and jerked his chin toward the dark hole, a command: *go in*. Ariadne realized too late that she hadn't thought about her father, who had now buried a son he had wanted because of her, his daughter who knew his lies, who was held under the god's hand, so he couldn't strike her down.

She stood frozen on the edge of the dark, for a single blank moment. She could have run away: she was farther away than the Athenian youth had been, and she could have fled into the dark, across the labyrinth. The god would take anyone chasing her, who tried to hurt her, surely. Surely. But if she ran, the golden Athenian boy would go down into the labyrinth. He would find her brother, her sleeping brother, and make a way for his friends to come out of the labyrinth at the other end: in the first light of morning they would come out, stained with her brother's blood, and there would be no more earthquakes, no piece of the god left under the hill, and the green grass would grow over the lines. Her father would reward him, call him blessed of the god, to have fought his way through the underworld. If Ariadne came back out with him, maybe Minos would even give the Athenian his own daughter to wife, and send him back to be a great lord in Athens, far away, where people wouldn't put her to death if she told them about her father's lies, because they wouldn't care at all.

She said instead, to the Oreth, "Come and help me down," and held her hands out to him across the dark hole. The man stood there a moment wary of her, his hand moving uneasily on the hilt of his sword. She remembered his face. He had helped to put the workmen down into this hatch. He had thrust them down roughly, pushing with his big arm and his sword held in his other hand, shoving them until they fell inside. He'd been ready to do that to her; he was ready to do it to the Athenians. He was slower to take a step to the edge, and reach out his hand to her. She gripped his hand and braced her foot against the far edge of the hole, and he let her down, kneeling to lower her into the dark, until her straining toes found the floor and she let go of his hand.

The torchlight made a golden circle of the hatch above. Inside there was only a cool dark, impenetrable. She could just make out the mouth of the passage, darkness on darkness, and a faint sense of the marble walls around her. There was a sluggish whisper of air coming out of it, like someone sighing faintly. She made herself start going, at once.

She heard the Athenians being pushed down behind her, cries and muted protests and soft weeping echoes, but worse than that footsteps, footsteps that she felt through the marble beneath her feet. She tried to run, for a little way, but she judged the distances wrong, and struck a wall before she expected it, ramming into stone with her forehead, although she'd thought she had a hand stretched out in front of her. She fell down hard, blinking away a dazzle that didn't belong, her eyes watering with the shock of pain.

But the dazzle wasn't just pain: a golden glow of light was coming down the hallway. The Oreth had given the Athenians one of the torches, too, along with the sword. They caught her, or nearly: she staggered up even as she saw them coming in a pack around the corner behind, staying close to their leader. She shut her eyes to keep the glare from getting into her eyes, and groped for the wall and went onward dancing instead, her stamping dance meant to wake her brother up, the dance her feet knew even in the dark.

That knowledge was what saved her. She kept her hand on the wall as she danced, along the familiar long curving stretch where the passage turned back outward, moving away from the center and back out to cross a great half-circle from one quarter to the other, and halfway along it, the wall fell away suddenly and unexpected from beneath her fingers: another way to go, a branching in the path, where there shouldn't have been one. She kept going several curving steps past it on sheer habit, until her seeking fingers bumped against the wall on the other side of the opening, and only then stopped, shivering. The passage air was warm and moist around her, but out of the branching the air came spring-cool and brisk, a scent of olive oil and wine.

She made herself keep going, keep the dance going, and before she reached the next turning she heard the Athenians arguing behind her in the mainland tongue: which way to go, which way the wholesome air was coming from. And the footsteps seemed fewer, afterward, as if some of them had gone the other way. Ariadne went on dancing, putting her feet down as quietly as she could. She passed another branching, another breath of clear air and freedom, even a hint of roast spring lamb, a smell of feasting. In the passage, the sense of something breathing was growing stronger: the slow rise and fall of enormous lungs. More of the Athenian footsteps fell off. Only a handful left behind her.

But she was coming closer. There was one more long curving, back into the last quarter. It wasn't far now to the seal, to the central chamber. When she passed another branching, a pungent waft of sweat came out of it, sweat and honeyed mead: a living, human smell, full of wanting and lust and strong liquor. On the other side, the thick air was so humid the walls were dewed with moisture, and they almost felt spongy, like the marble of a bathhouse worn into curves by years and bodies, next thing to flesh itself, yielding to an impossible pressure. Ariadne stood with just her very fingertips on the surface, her hand wanting to cringe away. She was afraid, so afraid. She wanted to turn around and run back to the torchlight flicker she could just see coming up from behind her. The god looking out of that golden youth's eyes wasn't the god down here. The god down here was the god in the dark, the god grown large and terrible, maybe too terrible to bear.

She remembered suddenly without remembering, a voice that burst into her ears and came out of her again, bloody. She still couldn't remember what it had said, but she remembered feeling it move through her like an earthquake, cracking open fault lines. She felt a whisper of it moving through her now, finding its way.

She had been pleased when the god had shook the earth under her, so pleased when she'd seen fear on her father's face, looking out of the high priest. She'd liked it, walking back up the hill to the shrine that made her a priestess and a power, that spared her the fate of her sisters. She'd been angry, and she'd been brave, and she'd brought her brother one offering after another to distract him in his prison, but there was the one thing she hadn't done, the one thing bigger than all the others: she hadn't told. She'd told Reja, and she'd told Staphos, small whisperings at night in dark places, but when the priest had come asking questions—Staphos's cousin, the one who had asked her in the light of day—she hadn't told him what was in the labyrinth. She hadn't told the high priest, either the first time he'd come up beside her father or in the palace—the high priest who would have cast her whole family down if he'd believed her. She hadn't told the people in the square, when she'd come out of the king's palace with the earth trembling beneath her feet, and she hadn't told the people come up the hill reveling. Her brother, her little brother, had pulled his hand out of hers and gone down into the dark to save her life, and she hadn't run down the hill shouting, begging a shepherd, a priest, a rich man for help.

So it was her lie, too. She was in the lie, and the lie was in her, and the lie couldn't go any farther into the dark. If she kept holding on to the lie, she could only take this last branching. It wouldn't take her to death. It would go somewhere living and human, because there was no death for her in the labyrinth. Her brother wasn't angry with her. He didn't blame her. It wasn't her fault, and he loved her, and he would never hurt her.

Anyway, she knew where it went. She had watched them dig every inch of the passage out of the ground. There were no branches. The only magic in the labyrinth was what was in it. Her, and her choice. If she followed the branching, she would come to the chamber at the end: and it would be an empty chamber, with a stagnant well, and an open hatch above that she would be able to reach. There would be no one else there. It had been three years. Her bastard half-brother had starved to death; his bones were somewhere in the passage, along with the bones of those poor workmen, and the priest, and Staphos, and soon the Athenians, who had all gotten confused and turned around in the dark. The lie would come up out of the ground with her and turn into that truth. And the people would see her come out of the ground, in the first light of morning, and they would kneel to her. Her father himself would kneel; he would make her high priestess, and she would have a voice that no woman had in Crete, and be safe and powerful, all her days.

She stood there, and then she turned around and waited while the torchlight came down the passage, until the last handful of Athenians came around. The golden one held the torch and the sword, and there were three others behind him, a young woman and two youths, all dark-haired, pale, shivering. They saw her and stopped. "Which way is it?" one of the dark-haired boys blurted, a little older than the others, and taller. "Tell us or we'll make you!"

"There's only one way," Ariadne said.

"There's a branching right there!" the girl said, a little shrill.

"No, there isn't," Ariadne said. She looked the golden-haired young man in the face. "There's only one way. The branching's in us, not in the labyrinth."

He looked back at her, his eyes clear and brilliant as jewels, but somehow familiar after all, and then he said, "Will you lead us?"

"Theseus!" the elder boy said. "Don't be a fool! The only way she'll lead you is straight into the maw of whatever thing they have penned up in here."

"Why would she help us?" the girl added. "Minos is her *father*; I heard them say so. Androgeos was her brother."

Then Theseus did pause, and looked at her. "Well?" he said, quietly. "Why would you show us the way?"

"I have another brother," Ariadne said. "And my father put him down here. If you'll help me get him out, get away with him, then I'll help you."

The other three Athenians wouldn't come. They stood at the branching, watching them go, holding the torch. The curve of the passageway swallowed them into the dark almost at once. Only Theseus came with her. She heard his footsteps following as she danced her way onward, finding the way with rhythm, the thick heavy damp smell ahead, a warm stink of sweat and musk, a breathing all around her, getting stronger, and then suddenly the wall slipped out from under her fingers, going not into a branching but into a round chamber, and there was a little brightness ahead of her. Not much, only the glimmer of starlight seeping in through the tiny grating, which she could see in darker lines against the night sky overhead and reflected in the still waters of the well.

"Minotaur," she said softly. "Minotaur, I'm here."

AUTHOR'S NOTE

I wanted to go further afield for my myth, but the Labyrinth has been occupying my head lately—not in the sense of a synonym for a maze, with many branching paths, but as Ariadne's dancing ground, the ancient pattern that pilgrims used to walk, the single road that winds incomprehensibly until it comes with a final turning to the conclusion. Our journey in time, where only one road can be taken, and the paths are pruned as we pass them; a journey toward truth and revelation, the journey to the story's end. The only way out is through.

NAOMI NOVIK

THE THINGS ERIC EATS BEFORE HE EATS HIMSELF

BY

—

CARMEN MARIA MACHADO

AT FIRST: A LOAF OF RYE, TWO PHEASANTS, HALF A goat. A wheel of blind Emmental cheese, wax and all. The cooking oil meant for the other half of the goat; then, the other half of the goat, uncooked. Seven oranges, a basket of berries that gives him the runs, a cluster of bitter rampion. Some kind of exotic reptile that belongs to his neighbor's son, cut into thin slices to make it last longer and sautéed in butter. Old Halloween candy. Boats of bone marrow. Honey from the hive, then the waxy comb, then the protesting bees. He sends his housekeeper out for more food, and when she returns he eats it steadily and sullenly at his table: cereal by the handfuls, shrimp (at least he lets her cook it first), beef stew, salted radishes, boiled dumplings tossed in vinegar and butter. Four eggplants; a dozen eggs, raw.

A pallet of single-serving bags of potato chips. A bushel of in-season apples.

He is still hungry. He empties his bank accounts and sends his house-keeper away with the cash; she comes back with duck hearts and pâté and caviar and rare Sardinian cheese leaping with maggots and illegal dead French songbirds and truffles and lobster and foie gras and a gold leaf cake. He folds all of it into his mouth with no comment and goes to bed. He tries to sleep, but is awoken an hour later by an indescribable hunger, as if he hasn't eaten since boyhood. His housekeeper gets up in the morning and finds him mixing the spices with water and eating the paste by the spoonful. She calls his daughter, Mia, who shows up with her famous banana-nut muffins and a Tupperware sloshing with soup. She asks him, "What kind of sick are you? Should we take you to the doctor?" But he drinks the soup and eats the muffins and tells her to get lost, applesauce, which she does.

Later that afternoon, his housekeeper finds him chewing on the house itself; the house he'd cleared the grove to build; the house that began all this trouble. She goes to the cottage on the hill where the women are gathered. She begs them to make it stop, but they decline. They tell her, "Look, you don't know our sister. She loves barrenness, hunger, destruction, and even more than that, she loves comeuppance. You cannot stop her any more than you can stop the tides. Have you explained to him the nature of consequences?"

The housekeeper is loyal, but she is also smart. She recognizes the unstoppable forces at work, the incontrovertible physics of the situation. She sends Eric a text message tendering her resignation, but he doesn't get it because he's already eaten his cell phone. (An experiment gone badly; now he has no way to order delivery, and it'd done exactly nothing to slake his hunger.)

Back at the house, Eric tries visualization exercises. He imagines that his stomach is a basket and the food he is eating is a thick quilt being folded into the basket, but as he eats, the walls of the basket fall away, and behind them is an infinite nothingness. He is wallowing in this sensation when Mia returns with more soup, more muffins.

As he eats he sends off an email to an old friend of his, who'd always admired Mia's shapely forearms. His friend, a businessman with unclear designs, arrives soon afterward, having purchased Mia for a handsome sum. Eric takes the proceeds and buys four pregnant cows from a local farmer. He knows he should be patient. He knows he should wait until the cows give birth, then breed them to ensure more cows—a self-perpetuating machine of food, the way mankind has fed itself since time immemorial—but as he lifts the unborn calf from the opened womb, he thinks, *Waiting is for suckers.* His father taught him that; his father taught him to strike while the iron was hot, to take what he wanted and suffer no fools. Consequences were for poor men, for effete men, for women. But soon the cows are gone, and he still feels as if his body is a whistling, barren tundra.

Mia returns. Her boyfriend freed her, she explains, though she does not specify how, precisely, her boyfriend freed her, or what, precisely, she was freed from. "I'm back," she says to Eric, "to take care of you."

"Thank goddess," Eric says with no small amount of sarcasm, and even as he says it he is putting an ad up on Craigslist, and soon another man has come to take her away. Eric takes the money and orders cases of MREs, and the deliveryman says to him, "You getting ready for the apocalypse, buddy?" "It's already here," Eric says, and as he eats the MREs in his living room—the wrappers scattered around him like leaves—he thinks about how the apocalypse is just a giant, disproportionate consequence, a consequence that has gotten distinctly out of hand.

The second time she escapes, Mia decides not to go back to her father or her boyfriend. She has learned what she needs to learn about the perils of duty. She flies to Cuba, and lives there still. The ad remains on Craigslist, though, and the men who show up hungry for her forearms have plenty of cash on hand. Eric steals it and sends them on their way, but when one of them fights back, Eric takes a minimalist Scandinavian sculpture that he recently purchased for his home office and bashes the man's skull in. *Great,* Eric thinks. There is some terrible jump between selling his daughter and the murder of a fellow businessman, and he has made it. Now he feels a vague sense of guilt as he sets about boiling the man's brains in a stockpot. (The jump between murder and cannibalism is, somehow, smaller.)

As he eats, Eric has a couple of regrets: Did he need to build his house right here, precisely? Did he need to hire such superstitious workers, the kind who would balk at the slightest impediment of a sacred grove? Did he need to chop down that beautiful ancient tree, which stood precisely where his new kitchen was supposed to go? Did he need to lift his axe above the dryad's body, bring it down through her crossed arms and wailing mouth and bare breasts? Maybe not, but did she need to curse him with her dying breath? Women were, he observes while sucking on the dead man's femur, chronic overreactors. She was wailing even as she split in twain, even as she bled sap, even when he buried her in the raised flowerbed next to the house. (Remembering this, he goes outside and unearths her body, which now more closely resembles a gnarled root. He roasts it in the oven and eats it piece by piece, and he is pretty certain she is still wailing even as the soft wood tumbles into the void of him.)

As he peels away the drywall and stuffs the house's insulation into his mouth, he has a memory of his boyhood, when his father took him to a county fair. His father was a real estate baron and not a particularly affectionate man, and he had never simply taken Eric somewhere on a whim, and yet they were out together! They ate cotton candy and funnel cake and went on a rickety Ferris wheel and threw darts at balloons, and then, finally, his father took him to a dark building where unknowable mysteries were on display. There, he directed Eric to a gnashing head in a cage, which you could feed a goldfish to for one dollar.

Eric asked his father for a dollar, and his father said he needed to earn the dollar and could do so by eating a goldfish himself. Eric watched as his father paid the attendant, and then did as he was told; it wiggled all the way down. After that, his father gave him a second dollar, and Eric fed the goldfish to the gnashing head, and even after it had swallowed the goldfish it continued to gnash and gnash and gnash. It did not seem to matter to Eric's father that he'd spent twice as much as necessary making Eric earn what might have been freely given. That was, in fact, the lesson. After that, Eric vomited little orange scales for days.

As he dices his couch into bite-sized pieces, he remembers the way his father displaced a marshland for a shopping mall, the way he evicted a neighborhood to build high-priced condos, the way he bought a struggling church and tore it down and used the materials to build himself a deck that he never went out on. He remembers asking his father when he would have enough money and no longer need to build, and his father laughed like he'd made a very funny joke. He remembers how, once, a topless woman showed up in front of his father's office with a sign: HAVE A HEART. It was not clear who she was with—she might have been an environmentalist, or a feminist, or a poverty activist, or an artist or a biologist or a mother. Her sign was not clear. But as the police hauled her away, his father said to him, *Your heart can't hurt if you don't have one.* His father was always saying such things: useful metaphors pregnant with unyielding practicality. Eric has always admired the unflappable structure of his wisdom. He supposes, were his father still alive, he'd say, *Your stomach can't gnaw with emptiness if you don't have one,* and it is a very good point.

Eric tourniquets his legs and saws them off one at a time. His non-dominant arm is next, and then the pale shells of his ears. (They tasted like shark fin, which had been one of his father's favorite meals.) He arrives at an impasse; how to feed himself more of himself without rendering himself incapable of feeding himself. He pokes out a message to Craigslist with his remaining arm, and the man who arrives an hour later is happy to assist, no payment required. The man is cheerful. He whistles while he works. He thoughtfully brings his own supply of aromatics, and the garlic and onions do improve the taste somewhat.

Eric's intestines taste different than he would have thought: sweeter. His heart tastes exactly like he expects: metal and muscle. His lungs are airy and light and the texture of tripe. When his stomach is cut away, he waits for the hunger to cease, but if possible, it redoubles, a compounded ache the breadth and width of the universe.

"How much can we take from your head before your mouth is no longer a mouth?" the man from Craigslist asks with genuine curiosity, and it is a very good question. A mouth is a space, a gap; it is only defined by what's around it (cheek and bone and cartilage), and once those elements have been peeled away, it becomes nothing more than a metaphor. It is the ultimate challenge, filling a void with matter so that the void might cease to be a void, except that the void is, by definition, eternal, and cannot be filled, and so the matter is used up in service of the void and then no longer surrounds the void and the void both ceases to exist and continues for all eternity.

You cannot fight an idea, Eric realizes as the man from Craigslist peels his skin down and folds it into Eric's mouth like a piece of burst bubble-gum. *You cannot fill true emptiness with substance,* he thinks as the man from Craigslist feeds him his own tongue, his own teeth, his own jaw. As he ceases to be—and yet remains as hunger incarnate—he intuits: *Ideas do not exhaust like horses. They do not set like the sun. It is possible to chase an idea forever; it will consume you even as it outruns you.* His father didn't teach him that; for once, he's learned something on his own.

Author's Note

I've always found the story of Erysichthon to be pretty straightforwardly delicious: a man who commits a terrible deed is punished with an appropriate and horrifying curse. (If only it worked that way in real life!) There are so many fun ways to potentially adapt it—including as a body-horror cozy mystery, which I still think is not a half-bad idea—but once I started writing "The Things Eric Eats Before He Eats Himself," I found myself unable to unsee Erysichthon as anything but a pawn. Not sympathetic, exactly. Rather, as a part of a larger system of entitlements and appetites, one that ultimately destroys almost everything it touches. Erysichthon learns too late what so many other people already know: if there's a list of things to be eaten—without compunction, without compassion, without mercy—chances are you'll eventually be on it, too.

Carmen Maria Machado

FLORILEGIA

OR

SOME LIES ABOUT FLOWERS

BY

AMAL EL-MOHTAR

"You can't have flowers made of claws."
—Alan Garner, *The Owl Service*

HER FIRST MEMORY IS A LOSS OF SUN. WHERE THERE was warmth on the white crown of her head, there is now cold shade, and two round shapes blotting out her light, blinking.

Her second memory is a loss of thorns. Where she was sharp, fierce, protected, she feels now smooth, soft, and vulnerable, pressed against green and yielding grass.

Her third memory is a loss of height. She has never felt so far from the sky, so lost to the wind.

Threaded through all this, the loss of roots unspools in her like a scream, the loss of rain, the loss of earth, the loss of everything she knows as food, and she has never, not in the bleakest midwinter or the driest midsummer, felt so hungry.

Small wonder, then, that she kissed Lleu Llaw Gyffes at their first meeting.

She was only trying to eat him.

Blodeuwedd lies naked in the orchard earth, trying to grow roots.

The day is miserable and gray, but not cold; her skin warms the mud beneath it. She breathes in long, deep breaths, and wills the hunger blooming in her center to still.

The hunger is always an ache, a shadow pushing against the inside of her skin. Today it is her head that hurts, her brow that pulses with pain; other days it is her calf, her breast, her belly.

She has been a year in the house of Lleu Llaw Gyffes, and has learned many things: how to run a household; how to use needle and thread; how to receive guests. She eats meat fresh from her husband's hunting, drinks beer from her women's brewing, listens to music from traveling minstrels singing the praise of great lords and wizards making marvels of the countryside. She has learned to endure her husband's presence and make use of his absence, and she has learned to treat the hunger in her like a sucking wound.

But she does not know how to cure it. All she can do is pack it with wet earth, fragrant air, and grit her teeth against being turned inside out.

Lying in the orchard helps. Whenever Lleu leaves—as he often does—to hunt, or fight, or do whatever else men do, she slips from the house to find a corner where none will seek her for the space of an hour. Whether it is the touch of loam against her body, or the fact that it is hers alone, her secret, she can't say—but it helps.

Bees thrill to her fingertips, buzz their puzzlement at her shape. She opens her mouth and lets them sip from her there, tastes the pollen on their dainty legs. She imagines the fields they've scoured for her; she imagines them carrying the wetness of her tongue over the walls, across meadows and arbors, spreading her across distances farther than her eyes or voice can reach.

The thought trembles in her like light on water, and she feels something release. She licks her lips and lies there, perfectly still, and does not stir when it begins to rain.

On their wedding night, Lleu told her the story of his birth, and hers too.

". . . and when Arianrhod was made to leap over my uncle Math's wand, I tumbled out of her, and my uncle Gwydion scooped me up. But because I was proof of her shame, my mother, Arianrhod, decreed that I would never have a name unless she named me, nor be armed unless she armed me, nor wed to any woman of any race on earth. But my uncles were cleverer than she. Between them they tricked her into naming me without knowing who I was; they tricked her into arming me by making her fear invasion. But last, and best, my uncle Gwydion gathered the blossoms of oak, meadowsweet, and broom, and he shaped them into you, Blodeuwedd, and that is how we come to be married, my love, and why we lie together this night."

His eyes were like clouds that bore no rain, like stone begging to be broken through.

It sounds, she thought, *as if your uncles forced you on the body of Arianrhod, and when she tried to deny you, made me for you to force yourself on.*

But his hand on her arm had the strength of a gale, and she knew this thing, this man, could kill her as easily as his uncles had plucked her from the fields—unless she swayed with him, kept quiet, and smiled.

All her words bent into a flower budding from her tongue. She bit it back. When he kissed her, she filled his mouth with blood and petals, planted her silence in his body like a seed.

* * *

"Blodeuwedd? Blodeuwedd!"

She hears the name as if from a distance, as if filtered through dark cloth. She opens her eyes: Lleu, in the mizzle and the gray, his face flushed so hot she fancies she can see steam rising from his cheeks.

Her peace shrivels, and her head pounds with pain.

"What are you doing, woman? What were you thinking? You'll catch your death—"

He drapes her in the wet, muddy robes she'd shed, scoops her up off the ground and covers her with his body.

She lets him. She does not ask why he's returned earlier than expected, and makes herself very small in his arms.

"The shame of it, my lady, if anyone but I saw you thus—"

She looks at him, and looks at him, and thinks, *You don't see me.*

"What's this," he says, lifting a gloved hand to her brow. "Have you bruised yourself, my love? Best you go to bed and warm up. I'll call my uncles—"

"No," she says, with her whole body. "No, no need to trouble them," in a voice like the rain. She reaches up, twines her fingers through his, and slowly draws his hand back from her cheek, smiling. "I will rest, as you say." Then, mechanically, "It is good to see you home so soon."

He relaxes. "I only returned to accompany a visiting scholar from the abbey, and must leave again quickly to make up the time."

She nods, winces as he kisses the dark space on her brow. It darkens further.

He sees nothing in her green and gold-flecked eyes of how much she longs to tear his gentle face apart.

A month after the wedding, Lleu's uncles, Math and Gwydion, came to visit.

Blodeuwedd felt the candles flicker at their arrival, remembered her world dimming in the shadow of their heads. But she received them as a lady should, calling for food and drink and entertainment, then drew back with women's work between her hands.

"Are you happy, Lleu?" asked Math, as if Blodeuwedd weren't there. "Is she everything a wife should be?"

Lleu, who was indeed happy, smiled. "I am; she is beautiful, gracious to guests, and keeps the household in order."

"That's as it should be," said Gwydion gruffly. "That's how we made her. Meadowsweet, useless but for its scent; broom for humility and neatness; oak for hospitality."

"I always wondered about that," said Lleu thoughtfully. "Has not the broom thorns, and the oak great strength?"

Blodeuwedd's hands hovered over her embroidery.

Math laughed. "Aye, Nephew, but we only took the flowers of each. Soft and pretty and fragrant they were, like cutting roses off at the head. Whoever heard of a blossom with claws?"

She pushed the needle through the fabric on her lap, and said nothing.

Lleu leaves again; meanwhile the purpling on her forehead spreads across her pale skin like a storm, and the pain hoods her eyes. She dresses her hair to cover it, and goes to the library.

It too is an orchard, after a fashion—full of dead trees, dead skins, dead plants, dead insects mounted on pins. She feels this in common with them. The library offers a different comfort: if she can no longer grow roots to sate her hunger, perhaps she can learn to die. To catch her death, as her husband says, by lingering with the dead.

Often she comes here to read of Arianrhod—gleaning, from half-mentions in tales and ballads, some sense of the mother-in-law she has never met. Arianrhod is almost as much a mother to her as to Lleu, after all; Blodeuwedd would not exist without her interdiction forbidding wives. But she has never been able to hate Arianrhod for that—only to feel, deep where her roots aren't, a fury that her life is a cheat, and to so little purpose.

She picks up a herbiary, opens it, looks at the drawings within. Some feel familiar, though she can't read the words beside them—a strange, toothy script in a language she hasn't been taught, proceeding from the wrong margin.

"May I help you, my lady," murmurs a voice from her side. She turns to look.

Dark hair and eyes, skin brown as branches. *Beautiful*, feels Blodeuwedd suddenly, in the heart of her, where her breath vanishes; *beautiful*, a strike and a searing, a jagged line of light.

She feels all this before she thinks to ask, "Who are you?"

"My name is Adain, my lady, lately of Penllyn." She smiles. "I am a scholar—I arrived today with your lord, to consult the library. I had heard you were . . . indisposed—"

Blodeuwedd nods. "My apologies for not meeting you on arrival. I've been unwell."

She can't stop looking at Adain's face.

"This book," she says brusquely, holding it out. "What does it say?"

Adain accepts it, looks at the open page. "It is a Levantine treatise on the oak; see, here it speaks of the different parts of the tree and their uses."

"What," she says, pointing, "does this part say?"

"Ah—that the oak is more likely to be struck by lightning than any other tree."

Blodeuwedd grabs the book back suddenly, shuts it with a snap. Her forehead throbs; she turns away, closes her eyes. "Forgive me; I have a terrible headache, and should rest."

She sets the book down, and walks away before Adain can say another word.

"Husband," said Blodeuwedd, hair spread over her pillow like a season, "were you not a man until you had a name, a weapon, and a wife?"

"No, my lady," he said, smiling, running his thumb along her cheek, "I was only a boy."

"You gave me a name; if I had a weapon, and a wife, could I also be a man?"

His laughter scythed a bright, hot line along her chest. "No, my lady." She wet her lips, and smiled. "Why not?"

"Because you were made by magic, my lady, from flowers."

"I do not understand, my husband," she said carefully. "Magic made you a boy, from your mother, and now you are a man. If I won myself a weapon and a wife, why should I not be a man, and conquer lands to reign over, as you do?"

Lleu thought on that. "It is because," he said finally, "you were made for me, belong to me, and I have decreed that you are my wife. And once you are my wife you can be no other thing."

Blodeuwedd spends a full day abed, sleeping fitfully, twisting her long yellow hair into her fists. The dull ache of hunger in her sharpens itself against thoughts of Adain—she hears her voice again, over and over, saying "my lady," so unlike when Lleu says it, the same words but the meaning as different as day from night, as bird from worm.

How could the same words mean so many things? Rain was rain, and sun was sun, and earth was earth. Only wizards could change one thing into another—honor into shame, maiden into mother, a mother's curses into a wife.

Her head hurts so much.

She instructs her attendants to have breakfast brought to her the next morning, and to summon Adain to share it with her.

When Adain arrives, a book in her hand, the noise in her head subsides.

"I apologize," says Blodeuwedd, gesturing for Adain to sit down, "for my rudeness yesterday. Is there anything you lack?"

"Nothing at all, my lady," says Adain quietly, looking at her. "Except to know the cause of your pain, and whether it is in my power to help with it."

Blodeuwedd shrugs. "It is a small matter that is always with me. But tell me of yourself, of your studies. Where does your interest lie?"

Adain holds her gaze a long moment. "In plants and animals, my lady. The study of natural history."

Silence lengthens like a shadow between them.

"How interesting," says Blodeuwedd at last, politely. "I hope you find many books on the subject."

"My lady," says Adain, lowering her voice, and her gaze, "I came especially because I heard of your own history."

Blodeuwedd holds very still.

"The marvel of Gwynedd," says Adain quietly. "A meadow made maiden. The fairest woman the world has ever known."

"And you wanted to see for yourself," says Blodeuwedd, trying to swallow the thorns in her throat, to keep the bitterness from her voice. "Well—I am as you find me. The work of wizards. A singular specimen."

Adain winces. "My lady, it is I who should apologize—"

"It is well, Adain," she says curtly. "I must beg you to excuse me—it goes ill with me again, and I would lie down."

Adain looks briefly miserable as she stands, and the glimpse of it lashes at Blodeuwedd, a mix of sorrow and triumph. To have caused her pain. To have spilled her own into her.

"I brought you this, my lady," says Adain, holding out the book she brought—a slender quarto volume with a bouquet of lilies embroidered into the cover and spine. "I hoped it might interest you. It speaks of the language of flowers."

Blodeuwedd stares at her. "What do you know of the language of flowers?"

"I know," she says, holding her gaze, "that they hunger for depth and height, for sun and rain, for the touch of insects, and that all men see of them are their pretty colors and sweet smells."

Blodeuwedd looks at the book for a long time. When she senses Adain about to withdraw, she says, "Wait."

Adain does.

. "Come closer," she says, and Adain obeys. Blodeuwedd reaches for her and draws her closer still, till she sits near enough that they can bend their foreheads together. Blodeuwedd lifts her hair from the spreading bruise at her brow.

"What can you tell me of this?"

Adain hesitates, hovers her fingers above the bruise. Blodeuwedd watches her, then closes her eyes as Adain touches her.

She shivers, and Adain gasps as petals push past Blodeuwedd's skin, unfurling toward her hand.

The relief of it is unspeakable. Blodeuwedd all but goes limp from it.

"It is an anemone, my lady," breathes Adain, tracing its edges.

Blodeuwedd shakes her head, dazed with how light, how clear, it feels. "That can't be. I was only made of three flowers."

"Aye, and people are made of flesh and blood and bone, but that isn't what comes out of our mouths in speech. You—" Adain looks at her with such tenderness that Blodeuwedd can't bear it, looks away. "Have you been biting your tongue all this time, my lady?"

Blodeuwedd bites her lip in answer, hardly hearing Adain over the peace of her body, the absence of pain. She fixes her eyes on the book Adain brought. "Tell me, then—what do anemones mean?"

"They signify fading hope and loss. But"—Adain brushes Blodeuwedd's hair away from the flower, smiles—"they are also said to mean anticipation."

"How," whispers Blodeuwedd, looking back to her, "do we know which it is?"

Adain holds her gaze while her fingers work delicately beneath the bloom.

"Context," she says, and plucks it.

* * *

There came a day when Lleu was knocked from his horse in war, shot through with many arrows, but he survived, prevailed, and his borders widened.

There came a day when Lleu was gored by a great boar during a hunt, but he survived, slew it, made a brush of its bristles for Blodeuwedd's hair.

There came a day when Blodeuwedd watched Lleu's naked body as he slept and made a knife of her eyes, a tusk of her teeth, and imagined unseaming his belly, imagined ripping into the meat of him and feasting on his heat. She made a noise deep in her throat, and his eyes opened, and she murmured, wanting him to hear—

"Can nothing kill you, Lleu?"

He smiled at her, and when he spoke his words had the ring of enchantment, incantation.

"I cannot be killed day or night, inside or outside, on horseback or on foot. I cannot be killed clothed or naked, nor by any weapon honorably made."

Blodeuwedd's chin trembled before her mouth made a smile of it.

"Then my husband is immortal, and shall never be parted from me."

"Just so, my lady." He laughed, bright as his name. "Unless the Almighty sees fit to dress me in netting and have me straddle a goat's back and a bathtub's edge by the side of a river at dusk, with a thickly thatched curve of roof above the tub, while a man stabs at me with a spear made of a year of Sundays. But if I were meant to die, would Fate have made my killing so difficult to arrange? Rejoice, then, Blodeuwedd, for you'll never be rid of me."

In the weeks that follow, Blodeuwedd and Adain are inseparable: reading in the library, walking along the grounds, sharing meals, sharing beds. Blodeuwedd cannot get enough of her, seeks always to be touching her, murmurs questions over their clasped hands and into the warmth of her neck.

"What does this mean," she asks, leading Adain's fingers to every ache in her body. Under her touch a deep red rose buds from her wrist, a bluebell from her breastbone, a heap of lilacs from her ankles, a crush of sweetpeas from her nape. Adain opens her mouth in answer against each bloom, until Blodeuwedd's cheeks flush from the heat of her breath, the tip of her tongue tracking light along the petals. Blodeuwedd feels every part of her clamoring to be read.

Adain reads her—but tells her, too, of what's outside her body, of all the plants and animals beyond the walls. Blodeuwedd listens keenly to her stories of the silent flight of owls, the cleverness of crows; the healing to be found in yarrow and willow bark, the soothing properties of raspberry leaf and mint. Blodeuwedd listens, but most thirstily for lessons on foxglove and mistletoe, hemlock and yew.

"These are plants that kill," Blodeuwedd says, astonished. "Plants that hide weapons inside them."

"In a sense. Though many poisons can heal if properly diluted and applied," says Adain. "A needle can stab and it can stitch; the same property can harm or heal. It is all a matter of context, of degree. Some poisons even heal each other's effects! Belladonna is dangerous, but it's also an antidote to wolfsbane." She smiles, just a little wan. "And anything is poison if you have too much of it."

The silence that follows her words has a shadow beneath its skin. Blodeuwedd sees it, reaches for it, gently.

"Is this too much, Adain? Am I poisoning you?"

"No," she says, swiftly, "no. Only I know this cannot last beyond your lord's return."

Blodeuwedd stills—then shrugs. "He is more often away than he is here. I am told he is at war, and while he will never die, he may yet be months, perhaps even a year away."

"But while he is here—"

"I will be bored, and hungry, and in pain, as I was before. But I will know you are here, and that will be—something. Better, if not enough."

Adain looks as if she would say something else—but Blodeuwedd's face is smooth, pleasant, any pain folded away behind it like a crocus in rain. But when Adain rests a hand on Blodeuwedd's shoulder, a whole hood of aconite stretches into her palm like a cat.

Blodeuwedd took to playing a pillow game with Lleu: she would hold a knife to his neck or stomach, spit her hatred of him, and cut into him while he moaned. The cuts never went deeper than paper, no matter where she dragged the blade. Sometimes they played with rope, some-times with fire; each time, Lleu trembled and cried out, lay spent and panting and infuriatingly alive.

He loved the games, though, and how she never played the same way twice.

"Shall I tell you," says Adain one day, as they walk together in the orchard, hand in hand, "about the flowers of which you were made?"

Blodeuwedd shrugs. "Those I know—meadowsweet for scent, broom for tidiness, oak for hospitality."

Adain shakes her head. "Those are only parts—"

"They only used parts. The blossoms, they said. There is nothing in me of root, thorn, branch—nothing that digs, cuts, climbs."

Adain looks at her sidelong, then back ahead, frowning.

"That may be, my lady," she says finally. "But blossoms carry seeds, and in that contain the whole of the plant. So I shall tell you all the same."

She stops walking, and Blodeuwedd stops with her; Adain crouches down, indicating Blodeuwedd's feet and legs.

"Meadowsweet is always underfoot, but the more it's bruised, the more scent it gives off; there is defiance in that, I think, like a song that won't be stopped up."

Adain touches Blodeuwedd's legs through the fine cloth that cov-ers them, standing slowly, working her way up. Blodeuwedd closes her eyes, feeling something like a breeze rustling the leaves and stems inside her.

"Broom," Adain continues, gesturing to Blodeuwedd's middle. "You know about the thorns, and it has a sweet smell too, but it's most notable for thriving in poor soil. It survives where little else could."

She places a palm over Blodeuwedd's heart. "And oak—"

"Is more likely," Blodeuwedd whispers, opening her eyes and covering Adain's hand with hers, "to be struck by lightning than any other tree of the same height."

"Full marks," says Adain, and stands on her toes to kiss her. "You were made of flowers, my love, but those are only pieces of you, the seeds from which you grew. You—you cannot be pressed into a book. You are so much more than the work of wizards."

Blodeuwedd is quiet for a space. Then she asks, "Are you a wizard, Adain?"

Adain blinks, then laughs. "Not at all! Why do you ask?"

"You . . . changed me, as they did. They saw plants, and made a woman—soft, sweet, biddable. You see the same plants, and make a different woman—hard, sharp, strong. How?"

"I like to think I see you as you are," she says, "and they see what they want to see. What flatters their vanity."

"Or am I the one thing when they look at me, the other when you do?" She chews her lip.

"Which do you want to be, my lady?"

"I want," she says, her voice a husk. "I want to eat. I want to change others. I want no one to tell me who or what I am, what I can or cannot be. I want"—she draws closer to Adain, wraps her arms around her, snakes her fingers into Adain's hair and tugs until she gasps—"to take what I please when I'm hungry, to ask no leave. I want a wife, and a weapon."

She releases Adain's hair, steps back. She looks at the ground.

"I want to be a wizard, though I hate them as I have never hated anything else."

"Is it a wizard you want to be," says Adain, looking up at her, "or a wizard's power you want to have?"

She chuckles. "Can I have the one without the other?"

"Certainly. Wizards—their power lies in naming. They shape reality because they tell a good story. Tell a different one—one of your choosing, one of your desire—and teach it to the world until it learns your truth and makes room for it."

Blodeuwedd raises an eyebrow. "That sounds like a pretty story itself."

"You were flowers, and they made you a woman," says Adain firmly. She hesitates for a moment, like an autumn leaf in a stiff wind before resolving to fall. "I too was once other than I am. I had a different name; I threw a mighty spear; I was lord of Penllyn, and did not want to be. And I gave them up—my name, my weapons, my lands—to be a woman among books, a woman among women. To be the blossom on the gorse instead of the thorn."

Blodeuwedd listens, and there is wonder in it, that Adain could ever have been other than she is; that Blodeuwedd, for all her failed hours in the orchard mud, could yet be something else—could be what she desired, instead of what she was before choice was taken from her.

"Teach me," she says at last. "Teach me how."

When Lleu returns from his business abroad, Blodeuwedd receives him as she never has before: there is a spark in her eyes she knows will thrill him, and her smile bares more teeth than she usually shows. She sees him surprised, and pleased.

"My lady," he says, "I've missed you," and leans forward to kiss her on both cheeks.

As he does, she whispers, "I've thought of a new game to play."

His eyes widen, and he grins, and sheds his armor as swiftly as is seemly, then follows where she leads.

"Not to the bedchamber," she says, coy. "I've thought of something much better."

She leads him out past the inner walls, and the outer; assures him there isn't far to go, until they arrive at the river.

There is a cauldron there, half covered with a thatched roof; next to it is a placid goat, an old fishing net.

"Blodeuwedd," he whispers, "what's this?"

"I want it to feel more real," she says smoothly. "The possibility of your death. Take off your clothes, husband."

He does as she says, tensing with desire and fear. She drapes the fishing net over him.

"Now," she says, "onto the goat."

"You don't have a spear," he observes.

She smiles. "I don't need one." She dips a tin cup into the cauldron, offers it to him. "Drink, my husband. We have thirsty work ahead."

Lleu does as he's told, keeping his balance on goat and tub the while.

As he drinks, she says, "Do you know what today is, husband?"

He hesitates, wiping his mouth. "Sunday, my lady."

"So it is. I've had much more than a year of them, you know, in your house—biting my tongue, speaking in flowers neither of us could read. I could have made you a whole other wife," she chuckles, "from the foxgloves I pulled from my fingers, the aconite I brushed from my hair. But I have learned something of my roots, while you were away."

Lleu frowns—coughs. He shakes his head, makes as if to step down.

"Stay," she says, "exactly where you are."

"Blodeuwedd—"

"Have you ever heard me speak so many words to you?" she wonders. "Have you ever thought to ask what I thought, what I wanted, what I needed, when you took me from my home and planted me in yours?"

"You are my *wife*," he gasps, and stumbles. The goat bleats in sudden panic as he loses his footing, falls backward, half into the river. Blodeuwedd watches him like an owl, but does not move. Lleu opens his mouth to speak further, but his tongue is swollen. His brow is fevered and wet. Blodeuwedd can hear his heart beating in furious rhythms.

"Adain!" she calls. "Adain, come out!"

Adain emerges from the trees, carrying another cup; she hurries to Lleu's side.

"Not yet," says Blodeuwedd, sharp as needles. "Lleu Llaw Gyffes, I am not your wife. Swear it now, and Adain will give you an antidote."

Lleu shakes his head, coughs blood—for a moment. Then he looks at Adain, and looks at Blodeuwedd, and nods. "I swear it," he spits through swollen lips.

"Swear," says Blodeuwedd, "that you will never take another wife, never make your manhood from another's pain."

Lleu stares for a long moment.

"*Swear!*" hisses Adain.

"I—swear—"

"Swear," says Blodeuwedd, "that you will never raise arms against me or mine, nor let your uncles seek to harm us in any way."

"I swear," he says in a voice of milkweed floss, more breath than words, and there is a sorrow in his eyes that makes her almost hate him less.

She nods, and Adain tips the antidote into the red of his mouth.

Blodeuwedd steps forward, squats down next to him as he pants. She dips her sleeve in the river, uses it to wipe the sweat from his brow.

"You gathered flowers and read *woman*. You read *woman* and gleaned docile, pretty, fragrant, weak. But you misread me, Lleu. I have in me the hearts of great ships, the bones of cathedrals. I have in me the sharpness of claws. And you, Lleu, what do you have? You cling like ivy. You smother like mistletoe. But what are you, besides wizard's work?"

She stands again, looks down at him.

"I will never again be what I was before you. But I will be *more*. And you—you will be a rogue, a rascal. You will be anything but a man."

Lleu cries out, pours his pain onto the air as Blodeuwedd never could. As she and Adain watch, Lleu's shape shrinks, shifts, blurs at the edges, as the magic called *man* leaves him, as he fights to hold on to it. A light flares from him, then dims. All that's left tangled in the net is a hawk, sour of body, sound of wing; no sooner do they lift the net's coils than the bird springs into the air, crying.

Blodeuwedd watches him go, speechless. She stares at Adain.

"I—did not know that would happen," she says. "Are all men hawks, without wives?"

"There was magic in his making, and magic in his unmaking," says Adain, looking up at the sky. "His uncles will know soon enough what happened, but his vows will bind them no matter his shape."

Then Adain draws her close, kisses her.

"You did it," she says. "You're free."

Blodeuwedd nods, silent, gazing into the darkness after Lleu's wings.

"Free," Adain insists, "from everything—from retaliation, from his uncles. You could rule his house if you wanted; you could come back with me to the abbey—we could keep studying together, make a life." Adain takes her hand. "You have everything you wanted—a name, a weapon—"

"Adain." Blodeuwedd kisses her. "I think we can do better than that."

The moon rises fat and bright over the river; Blodeuwedd looks long at its reflection on the water rippling the coin of it into white and silver lines.

"I want to meet Arianrhod," she says at last. "My former mother-in-law. I want to know what she's like. Will you come with me? Before you answer," she says, cutting off the passion in Adain's eyes, "I cannot say whether I will stay as I am, now that you've taught me to read between my lineaments. I may hunger again. I may change."

"I wouldn't have you otherwise," says Adain firmly. "And so long as you'll have me, I will stay with you to the earth's end."

Adain kisses her hand, then turns from the water, and begins calling gently for the goat.

Blodeuwedd takes her time before following; she stretches her hand out in the moonlight, turns her wrist to the sky. She feels no blooming pressure there, or anywhere. Nothing hurts.

For the first time, the blue branches of her veins look like roots.

Author's Note

I first read the Mabinogion *as a young teenager, and loved Blodeu-wedd's story for its strangeness as much as I hated it for its unfairness. When you read a lot of folklore and fairy tales, you get used to a certain amount of sameness as types repeat and accrete, but Blodeuwedd was unlike anything else I'd encountered. I was always fiercely of her party, and tended to forget her surrounding details. What was her lover's name? Her husband's? His uncle's? I could never keep those jerks in my head, because this fierce husband-murdering flower-owl-woman was so power-fully provocative. If ever a story wanted subverting, this one did.*

This isn't the first time I engage with the myth—I wrote a poem about Blodeuwedd in 2005, a short story ("The Truth About Owls") nine years after that, and still don't feel done exploring the story's ten-sions or arguing with other people's interpretations. (This story was definitely partly written out of irritation with Alan Garner's The Owl Service.*) There are so many flowers, and so many birds, and so many women in the world, and they all deserve to be more than set dressing in men's stories.*

Amal El-Mohtar

ACKNOWLEDGMENTS

Thank you to everyone at Saga Press and Gallery Books who had a hand in making *The Mythic Dream*: Michael McCartney and Erika Genova, who made our book look beautiful; Caroline Pallota, Kaitlyn Snowden, Stephen Breslin, and Allison Green, who kept things on track and made sure the book came together; Serena Malyon, whose gorgeous art is on the cover; LJ Jackson, publicity and marketing manager extraordinaire; Erin Larson, Allison Light, and Samantha Desz, who made it sound so good; and our publishing team, Jen Bergstrom, Jen Long, Justin Chanda, Joe Monti, and Madison Penico. We feel remarkably lucky to have gotten to make this book with the best people in publishing.

And the biggest thank-you to the writers whose stories make up this anthology: we quite literally could not have done it without you. We are so grateful that you loved mythic stories this passionately, and reinvented them so powerfully.

Dominik would like to thank André and Ginette Parisien, as well as Sophie, Luigi, Théa, and Livie Zaccardo for their unparalleled support. Thanks to Ann VanderMeer for her guidance over all these years. Thanks to Nicole Joanisse and Joanne Larocque, Nicole Kornher-Stace, Mike Allen, Elsa Sjunneson-Henry, Kit, John, and Andrew F. Sullivan, and Amy Jones. A heartfelt thanks to Navah for this last editorial venture—what an incredible journey we've had, truly one of mythic proportions in my eyes. I will be forever grateful for all we've done together, and for your friendship. Finally, thank you, of course, to Kelsi Morris, who continues to believe in and supports all of my wild projects—it means so very much to me.

Navah would like to thank her parents, Debbie and Judah Rosensweig, who always believed she'd make books one day; her siblings (and siblings-in-law), Talya and Yechiel, Hillela and Noah, Chayim and Shayna, Moshe, and Elisha; and her extremely excellent tiny nieces and nephews, Maya Ellie, Miriam, and Rafael. Thanks for friendship and moral support go to the Second Saturday game folks, the 9pm Heavy Hitting boxing crew, the BAMS family, the Murder Friends, and especially Maruja Ivri (even though it's not Galentine's Day). Thank you to Dominik, for being the best co-editor and friend a person could wish for. Thank you thank you to Naftali Wolfe, for all the things, always. And finally, thank you to Eliora and Ronen, story readers, adventure-havers, myth-believers. Of all the stories I know, you two are the best.

ABOUT THE EDITORS

Dominik Parisien is the co-editor, with Navah Wolfe, of *Robots vs. Fairies* and *The Starlit Wood: New Fairy Tales*, which won the Shirley Jackson Award and was a finalist for the World Fantasy Award, the British Fantasy Award, and the Locus Award. He also co-edited, with Elsa Sjunesson-Henry, *Disabled People Destroy Science Fiction!* His work has appeared in various journals and magazines, including *Quill & Quire*, *The Fiddlehead*, and *Uncanny Magazine*, and he is the author of the poetry chapbook *We, Old Young Ones*. Dominik is a disabled, bisexual French Canadian. He lives in Toronto.

Navah Wolfe is a three-time Hugo and Locus Award–nominated senior editor at Saga Press. She is also the co-editor of *Robots vs. Fairies* and *The Starlit Wood: New Fairy Tales*, which won the Shirley Jackson Award and was a finalist for the World Fantasy Award, the British Fantasy Award, and the Locus Award. Her books have been finalists for the Hugo, Nebula, World Fantasy, Stoker, Tiptree, and Locus Awards. In her past life, she was an editor at Simon & Schuster Books for Young Readers, where she worked on many bestselling and award-winning young adult and middle-grade books. She loves tea, Eurovision, and gorgeous storytelling, and lives in Connecticut with her husband and two small humans. Find her on Twitter as @navahw.

ABOUT THE CONTRIBUTORS

John Chu is a microprocessor architect by day, a writer, translator, and podcast narrator by night. His fiction has appeared or is forthcoming at *Boston Review*, *Uncanny*, *Asimov's Science Fiction*, *Clarkesworld*, and Tor.com, among other venues. His translations have been published or are forthcoming at *Clarkesworld*, *The Big Book of Science Fiction*, and other venues. His story "The Water That Falls on You from Nowhere" won the 2014 Hugo Award for Best Short Story.

Leah Cypess is the author of four young adult fantasy novels, starting with *Mistwood* (HarperCollins 2010). Her short fiction has been published in *Asimov's Science Fiction*, the *Magazine of Fantasy & Science Fiction*, and *Daily Science Fiction*, among other places. Leah lives in Silver Spring, Maryland, with her family. You can read more about her and her writing at www.leahcypess.com.

Indrapramit Das (aka Indra Das) is a writer and editor from Kolkata, India. He is a Lambda Literary Award winner for his debut novel *The Devourers* (Penguin India/Del Rey), and has been a finalist for the Crawford, Tiptree, and Shirley Jackson Awards. His short fiction has appeared in publications including Tor.com, *Clarkesworld*, and *Asimov's Science Fiction*, and has been widely anthologized. He is an Octavia

E. Butler Scholar and a grateful graduate of Clarion West 2012. He has lived in India, the United States, and Canada, where he completed his MFA at the University of British Columbia.

Amal El-Mohtar's short fiction has won the Hugo, Nebula, and Locus Awards, and her poetry has won the Rhysling Award three times. She writes the "Otherworldly" column for the *New York Times Book Review*, and is the author, with Max Gladstone, of *This Is How You Lose the Time War*, an epistolary spy vs. spy novella co-written across time and space. Her work has appeared in numerous anthologies, including *The Starlit Wood: New Fairy Tales*, *The Djinn Falls in Love & Other Stories*, and *The New Voices of Fantasy*; in magazines such as Tor.com, *Lightspeed, Strange Horizons*, and *Fireside*; and in her own collection of poems and very short stories, *The Honey Month*. She lives in Ottawa with her spouse and two cats. Find her online at amalelmohtar.com or on Twitter as @tithenai.

Jeffrey Ford is the author of the novels *The Physiognomy, Memoranda, The Beyond, The Portrait of Mrs. Charbuque, The Girl in the Glass, The Cosmology of the Wider World, The Shadow Year*, and *Ahab's Return*. His short story collections are *The Fantasy Writer's Assistant, The Empire of Ice Cream, The Drowned Life, Crackpot Palace*, and *A Natural History of Hell*. Ford's fiction has appeared in a wide variety of magazines and anthologies and has been widely translated. He lives in Ohio in an old farmhouse surrounded by corn and soybean fields and teaches part-time at Ohio Wesleyan University.

Hugo Award winner **Sarah Gailey** lives and works in beautiful Portland, Oregon. Their nonfiction has been published by *Mashable* and the *Boston Globe*, and their fiction has been published internationally. They are a regular contributor for Tor.com and the Barnes & Noble Sci-Fi & Fantasy Blog. You can find links to their work at www.sarahgailey.com. They tweet as @gaileyfrey.

Carlos Hernandez is the author of the critically acclaimed short story collection *The Assimilated Cuban's Guide to Quantum Santeria* (Rosarium 2016) and most recently, as part of the Rick Riordan Presents imprint of Disney Hyperion, the novel *Sal and Gabi Break the Universe* (2019). By day, Carlos is an associate professor of English at the City University of New York, with appointments at BMCC and the Graduate Center, and a game designer and enthusiast. Catch him on Twitter as @writeteachplay.

Kat Howard is the author of the novels *Roses and Rot* and the Alex Award–winning *An Unkindness of Magicians*, as well as the short fiction collection *A Cathedral of Myth and Bone*. Her novella, *The End of the Sentence*, co-written with Maria Dahvana Headley, was an NPR best book of the year in 2014. She currently lives in New Hampshire.

Stephen Graham Jones is the author of sixteen novels, six story collections, and, so far, one comic book. Stephen's been an NEA recipient, has won the Texas Institute of Letters Award for Fiction, the Independent Publisher Book Award for Multicultural Fiction, a Bram Stoker Award, four This Is Horror Awards, and he's been a finalist for the Shirley Jackson Award and the World Fantasy Award. He's also made *Bloody Disgusting*'s Top Ten Horror Novels. Stephen lives in Boulder, Colorado.

T. Kingfisher is the pen name for Ursula Vernon, or possibly the other way around. She is the Hugo and Nebula Award–winning author of *Digger*, "Jackalope Wives," *Clockwork Boys*, and various other oddities. She lives in North Carolina with her husband and his chickens.

Ann Leckie is the author of the Hugo, Nebula, and Arthur C. Clarke Award–winning novel *Ancillary Justice*. She has worked as a waitress, a receptionist, a rodman on a land-surveying crew, and a recording engineer. She lives in St. Louis, Missouri.

Carmen Maria Machado's debut short story collection, *Her Body and Other Parties*, was a finalist for the National Book Award, the Kirkus Prize, LA Times Book Prize Art Seidenbaum Award for First Fiction, the World Fantasy Award, the Dylan Thomas Prize, the PEN/Robert W. Bingham Prize for Debut Fiction, and the winner of the Bard Fiction Prize, the Lambda Literary Award for Lesbian Fiction, the Brooklyn Public Library Literature Prize, the Shirley Jackson Award, and the National Book Critics Circle's John Leonard Prize. In 2018, the *New York Times* listed *Her Body and Other Parties* as a member of "The New Vanguard," one of "15 remarkable books by women that are shaping the way we read and write fiction in the 21st century."

Her essays, fiction, and criticism have appeared in the *New Yorker*, the *New York Times*, *Granta*, *Harper's Bazaar*, *Tin House*, *VQR*, *McSweeney's Quarterly Concern*, the *Believer*, *Guernica*, *The Best American Science Fiction & Fantasy*, *The Best American Nonrequired Reading*, and elsewhere. She holds an MFA from the Iowa Writers' Workshop and has been awarded fellowships and residencies from the Michener-Copernicus Foundation, the Elizabeth George Foundation, the CINTAS Foundation, Yaddo, Hedgebrook, and the Millay Colony for the Arts. She is the Writer in Residence at the University of Pennsylvania and lives in Philadelphia with her wife.

Arkady Martine is a speculative fiction writer and, as Dr. AnnaLinden Weller, a historian of the Byzantine Empire and a city planner. Under both names she writes about border politics, rhetoric, propaganda, and the edges of the world. Arkady grew up in New York City and—after some time in Turkey, Canada, and Sweden—lives in Baltimore with her wife, the author Vivian Shaw. Find her online at arkadymartine.net or on Twitter as @ArkadyMartine.

Seanan McGuire is an American author living and working in the Pacific Northwest. Since her debut in 2009, she has published more than forty novels and has been the recipient of the Campbell, Alex, Hugo, Nebula, and Pegasus Awards. Seanan spends a somewhat daunting amount of time wandering through cornfields, and knew how to take a Ferris wheel apart by the time she was twelve. Strangely enough, this is not a particularly marketable skill. Seanan watches too many horror movies, can be located in a crowd by singing the opening phrase of almost any Broadway show, and can be found most easily at www.seananmcguire.com.

Naomi Novik is the acclaimed author of the Temeraire series and the Nebula-winning novel *Uprooted,* a fantasy influenced by the Polish fairy tales of her childhood. She is a founder of the Organization for Transformative Works and the Archive of Our Own. Her latest novel, *Spinning Silver*, is a retelling of Rumpelstiltskin.

Rebecca Roanhorse is a Nebula and Hugo Award–winning speculative fiction writer and the recipient of the 2018 Campbell Award for Best New Writer. Her short fiction has also been a finalist for the Sturgeon, Locus, and World Fantasy Awards. Her novel *Trail of Lightning* (Book 1 in the Sixth World Series) was selected as an Amazon, B&N, Library Journal, and NRP Best Book of 2018, among others, and is a Nebula, Hugo, and Locus Award finalist for 2019. Book 2 in the Sixth World Series, *Storm of Locusts*, has received starred reviews from Publishers Weekly and Booklist. Her next novel, *Resistance Reborn*, is part of *Star Wars: Journey to the Rise of Skywalker* and is out in November 2019. Her middle-grade novel *Race to the Sun* for the Rick Riordan Presents imprint will release in January 2020. Her short fiction can be found in *Apex Magazine* and in *New Suns* and various other anthologies. Her nonfiction can be found in *Uncanny Magazine, Strange Horizons*, and *How I Resist: Activism and Hope for a New Generation* (Macmillan). She lives in northern New Mexico with her husband, daughter, and pups. Find more at rebeccaroanhorse.com and on Twitter at @RoanhorseBex.

JY Yang is the author of the Tensorate novellas from Tor.Com Publishing (*The Red Threads of Fortune*, *The Black Tides of Heaven*, *The Descent of Monsters*), which have been nominated for the Hugo, Nebula, World Fantasy, and Locus Awards and were on the Honor List for the Tiptree Award. Their short fiction has been published in over a dozen venues, including Tor.com, *Clarkesworld*, *Strange Horizons*, and *Lightspeed*. Find them on Twitter as @halleluyang.

Alyssa Wong's stories have won the Nebula Award, the World Fantasy Award, and the Locus Award. She was a finalist for the John W. Campbell Award for Best New Writer, and her fiction has been shortlisted for the Hugo, Bram Stoker, and Shirley Jackson Awards. She lives in California.